THE TREASURY OF SHERLOCK HOLMES

The Further Adventures of Sherlock Holmes

Craig Janacek

The New World Books

Grateful acknowledgment to Sir Arthur Conan Doyle (1859-1930) for the use of the Sherlock Holmes characters.

Some excerpts of 'The Lost Legion' are derived from 'The Terror of Blue John Gap' (1910) by Sir Arthur Conan Doyle.
Some excerpts of 'The Adventure of the Double-Edged Hoard' are derived from 'The Silver Hatchet' (1883) by Sir Arthur Conan Doyle.
Some excerpts of 'The Adventure of the Dawn Discovery' are derived from 'Our Midnight Visitor' (1891) by Sir Arthur Conan Doyle.
Some excerpts of 'The Adventure of the Queen's Pendant' are derived from 'The Jew's Breastplate' (1922) by Sir Arthur Conan Doyle.
Some excerpts of 'The Adventure of the Sunken Indiaman' are derived from 'Sidelights on Sherlock Holmes' (1924) by Sir Arthur Conan Doyle.

'The Adventure of the Double-Edged Hoard' first published in 'The MX Book of New Sherlock Holmes Stories, Part IV: 2016 Annual'; David Marcum, Editor; MX Publishing.
'The Harrowing Intermission' first published in 'Holmes Away from Home: Tales of the Great Hiatus'; David Marcum, Editor; Belanger Books.
'The Adventure of the Sunken Indiaman' first published in 'The MX Book of New Sherlock Holmes Stories, Part VI: 2017 Annual'; David Marcum, Editor; MX Publishing.

ISBN-13: 9781976782985

Cover illustration by Frank Wiles for 'The Valley of Fear' in 'The Strand
Magazine' (1914), in public domain.
Printed in the United States of America
The New World Books

First Printing: January 2018
Second Printing: April 2020
Third Printing: October 2020

To Margaret

"All the chance events of our lives are materials
From which we can make what we like.
Whoever is rich in spirit makes much of his life.
Every acquaintance, every incident would be
For the thoroughly spiritual person –
The first element in an endless series –
The beginning of an endless novel."

'MISCELLANEOUS OBSERVATIONS' (1798)

GEORG PHILIPP FRIEDRICH VON HARDENBERG (WRITING
AS 'NOVALIS')

CONTENTS

LITERARY AGENT'S FOREWORD TO TREASURE TROVE INDEED!

"Sherlock Holmes sat up with a whistle. 'By Jove...' said he, 'this is treasure-trove indeed!'"

— The Adventure of the Blue Carbuncle

T hings get lost very easily in England. Perhaps the vast weft of centuries that have passed since the Neolithic days, through the successive reigns of the Celts, the Romans, the Angles, the Saxons, the Danes, the Normans, and all who followed, has contributed to this peculiar phenomenon.

But once was lost, shall surely be found. Since the late 1700's, over two-hundred-and-fifty treasure hoards, some dating back over five thousand years, have been unearthed throughout the British Isles, with more being found seemingly every month. As noted in The *Adventure of the Golden*

Pince-Nez, some – such as the contents of the ancient British barrow – have led to great tragedy. The discovery of buried treasure is in fact so common that there are common laws dealing with the subject. These date from the time of Edward the Confessor (1003-1066), and draw a distinction between objects lost or abandoned, which belong either to the first person who found it or to the landowner, versus treasures hidden with *animus revocandi* (intention to recover later), which belong by prerogative right to the Crown.

Before the Age of Victoria, perhaps the most famous treasure discoverer was Sir Walter Scott (1771-1832), the great Scottish novelist. The fabled 'Honours of Scotland,' also known as Scottish Crown Jewels, consisted of a jewel-encrusted golden Crown (from 1503), a silver gilded Sceptre (from 1494), and a etched Sword (from 1507). They had been used in the successive coronation of Scottish monarchs, both independent (beginning with Mary, Queen of Scots) and joint (concluding with Charles II). During the English Civil War, they were successfully hidden from the rapacious grasp of the usurper Oliver Cromwell. However, after the 1707 Acts of Union, they became superfluous and were lost for over a hundred years. Lost until Walter Scott set out to discover them in 1818, and in a now legendary moment, they were found locked away in a chest deep in Edinburgh Castle.

§

"Buried treasures are naturally among the problems which have come to Mr. Holmes." So said Sir Arthur Conan Doyle, Dr John H. Watson's first literary agent, in an essay entitled 'Sidelights on Sherlock Holmes' in *Memories and Adventures* (1923). And he was right. In the sixty Canonical tales, there are no less than five cases that revolve around treasures, buried or lost in a variety of fashions, such that Holmes' fame as a 'treasure-hunter' has surpassed that of even Sir Walter. First, as a young man, Holmes followed in the footsteps of Scott when he successfully unravelled the mystery of *The Musgrave Ritual*. This led to the recovery of nothing less than the ancient crown of the Kings of England (also hidden away from the plundering Cromwell), which had been lost when Sir Ralph Musgrave's untimely death prevented him from passing on to his son the full import of secret.

Many famous jewels were also recovered in large part due to the efforts of Sherlock Holmes. In *The Adventure of the Beryl Coronet*, Holmes was directly responsible for recovering for Mr. Alexander Holder three of the beryls ripped from the precious coronet by Sir George Burnwell. Holmes also recovered the Countess of Morcar's blue carbuncle, stolen from her room at the Hotel Cosmopolitan by the head attendant, James Ryder. It was found 'buried' in the crop of a Christmas goose by the wife of Commissionaire Peterson, who promptly rushed to Holmes for advice. *The Adventure of the Blue Carbuncle* does not relate whether Holmes shared with Peterson the thousand-pound reward that had been offered for its return. The black pearl of the Borgias was stolen from the room of the Prince of Colonna at the Dacre Hotel by his wife's maid, Lucretia Venucci. Holmes found this 'buried' in the plaster bust of Napoleon, where it had been hidden by Beppo. *The Adventure of the Six Napoleons* does not related what precisely Holmes did with the pearl after he had Watson place it in the safe, but we must assume that he eventually returned it to the Prince. Finally, there was the Crown Diamond, the great seventy-carat yellow stone, one of eighteen once owned by Cardinal Jules Mazarin of France. It had been stolen by Count Negretto Sylvius from the English State and Holmes' efforts restored to its representative, Lord Cantlemere in *The Mazarin Stone*.

There are hints of Holmes' efforts to recover other treasures in both unrecorded and non-Canonical adventures. In *The Sign of Four*, Inspector Athelney Jones recalled how Holmes had lectured the C.I.D. about 'causes and inferences and effects' in the Bishopgate jewel case. In *The Adventure of the Speckled Band*, Miss Helen Stoner recounted how Holmes assisted Mrs.

Farintosh in a case concerning an opal tiara. Holmes once referred to the theft of the Duchess of Ferrers' Topaz Pendant as an example of what occurred whenever he absented himself from London for an overly long time.[1] It seems as if the nobility were often misplacing their valuables, for during his attempt to save Dr Lowe, Holmes mentioned the recovery of the Duchess of Ulster's Amethyst Pendant, which he believed was stolen by Mr. Archibald Hatton of Homer Street.[2] One of the most ruthless foes of Holmes and Watson was Mrs. Simone Elizabeth Kirby, whose lust for the Coronation Ring of William IV, part of the British Crown Jewels, led to her terrible fate.[3] And perhaps most remarkable of all was Holmes' recovery of the fabled Star of India, a centrepiece of the British Crown Jewels which had been lost for a dozen years, despite the best efforts of the government to cover up the crime.[4]

Surely, with these fantastic cases upon record, their provenance undisputed, there can be little doubt that additional tales of Holmes and Watson encountering 'buried treasures' of an assorted variety may also be authentic works by the pen of Dr John H. Watson. One can even consider these recently unearthed tales to be treasures of a sort.

Holmes himself reported in *The Hound of the Baskervilles* (Chapter V) that by 1889 he had investigated some five hundred cases of "capital importance." And only two years later, in *The Final Problem*, he noted that he had handled a thousand in all. As noted in The *Adventure of the Solitary Cyclist*, from 1894 to 1901, he handled hundreds more. Although it seems unlikely that Watson could have accompanied Holmes upon absolutely every case, between those where he was physically present, and those where Holmes related to him the details after the fact, we could safely assume that Watson was cognizant of at least half of the cases, or roughly six hundred. This is a particularly fine number, for the sixty Canonical cases then represent precisely ten percent of the total.

There is no doubt that Watson preserved very full notes of hundreds of Holmes' cases, which he chose for various reasons not to lay before the public at the time. Most famously, many these records were crammed into a "travel-worn and battered tin despatch-box with his name, John H. Watson, M.D., painted upon the lid" deep in the vaults of the bank of Cox and Co. at Charing Cross. However, arithmetic dictates that one tin-despatch box could not possibly hold all of Dr Watson's writings. Each of the fifty-six shorter tales runs to some ten thousand words, or roughly thirty double-spaced typed pages. With a two-inch modern ream of paper containing five hundred pages, as Holmes would have noted, the calculation is a simple one. Five hundred and sixty missing accounts would run to approximately thirty-two reams of paper, or some sixty-four inches high. Many adult men of the Victorian era barely reached that height!

Below, we show an advertisement from the Gamages catalogue of 1914, with a Bombay Despatch Box of Japanned Polished Ebonite and Gold, "fitted with Tray, with Partitions for pens, pen-holders, inks, stationary and ruler, with Brass Lever Lock and Duplicate Keys, and Strong Leather Strap all round." It could be ordered in widths of 14, 16, or 18 inches, but the height did not vary. Even with the tray removed, one suspects that the storage space of such boxes was no more than six inches tall.

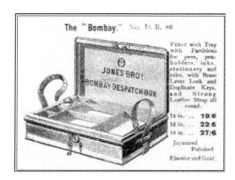

Therefore, Watson would have needed at least nine, and possible many more, such boxes to contain the accounts of all of the missing cases. Watson was clear that only one such case was stored at Cox and Co. and, despite many slanders to the contrary, the doctor was no fool. He would have never kept these cases all in one locale, but would have scattered them about London, and possibly even further abroad, for safekeeping.

In summary, there is no doubt that the multitude of newly discovered cases of Sherlock Holmes may very well be authentic. Only a careful scrutiny of their provenance, linguistics, and mannerisms can say with any degree of certainty. But to whom do these unearthed tales belong? We must return to the English Treasure Trove law, which dictates there can be only two answers. If the papers were lost or abandoned by Watson, they belong either to the first person who found it or to the landowner where it was found. If the papers were hidden by Watson with *animus revocandi* (intention to recover later), which belong by prerogative right to the Crown. It should be noted that in no instance do they belong to non-linear distant relatives of Sir Arthur Conan Doyle, Watson's first literary agent.

So do they belong to the Crown? Certainly an argument could be made that Watson hid them with the intent to recover and publish later. The final moments of Watson's life have been lost to posterity, nor has his will ever come to light, so we cannot be absolutely certain what his precise wishes were regarding the unpublished tales of his friend and companion, Sherlock Holmes. However, we think the Queen is doing rather well for herself at the moment, and it seems unlikely that she will attempt to seize possession over various and sundry papers which detail the adventures of a man who once performed many extraordinary services for her great-great-grandmother.

Thus, we would argue that any such unearthed tales were in fact abandoned by Watson. They exist out there, in various locales hidden both within Britain, but also dispersed throughout the world at large. For Watson had experiences that ranged over many continents. Who knows from where the next tale of Mr. Sherlock Holmes and his friend and biographer, Dr John H. Watson, will be unearthed?

§

The Lost Legion (1875)
The Musgrave Ritual (1879)
The Adventure of the Queen's Pendant (1887)
The Adventure of the Pirate's Code (1888)
The Adventure of the Beryl Coronet (1890)
The Adventure of the Six Napoleons (1900)
The Adventure of the Mazarin Stone (1903)
The Adventure of the Silent Drum (1903)

LITERARY AGENT'S FOREWORD TO FORTUNES MADE & FORTUNES LOST

"He had been a pioneer in California, and could narrate many a strange tale of fortunes made and fortunes lost in those wild, halcyon days."

– A Study in Scarlet

When Dr John H. Watson first agreed to share a suite of rooms with Mr. Sherlock Holmes at 221B Baker Street, he quickly discovered that his new companion displayed a remarkable ignorance regarding several matters near to the heart of the contemporary man about town. Of contemporary literature, philosophy and politics Holmes appeared to know next to nothing. And yet, when Holmes retired to his villa on the South Downs, it was to practice apiculture and study philosophy.

We can assume that during this time Holmes came across

the treatise *Leviathan* (1651) by Thomas Hobbes. In that work, Hobbes argued that: "The passions which most powerfully urge people to crimes are anger, greed, and the other more vehement desires, but not without hope. For no one would commit a crime for the sake of a good which he had no hope of possessing." Reading those words, Holmes likely would have been reminded of a passage of an older book, one he would have encountered during the Great Hiatus, when he passed through India on his way to Tibet. The *Bhagavad Gita* says (c.400 BCE): "There are three gates to self-destructive hell: lust, anger, and greed."

Surely, when Holmes thought back over his career as a consulting detective, he would have seen the truth in those words. Of those passions, it might be argued that the most common was greed. A great number of the adventures that Holmes and Watson embarked upon were precipitated by a man's greed, typically for some rare bauble – such as gold and gems – to which the vast majority of humankind has collectively agreed to represent earthly value.

Of course, Holmes recognized that it was a dull world without lunatics who preferred to bury treasures in locales more exotic than their bank.[5] Such was the lesson of the greatest treasure of them all, one that once belonged to a rajah of the northern provinces of India, consisting of: "one hundred and forty-three diamonds of the first water, including one which has been called 'the Great Mogul,' and is said to be the second largest stone in existence. Then there were ninety-seven very fine emeralds, and one hundred and seventy rubies, some of which, however, were small. There were forty carbuncles, two hundred and ten sapphires, sixty-one agates, and a great quantity of beryls, onyxes, cats'-eyes, turquoises, and other stones.... Besides this, there were nearly three hundred very fine pearls." As reported in *The Sign of Four*, the combined value of this Agra treasure was computed to be "not less than half a million sterling," which would have made Mary Morstan "the richest heiress in England" if Jonathan Small had not madly scattered it over five miles of the bottom of the Thames. Still, we must suppose that Dr Watson was happier for its loss.

Thus, for most men greed is the path to madness, as Major John Sholto finally learned when he was on death's door.[6] The four recently unearthed adventures compiled herein continue to relate Holmes and Watson's experiences with the dark side of hunts for various treasure troves. Dangers both physical and spiritual lurk around every corner, and some items are seemingly cursed by the gods themselves. Fortunes may be easily made, but just as easily lost, and sometimes the price of infinite riches is either terrible pain or death everlasting.

§

The Adventure of the Double-Edged Hoard (1881)
The Adventure of the Dawn Discovery (1887)
The Sign of Four (1888)
The Harrowing Intermission (1891)
The Adventure of the Sunken Indiaman (1897)

THE LOST LEGION

Having lived with Mr. Sherlock Holmes for many years, I knew well his propensity for sudden interjections seemingly apropos of nothing. "Would you say, Watson, that I am the sort of individual who would invent an abnormal series of events solely for the sake of producing alarm?" asked my friend one morning towards the end of 1894.

It was a cold winter day, and snow had fallen heavily the night before.[7] Baker Street was thickly covered, such that any attempts to brave the outdoors would have guaranteed sodden pant legs. As such, I was sitting with my feet by the fire reading a black-letter edition of Haggard's newest novel, while Holmes was fiddling about by his chemical bench, where he had managed to produce a rather mephitic odour.[8]

I looked up from the page and stared at him in wonderment. "On the contrary, Holmes, I would assert that you are a man of a particularly sober and scientific turn of mind, absolutely devoid of poetic imagination, and therefore most unlikely to do such a thing."

"Then it may interest you then to learn that Mr. Haggard may in fact be not that far from the truth."

"How could you know possibly that I doubted the plausibility of Mr. Haggard's words?"

He snorted in amusement. "Did you realize, Watson, you

often mutter under your breath when you are reading? This charming trait makes it quite simple to know what you are thinking."

I frowned in bafflement, for I was not aware of any such habit. "And what did I say in this particular instance?"

"You first muttered something about 'ineffable twaddle' and later that you had 'never read such rubbish in your life.' Hence my observation."

"But, Holmes," I cried, "this story purports to tell of a penniless adventurer who, seeking his fortune in unexplored Africa, discovers both a lost race and a fortune in jewels. Listen to this florid prose." I flipped back to the beginning and proceeded to read from the page: " 'To his right were two stately gates of iron fantastically wrought, supported by stone pillars on whose summit stood griffins of black marble embracing coats of arms and banners inscribed with the device *'Per Ardua ad Astra.'*[9] ' It gets much more improbable henceforth." I looked up at my friend. "Can you possibly say that such a thing is truthful?"

"Not truthful, Watson, but containing, perhaps, a kernel of veracity. Certainly, I have seen some strange things in my travels."

"Where? During your two years in Tibet?" I asked, a small note of residual bitterness creeping into my tone. "Did you stumble upon Shambhala?"[10]

He smiled enigmatically. "The stories of Sigerson will have to wait for another day, Watson, as I am not certain you are prepared to hear them." He shook his head. "No, the events I have in mind took place before I made the fruitful acquaintance of my biographer in the laboratory of St. Bart's. Before I had even fully determined the path of my particular life's work. It was, in fact, shortly after my trip to Donnithorpe where I had my attention arrested by the horrific demise of Old Trevor."[11]

"Another case?" I asked, interested in spite of myself.

"One of the most peculiar nature; which I have not thought

THE TREASURY OF SHERLOCK HOLMES

about for some twenty years. However, the combination of the words from your novel and the smell of this vial of hydrogen sulphide have stimulated a memory from deep within my brain-attic."

"I admit that I would be most curious to hear about it."

"There is a relic here at Baker Street which is connected to the case in a fashion. If you would fetch it down, I will pluck some cigars from the coal scuttle and pour us something from the tantalus."

"What is it?"

"A cup carved from blue stone."

I glanced about our chambers in confusion. Holmes was never the neatest of fellow-lodgers, but even amongst his jumble of papers, chemical apparatuses, and criminal relics, I could not have missed such an item. "I may not have your powers of observation, Holmes, but I can confidently state that we have no such cup at Baker Street."

He waved his hand. "I stuck it in the lumber-room years ago. I had run out of room upon my bookshelf, and during one of my rare attempts to make this place a tad more habitable, I put it away."

"Very well. Which one?" I inquired.

"Obviously, not the room packed with my old papers, Watson. The other one," he replied, imperiously.

I climbed the steps that led up to the lumber-rooms, and I rummaged around for a few minutes in the specified locale. I soon determined that this was likely a vain endeavour, for the place was cluttered with the detritus of Holmes' varied career. He had a horror of discarding anything which might come in use again, so the shelves were clogged with an assortment of wigs, hats, and clothing which Holmes could never wear out in respectable society, but which had formed the basis of many successful past disguises. However, just as I was about to abandon the search, I spotted a small stemmed cup carved from the most distinctive mineral. It almost shone with a great variety of colours: shades of purple and white, interlaced with mixtures of the two. I realized that it must be the item to which Holmes referred. I descended the steps slowly as I studied the unusual goblet.

"Ah, I see you have found the Blue John," said Holmes, an impish gleam in his eyes. "Do you know it?"

I shook my head. "No, I have never seen such an item."

"That is not surprising. I myself was unfamiliar with the stone until I spent a few weeks up in Derbyshire."[12]

"Derbyshire?" I echoed. "The Peak District?"

"Indeed. You see, Watson, although I have a vigorous constitution, my system is still prey, upon rare occasions, to various infectious complications."

"Yes, I recall the dreaded Tapanuli fever," said I, dryly.

Holmes's cheeks flushed with a modicum of chagrin. "Upon this occasion, the scarlatina was most real, and I was prostrate for several weeks."[13] I was, at the time, under the care of one Professor Alexander. Eventually, he decided that the stale college atmosphere was impeding my recovery, and prescribed a regimen of country air. When I expressed a reluctance to visit my own family's country estate, the Professor instead suggested a farm near Castleton, run by two old ladies, sisters by the surname of Vermilion. Alexander confessed that he himself had recuperated from rubeola there as a lad.[14] He recalled scaring crows in the Vermilion fields as one of the pinnacles of his boyhood. In any case, I was in no shape to argue, and the next morning I was shipped off via train to Edale, where the closest station to the sisters' farm was situated. There an old field hand driving a rough single-horse-drawn cart met me. By the end of the twenty-minute ride along Arthurs Way, I was already beginning to feel the benefit of the wonderful upland air.

"The farm of the Vermilions lay some fourteen hundred and twenty feet above sea-level, so it was a bracing climate in that early spring month. The first two days I spent laid up in my bed, recovering from the strain of the travel north and devouring the scant news captured in the pages of the local

Castleton Courier by its lone reporter, one Mr. Charrington. Beyond the usual morning cough, I had very little discomfort, and, what with the fresh milk and the home-grown mutton, I soon began to put on some weight, the prior loss of which had so displeased Professor Alexander. Miss Alma and Olivia Vermilion were charmingly quaint and kind, little hard-working old maids, who were ready to lavish all the heart which might have gone out to husband or to children instead upon an invalid stranger. Truly, Watson, the old maid is a most useful person, one of the reserve forces of the community. Their neighbours were quiet sheep farmers, Mr. Appleton on one side, and Mrs. Miller on the other.

"It was a most lonely spot, and the walks were picturesque in the extreme. The farm consisted of grazing land, which lay at the bottom of an irregular valley, and through which ran one of the region's innumerable streams, this one with the recherché name of Odin Sitch. On each side were fantastic limestone hills, formed of rock so soft that you could break it away with your hands. I deduced that all the country around was effectively hollow. Could you but strike it with some gigantic hammer it might boom like a drum, or possibly cave-in altogether and expose some huge subterranean sea. Across the way, the forlorn ruins of a Norman fortress stood guard over the valley.

"It was upon one of those walks that I made the acquaintance of one Mr. Richard Handsacre, a young man of those parts. He had spent a few years at the university in Durham, and I found him to be a man of some education and character. Although he had returned to the family business of sheep farming, he had a peculiar passion for the history of the area, and was a considerable fund of local lore. We would go on walks about the Mam Tor, scrambling over the prehistoric stones upon its summit, and he would regale me with the legends he was collecting for a planned book upon the subject.[15]

"Handsacre had conceived the idea that that the events recounted by Homer had taken place not in Asia Minor as commonly believed, but rather in ancient Britain. He also supposed that our island home was once connected to the rest of Europe by a vast land bridge, and that rising sea levels swallowed many now-lost cities, including Lyonesse off the Cornish peninsula, Ys off the coast of Brittany, and Vineta in the Baltic.[16] And over in Wales, deep in the mountains, he claimed that entire settlements still existed which had never been visited by the modern world. These notions struck me as a bit eccentric, though quite harmless.

"Upon our walk one day Handsacre pointed out the entrance to a cave, which was a clean-cut arch in the rock, the mouth all overgrown with bushes.

'That is the entrance to the Shivering Cavern,' said he.[17] By the rise of my eyebrows, he understood that I was interested in the cave, so he continued. 'It is one of only three places in the world where the precious Blue John mineral can be found. The stone is so rare that even an ordinary vase carved from it can command great prices.'

" 'The mine doesn't look as if it is much in use,' said I.

"Handsacre shook his head. 'Not anymore. It was abandoned decades ago when it was determined that this vein has been played out after being continuously mined for some nineteen hundred years.'

" 'Surely that dates back to the time of the Roman occupation of Britain?'

" 'Indeed. Pliny the Elder called it *murrhine*, and the most affluent of Romans coveted it for their drinking vessels, as the stone imparted a strange, pleasing taste to any wine drunk from it. The story goes that one debauched consul of Rome went so far as to gnaw upon the edges of his cup in order to demonstrate his great wealth. I hear that a few vases of Blue John were recently recovered from the buried city of Pompeii.[18] The Romans, with that extraordinary instinct of theirs, discovered that it was to be found in this valley, and they sank a horizontal shaft deep into the mountainside. It is a goodly passage which the Roman miners have cut, and it intersects some of the great water-worn caves that naturally tunnel through these hills,' he concluded.

"Handsacre led me across the field over to the mouth of the arched tunnel, where we peered down into the black recesses beyond. I found myself wishing for a bicycle lamp, so I could journey a bit deeper into the calming solitude of the cave.

" 'If my health returns, I might be interested in devoting some of my holiday to exploring those mysterious depths,' said I.

"Handsacre shook his head. 'There are plenty of other caves that I would recommend instead of the Shivering, Mr. Holmes. There are gaps in the rocks everywhere in this district, and when you pass through them, you find yourself in great caverns that wind down into the bowels of the earth. I have gone deeply into a few, and it is a joy to see the wonderful silver and black effect when one throws the light of a lantern upon the stalactites that drape their lofty roofs. Shut off the lamp, and you are in the blackest darkness. Turn it on, and it is a scene from the Arabian Nights. Of course, you would do well to mark your steps and to have a sufficient store of candles, or you may never make your way back to the daylight again.'

" 'But what of this particular cave? Surely it too has some fine stone formations?'

" 'No one knows,' said Handsacre with a shrug of his shoulders. 'No soul is brave enough to venture into the Shivering. They are too afraid.'

" 'Afraid!' I answered. 'Afraid of what?'

" 'Of the Terror that lives inside,' said he, with a point of his finger towards the black vault.

"Strange how superstitious these countrymen are, I thought to myself! How absurdly easy it is for a legend to arise in a lonely countryside! I soon questioned him as to the reasons for his strange belief. It seemed that, from time to time, sheep have gone missing from the fields, carried bodily away by the supposed Terror, according to Handsacre. That they could have wandered away of their own accord and disappeared among the mountains was an explanation to which he would not listen. Upon one occasion a pool of blood had been found, and some tufts of wool. That also, I pointed out, could be explained in a perfectly natural way: although wolves had long ago been exterminated, surely young sheep are still pretty to foxes and kestrels? Furthermore, he countered, the nights upon which sheep disappeared were invariably very dark, cloudy nights with no moon. This I met with the obvious retort that those were the nights that a commonplace sheep-stealer would naturally choose for his work. Finally, he reported that upon one occasion, a gap had been made in a wall, and some of the stones scattered for a considerable distance.

" 'Human agency again,' I argued.

" 'Is that so, Mr. Holmes? Then what if I tell you that I have actually heard the Terror myself? Indeed, anyone could hear it should they remain long enough at the cave entrance. It sounds like the distant roaring of an immense creature.'

"I could not but smile at this, knowing, as I do, the strange reverberations which may be produced by an underground water system running amid the chasms of a limestone formation. My incredulity annoyed Handsacre, such that he turned and left me with some abruptness.

"And now comes the strange point about the whole business, Watson. I was still standing near the mouth of the cave, turning over in my mind the various statements of Handsacre, and reflecting how readily they could be explained away, when suddenly, from the depth of the tunnel beside me, there issued a most extraordinary sound. How shall I describe it? First of all, it seemed to be a great distance away, far down in the bowels of the earth. Secondly, in spite of this suggestion of distance, it was very loud. Lastly, it was not a boom, nor a crash, such as one would associate with falling water or tumbling rock, but it was a high whine, tremulous and vibrating, almost like the whinnying of a horse. It was certainly a most remarkable experience, and one, which for a moment, I must admit, gave a new significance to Handsacre's words, as absurd as his explanation was.

I waited by the entrance to Shivering Cavern for another half an hour or more, but there was no return of the sound, so at last I rambled back to the farmhouse, rather mystified by what had occurred. The sound was certainly very strange, and I fancied that I could hear ringing in my ears for several hours after the event, though that was likely a residual symptom of the scarlatina. I determined to explore that cavern, and learn the secret of the old mine, as soon as my strength was fully restored.

"Three days later, I decided that I was finally fit for such an expedition. I said nothing of my plans to the Miss Vermilions, for I had learned from various conversations that they were quite superstitious enough already. However, I begged a small oil lantern from them and set off that morning to investigate for myself. Utilizing the methods that I had been developing at school, I first systematically inspected the area around the opening of the old Roman-hewed arch. I noted that the bushes at the entrance of the cave presented an appearance as if some heavy creature had forced its way through them. There I observed that, among the numerous tufts of sheep's wool that lay among the bushes, there was one plant that was smeared with a splash of crimson blood. Of course, my reason told me that if sheep wander into such rocky places they are likely to injure themselves, however, I began to be keenly interested. I therefore availed myself of my other senses, and sniffed the air. A fetid breath seemed to ooze from the black depths into which I peered, which I knew was most likely the result of escaping sulphuric gasses. I heard no sound at all, and could almost believe that I had been the victim of some febrile hallucination induced by my illness and suggested, perhaps, by my melodramatic conversation with Handsacre.

"Determining that there was nothing more to be learned from the entrance and resolved to learn the secret of the old mine, I set a light in my lantern, pushed my way through the briars, and descended into the rocky shaft. It went down at an acute angle for some fifty feet, the floor being covered with broken stone. At the bottom, a long, straight passage cut in the solid rock extended deeper into the heart of the mountain. My training in geology was, at the time, rather limited, however I could infer that the lining of this corridor was certainly of some harder material than limestone, for there were points where I could actually see the tool-marks that the old miners had left in their excavation, as fresh as if they had been done yesterday. Down this strange, old-world corridor I carefully treaded, my feeble flame throwing a dim circle of light around me. Finally, I came to a spot where the Roman-carved tunnel opened into a natural water-worn cavern. This proved to be a huge hall, hung with long white icicles of lime deposit. From this central chamber, I could dimly perceive that a large number of passages, worn by the subterranean streams, wound away into the depths of the earth. I was standing there considering whether I had better return, or whether I should venture any farther into this dangerous labyrinth, when my eyes fell upon something at my feet, which strongly arrested my attention.

"The greater part of the floor of the cavern was covered with boulders of rock or with hard incrustations of lime, but at this particular point there had been a drip of water from the distant roof, which had left a patch of soft mud. In the very centre of this there was a huge mark – an ill-defined blotch, deep, broad and irregular, as if a great boulder had fallen upon it. No loose stone lay near, however, nor was there anything to account for the impression. It was far too large to be caused by any possible animal, and besides, there was only the one, and the patch of mud was of such a size that no reasonable stride could have covered it. And yet, a portion of my mind was convinced that the shape resembled nothing so much as the print of some gigantic animal's paw. As I rose from the examination of that singular mark, I looked round into the black shadows for any other clues, but could see nothing of note.

"Given that I was determined to conduct the investigation of this cavern and its mysterious legend in a systematic fashion, I abandoned any further attempts to penetrate its depths for the moment. Instead, that afternoon I set my footsteps towards the town of Castleton. My first stop was at the local ironmongers, where I purchased a good supply of gypsum plaster. This I planned to use to preserve the impress of the possible footstep, so as to facilitate easier examination and eventual identification.[19]

"I then paid a visit at the practice of Dr Matthew Lukeson, to whom Professor Alexander had given me a note of recommendation as someone who could pronounce me fully recovered from the bout of scarlatina. Lukeson appeared to have an unabsorbing practice, as he welcomed me in and bade me tell him how I had been spending my days. He appeared most interested by the strange story of Handsacre's Terror, as well as by my discovery of the print and my plans to produce a facsimile from it. After listening intently, he then carefully examined me, paying special attention to my reflexes and to the pupils of my eyes. When he had finished, Lukeson refused to discuss my adventure, saying that it was entirely beyond him, but he gave me the card of a Mr. Stephen Gaelton over at Buxton, with the advice that I should instantly go to him and tell him the story exactly as I had done to himself. He was, according to my adviser, the very man who was pre-eminently suited to help me.

"Eager to obtain some assistance in this matter, I therefore went on to the station and bought a ticket to the little town of Buxton, which was some ten miles away. Inquiring of the local stationmaster, I was soon directed to the address I sought. Mr. Gaelton appeared to be a man of importance, as his brass plate was displayed next to the door of a considerable building upon the outskirts of the town. I was about to ring his bell when some misgiving came into my mind, and, crossing to a neighbouring shop, I asked the shopkeeper behind the counter if he could tell me anything of Mr. Gaelton. 'Why,' said the man, 'he is the best mad doctor in Derbyshire, and yonder is his asylum.'

"Upon receipt of this news, I began to heartily laugh, for clearly I had professed too great an interest in this supposed Terror, and Dr Lukeson had felt that my brain had been touched by the scarlatina. If I hadn't similarly dismissed Mr. Handsacre's stories myself, I would have been most put out by the unimaginative nature of that country doctor, who clearly required a re-reading of Hamlet's advice to Horatio. Needless to say, I did not pay a visit to Mr. Gaelton, but instead returned to the Vermillion farm.

"The following morn, I set out shortly after dawn in order to make my preserve of the giant print. As I took prodigious care in the matter, a great deal of time elapsed for the setting of the plaster. Once complete, I lifted the cast from its mould, wrapped it in a blanket, and brought it back into the sunlight outside of the cave; for I knew any inspection in those dark shadows would risk missing some critical element. When I reached the surface, I examined my handiwork, which showed the impression of a gigantic clawed foot, far larger than any animal I had ever before laid eyes upon!

"I considered this for a moment, Watson. My first hypothesis was that this print was proof of the existence of some remnant of Pleistocene megafauna, some sort of gigantic cave bear.[20] Could such a beast actually exist? I knew that several lochs in Scotland were popularly supposed to be the dwelling places of massive water reptiles, but had never considered this to be anything other than folklore. Could it be that in this part of England there is a vast subterranean lake or sea, which is fed by the great number of streams which pass down through the limestone? Where there is a large collection of water there might also be some evaporation, mists or rain, and perhaps a possibility of sunless vegetation. This in turn suggests that there may be animal life, arising, as the vegetable life would also do, from those seeds and types that had been introduced at an early period of the world's history, when communication with the outer air was easier. This place may have then developed a fauna and flora of its own, including such monsters as the one who left this print, which may well have been the old cave-bear, enormously enlarged and modified by its new environment. For countless eons, the internal and the external beasts may have been kept apart, evolving steadily away from each other. Then could there have come some rift in the depths of the mountain, which had enabled one creature to wander up and, by means of the Roman tunnel, to reach the open air? Perhaps there was an astonishing truth to Handsacre's Terror?

"However, upon further inspection I realized that there was an irregularity with the print. The claws were divided from each other by a precise measurement, which seemed to me to be rather unnatural. Surely, when such a beast steps, their foot splays out upon the ground in a way that produced varying degrees of separation of the digits? It was a theory that needed experimental confirmation, though that would have been challenging from a practical standpoint at the moment. Nonetheless, if true, what could such a finding mean? Was this print counterfeited? For what possible motive would someone go to such pains? I realized that only another foray into the cavern could answer these questions.

"As there was still considerable daylight left, I decided to attempt this expedition immediately. I retraced my steps to what I will now call the 'Bear-cave' and before proceeding any further, I took good note of a curious rock formation in the wall by which I could recognize the entrance of the Roman tunnel. The precaution was very necessary, for the great cave, so far as I could see it, was intersected by innumerable passages. Having made sure of my position, and reassured myself by examining my spare candles and my matches, I advanced slowly over the rocky and uneven surface of the deepest recesses of the cavern.

"I had progressed some forty yards when the tunnel split. I stopped and considered the options. After a moment, I realized that the featureless ground was not as unrevealing as I first thought. Although there was a distinct lack of additional prints upon the hard ground, I began to discern that this was because someone or something had carefully swept the passage. Once I knew to be on the lookout for such disturbances, I could see that the right hand path was the one to follow, for the left appeared completely untouched. This route twisted and turned for another seventy yards before, to my great surprise, it ended at a locked gate which blocked the entire tunnel so that nothing could be seen beyond. The gate was made of a hard wood, and bonded by bars of black iron. In the stone above it was carved the following inscription: '*Ut omnis homo super terram / Mors venit cito vel tarde.*' I translated this to read: 'To every man upon this earth / Death cometh soon or late.' For a brief moment, I imagined that I had reached some Tartarian entrance straight out of the feverish dreams of Alighieri.

"As I had no tools with me that might be used to open such a formidable lock, I abandoned any further spelunking for the moment. On my way back up to the surface, I considered what I had learned. Although the Latin inscription might be nineteen-hundred years old, the gate was surely not, for any such wood and iron would have rotted and rusted centuries ago. Therefore, someone had recently replaced the structure. But to what end? What secret deep within Shivering Cavern did it protect?

"I reviewed the clues that I had unearthed thus far. One: many sheep were missing from the local fields. Two: the cave was known to produce strange sounds. Three: someone had most—likely produced an artificial track of an enormous cave-bear. And four: this Latin-inscribed door. I realized that my knowledge of the Roman occupation of Britain was completely inadequate and promptly set out to rectify that situation.

"As the last rays of the sun fell, I paid a visit to the small library situated in Castleton, whose shelves upon the subject were remarkably well-stocked upon the matter. There were several interesting tomes, which comprised every known detail of that Late Antiquity period. Most notable of all was a small monograph entitled *'The Eternal Flame of Rome'* written in 1870 by none other Mr. Stephen Gaelton, the Buxton asylum-keeper. His work described how in the year 411, Constantine III, the last Roman Emperor to have been born in Britannia, was captured by rival troops near Ravenna during a civil war with Emperor Honorius and subsequently beheaded. His sons, Constans, Aurelius, and Uther, fled back to the Albion isle, where they and their descendants valiantly attempted to keep the Roman spirit alive in the face the hordes of invading Saxons. Mr. Gaelton's theory was that the Peak District around Castleton served as their base, due to both its distance from the easily assaulted shores of Sussex and Kent, and to its combination of formidable heights and defensible caves. In his conclusion, Gaelton supposed it conceivable that some remnant of a Roman legion still existed in a remote subterranean fortress.

"I leaned back in my chair and reflected upon this possibility. Although it was not common for humans to dwell permanently in underground cities, I was well aware that pertinent examples existed in the plateaus of Cappadocia. At the time, I had not yet fully formulated my own maxim and instead relied upon that of Occam: *'Entia non sunt multiplicanda praeter necessitate.'*[21] Surely, the theory of Mr. Gaelton could, on its own, explain the sum of Shivering Cavern's mysteries?

"I sat up for many hours of that cloudy and moonless night pondering these questions, consuming an ounce of shag tobacco in the process. When the morning finally dawned, I discovered that there had been new developments in the case. During the night, several additional sheep had disappeared from farms in the neighbourhood, including one belonging to the two Miss Vermilions. No trace had been left of them, and my hosts passed along the rumours buzzing through the countryside of both sheep-stealing gypsies and strange terrors in the night. However, there was something more serious than a few missing ungulates: Mr. Handsacre had also disappeared! He had left his moorland cottage early on the two nights prior and had not been heard of since. He was an unattached man, so there was less sensation than would otherwise be the case. The popular explanation, per Miss Alma, was that Handsacre owed someone money, and had found a situation in some other part of the country, whence he would presently write for his belongings.

"But I had grave misgivings, Watson. I considered it much more likely that the recent disappearance of the sheep had caused him to take some steps which may have ended in his own destruction. He may, for example, have lain in wait for the Terror and instead been carried off by the lost Romans into the recesses of the mountains. What an inconceivable fate for a civilized Englishman of the twentieth century! And yet, I felt that it was possible and even probable.

"I resolved that I would set off at once to rescue Handsacre. I briefly considered enlisting the aid of a companion, but who could be trusted? Back at the university, I had the reputation of being a man of courage and enterprise. When there was a ghost-hunt at Chargeford, it was I alone who sat up in the haunted house until the mystery was solved.[22] I prepared for this final expedition more deliberately and better considered than the last. As a first step, I went round to Castleton and obtained a few essentials – a large acetylene lantern for one thing, and a good jemmy for another. The latter I judged to be sufficient for opening the gate's lock. I was now ready for my troglodyte friends. Give me better health and a little spate of energy, and I should try conclusions with them yet. But who and what are they?

"It was shortly after noon when I once more entered that Tartarian realm and carefully retraced my steps to the in-scribed gate. I made short work of the lock and pushed my way past, only to find myself in a further labyrinth of tunnels. As I went along, I recalled the lesson of Knossos, and I made some subtle marks in chalk in order to guide my way back to the surface. And then, I came to the point where I met with a sudden and desperate disaster. A stream, some twenty feet broad, ran across my path. I judged it to be at least three or four feet deep, so I walked for some little distance along the bank to find a spot where I could cross dry-shod. Finally, I came to a place where a single flat boulder lay near the centre, which I could reach in a stride. However, the rock had been cut away and made top-heavy – either by the rush of the stream or the cunning hand of man – such that it tilted over as I landed on it and shot me into the ice-cold water. My lantern flew from my hand, and I found myself floundering about in utter and absolute darkness.

"I staggered to my feet again, more amused than alarmed by my adventure, for the current was not very strong. The lantern was lost in the stream, but I had two candles in my pocket, so that it at first seemed to be of no importance. I got one of them ready, and drew out my box of matches to light it. Only then did I realize my position. The box had been soaked during my fall into the river. It was impossible to strike the matches!

"I frowned as I considered my options. The darkness of the cavern was quite opaque. It was so utterly black, that even when I put my hand up to my face I could discern nothing different. I tried to reconstruct in my mind a map of the floor of the cavern as I had last seen it. Unfortunately, the marks that I had made upon the wall were visual in nature and not able to be found by touch. I should have used Ariadne's thread! Still, I remembered in a general way how the sides were situated, and I hoped that by groping my way along them I should at last come to the opening of the Roman gate. Moving very slowly, and continually striking against the rocks, I set out upon this quest.

"However, I very soon realized how impossible it was. In that black, velvety darkness, one lost all of one's bearings in an instant. Before I had made it fifty paces, I was frustratingly baffled as to my whereabouts. The rippling of the stream, which was the one sound audible, showed me where it lay, but the moment that I left its bank I was utterly lost. The idea of finding my way back in absolute darkness through that limestone labyrinth was clearly an impossible one. I resolved at that moment that, once this adventure had passed, I would henceforth hone my other senses so that never again would I need to rely upon sight alone.

"I sat down upon a boulder and reflected upon my plight. I had not told anyone that I proposed to explore the Shivering Cavern mine, and it was unlikely that a search party would come after me. Therefore, I knew that I must trust to my own resources in order to get clear of the danger. There was only one hope, and that was that the matches might eventually dry. When I fell into the river, only half of me had got thoroughly wet. My left shoulder had remained above the water. I took the box of matches, therefore, and put it into that armpit. The heat of my body might possibly counteract the moist air of the cavern, but even so, I knew that I could not hope to strike a light for many hours. Meanwhile, there was nothing for it but to wait.

"By good luck I had slipped several biscuits into my pocket before I had departed the farm-house. Although somewhat damp, these I now devoured, and washed them down with a draught from that stream which had been the impediment to my mission. Then I felt about for a comfortable seat among the rocks, and, having discovered a place where I could get a support for my back, I stretched out my legs and settled myself down to wait. I was damp and cold, and I reflected that should Professor Alexander ever hear of this, he would be most exasperated apropos of how I had attended to my health during this time of supposed rest from my recent illness. Gradually, lulled by the monotonous gurgle of the stream, and by the absolute darkness, I sank into an uneasy slumber.

"How long this lasted I cannot say with certainty, but I suspected a span of some six to eight hours. Suddenly I sat up from my rock bench, with every nerve thrilling and every sense acutely on the alert. Beyond all doubt, I had heard a sound – some sound very distinct from the gurgling of the waters. It had passed, but the reverberation of it still lingered in my ear. Was it a search party? I almost called out, and then realized that they would most certainly have shouted, and vague as this sound was which had wakened me, it seemed to be moving furtively, and not like a group seeking a missing man. It soon became a continuous noise, and it was coming in my direction. From the regular beat of the muffled tread, it was clear that it derived from a crowd of men moving decisively, as if they knew the paths upon which they strode. And then, a light began to flicker from the mouth of a tunnel, which I soon recognized as the one that had led me to this locale. Within a minute, I watched curiously as a party of some thirty men, all dressed in white robes and carrying torches, filed past. When they came to the bank of the stream, I noticed that they avoided the obvious crossing place where I had fallen, and instead utilized a spot where the stepping-stone was almost completely covered by water. Once across, they moved towards another tunnel opening, and I realized that I had mere moments of light remaining in order to copy their actions.

"Never did it occur to me to seize this moment to make my escape back to the surface. I placed the matches back in my pocket, hoping they were now dry, and instead moved to follow the mysterious men. I had no wish to lose sight of their torches! I kept as much distance between us as feasible, but at the trade-off that I could little see where I placed my own feet. At one point, I accidentally kicked a few stones, which rattled loudly in the echoing tunnel. I heard the group pause. Had they caught the sound of my pursuit? Hardly daring to breathe, I crouched behind a rock, knowing it offered little actual shelter should they decide to backtrack and investigate. Fortunately for me, they must have determined that my kicked stones were merely a delayed slide stirred up from their own passage, and I eventually heard their steps resume and draw away into the distance.

"I continued my chase of this band deep into the bowels of the earth. I will admit that my blood was up, and my quarry seemed to be hastening to some nefarious end. An old primeval hunting-spirit awoke within me, and prudence was cast to the wind. I ran at the top of my speed upon the trail of the band, hoping to obtain absolute proof of their nature and deeds. I soon realized that the light that I was tracking began to grow brighter, which suggested to me that the group had stopped, perhaps even reaching their final destination.

"I slowed down in turn and then drew up my steps and paused at what seemed to be the end of the tunnel. Concealing myself as best as possible, I peered around the corner. The most fantastic sight greeted my eyes. Within was an enormous central cave, far larger than any I had yet encountered in those depths. Here the stalagmites and stalactites had fused into pillars of stone, which had been carved to resemble Ionic columns. Brass braziers filled the room with vivid light, black smoke, and a mephitic odour. By means of this glow, I was able to see that the band of men had spread out to fill the space, which had been adorned as a Roman temple. Most were turned away from me and towards an ornate marble altar. Upon this rested a curious goblet, through which the light shone and reflected vivid blue rays about the room, and which I presumed had been carved from the fabled Blue John stone.

"Behind the altar – where classically the statue of the patron god would have resided – was instead the skeleton of a great beast, reared up on his hind legs as a bear would, though this bear was twice the size of any bear seen upon the earth. His great crooked forelegs shone with their ivory-white claws, and his gaping mouth was fringed with monstrous fangs. I could just make out that the skeleton had been cleverly wired together and hung from a rope that vanished into the dark shadows of the ceiling.

"Facing me were two men, their faces covered with white

masks through which their eyes gleamed in the flickering candle light. Despite this attempt at disguise, it would not be immodest to claim that even then my powers of observation were finely honed, and it was only the dim light and great distance that prevented me from making a positive identification. Nonetheless, I felt confident that the man closest to the altar was none other than the local medico, Dr Lukeson. Though I had not met him face to face, I suspected that the man behind Lukeson was therefore his accomplice in crime, Mr. Gaelton of Buxton.

"I then realized that before the altar was the kneeling figure of a man, his hands bound behind him and his mouth gagged. His face was turned away from me, but I was certain that it was none other than the unfortunate Mr. Handsacre. My mind raced at this new development. How was I to effect Handsacre's rescue? Although my training in baritsu was progressing, I knew that I stood little chance against a gang of some thirty men, even with the element of surprise in my favour. As I pondered this question, the leader turned his glare upon Handsacre.

"When he spoke the man's voice echoed perfectly around the enclosed chamber. 'Richard Handsacre, you stand accused of violating our sacrosanct temple upon our most sacred day, and observing that which is forbidden to all outsiders. To every man upon this earth, death cometh soon or late. And how can man die better than facing fearful odds, for the ashes of his fathers, and the temples of his gods? Your fate will be determined by the omens divined by the sacrifice of your own beast. Only they may determine if you should ever again see the light of day, or if you are to be condemned to wander the underworld forever.'

"The man I took to be Dr Lukeson turned and motioned to an area of the chamber that was outside of my line of sight. As I watched with some amazement, a sheep – its hooves bound together – was carried out of what I presumed to be a side cave. Struggling feebly, it was laid upon the stone altar and the man I thought to be Mr. Gaelton stepped forward to raise a curved dagger above the poor beast. Without warning, he plunged the blade down into the sheep's heart and a spurt of blood showered the front of his white robes. He quickly eviscerated the liver and held it forth in his hands, as if studying it. I realized that the man was a *haruspex*, a priest trained to read such entrails.[23] I had stumbled upon a lost legion of Roman soldiers, still carrying on traditions that had otherwise vanished from the earth centuries prior!

"However, then something else dawned upon me. The first words the other man – Dr Lukeson – had spoken were also carved above the gate. And they were not Latin – at least not originally. They were from Macaulay's *Lays* and were therefore but half-a-century old.[24] The *Lays* were standard reading in my public school, otherwise I would have taken little note of these words. At one point, I had memorized a critical bit about Captain Horatius and a bridge in preparation for an examination, and it stuck with me still.

"I suddenly realized that these men were no lost vestige of a Roman legion. They were members of some previously unknown secret society, using the cave to enact their arcane rituals. Like the Masons, who took inspiration from the vanished Knights Templar, these men found their cues in the hidden mysteries of ancient Rome. So I read the riddle. If I was correct, these men simply planned to scare Handsacre witless; they would not do him actual harm. I could safely withdraw and wait them out.

"I retreated a ways back down the tunnel and pulled out my matches. They seemed perfectly hard and dry. Stooping down into a crevice of the rocks, I tried one of them. To my delight, it took fire at once. I lit the candle, and, with a quick backward glance into the obscure depths of the cavern, I hurried in the direction of the Roman passage.

"When I emerged back into the world above, I found that night had fallen. The clouds were drifting low, and there was not a star in the sky. I scrambled up the slope of stones, careful to avoid the tangle of briars, and found a patch of soft grass nestled between the rocks. There I perched above the mouth of the Roman shaft and doused my candle. I waited patiently for the group of men to emerge. It was a lonely vigil. All down the winding valley, I could see the scattered lights of the farm-houses, and the sound of the church clock of Edale tolling the hours came faintly to my ears. Twelve o'clock struck in the distant church, then one, then two. It was the darkest hour of the night. An owl was hooting somewhere among the rocks, but no other sound – save the gentle whistling of the wind – came to my ears. And then suddenly I heard them! From far away down the tunnel came those muffled steps, marching in unison. I heard also the rattle of stones as they gave way under the tread of the band's feet. They drew nearer. They were close upon me. I heard the rustling of the bushes round the entrance, and then dimly through the gloom I saw the group emerge.

"As they passed me, I counted their number until I was certain of two things. First: all of the members of that secret society had actually departed the cave. And second: Mr. Handsacre was not amongst their band. I began to fear that I had sorely miscalculated the fatal resolve of this society. I watched as they were swallowed up in the darkness of the night, and counted to sixty before I made my move. Relighting my candle and shading its light from any members who chanced to look behind them, I once more plunged into that rocky archway.

"I immediately made for the great cavern where their ceremony had taken place, pausing only briefly to once more unlock the supposed 'Roman' gate, and to carefully ford the subterranean river at the proper spot. The room looked like a different place entirely by the dim light of my candle rather than the bright light of the now-cold braziers. The enormous cave-bear skeleton looked even more fearsome, if such a thing was possible. To my eternal relief, however, I found a still-breathing Handsacre near where I had abandoned him. Whether it was the words of the men who had captured him, or the thought of being left alone all night in the pitch-black cavern with only the looming bear for company, he had fainted in a surge of taphophobic terror.[25] Undoing his bonds and gag, I struggled to arouse him. I cursed myself for forgetting to bring along an invigorating flask of brandy, but eventually Handsacre came around. His reason was nearly unstrung after his unwilling adventure, and his limbs quivered uncontrollably. He had sustained a terrible shock to both his mind and his body, but with one arm thrown over my shoulders, I managed to guide him back to the surface.

"Before we left that chamber, however, I decided to relieve the society of one of its artefacts. The *haruspex* had left his Blue John goblet upon the altar, which I tucked into my coat pocket. Upon our exit from Shivering Cavern, Handsacre insisted upon being brought round to his farmhouse. A cursory inspection by my untrained eye suggested that his left arm and at least two ribs had been badly fractured during his rough capture. However, I hesitated to summon the local medico, for I was certain that Dr Lukeson had been one of the perpetrators of Handsacre's torture. For a few moments, I worried that Handsacre would pass into high delirium, but he seemed to have been made of firmer stuff and soon regained his wits.

"After I splinted his arm, we discussed his misadventure and what response we should make. He argued that with the knowledge that he had gained, it was his duty to see something done that would prevent any further conventicles of that treacherous society. He wished for no man to ever again undergo the mishaps that he had suffered over the last four and twenty hours.

"Handsacre recounted to me that when he had returned home from the walk where we had argued, he found that one of his sheep had gone missing. He discovered a strange boot-print in the mud of his fields, which he tracked back to the entrance to Shivering Cavern. Realizing that I was correct during our argument, and that a human agency was responsible rather than a monstrous beast, Handsacre returned to his house for a lantern and gun. However, he had only penetrated as far as the inscribed gateway when he was struck from behind and lost consciousness. When he awoke, he found himself in the great cave, where two men were engaged in a heated argument. They did not realize that Handsacre was listening, so he was able to learn that Gaelton and Lukeson had founded what they had entitled the Artus Society.[26] From what he was able to piece together, Handsacre determined that the pair had recruited prominent members of the local towns' governments with grandiose promises of progressive teachings available only to selected individuals. These teachings, based on the Mithraic mystery cults of the Roman age, supposedly led to hidden and unique truths, which would bring about personal benefits beyond the reach and understanding of the uninitiated.[27] Because their rituals were so secret, they had to be practiced deep below the mines of Shivering Cavern, where non-members could neither observe them, nor even learn about the existence of their society. To those ends, the members of the society spread rumours of the Terror across the countryside, made special tools to counterfeit its foot-print, and would upon occasion even ensure that strange smells and sounds emanated from the cavern's mouth.

"Nonetheless, it was all a sham. In reality, Gaelton and Lukeson were using the Artus Society as a front for their illegal mining of Blue John. For it seemed that the Shivering Cavern vein was not fully mined out. However, the rights belonged to a Manchester man named Swinburne, who was already well off and therefore had no intention of excavating the vein. The conspirators wished to keep their activities quiet, as the surreptitious sale of the Blue John was making them vastly wealthy. As Handsacre listened, he heard Gaelton and Lukeson argue about his own fate, for his sudden appearance threatened the secrecy of their entire operation. Lukeson had implied going so far as to permanently silence Handsacre, but the other man instead argued to spare him and, if need be, to ensure that Handsacre was involuntarily confined to Gaelton's mad asylum. Although Gaelton's less-fatal argument had ultimately won out, Handsacre still wished to see both men pay for his suffering, not to mention the chronic theft of his sheep for their gruesome rituals.

"I, however, counselled against any such action. There was little evidence to prove what he said was true. Handsacre had never seen their faces. It would be his word against theirs. I had procured the Blue John cup, but I was certain that by the time we returned to the cave tomorrow, the society members would have learned of Handsacre's escape and hidden the great bear skeleton. Furthermore, there were close to thirty men in that cave with Gaelton and Lukeson. How could we know precisely which local men were their accomplices in the Artus Society? Even if we could locate a sympathetic constable, one willing to hear us out, how were we to be certain that he had not himself participated? I instead argued that we should turn the society's own ruse against them. If they wished to jest with the credibility of their poorer folk of the countryside, we would harness such beliefs.

"Perhaps the educated and the scientific inhabitants of Castleton smiled knowingly at Handsacre when he narrated his fictional adventure the following morning to a transfixed crowd in the town square. He told them of his supposed encounter with the Terror, and how he had barely escaped its clutches. For a few hours, local opinion was fiercely divided upon the subject. On the one hand were those who suggested that Handsacre had suffered from some strange hallucination, perhaps induced by an escaped bubble of Pythian gas.[28] Some *idée fixe*, according to these gentlemen, caused Handsacre to wander down the tunnel, and a fall among the rocks was sufficient to account for his injuries. On the other hand, a legend of a strange creature in the cavern had existed for some years back, and the farmers looked upon Handsacre's narrative and his personal injuries as a final corroboration. So the matter stands, and so the matter will continue to stand, for no definite solution will ever be possible.

"On that afternoon, less than twelve hours after I had recovered Handsacre from the depths of Shivering Cavern, the locals assembled in their hundreds round the great stone maw. Over the protests of several seemingly adventurous gentlemen from Buxton and Sheffield, who had offered to descend into the cave and explore for any evidence of a prehistoric beast, the country people took the matter into their own hands. From a late hour of the morning, they had worked hard in stopping up the entrance of the tunnel. There was a sharp slope where the shaft begins, and great boulders, rolled along by many willing hands, were thrust down it until the mouth was absolutely sealed.

'As the headlines of the *Castleton Courier* said about the matter: 'Shivering Cavern's Terror No More.' Mr. Charrington's article was remarkably lurid and concluded that: 'it transcends human wit to give any scientific explanation which could cover the alleged facts.' Since Handsacre and I, with the unwitting help of the Artus Society, had invented the Terror whole cloth, I suppose that Charrington was absolutely correct.

"Once that cavern was sealed, it seemed obvious that both Handsacre and I had worn out our welcome in the vales of Derbyshire. We met for one last time opposite the steep hillside, grey with shale rock. Upon its flank was the dark cleft which once marked the opening of the Shivering Cavern. Never again through that ill-omened tunnel should any strange band flit out into the world of men. The men of the Artus Society officially went unpunished, but I later learned that after we deprived them of their illicit livelihood, both Lukeson and Gaelton were ruined financially. So, perhaps a form of justice had indeed been handed out. One that Jove himself, I like to think, would have appreciated.

"For his part, Handsacre abandoned sheep-farming, and the last I heard, he had moved to Ashford and become the principal of a preparatory school of no small repute, as well as the author of several fine scholarly books. Meanwhile, I returned to university where I redoubled my efforts to acquire the unique set of skills and knowledge that would eventually allow me to make my way in the world. I did, however, retain the Blue John cup as a memento of that early adventure."

Holmes leaned back in his chair and smiled at me. "So you see, Watson, there is a possibility of lost worlds or antediluvian beasts anywhere, even a place as prosaic as the hills of northern England. Who knows what might exist in the distant reaches of Africa or South America? You should not doubt the merits of Mr. Haggard's writings. Of course, in this instance, the matter was rather simpler than a centuries-enduring Roman legion. Still, I have it on good authority that such secret societies are the wellsprings of an ancient desire for an all-male warrior band. Perhaps in that way the ordinary members of the Artus Society were, in spirit, a remnant of a lost company of Rome. And one with which I can undoubtedly sympathize, for – with the exception of spinsters such as the two Miss Vermilions – I am not a whole-hearted admirer of womankind."

Ignoring Holmes' unreasonable attitude towards the fairer sex, I instead spluttered incredulously, "Holmes, if I didn't know you as well as I do, I would be certain that this recitation is a complete fiction. Why have you never told this story before?"

"I have, Watson. Once before I spoke of it to someone I trusted, and the scepticism with which it was met has prevented me from ever opening my mouth upon the subject again.[29] It goes without saying that this is one tale which can never be recorded, for I fear that your readers will lose all confidence in me and business may suffer."

§

THE ADVENTURE OF THE DOUBLE-EDGED HOARD

I t was an early December day, the snow still fresh on the ground, when Sherlock Holmes inquired if I would be interested in assisting him with another one of his cases. As it was only towards the tail end of the first year of our association, there were but a rare few adventures in which he had to date deigned to include me, despite my great curiosity regarding the matters of the mystery at Lauriston Gardens, or the disappearance of Mr. James Simmons from the Savoy.[30]

On the day in question, Baker Street was still enjoying its morning quiet before the roar of passing hansoms and omnibuses would begin to fill the air, which itself was happily free of the typical gloomy winter fogs. The two of us had recently finished breaking our fast. I was absently perusing the morning editions, while in the armchair across from me, Holmes was smoking his morning dottles and reading Langemann's *Textbook on Metallurgy*.

"Hark to that!" said Holmes, snapping closed the book and pulling his long legs back from the cheery fire. "Why, if I am not mistaken, I think we are about to have a caller."

I glanced up. "Why do you say that, Holmes?"

"The overwhelming majority of people, Watson, rarely utilize the full gamut of their senses. Vision, of course, is employed, though there is a vast chasm between seeing and observing. However, the others are sadly neglected except during unusual occasions when a person turns his complete attention to the sense in question, such as during a concert by Norman-Neruda at the Albert Hall, or while enjoying an epicurean repast at Simpson's. I, on the other hand, have engaged in a systematic training that enables my senses to be alert at all times. That is how I can tell that a police wagon has just pulled up in front of our rooms."

I stood and made my way over to the half-parted blinds in order to verify his statement. As he had predicted, I noted the presence of a Black Maria at the curb of the snowy street.[31] I shook my head in amazement. "I fail to see, Holmes, how you could tell it was a police wagon rather than any other four-wheeled carriage?"

"The bell, Watson, the bell."

Any further explanation was cut short by a knocking upon the door. The boy in buttons entered to announce our visitor, which proved to be our old-acquaintance Constable John Rance. Despite Holmes' previous ill-treatment of the man, the constable had come around to the opinion that Holmes was a bit of a magician and had forgiven Holmes' once harsh words.

Holmes peered at the man. "From whom do you bring a message, Mr. Rance?"

Rance pulled a note from his coat pocket. "From Inspector Lestrade," he replied, handing it over.

Holmes nodded, as if this confirmed a theory of his, and without looking at it, he glanced over at me. "What do you, say, Watson, to a trip up to Cambridge?"

Rance gave a little jump of surprise, and his features assumed a mystified expression. "Have you been hiding in the telegram room at Scotland Yard, Mr. Holmes?"

Holmes chuckled. "No, that sounds like a dull occupation

indeed, constable. If I recall my Bradshaw's correctly, pray inform Lestrade that we will arrive upon the eleven o'clock train."

The man's brows furrowed in utmost astonishment and he tipped his hat. "Very good, sir."

When Rance had departed, Holmes turned to me with a smile. "Well, Watson, are you coming?"

I nodded my agreement. "Why not? It is a case, I presume?"

"Oh yes, and quite a peculiar one. Certain elements bring to mind the Williams case of '11 or the more recent Greenwich hammer attack.[32] The official forces are completely puzzled, of course. Hence they are calling me in to shed some light where all is dark."

I shook my head. "How could you possibly know that, Holmes? You haven't even opened the note. I admit that I am as mystified as Constable Rance."

Holmes laughed. "I am afraid that was rather simple, Watson. There was a note of the case in last night's paper, which mentioned that our old friend Lestrade had been called in to assist the local force. As soon as Rance told me the sender of the note, I knew exactly what it must comprise."

"Ah, that is rather simple then."

"Everything unknown passes for something splendid, Watson. The sad part of science is that it can – at times – take some of the wonder out of the world. For myself, I prefer to maintain a bit of mystery to my methods. It elevates my little reputation amongst the official police force."

I glanced at my pocket-watch. "If we are to meet Lestrade as promised, we must set off at once. Should I pack a valise?"

Holmes shook his head as he threw on his long grey travelling cloak and close-fitting cap. "No, I imagine we should be back well before the bell strikes midnight. I expect this to be a simple matter."

Thirty minutes later, when we had finally settled into the otherwise empty train carriage, Holmes pulled out his briarwood pipe and crossed his legs. "Would you care to hear an account of the case, Watson?"

"Of course, Holmes. I am all ears," said I, leaning forward.

"Both Lestrade's note and the London dailies are rather vague, but I tracked down a copy of yesterday's local paper which has a concise account of the circumstances. Here are the facts as I know them, Watson. Two nights ago, Dr Everett Ackroyd, Regius Professor of History at Cambridge University[33] and Director of the Fitzwilliam Museum, was murdered within a stone's throw of the entrance to the Old Court at Pembroke College. It appears that the eminent professor was highly beloved by both his students and the townsfolk, therefore his sudden slaying has excited strong concerns that others may be in danger."[34]

"A tragic story, to be sure, Holmes, but hardly that unusual. Why the concern that anyone else is at risk?"

"Because of the particularly brutal form of the murder. It seems, Watson, that Dr Ackroyd left the Museum about half-past five in the afternoon in order to meet the train due from York at three minutes after six. His old friend and comrade, Professor William Sidney, Sub-Curator of the Museum and Bosworth Professor of Anglo-Saxons accompanied him.[35] The object of these two esteemed gentlemen in meeting this particular train was to receive the legacy bequeathed by the late Earl of Chesterfield to the Museum."

"The same Earl of Chesterfield who recently was killed by his assistant?" I interjected, the lurid details still somewhat fresh in my recollection.

"Precisely, Watson. While it is far too early to form any definitive hypotheses, we must consider that the Earl's recent demise may in some way be connected to the mystery at hand. It appears that Chesterfield left his personal collection of medieval weapons, as well as several priceless illuminated manuscripts, to enrich the museum of his *alma mater*. Dr Ackroyd refused to entrust the reception and care of this valuable legacy to a mere subordinate. Therefore, with the assistance of Professor Sidney, the two men proceeded to remove the entire collection from the train, and packed it away into the Museum's gig."

"Hold a minute, Holmes. How old was Dr Ackroyd?"

Holmes smiled. "An excellent question, Watson, and one that had also occurred to me. The paper is silent on this matter, but a quick perusal of *Bulmer's Directory* before our departure from Baker Street informed me that Dr Ackroyd was born in 1806."[36]

"So, he was seventy-five years old? And his colleague, Professor Sidney, was he of a similar age?"

"Much the same, Watson. He was only two years younger than Dr Ackroyd."

I shook my head. "That is most unusual, Holmes, for two such distinguished and elderly men to perform their own manual labour."

"I concur, Watson. Most of the manuscripts and more fragile items were packed in cases of pinewood, but many of the weapons were simply done round with velvet, so that considerable effort was involved in moving them all. However, it seems that Dr Ackroyd was so nervous that any object be injured in the process that he refused to allow any of the railway employees to assist. Every article was carried across the platform by Professor Sidney and handed to Dr Ackroyd in the cart. When everything was in its place, the two gentlemen personally drove the cart back to the Museum. It appears that Professor Sidney later testified that Dr Ackroyd was in excellent spirits, and not a little proud of his feat of physical exertion. He even made some jest in allusion of his prowess to a Mr. Ramsey, the museum's janitor. The latter had met the cart upon its return, and enlisting the help of his friend Walton, the pair of them unloaded the contents under the watchful eyes of the two older gentlemen. Once Dr Ackroyd was satisfied that his new curiosities were safely tucked away in the storeroom and the door locked, he entrusted the key to his sub-curator. He bid the three men 'good evening' and departed in the direction of his college. He was never seen alive again."

"What happened?" I asked, aghast.

"At eleven o'clock, about an hour-and-a-half after Dr Ackroyd's departure from the Museum, a commissionaire was passing along the front of Pembroke College and came across the lifeless body of the professor lying a little way from the side of the road. According to the paper, Dr Ackroyd had fallen upon his face, with both hands stretched out. His head was literally split in two halves by a tremendous blow, which it is conjectured must have been struck from behind."

"Why would they conclude such a thing?"

"Because Dr Ackroyd had a peaceful smile upon his face, Watson. It was as if he had still been dwelling upon his new archeologic acquisitions when the blow suddenly fell. There was no other mark of violence upon the body, except a bruise upon his left kneecap, presumably caused by the fall itself."

"Have they determined a motive?"

"Ah, that is the most mysterious part of the affair. Dr Ackroyd's purse still contained forty-two pounds, and his golden pocket-watch was untouched. Robbery cannot, therefore, have been the incentive to the deed."

"Unless the assassin was disturbed before he could complete his work," I suggested.

Holmes shook his head. "It will not do, Watson. This idea is refuted by the fact that nobody reported such a thing. In addition, the body was stone-cold when it was discovered by the commissionaire. I highly doubt whether the local coroner is capable of fixing a precise time of death, but even on a mid-winter's night, it would take some time for that to occur."

"So why precisely are you involved, Holmes?"

"The local police, headed by a man named Sergeant White, investigated the case; however their research has failed to throw the least glimmer of light upon the matter. White could find no trace of the murderer, nor does he appear to possess sufficient ingenuity to imagine a reason that would have induced someone to commit the deed. By all reports, Dr Ackroyd was a man so consumed by his own studies and pursuits that he lived much apart from the world. As far as the police can tell, he never raised the slightest acrimony in any human heart."

"Then it must have been some brute, some savage, who loved blood for its own sake, who struck that cruel blow," I concluded.

Holmes shook his head. "Not necessarily, Watson. It is far too soon to postulate the existence of a random lunatic. Simply because the local police force has failed to turn up a *raison* for this crime, does not denote that one fails to exist. However, since the local police were completely dumfounded as to both means and motive, they called for assistance from Scotland Yard. They in turn sent up the good Inspector Lestrade, who you likely recall from the little matters of Brixton Road and the Holloway forgery case."[37]

"Of course."

"Not surprisingly, given his own limitations, Lestrade was also unable to come to any conclusions upon the matter. As his note informed me, an anonymous letter has cast suspicion upon the janitor's friend Walton. However, Lestrade has been unable to locate the tiniest morsel of evidence against him, so no arrest has been made. Fortunately, Lestrade has made the wise choice of promptly requesting my assistance with the investigation and here we are." He waved out the window to the passing bucolic scenery of the Essex countryside.

§

The lean, ferret-like form of Inspector Lestrade was waiting for us when the train arrived at the Cambridge railway station. He held out his hand for a quick greeting, but the look on his face was grave.

"I take it that you have made no further progress, Lestrade?" asked Holmes mildly.

"It's worse than that, Mr. Holmes," replied the inspector morosely. "There's been another killing."

"Another?" exclaimed Holmes, his right eyebrow arched and his eyes gleaming with interest. "Pray tell. Spare no details, Lestrade."

"Was it Professor Sidney?" I asked. For I had, during the remainder of the train ride, begun to construct a theory in which Dr Ackroyd had been targeted because of his academic affiliation.

Lestrade eyed me and shook his head. "No, Doctor. It is Walton, the labourer. He was found this morning lying in the north-western corner of the yard at King's College Chapel. He was so mutilated that he was hardly recognizable. His head was hacked open in very much the same way as that of Dr Ackroyd, and his body exhibited numerous deep gashes, as if the murderer had been so possessed with fury that he had continued to hack at the body long after all life had fled."

Holmes frowned at this horrific news. "Have you disturbed the body, Lestrade? Snow fell heavily yesterday and through the night. If we go at once, we may be able to read traces in the prints of the assassin."

Lestrade shook his head. "The body was in plain sight of the road, so we were forced to remove it to the local mortuary. We can examine the scene if you like, Mr. Holmes, but knowing your methods, I am afraid it will not make you very happy. You are correct that there is snow, almost a foot deep in places, and when the body was discovered there was a thin layer coating the man. However, a passing coal heaver, who in turn called for help, discovered Walton's body. A number of folk rushed over to discover the source of the commotion, and by the time the local constables thought to make a cordon around the body, I am afraid the scene became a blurry mess of footprints. I think that it is nigh impossible to draw any trustworthy evidence from them."

"I will look at them all the same." Holmes scowled in evident frustration at this potentially wasted clue. "But you simply must instruct these local men in the proper respect for a crime scene. They should attempt to emulate a solitary statue rather than a herd of buffaloes. Now, Lestrade, have you discerned a motive to the attack?"

"That's just the thing, Mr. Holmes," cried Lestrade in despair. "We have the same impenetrable mystery and absence of motive as with the murder of Dr Ackroyd. In Walton's pocket, we found a notebook which contained a considerable sum in gold and several fifty pound bills from the Bank of England."

"The attacker left behind all of that money!" I exclaimed.

"Yes, Doctor," replied Lestrade. "Of course, it is hardly conceivable that anyone in their right mind would leave such a spoil untouched. Therefore, the town-folk have concluded that a madman walks the streets."

"Yes, well, perhaps we should start with the scene of the most recent attack?" suggested Holmes.

"As you wish, Mr. Holmes," nodded Lestrade, waving towards a row of waiting hansoms.

A quarter of a mile ride down Regent Street soon brought us to the site in question, in the snowy corner of the yard surrounding the city's most magnificent structure. The Gothic spires soaring into the crisp blue sky proved to be a stark contrast to the sad scene below, where a red-splattered area still bore witness to the gruesome crime. The area remained under the guard of a tall and thin man, whom Lestrade introduced as Sergeant White. His official uniform was crisp and neat, and he had an expression of alertness. At his side were two stalwart constables armed with large whisk-brooms.

"What are you doing, man?" Holmes asked, a note of alarm in his voice.

"We are about to sweep the area," said White, mildly.

"Whatever for?"

"There was no sign of the murder weapon next to the body, so we thought it might have been discarded in the snowdrifts nearby."

Holmes shook his head. "You are as likely to find the crown jewels in that snow pile as you are the murder weapon. The assassin would never be so foolish. He would either maintain possession of it, or if he wished to dispose of it, the presence of the nearby River Cam would be much more amenable than a drift of snow which may melt away in a few days' time."

"That's an excellent idea, Mr. Holmes," exclaimed Lestrade. "White, have your men drag the river."

"Hold a minute, Lestrade. Let us see if we can determine the whereabouts of the weapon with rather less effort." Holmes proceeded to stroll nonchalantly up and down the blood-soaked area where the body had been found. He gazed fixedly upon the ground and at one point he stopped, his eyes betraying a glimmer of satisfaction. He knelt down and pulled a large rosewood-handled magnifying glass from his pocket in order to inspect one particular area more closely. Finally, he rose, brushed some snow from his pant-legs, and replaced his glass. Glancing over at us, he shook his head. "Well, Lestrade. I can see why you determined that the ground is far too trodden over to make anything of it. But there are one or two peculiarities of note."

Lestrade frowned. "What? Where?"

"They may be nothing, only further investigation will say for certain. I suggest we commence with a trip to examine Mr. Walton's chambers."

Lestrade pulled out a notebook and consulted it. "He boarded with the widow Green at 25 Victoria Street. However, I am not certain, Mr. Holmes, what we might find there that could possibly tell us anything? Surely this was a random attack."

"We shall see," replied Holmes evasively. "Sergeant White, if I may request that you and your men refrain from demolishing the area for a few minutes longer, I shall attempt to locate your murder weapon in another locale altogether." He then set off briskly for the street in question, with the two of us close upon his heels, our breaths curling in the crisp, frosty air. As we walked, Holmes questioned the inspector. "Tell me, Lestrade, what is your theory as to the sum of money in Mr. Walton's pocket?"

"Well, Sergeant White supposes that Walton may have lent money to someone, and when he went to collect, the assassin utilized this method as a means of evading his debt."

"So you have discounted the madman hypothesis?"

"Not at all. I was just telling you the competing notion. I, for one, favour the rogue lunatic. But I don't know how to identify him before his next attack."

"Hmmm," murmured Holmes.

"You don't agree, Mr. Holmes?" said the inspector irritably.

"I have yet to form a complete theory, Lestrade. It is far too premature, as we are not yet in possession of all of the facts. But in my experience, there is often a method to madness."

Number 25 Victoria Street proved to be a modest dun-coloured brick row-home tucked behind one of the colleges, where resided the common folk who maintained the apparatus of the great university. The street was exceedingly narrow, such that the houses crowded right up to the sidewalks, while an appropriately painted front door marked Mrs. Green's house. The widow herself was a mousy-faced woman of some thirty-odd years. Over the course of the next few minutes, we discovered that her husband had died two years prior from diphtheria, and so she had opened three of her rooms to boarders. Walton had been with her from the start and was considered an affable man with little ambition other than enjoying a pint at the local pub.

"Tell me, Mrs. Green," asked Holmes, "what was the source of Mr. Walton's income?"

She shrugged. "He did odd jobs around the town. Nothing steady. His friend Ramsey often turned him on to work."

"So you are acquainted with Mr. Ramsey?"

"Oh yes, he would come by often to have a smoke with Mr. Walton."

"Do you know the nature of their friendship?"

She shrugged. "From what I could tell by their conversations, they were once soldiers together. Bengal Army, I think."

"So Mr. Walton was not a wealthy man?"

She scoffed. "Quite the contrary. It was a rare month that he paid his rent on time."

"You may have heard that Mr. Walton was found with a considerable sum of money upon him. Do you have any idea where it would have come from?"

"I heard it all right, but can hardly credit it. The man seldom had two pence to rub together."

"And what exactly did Mr. Walton do on the day of his demise?"

She shook her head. "I don't rightly know. He was shut up in his room most of the day. He seemed deeply downhearted about the suspicion that has been affixed upon him."

"But he eventually went out?"

"Oh, yes. It was around eleven o'clock in the evening when I heard him depart."

"Surely that is a late time to go for a stroll?"

She shrugged. "He had said earlier he didn't want to show his face on the streets. Possibly he thought that there would be fewer folks about at that hour and he might be able to pass unrecognized?"

"Perhaps. You did not wait up for him to return?"

"Oh, no! He had a latchkey and could let himself in at any time. I went to bed and by the time I realized that he had not come down for breakfast, Sergeant White was already knocking at my door to tell me that poor Mr. Walton was dead."

"Thank you, Mrs. Green. You have been most helpful. Would you mind if we took a quick look at Mr. Walton's room?"

She shrugged. "A couple of constables have already been over it and said there was nothing to be seen."

"Hmmm, yes," murmured Holmes non-committedly. "My methods are, shall we say, slightly different from those employed by the local aid."

Mrs. Green nodded her assent, and Holmes spent the next ten minutes carefully inspecting the small area while Lestrade and I watched from the doorway. If the room had once been tidy, the onslaught of the searching constables had certainly altered that. Holmes puttered around, shaking his head in dismay at the disorder that had been inflicted upon the space. He only paused to contemplate the ashes in a small tray, even bending over so as to sniff at its contents.

Knowing his especial expertise in such matters, I called out, "Something interesting about the man's tobacco, Holmes?"

"The man primarily smoked a cheap Trichinopoly, Watson, but the most recent ashes are the far more expensive Cavendish. This confirms Mrs. Green's observation that Walton was poor, at least until the last day of his life, when he suddenly felt capable of splurging upon something finer."

"And how does that advance us?" I asked.

Holmes smiled. "There are but a few ways for a poor labourer to suddenly come into wealth, Watson. It provides a reasonable frame-work for a motive to his slaying." However, per his usual reticence, Holmes refused to say anything more upon the matter.

§

It was going on four o'clock when we left the former quarters of Mr. Walton. "What do you suggest now, Mr. Holmes?" asked the inspector.

"We must interview the remaining witnesses to the pivotal moment."

Lestrade frowned in incomprehension. "What are you talking about, Mr. Holmes?"

"Come now, Lestrade. Surely, it must be evident that the two attacks are connected? The resemblances between the cases of Ackroyd and Walton are far too great to be a simple coincidence." He began to count off on his long fingers. "One: the absence of motive and robbery. Two: the lack of any clue to the identity of the assassin. Three: the nature of the wounds, evidently inflicted by the same or, at least similar, weapon. This all points in one direction – that the meeting at the museum of the four men, including Professor Sidney and

Mr. Walton, somehow precipitated these murders. Since there are only two men left, we must speak with them before they too are struck down."

"But surely Holmes," I interjected, "if another is killed, then the assassin must be the remaining man?"

He smiled wryly. "That is a reasonable hypothesis, Watson, but perhaps not one we wish to put to the test. In an ideal world, the goal would be to identify the guilty party before he has time to take a third life."

"Well, yes, of course," I muttered.

"Let us start with Professor Sidney, shall we? I expect at this hour we shall find him at the Fitzwilliam."

The white marble of that fabled institution gleamed in the rapidly dropping red rays of the sun. As classes were out of session and the museum closed for the evening, the nearby lantern-illuminated pubs were crowded with students roaring drinking songs at the tops of their lungs. As we strode through the Corinthian capitals onto the museum's portico, we stopped to knock some of the snow from our boots.

"Stop, Watson!" Holmes suddenly exclaimed. "Don't move a muscle!"

I froze with my right foot in the air. "Whatever is it, Holmes?" I said, tightly.

Instead of answering, Holmes moved over to my side and inspected the snow beneath my feet. All I could see was a jumble of prints and I was mystified what precisely Holmes could possibly conclude from it. Finally, his face satisfied, he motioned for me to proceed with placing down my step, before he himself strode into the museum.

On the first floor, we located the eclectically decorated office belonging to Professor Sidney. He proved to be a man of medium-height and he looked even older than his supposed seventy years, with great lines of care etched upon his face and his grey hair much thinned. His temperament was far more tense and excitable than I would have typically expected from a man of letters, though some of those nerves could easily be attributable to the recent death of his friend, and perhaps concerns that his own life may be in danger.

As Holmes introduced the three of us, Sidney rose from behind his desk and came around to shake our hands half-heartedly. "Professor Sidney," said Holmes, "I am most sorry for the loss of your friend. On the night in question, what exactly did you do after Dr Ackroyd departed?"

The man shrugged. "I took a last look into the store-room to reassure myself that all was right with our new acquisitions and then also went off to my chambers."

"What about Walton and Ramsey?"

"I recall that they were sitting in the janitor's room drinking a pot of coffee."

"Did you ever consider the possibility that one of them was responsible for the attack on Dr Ackroyd?"

Professor Sidney shook his head vigorously. "Never. I have heard the rumours that Walton was involved, but I thought that impossible even before the man was killed."

"And why is that?"

"Because Ramsey declared solemnly that Walton was with him until the moment that they heard the commissionaire's startled cries, which caused both of them to run out to the scene of the tragedy."

"And you have no reason to doubt his truthfulness? Walton was his friend. Old friendships may induce one man to tell a falsehood in order to screen his compatriot."

"No, I don't believe that to be the case, Mr. Holmes. Ramsey has been part of Cambridge for longer than anyone can remember. He has been here since shortly after I came up, and I am no young man. The stones of this college are his bones, and the river Cam, his lifeblood. Ramsey would not lie, especially not if it endangered the college. In any case, Walton's innocence is now sadly proven beyond a doubt."

"Why do you say that?" inquired Holmes.

Professor Sidney frowned at Holmes as if he were daft. "The man is dead, sir!"

"As far as I am concerned, that only exonerates him from the second murder. He is still very much a suspect for the first."

The professor looked astonished by this statement. "Surely there are not two men running about Cambridge killing men with hatchets?"

"Until disproven, it must be on the list of possibilities," said Holmes, mildly. "However, even if Walton was responsible for the murder of Dr Ackroyd, we no longer need concern ourselves about two murderers on the loose. We must only determine the final link in the chain."

"If you say so," replied Sidney uncertainly.

"Tell me, Professor Sidney, about the collection of weapons from the Earl of Chesterfield. Where precisely did they originate?"

The man's sad face lit up somewhat. "Ah, yes, that is a fascinating story. The Earl was quite an excellent amateur archaeologist. He had found the Apollo sanctuary, you know.[38] Most recently, he became convinced that a forest clearing near his home was actually the location of a Viking-era assembly place. The site in question was remarkable for the presence of a low hill, which further inspection of the soil sub-layers revealed to be artificial in nature."[39]

"A barrow?" asked Holmes.

"Precisely. The Earl commenced the digging of tunnels and, after the span of a few weeks, he and his men penetrated to the central chamber, where they found the grave of what was obviously a great Jarl, surrounded by the bodies of four of his warriors. He had lain there, untouched, for almost a thousand years. Around him was arranged an extraordinary hoard of silver and golden objects. There were coins, ornaments, ingots, and drinking vessels, not to mention the weapons and armour of the five men."

"A mighty treasure!" I exclaimed.

"It certainly was, Doctor," replied Professor Sidney. "It is the first instance we have of a burial mound from the Danelaw, when the Vikings held sway over the entire eastern seaboard of England. That is what made the Earl's death all the more tragic."

"What happened, exactly?" I asked.

The professor shook his head sadly. "I am surprised that you did not follow the case more closely, Doctor. Certainly, public interest in the matter was very high. His assistant, a man by the name of Neal Scott, who had worked closely with the Earl for a dozen years, suddenly shoved him from the balcony of the Earl's estate. At first, it was assumed that the Earl's fall must have been accidental, but later that night, Scott took his own life. His wife found him hanging from a hook in the wall of their bedroom, a rope tied round his neck and an overturned chair beneath him. On the table was a note in which Scott admitted to committing the fatal deed, though he gave no explanation for his actions. Witnesses did not report any signs of conflict between the men, nor any recent arguments. It is a sad tale."

"And thus, in conformity with the Earl's will, his entire collection, both old and newly acquired, came into possession of the Fitzwilliam Museum?" said Holmes. "But why the special care in transport, Professor Sidney? Surely that was unusual for two such men as yourself and Dr Ackroyd?"

"Everett was always fastidious about such things, especially such an important find. As I said, we have no other example of an intact Viking burial in all of England."

"Very good, Professor. We shall return if we have any other questions for you." Holmes turned to the inspector. "Have you looked over the weapons which Dr Ackroyd was so concerned about on the day he met his death?"

Lestrade shrugged. "Of course, but I saw nothing of note."

"Yes, well, I think they may be well worth another visit. We shall kill two birds with one stone and ask the janitor, Ramsey, to show us about the storeroom."

We found the man in question huddled in a small room tucked off the main corridor of the first floor. The space was filled with brooms, mops, and other items of use in the man's trade, but Ramsey had also transformed the area into a miniature sitting room, with two well-worn chairs gathered around a small table. On that lay a tray filled with ashes, and as Holmes gazed about the area, I could see him glancing carefully at those remnants. Ramsey himself was a small, wiry man, who appeared to be in his late sixties. Although no longer young, I could plainly see that the effects of his years of military service had not completely vanished, and he remained trim and likely quite strong. I was certain that, if he wished, he surely could have wielded the blade by which both Dr Ackroyd and Mr. Walton had been struck down.

Ramsey looked up as we entered and shook his head morosely. "It's no use, gentlemen."

"What is no use, Mr. Ramsey?" asked Holmes.

"Trying to figure out who is responsible for this madness. This goes beyond the realm of man."

Holmes smiled. "I assure you, Mr. Ramsey, that magic and charms have little role in my vocabulary. The answer will be much simpler. If you would be so kind as to show us now to the storeroom where the various items comprising the bequest of the Earl of Chesterfield are kept?"

The man sighed heavily. "Very well, follow me."

He led the way along the corridor and down the stairs to the ground level. As we walked, Holmes made a few seemingly innocuous inquires, but which I presumed must be advancing his case. The most unusual request was when he told Ramsey that he needed to withdraw some funds and asked the janitor to recommend a local banking establishment. The man suggested a branch of the Capital & Counties Bank, which appeared to satisfy Holmes. I, for one, was mystified as to the purpose of this question, as I well knew that Holmes would not have departed Baker Street short of ready currency. Eventually, in the rear of the museum, we stopped at a door marked as 'Private.' From his pocket, Ramsey took a steel hoop holding numerous keys, but before he could use one to open it,

Holmes stayed his hand.

"A minute, sir." Holmes knelt down in front of the door and examined the lock with his glass for a moment. "You will note, Lestrade, that there is no sign of tampering of the mechanism. It has been opened with its key alone."

The inspector frowned, but made no comment. He nodded for the janitor to proceed and the man moved forward in order to unlock the door. This opened into a musty room, without windows, such that it took Ramsey a few moments to light a sufficient number of the gas lamps so as to allow us to take it all in. What we found was a space of some ten yards square, the front occupied with several low tables, and the back filled with numerous tall shelves. From what I could ascertain, the shelves were arranged roughly chronologically, with the ones to the far left holding an Egyptian sarcophagus and several Canopic jars, while the ones to our right held relatively recent Bantu artefacts from our country's recent occupation of Whale Bay.[40]

However, the items of greatest interest were either scattered about on the tables or occupied the nearest of the shelves. This included a large pot filled with silver coins, as well as several golden armlets, neck rings, and brooches. In my mind, the highlight was the four exceptionally large round-pommelled swords, which – despite their great age – remained remarkably free of rust or deterioration. It appeared that many of the items had been recently labelled. Holmes motioned for us to remain near the doorway, while he moved deeper into the room in order to discern fully all of the items it contained.

After the span of a few moments, he turned back to us. "Mr. Ramsey, I am desirous of examining that particular shield upon the top shelf." He pointed to the item in question, which was one of five similar bulwarks lying next to what appeared to be corroded iron helmets. "Would you be so kind as to fetch it down for me?"

The man nodded. "Of course, sir." He moved over to a corner of the room where he picked up a ladder. He set it down in front of the shelf in question and proceeded to climb the rungs.

In a heartbeat, Holmes slipped over to beneath the ladder, where he proceeded to grasp hold of it. "Let me steady this for you, Ramsey," he said, as he looked up at the man. "We want no more blood spilt in these halls, metaphorically-speaking."

The man grunted his appreciation and took hold of the item that Holmes had requested. Once he descended the ground, Ramsey handed it to my friend. "Is this what you needed, sir?" His tone clearly conveyed grave doubts over how this particular shield could play any role in the deaths of either his employer or his friend.

Holmes carefully took the item, which proved to be a circle of blackened wood banded in rusted steel, with great scars along the top. "Yes, I think it just may be." He again took out his glass and scrutinized the scars closely. His face split into a smile. "Ah, yes, this is precisely what I had hoped to find."

Lestrade could take no more. "Come now, Mr. Holmes," protested the inspector. "Dr Ackroyd and Walton were hacked to death, not battered with a shield."

"You might be surprised, Lestrade, but the scars on this shield explain exactly why the two men were killed."

"What!" exclaimed Lestrade. "You are having sport with me, Mr. Holmes! This is no time for jesting."

Holmes merely smiled and shook his head. "I speak nothing but the truth, Inspector. However, I admit to having an advantage over you."

"And what is that?" huffed Lestrade.

"The power of imagination. You see, Lestrade, I considered all of the possible evidence and then reflected on how it could possibly tie together. The answer, while quite fantastic, is the only one that fits. I must say, Lestrade, that I am deeply in your debt for asking me to join you in this investigation. It is surely unique in the annals of crime."

"Do you mean to say that you have solved it?" I exclaimed.

"There are one or two things that are still not clear, Watson, but yes, I think my case is essentially complete." He turned to the janitor. "Tell me, Ramsey, is there a catalogue of what precisely comprises the Earl's collection?"

The man looked puzzled. "I don't rightly know, Mr. Holmes."

"Would you do me the favour of inquiring of Professor Sidney, and if possible, bring the catalogue back for me to peruse?"

The man nodded and silently departed.

Holmes turned to Lestrade and me. "Now, gentlemen, what do you observe in this room?"

Lestrade and I glanced at each other. The inspector merely shrugged, so I proceeded to describe the various pieces of armour and the weapons to the best of my ability.

When I was complete, Holmes shook his head, as if disappointed that I failed to notice something of importance. "That's it?" he asked.

"Yes, Holmes," I replied. "Wait, do you think one of these swords could have been used to strike down Dr Ackroyd and Mr. Walton?" I leaned in to inspect the blades, hoping to find some glimpse of residual blood upon one of them.

Lestrade stroked his chin thoughtfully. "It would take a mighty man to wield such a blade. They must be thrice the weight of a modern sabre."

However, from the look upon his face, it was clear that neither Lestrade nor I understood Holmes' point. "Tell me, Watson, how many weapons do you count?"

I studied the contents of the shelves to see if I was missing anything. "I see just these four swords, Holmes."

"Precisely. However, there were five men in that tomb. So where, pray tell, is the weapon of the Jarl?"

"Of course!" I exclaimed. "The missing weapon was used to kill the two men."

"I expect it will prove to be an axe," said Holmes mildly.

"That is excellent, Mr. Holmes," said Lestrade excitedly. "I see it now. The burglar, a strong man, broke into the storeroom, and stole the missing axe. To his eternal misfortune, Dr Ackroyd must have decided to return and re-inspect some item or another. The curator discovered the burglar and ran for help, but the burglar chased him down, axe in hand, and killed him."

"Very good, Lestrade," said my friend, nodding. "That is a most interesting hypothesis. But then how do you explain the murder of Walton?"

Lestrade waved his hand. "Who knows, Mr. Holmes? Perhaps he developed a taste for violence? But it is of little matter. We can ask the man once we catch him. The axe will prove to be his undoing. It is simply far too valuable to discard. He will attempt to sell it, and once he does, we will have our murderer."

Holmes shrugged. "Unfortunately, Inspector, I do not believe that there was ever a burglar. As I showed you earlier, the lock shows no sign that it was ever opened in any fashion other than with its intended key."

"You know as well as me, Mr. Holmes, that a very skilled lock-pick can leave no mark. Do you have some other reason to doubt the existence of the burglar?" Lestrade scowled.

"Only that the murderer of Mr. Walton was no more than five-foot-six inches tall."

The inspector stared at my friend incredulously. "How can you make such a claim?"

"All in good time, Lestrade." He glanced over the inspector's shoulder. "Ah, Ramsey, excellent. What do you have for me?" The janitor returned holding a large ledger, which he promptly handed over to my friend. "Thank you, my good man." Holmes flipped through it for a moment. "Ah, here we are: 'a large antique two-handed battle-axe, with a head of steel, and a handle of chased silver wrapped with golden bands.' I think we have our murder-weapon, gentlemen." He gazed at the janitor. "Do you recall seeing this particular item during the un-loading process?"

The man frowned. "No, sir."

"Come now, man," interjected Lestrade angrily. "There is no sense in lying! Out with it!"

"Wait," Holmes forestalled the inspector's wrath. "He is not lying, Lestrade. I apologize for failing to read the rest of the description. This particular battle-axe was, per our catalogue here: 'preserved within a fine silver casket, itself covered in runic inscriptions, whose meanings have yet to be deciphered.'" Holmes paused to look around for a moment, and then pointed. "Like that casket, right there."

We all turned to follow the aim of his finger, which was directed at an unusually shaped coffer. It was some four-feet long, two feet deep, and perhaps one-foot high, with a somewhat lopped-off pyramidal lid fastened by a solid clasp. The silver had clearly been recently polished, removing the tarnish of the centuries and allowing us to appreciate its elaborate chasing and engravings.

"You think that the murder weapon is within?" said I in a low voice.

"I do," Holmes replied calmly.

"Well, let's find out," snapped Lestrade, who stepped towards the silver casket.

"Hold a minute, Lestrade. We must do this properly. Professor Sidney should be here when we open it, don't you think?"

The inspector scowled. "If you insist."

"It will only take a moment."

Lestrade waved at the janitor, instructing him to fetch the museum's assistant director, but Holmes pre-empted him again. "No, let us go to him. Watson, Ramsey, if each of you gentlemen would deign to take one end, we can surely manage to carry it up to the Professor's office."

Over Lestrade's protests, the two of us lugged the surprisingly heavy coffer up the stairs and back to the locale requested by Holmes. When we entered, Professor Sidney looked up from his work. For a moment, simple puzzlement shone on his pale features, but when he saw what we carried, he shrank back in a paroxysm of terror. "What are you doing?" he exclaimed. He pointed at the coffer convulsively with an emaciated hand. "Don't touch that!"

So strident was the fear in his voice that Ramsey and I quickly deposited the box upon the man's desk and backed away. The professor pushed his chair against the far wall, as if to put as much space between him and the casket as possible.

"Why not, Professor?" asked Holmes mildly.

"It is cursed," replied the man, his tone husky.

"So you have interpreted the runes?"

"Of course. I am the foremost authority in all of England on such inscriptions," said he, some measure of pride creeping into his voice. "They warn of a great horror which will befall any who opens it."

Holmes nodded. "I would be most obliged if you would provide an exact translation."

The professor closed his eyes and shook his head, his face ashen. "It says: 'He who opens this box will deal in grief. Midnight will shade his eyes. His hands will run red with the blood of foe and friend alike.'"

"If you knew what the runes said, Professor, I wonder why you ever dared to open it?"

The man threw his hands to his face. "How did you know?" he cried. "It was the most terrible mistake of my life. Would that I had never seen it! Yes, I admit it. I can take it no longer. I would ease my soul of the weight of these terrible crimes. It was I who killed my old friend." He seemed utterly prostrated with grief.

"What did you say!" exclaimed Lestrade, flabbergasted at this sudden confession. "You committed the murder of Dr Ackroyd? Why would you do such a thing?"

"I know not!" the professor wailed. "I was consumed with such a rage; it could not be satiated until I felt blood running over my hands. Under such an unnatural passion, I chased after my dearest friend and struck him down. I can only repeat that the runes do not lie. There is a curse upon that blade."

Lestrade looked much discombobulated. "Surely, Professor, you are distraught with grief," said he sternly. "You couldn't possibly wield such an axe."

However, in response the man silently collapsed onto a chair and sobbed piteously into his hands.

Holmes looked at the professor for a moment and then shrugged. "It is indisputably unlikely, Lestrade, but not entirely impossible. Nevertheless, I am afraid that Professor Sidney is also responsible for the murder of Mr. Walton."

"What?" cried the inspector. "How can you be certain?"

"Although I had not formed any conclusions with the meagre amount of information in the papers, I suspected from the minute that I heard Walton was dead that the deed must have been committed by either Professor Sidney or Mr. Ramsey here. When we arrived at the scene of Walton's murder, I found a single heel-print of a distinctive nature. It had a divot in it which was quite unique."

"That could have belonged to anyone," spluttered Lestrade.

"True enough, Inspector. However, I soon observed the same print again in the snow that had recently been tracked in the front door of the museum. Hence my ruse which allowed me to inspect the bottom of Mr. Ramsey's boots as he climbed the ladder. His heels did not possess that particular divot. Thus, Professor Sidney became my primary suspect. Of course, Ramsey was always the less-likely of the pair."

"Why is that, Holmes?" I inquired.

"Did you forget about the money in Walton's pocket, Watson?"

"No, but I fail to see how it relates?"

"Come now, Watson. Mr. Walton was a common labourer. He assuredly did not come to that fortune honestly. Walton had plainly blackmailed someone. He possessed a clue about the identity of the murderer, but rather than come forward and relate his news to the police, he decided to attempt to profit from it. Walton approached the murderer and extorted all of his ready money, which is surely far more than a janitor such as Mr. Ramsey here would have had on hand, especially when he clearly kept his savings in the local bank."

"But if the Professor had paid off Walton, why murder him? And once he did so, why not re-claim his money?"

"I suspect he was under the influence of a similar rage attack as when he struck down Dr Ackroyd."

"Are you saying you believe his tale, Mr. Holmes?" interjected Lestrade.

"Oh, yes. It fits all of the evidence precisely."

Lestrade looked puzzled. "But what was his motive? The two men have been friends for years."

Holmes shook his head. "There was no motive, Inspector. Professor Sidney could no more control his actions than he could fly to the moon. I believe that he is not feigning his distress at the realization of his actions. I cannot be absolutely certain until confirmed by the professor here, but I think that he unlocked the store-room after the departure of Dr Ackroyd, and – heedless of the warning runes – opened the casket. Under the sway of its ill humours, the professor then seized the axe, rushed after his friend, and killed him. Sidney soon returned to his senses, however, in his confusion, he simply brought the axe back to the museum rather than attempting to dispose of it, as a pre-meditated murderer surely would have done. At some point in this process, Mr. Walton observed Professor Sidney. Under suspicion himself, Walton decide to leave the local area, but not without some currency in his pocket. He sought out the professor, who initially agreed to his pecuniary demands and watched Walton depart. Shortly thereafter, the Professor must have returned to the casket. Perhaps he wished to stare at the axe, as if to verify that it was not all a horrible dream. Again his rage was kindled by the contents of the coffer, and snatching up the axe, he chased after Walton, ensuring that the man met the same fate as Dr Ackroyd."

"There are many strange things in the world, Mr. Holmes," said Lestrade, shaking his head. "But you won't have me believing that this thing is cursed. I am afraid we still must present the murder weapon to the magistrate." He stepped towards the casket.

Holmes held out his arm to bar the inspector's way. "I would strongly counsel against opening that casket, Lestrade. All who have done so before you have come to ruin."

Lestrade smiled contemptuously. "Come now, Mr. Holmes. As you said yourself, magic and charms have no role in the legal system. You cannot possibly believe that the casket carries some misfortune?"

Holmes smiled grimly. "There is no need, gentlemen, to fall back upon magic for an explanation of what has transpired. What I am about to say is merely a hypothesis, of course, and would require additional chemical testing to confirm, but I believe it is the only possible explanation for this extraordinary case. The coffer originally belonged to an honoured Danish warrior, on that we can all agree, yes? The Norsemen were the most feared raiders of the medieval world, in no small part because of a particular subset of them who fought with a nearly uncontrollable, trance-like fury. They could perform remarkable feats of strength far beyond what you might typically expect from their already formidable size, and they could sustain numerous terrible wounds before finally succumbing. They were called the 'berserkers,' and are well described in the literature of the time. One of their hallmarks was that, in their great rage, they would bite furiously on the tops of their shields."

"Like the shield in the store-room!" I exclaimed.

"Precisely, Watson."

Lestrade shook his head. "What can that possibly have to do with the matter at hand, Mr. Holmes? We are talking about modern times, not the Dark Ages!"

"Ah, but there are many similarities are there not? Why else would Professor Sidney strike down his dear friend? How else could he even lift the weapon which dealt the blow?"

"I still don't see how opening this casket could induce such an effect?" said Lestrade incredulously.

"That, Lestrade, is a topic of much debate among historians as to how precisely the berserker came to achieve his trance-like state. It is surely not a natural one. It required some sort of transformative process."

The inspector shrugged. "I suppose that I've seen some men who can fight like demons after too many rounds at their local public house."

Holmes nodded. "The consumption of massive amounts of alcohol is certainly one possibility, Lestrade. However, the majority of men simply collapse into a stupor before becoming so agitated. And it is well known that the berserkers fought as gangs."

"So what is your theory, Holmes?" I asked.

"I have read that there is a particular fungi endemic to the Danish isles, which when consumed, can bring upon such a trance."[41]

"Surely Professor Sidney would not have eaten any mushrooms that he found within that casket!" protested the inspector.

"No, Lestrade, of course not. But would a growth of fungi be intact after a span of some nine hundred years? Alternatively, would it have decayed to the merest flecks of spores, so easy to accidentally inspire as you breathed over the axe, examining it? I submit, gentlemen, that this is what drove Professor Sidney to commit his acts."

"By Jove!" I exclaimed.

"No, Watson. By Odin," Holmes chuckled wryly.

The inspector stared at Holmes incredulously. "You would have me argue this in front of the magistrate? They will laugh me out of court."

Holmes shrugged. "That is your concern, of course, Lestrade. You now see the advantage of being an independent agent. I suppose that you may be able to fashion some sort of mask, which might serve to protect you.[42] On the other hand, if you follow my advice, you could ensure that no further attacks occur by preventing that casket from ever being opened again. Of course, you would be forced to record that the murders were caused by a 'person or persons unknown,' and your failure to bring this case to a successful conclusion, at least in the eyes of the public, may cast some aspersion upon your professional competence."

Lestrade looked anguished at this Solomonic-choice. I watched as a play of emotions traversed his face, which finally settled upon something resembled resignation. "Very well, have it your way, Mr. Holmes. What should we do with this blasted casket?"

"You could re-bury it," I suggested.

Holmes shook his head. "It will not do, Watson. Someone foolish will simply dig it up again, if not now, then in a hundred years when the sad fates of the Earl of Chesterfield and Dr Ackroyd have long been forgotten. I would recommend its definitive destruction."

"Surely it is the property of the museum," I demurred.

"Not anymore, Watson, it is both the evidence and the inciter of several capital crimes. As there will be no trial, the C.I.D. may dispose of it however they wish. Unfortunately, we now have proof that not all treasures of the past are worthy of preservation, Lestrade. While it may be possible to remove all traces of the contamination via its immersion in some acidic solution, it hardly seems worth the risk. I would instead advocate that you have it dropped forthwith into the deepest reaches of the North Sea. Perhaps there the restless spirit of the berserker Jarl, if you give credence to such things, will shield our shores from any future foreign incursions."

§

Inspector Lestrade agreed straightaway with Holmes' suggestion and, enlisting the aid of a pair of trustworthy men from the local constabulary, the trio boarded the first train to Ipswich. From there I knew that they could hire a boat to take them several miles away from shore, where they would intern the casket for all of eternity.

Professor Sidney, having confessed to his involuntary misdeeds, was nonetheless a broken man. He was quietly retired and re-settled in a sister college at Oxford, far from the sight of the once-bloody streets of Cambridge. In seclusion, he could attempt to turn his shattered mind to areas of inquiry far removed from the doings of the Danelaw.

As for Holmes and I, on the evening train back to King's Cross Station, I jotted down my notes of the terrible events of the last few hours while they were still fresh in my brain. Although at the time, I had already begun to entertain the idea of someday publishing my adventures with Holmes, I knew that, in respect to poor Professor Sidney, this was one story that should not see the light of day until long after he had drawn his last breath. He had suffered enough.

I shook my head sadly at the great tragedy of it all. "To think, Holmes, that all of this came about from the Earl's passion for the scientific art of archaeology."[43]

Holmes pursed his lips and lit his long cherry-wood pipe. He puffed on it for a moment before answering. "It is a matter of perspective, Watson. What we today might call archaeology, the ancients would call grave robbing. To them it made no difference if their treasures were melted down by their modern rivals, or displayed in some future museum. It was all a violation of their journey into the after-life. And they would do whatever was necessary in order to prevent such a theft. Therefore, for Chesterfield, Ackroyd, and even Sidney, this supposed treasure turned out instead to be a terrible curse. As the Bard once said, 'Had you been as wise as bold, gilded tombs do worms enfold, all that glisters is not gold.'"[44]

§

THE ADVENTURE OF THE DAWN DISCOVERY

The year '87 proved to be the busiest of Holmes' career to date. Amongst the cases provided to us during those twelve months were the colossal schemes of Baron Maupertuis, the tragic death of John Openshaw, and the nefarious deeds of the Cunninghams. But of all of them, perhaps the most distinguished was the singular adventures of the Grice Patersons in the island of Uffa. This latter case, which I will now take up my pen to describe, began in his suite of rooms at 221B Baker Street. My wife was away for the week, so I had given the maid a paid holiday and had taken the opportunity to bunk in my friend.

"But why Roman, Watson?" asked Holmes suddenly, one early summer afternoon, as I sat in my old armchair reading the *Dundee Courier,* which contained an account of an ingenious device installed at Marykirk by a Scottish engineer in order to capture the power of the wind and convert it to electrical energy.[45] Holmes had just looked up from his desk, where he appeared buried in the task of writing a monograph, undoubtedly upon some obscure aspect of the art of detection.

I glanced up frowning in confusion. "Whatever are you talking about, Holmes?"

"Your bath today."

"Have you been following me?"

He smiled with amusement. "Hardly, Watson. It was a simple deduction."

"I see nothing simple about it."

"Shall I show you the chain of logic which led me to this conclusion?"

"Please do."

"Very well. 1. When you went out earlier, you mentioned that you were going to your club. 2. When you go to the club on Thursdays, you always play cards with Lomax. 3. When you play cards with Lomax, you revert to the use of Ship's tobacco. 4. However, I detect no scent of that strong blend upon you, suggesting that you and your suit underwent a good cleaning afterwards. 5. You are reading a regional paper, which – in all of London – is only carried at Carter's stall. 6. Carter's stall is located at the junction of the Strand and Lancaster Place. 7. Carter's stall is not situated on the route between your club and your typical bath in Northumberland Avenue. 8. The closest such establishment to Carter's stall is the Old Roman Bath at Surry Street next to the Norfolk Hotel."[46]

I clapped in amazement. "Astonishing, Holmes. Yes, afterwards I felt my energy flagging in the summer heat and decided to have an invigorating dunk in the cold pools of the Roman spring. For a moment, I thought you read my mind."

"Yes, well, any sufficiently advanced reasoning is indistinguishable from omniscience. Finally, and perhaps most importantly, your hair is still wet. However, if I am not mistaken, that is the sound of the bell, suggesting that we are about to have a visitor. Let us hope they prove to have an interesting problem for us."

A few moments later, Billy showed in a man of roughly sixty years, with a lean face and thinning brown hair. His face was drawn and his eyes dim, like those of a man who is weighed down by a terrible sorrow. He wore a black suit and held a bowler in his hand.

Silently, he presented his card to Holmes, who glanced at for a moment before handing it to me. It read, *Winston Grice Paterson, Naturalist.*

"I see that you are in mourning, Mr. Grice Paterson," said Holmes. Your wife, I presume?"

"Yes," the man stammered. "How did you know?"

"By the dust upon your collar and the moth hole on the right sleeve, it is plain that your suit has clearly not seen use for many years, but it is one whose style is best suited for a funeral. We may deduce from your ring that you are married, yet you come without your wife. Therefore, it is probable that it was your wife who has recently passed on."

"You are correct, Mr. Holmes. I have come down to identify the body of my poor Clare. She was found yesterday, and I was summoned to collect her."

"And you believe that her death was unnatural?"

"How did you know that?"

Holmes spread out his hand. "Otherwise, what use would you have for my service?"

The man nodded slowly. "You are correct, Mr. Holmes. I have tried explaining my concerns to one of the inspectors down at Scotland Yard – a Mr. Lestrade, if I recall correctly. But he was unconvinced."

"Yes, well, if I had a pound for every time Lestrade prematurely jumped to an erroneous conclusion, I would be able to start my own bank," said Holmes, dryly. "Why don't you start at the beginning, sir? It is a method which I heartily recommend to Watson, here."

"Very good, Mr. Holmes. As you can see from my card, I am by profession a naturalist. Until recently, my wife and I resided in the town of Liss. For years, I have been collecting phenologic observations regarding the various animals and plants of Hampshire. It is my life's work to collect these notes in a volume which will be the successor to Gilbert White's *Natural History of Selbourne*."

"Why does that book require a successor volume?" I interjected. "I thought it was the definitive work on the subject."

The man's head bobbed up and down. "Oh, it is indeed, Dr Watson. But how things have changed in the course of one century! White wrote his treatise in the days when the handloom and the ironsmith were the only industry in the countryside. However, today is the Age of the Factory, which has had significant violent repercussions on the land. I hope to make this plain to the public. White's book was first published in 1789, and I planned to have mine ready for its centennial anniversary. But now I don't know what I shall do!" His voice wavered, and for a moment I thought he was about to burst into tears.

With uncharacteristic restraint, Holmes permitted the man sufficient time to collect himself. Mr. Grice Paterson then resumed his narrative. "Word got round about what I was working upon, and I found myself the object of attacks by some of the local factory owners, who were unhappy when they considered the potential negative publicity my book might bring upon them. In short, Clare and I decided to retire to some other part of the country, where I could complete my book in peace. As a child, I had once visited the misty and craggy west coast of Scotland, and I thought it might be the perfect locale for us, even though Clare had never visited. I have a small income – left to me from my parents – which has dwindled over the years, so I could not afford anything grand. We therefore sought the assistance of Mr. McNeil, the well-known Wigtown factor, who said that he had just the place for us.

"It was as remote a place as one could possibly wish for, the former farming croft of Carracuil upon the little island of Uffa, in the Firth of Clyde. It had once belonged to a Paisley doctor named MacDonald, but he never lived there after the death of his father in a boating accident back in '65. He sold the holding of it – for the rents are due to the Duke of Hamilton – to a Mr.

Gavin McBane, a fisherman from Troon. McBane lived there for a few years, but he later married a lass who was in possession of a larger homestead on the island, into which the two of them moved once their family began to grow. The house-agent explained that the Carracuil place had therefore been deserted for a dozen of years. However, with a little time and energy, he assured us that it could be brought round to a state of comfortable snugness. Clare thought the situation sounded perfect and that the work of fixing up the place would keep her occupied while I wrote. She was also an amateur ornithologist, and hoped to enjoy the spotting of various sea birds, so different from those native to our old home.

"We therefore moved to the island of Uffa about four months ago. The house needed work, of course, but it was a very quiet corner of the world, and well suited my purposes. Even the air seemed fresher than it did down in Hampshire. It took us some time to earn the good graces of our neighbours who – like most Scotsmen are not overly fond of strangers. Given that these folk have resided upon Uffa for many generations, we certainly qualified for that classification. But recently, it seemed like we had settled in nicely, and work was progressing well upon my book. Clare was happy. That is why I find this whole thing so incomprehensible, Mr. Holmes!" he cried.

"And have there been any incidents of note recently upon Uffa?"

Grice Paterson considered this for a moment. "Well, yes, there was the great storm of two weeks ago. It was rather late in the season, far past the typical equinoctial gales of spring. It was also certainly remarkable for its violence and for what it brought forth from the sea."

"Which was what?" asked Holmes, leaning forward slightly.

"A body!"

"What?" I exclaimed. "You found a body washed ashore?"

"Well, more of a skeleton, to be accurate, Doctor. Moreover, it wasn't I who found it, of course, but rather the Gibbs brothers. They live over at Arden, the third croft upon the island."

"Surely it must be related, don't you think, Holmes?" I asked.

He shook his head. "It is far too early for such conjectures, Watson." He turned back to our guest. "What came of the skeleton, Mr. Grice Paterson?"

"It was quite the event on the island, you understand, Mr. Holmes. With only three farms and the occasional visit from a Lamlash boat with the papers and the news, such a thing was bound to excite much curiosity. I was busy working on my book, but I recall that Clare walked over to see the thing, though I advised her against it. When she returned, her mood was rather odd. She was both pensive and excited at the same time. I suppose she found it a visceral reminder that our days upon this earth are numbered."

"Perhaps," said Holmes. "And the authorities? What did they make of this skeleton?"

"An inspector came over to the island, all the way from Glasgow. He brought with him a surgeon, who examined the bones and teeth. He determined that they belonged to a once powerful man in his fifties. The only remarkable thing was a well-healed break of his right arm. When Geordie and Jock Gibbs, and Minnie McBane, heard this description, they promptly declared that the bones must belong to old Fergus MacDonald, the one-time owner of our croft at Carracuil. For Fergus had once been possessed of just such a frame, and he had famously broken his arm back in the winter of '55, which was well-remembered because the injury had severely curtailed his fishing season.

"As you might imagine, this news soon brought round Fergus' son, Archie, from his home in Paisley. Clare heard from Minnie McBane that Dr MacDonald had not been back to the island since he had left some twenty-two years earlier, following the death of his father. Therefore, his reappearance was of considerable curiosity to the local inhabitants – and to Clare as well, if truth be told. A presbyter came round with Dr MacDonald and helped ensure that Fergus' bones got a proper burial in the grounds of the small chapel near the harbour at Carravoe. Several interested parties came over from the mainland for the funeral, such that the population of the island was for a short time, tripled. I took a pause from my writing to pay my respects to this man who I had never met. The only thing that struck me as peculiar about the service was that Dr MacDonald refrained from speaking about his father.

"Later, Clare related to me that the doctor and his father had not seen eye-to-eye on quite a few things – a fact which she had learned from Minnie McBane. Minnie recalled Fergus MacDonald as a grim, stern old man, and she did not fault Archie for his feelings on the matter."

"Is there any chance that Archie was responsible for the death of his father?" asked Holmes.

Mr. Grice Paterson shook his head. "I can't rightly say, Mr. Holmes. I do not know the entire story. I heard that Dr MacDonald and his father were ferrying a guest over to the mainland one day when a sudden squall blew up and the old man and the guest were lost overboard. Dr MacDonald alone eventually returned to shore. But I cannot see how this relates to my poor Clare?"

"It may not, sir. However, I find that such singular events are often interconnected. Tell me, what did your wife do after the funeral?"

He shrugged. "She went back to her ways, more or less. Taking care of the croft, and watching the birds. However, I did sense something was wrong. She was not quite herself. She was less talkative in the evenings after dinner. More thoughtful. Secretive even."

"When did she decide to come down to London?"

"Just two days ago. She announced that she wanted to buy me a present for my sixtieth birthday, which is in less than a week. I protested that I needed nothing, nor could we afford anything. But she insisted. She said that she had a surprise for me, and that the cost would be minimal. She crossed over to Ardrossan and caught the train to Euston Station. She said she would only be one night in town, and to expect her back today. However, when the boat came over – instead of my Clare – it held a constable from Ayr with a telegram informing me of her death. I dropped everything and came at once."

"And what did Scotland Yard tell you?"

The man paused, clearly distraught at having to relive the matter. "Her body was found in an alley off Fleet Street, near some dragon-topped plinth," said he, his voice taut with emotion.

"The new Temple Bar," I deduced.

"Yes, Watson, I know it well," said Holmes. "Mr. Grice Paterson, can you think of a reason why your wife would be passing by the Temple Bar?"

The man considered this for a moment. "Well, our bank is Tellson's.[47] It is on Fleet Street very near there, I believe. But what she would be doing at the bank is beyond me. She said she didn't require any money, nor could she have withdrawn more than a pittance without my being present as a cosignatory."

"And how was she killed?" asked Holmes.

The man's face quivered and water rose to his eyes. "They tell me it was a head wound, Mr. Holmes. They believe she was admiring the new Royal Courts of Justice when she tripped and fell backwards. She hit the back her head upon a concrete projection from the side of a building and never awoke."

I frowned. "That seems like a rash conclusion! It could have just as easily been a robbery. Someone may have hit her from behind with a tosh."

The man shook his head miserably. "The inspector said that was an unlikely scenario, Doctor, for her wallet was still in her pocket and her rings were untouched."

"But…" said I, before Holmes held up a forestalling hand.

"Enough, Watson. Mr. Grice Paterson does not need to relive this scene. We can ask Lestrade about it ourselves. What would you ask of me, sir?"

"I need to know what happened, Mr. Holmes," the man wailed. "My Clare was sure-footed. Every day she climbed the Combera cliffs behind our estate in order to watch the birds gliding over the Irish Sea. She would not have tripped and fallen as they said. Something drew Clare to London, and someone killed her. However, the police intend to ignore it. I need you to bring her justice, Mr. Holmes, if it costs me my last penny."

My friend stared at our visitor for a moment, and then stood. "Your case intrigues me, Mr. Grice Paterson. You should return home on the next train, where Watson and I will join you forthwith. My professional charges are on a fixed scale. I do not vary them save when I remit them altogether. Given the circumstances, I can confidently expect the latter situation to be in effect."

§

Once Holmes' newest client had departed, he turned to me with a smile. "What do you think, Watson?"

I shook my head. "I hardly know where to begin. It seems an impenetrable mystery to me."

"Yes, well, there are one or two points of interest. Most notably the skeleton of old MacDonald. As you noted earlier, it would be a grave coincidence if it were not somehow linked to the death of Mrs. Grice Paterson." He stood and walked over to his row of reference books, where he took down Wilson's *Imperial Gazetteer of Scotland*. Perusing the index, he emitted a sharp laugh. "Ha! Uffa is not even mentioned. It must be nearly unknown to tourists." He then pulled out Cary's *English Atlas*. He flipped though this until he came upon the page he required. He pointed with his finger. "There, in the Firth of Clyde, do you see that little speck of land off the southern side of the island of Arran, Watson? That is the lonely isle of Uffa. Arran herself is only ten miles wide by twenty long, so you may judge how small poor Uffa is. All in all, it seems rather insignificant, and yet something important happened there. Something important enough to bring about the death of a presumably blameless woman. We must determine what."

"You intend for us to travel there?"

"I do indeed. In fact, if you would be so good as to go round to Euston Station and obtain tickets for the express train, I will soon join you there. Pack a valise, of course, for we may be gone a few days."

I followed Holmes' instructions, and a few minutes later, I saw Holmes' tall, gaunt figure making his way up the platform. He had changed into his long grey travelling-cloak and close-fitting cloth cap, which always put me in the mind that an adventure was afoot.

"Where did you go, Holmes?" I asked.

To my surprise – for Holmes was usually rather reticent with his findings this early in a case – he was loquacious with his explanation. "I wished to see the location of Mrs. Grice Paterson's fatal fall. I needed to assure myself that it was not an accident."

"And what did you find?"

"Oh, there is no doubt about it, Watson. Someone likely smeared a bit of blood upon the wall, which might perhaps fool a rather dull-witted C.I.D. man, but there is little doubt that she was deliberately killed."

Since I had splurged for first-class tickets, the seven-hour ride aboard the *Caledonian* was pleasant enough.[48] Holmes alternated between smoking his paper and reading the agony columns, while I was engrossed in a recently published Gothic epistolary novel set in Whitby.[49] It was the best story of deviltry that I had read for many years. Eventually we changed onto the branch line that would take us to Irvine, the largest settlement in the area.

That town's station was situated very near the harbour, where some questioning brought us around to a boat owned by one Tommy Gibbs. He proved to be a garrulous man in his late forties, with bright blue eyes and a weather-lined face. When we arrived, he had been engaged in the task of mending some nets.

Holmes explained his desire to visit Uffa. After studying the sky for a moment, Gibbs appeared to hesitate. However, he readily agreed to assist when he heard Holmes' offered price. "It looks like the weather will hold off for a bit longer. I suppose can check in on my brothers while I am there," said he.

"Your siblings reside upon the isle, do they?" asked Holmes.

"Yes, sir. I was born and bred there myself, though I left the old place to Geordie and Jock. Between farming and fishing, my brothers are able to lay by a penny or two. However, eventually the place got to be a little tight for me, and I decamped over here to the mainland where I met a nice girl. I can locate the herring just as easily from Irvine as I could from Uffa. They are rather thick on this part of the coast."

Gibbs motioned to a small fishing boat, its planks recently calked. After we climbed aboard, he set the foresail, jib, and mainsail, and we shot away from the dock. When we were out in the water, Holmes inquired whether we were going to call upon Arran first.

"Oh, no!" Gibbs exclaimed. "You don't want to travel to Uffa from Arran, sir. There is a dangerous current that sets in from the north in that narrow straight between the two. Even on the calmest day, a wise man may note the presence of ripples and swirls, which portend deep impacts. But when the wind blows from the west and the terrible North Atlantic waves rush up the inlet between the Argyll peninsula and County Antrim in Ireland, they collide with those coming down the Firth to form such a seething turmoil that Odysseus himself would rather face Charybdis than the Uffa current. They call that stretch of water the Roost and he is a foolish man who does not respect it."

Holmes indicated that he put his trust in Gibbs' knowledge, and then began to ask about the island. Gibbs described the inhabitants of the three farms. This roughly matched what we had learned from Mr. Grice Paterson. He noted that the bulk of the isle was made up on barren undulating moorland, which slowly stretched up to two rugged knolls in the centre, called Beg-na-sacher and Beg-na-phail. Legend held that they were once giants who had been turned to stone by an ancient sorcerer, perhaps even Merlin himself.

As we passed the island of Arran, I admired the peak of Goatfell, which was partly surrounded by clouds. A wind was blowing freshly from the northwest, and the sea was dancing with alternating waves of light green and dark brown. In the far distance, I spied a colossal ocean liner making its stately progress towards the Irish Coast. The whole air was brisk with the tang of the sea.

"If you don't mind my asking, sir, what is your business on Uffa?" Gibbs suddenly asked from his post near the tiller.

"Did you know Mrs. Grice Paterson?" Holmes asked in turn.

"You speak as if she were no more, sir."

"That is the sad truth, Mr. Gibbs. She was killed in London not two days ago."

The man shook his head. "I am most sorry to hear that. She was a very nice lady. Would not hurt a fly. Are you the police then?"

Holmes shook his head and refrained from giving his opinion of the official force. "No, Mr. Gibbs. We were retained by her husband to inquire into the nature of her death."

Gibbs' eyebrows rose with interest. "So it wasn't an accident?"

"An accident is the working theory of Scotland Yard. We are merely attempting to verify a few facts."

"I see, sir," said Gibbs, as he clamped his lips closed. It was plain he wished to ask more.

Once Tommy Gibbs put into the rough little harbour at Carravoe, he explained it was an easy walk to Carracuil. He pointed us in the right direction and away we went. Five minutes later, we were walking along a winding, thistle-bordered, narrow gravel path. This ended at a recently mended rail fence that surrounded the homesteading where the Grice Patersons resided. Carracuil consisted of a rather bleak-looking grey-stone house, with a thatch roof and a red-tiled byre buttressed against one side of it. The enclosure was only several hundred yards wide, and about the same broad. It held a couple of cows, about a dozen egg-laying hens, as well as a few blackface sheep, which looked about ready to be sheared. I spotted a few ears of corn and the purple and yellow flowers of some potato plants, but assumed that the inhabitants must primarily subsist upon tinned food brought round from the mainland. The land tapered down to a fine, pebble-strewn beach.

Holmes' client had reached his home on the earlier train, and he promptly showed us into a dark kitchen. Grice Paterson struck a match and lit an oil lamp. "I apologize, gentlemen. I was working in my study and did not expect you so soon. Normally Clare would have the lamps ablaze and a pot of tea upon the stove." He glanced miserably at the unburned faggots behind the cold metal grate. "I scarcely know what to do with myself."

I patted him consolingly on the shoulder. "Work is the antidote to sorrow, Mr. Grice Paterson. You should finish your book."

"It is very hard, Doctor. My mind keeps wandering. I cannot stop trying to think about what happened in London."

"That will end soon enough. Holmes will determine who wished harm upon your wife."

He turned to my friend. "Do you think so, Mr. Holmes?"

He shrugged. "It is a very unusual crime, sir. Those tend to be the easiest ones to solve. So, Dr Watson is likely to be correct. Now then, do I have your permission to search the premises?"

The man waved his hands about. "Of course. The place is yours. I have nothing to hide. But what do you hope to find?"

"Some clue as to what your wife was thinking. As you said, sir, she had some secret from you in her last few days. It is likely that this secret got her killed. If we can determine its nature, it will go a long ways to identifying her murderer."

The man shook his head. "I shudder to hear you say such words, Mr. Holmes. To think that something so violent could transpire in this day and age. And in such a remote locale."

"There are just as many terrible passions in the countryside as in the rankest depths of Wapping. We have not come so far, Mr. Grice Paterson, from the days when the Norsemen raided these shores looking for thralls.[50] We may have invented telegraphs and locomotives, but the soul of man is still that of animal."

§

On that unhappy philosophy, Holmes and I proceeded to search the small house. Truth be told, there was little to see, and I soon abandoned hope of finding anything of note. Even Holmes looked disappointed in his haul, though in a wooden dresser he did find a train ticket, dated a week prior, which permitted passage from Ardrossan to Glasgow.

When questioned about the ticket, Mr. Grice Paterson said that his wife had gone round to Glasgow to do some shopping.

"What did she buy?" Holmes inquired.

The man frowned. "Now that you ask, Mr. Holmes. I cannot rightly say. I don't recall her carrying anything back with her."

"Ah, well," said Holmes, lightly. "Sometime women just like to look in the windows," he pontificated, as if he were an expert on the fairer sex.

I could not refrain from a snort of amusement. "What now, Holmes?"

"I think it is high time to interview some of the other denizens of Uffa."

This entailed taking a path through the furze bushes. Everything on the isle of Uffa was some shade of grey, brown, or dark greens. I thought it a place in desperate need of some colour. By the time we reached the moderately prosperous croft of

Arden, Tommy Gibbs had already departed for the mainland. We soon discovered that his brothers, Geordie and Jock, were rather loutish fellows. It was plain that they were already deep in their cups, though the sun was still shining in the sky.

"Now, then, which of you found the body of Fergus Mac-Donald?" asked Holmes.

"I saw it first," replied Jock. "After the great storm, we were beachcombing, even though most good things get swept round to Lamlash Bay or the Holy Isle by the awful undercurrent in these parts. But one never knows when a part of a ship might turn up. See that panelling over there?" he pointed to a section of a wall. "That came from a wrecked brigantine."

"Half the house's timbers came from some ship or another," added his brother. "One day we will haul in a sea chest filled with gold napoleons, and we'll be rich as Mr. Midas."

"But the body?" persisted Holmes.

"Well, I sort of just stumbled across it, I did, Mr. Holmes. It was just sitting there on the beach, surrounded by great masses of seaweed."

"Mr. Gibbs, you said it was a skeleton?"

"Oh, yes, indeed, Mr. Holmes. The fishes got at it, I reckon."

Holmes shook his head. "Weren't the bones all jumbled?"

"A skull's a skull, Mr. Holmes," said Jock. "Once you see that staring back at you, it's pretty plain what you have found. We did not turn up every bone, of course. The Glasgow doctor counted 'em and said we had gotten one hundred twenty-nine, which I thought was a rather good haul. There are only one hundred sixty, you know."[51]

As I listened to them talk, it soon became clear to me that the Gibbs brothers were not clever enough to manage the business of following Mrs. Grice Paterson to London and doing her harm. Holmes also must have sensed that they had little to tell us, for he soon took our leave of the brothers. As we walked away, he indicated that we should take the footpath to Corriemains, which was about a mile from Carracuil.

The third of the Uffa's crofts structurally appeared much

like the other two, though it was far neater than Arden and more productive than Carracuil, with an abundance of animals and crops in evidence. A tuft of blue smoke rose from the chimney. When we arrived, we were greeted by a buxom, fresh-faced woman with a mass of brown hair that refused to be contained by a loose French plait. Minnie McBane was not exactly beautiful, but neither was she homely. We could hear the sounds of children playing in the fields behind the house.

Once we introduced ourselves, she offered us a seat and explained that her husband Gavin was at sea. Her voice was mellow and carried the peculiar accents of this distant corner of the Empire. "So it's true, then?" she asked. "Mrs. Grice Paterson was murdered?"

Holmes frowned. "How did you hear that?"

"It's a small island, Mr. Holmes. News travels fast. I heard it from Tommy Gibbs, I did."

"You have lived here all your life, Mrs. McBane?"

"Aye," said she, smiling. "Look about you." She waved her hand at the view of the sea, its dark blue waters rippling gently under a slight breeze from the north. Across the water, we could see the Carlin's Leap and Goatfell bathed in purple mist, while beyond them along the horizon loomed the long line of the Argyleshire hills. Away to the south, the great bald summit of Ailsa Craig glittered in the sun, and a gaggle of fishing boats were beating up the Scotch coast. It was a stunning locale. "What more could a body need?"

"No siblings?"

She cocked her head. "My brother is a corn chandler in Ardrossan, so there is a still a Fullarton to carry on my father's name, may he rest in peace. Robert is rather successful, I suppose. But it be numbers and figures which make him happy, not the smell of the sea, nor the caress of the wind whipping through your hair."

"And what is your relationship with Dr MacDonald?"

Her cheeks bloomed red. "There is no relationship, sir. Happily married, I am."

"You were children together upon a small island. Surely there must have once been some contact between the two of you?"

She paused and pursed her lips. "Perhaps there was once. I suppose there is no harm in you knowing that he once spoke tender nothings into my ear upon the Combera cliffs. But that was a long time ago. Water under the bridge."

"What happened?"

She shrugged. "Your guess is as good as mine. One day our friendship was rather warm, the next he was off to Glasgow for good."

"So this was about the time his father died?"

"Aye."

"This may be a touch indelicate, but as you say, Mrs. McBane, water under the bridge. Perhaps he was only pursuing you to make his father happy?"

She laughed aloud. "Quite the contrary, Mr. Holmes. Old MacDonald had something against me, which was a stance neither Archie nor I ever understood. Was I not an eligible match for his son? No, not in his eyes! Though at the time Archie cared little for the old man's attempts to frighten him away from me."

"I see. And were harsh words ever spoken between them?"

"Harsh words?" she said. "You might say that. Old MacDonald had an angry streak as wide as the Roost. From time to time, I would see his face turn livid with rage, his mouth foaming, and his great bony hands shaking with passion. And Archie himself was rather hot-headed, though he often jauntily laughed off his father's moods, as if he feared neither the man's powerful hands nor his loaded shotgun. Of course, occasionally the old man's bullying got under Archie's skin and vexed him mightily. I remember one violent row after which Archie partook of rather more whisky than was good for him." She paused, as if she suddenly realized that she had said too much. Her lips clasped shut.

"Was there anything peculiar about the death of Old Mac-

Donald?"

"Now don't you go blaming that on Archie!" she exclaimed. "That was caused by the ghost."

Holmes' eyebrows rose. "A ghost? I am afraid I find that a hard theory to lend credence. In my experience, there is no such thing as ghosts."

"My cousin Steevie, who lived over in Loch Ranza, died of seeing a ghost, Mr. Holmes," said she, defensively. "But you are correct. This was not a real ghost, mind you. That is only what I first thought when I found him pressing his face against the glass of my window in the middle of the night. My very blood ran cold and I couldn't scream for fright." She paused and furrowed her brow. "There are times I heartily wish he had been a wraith or a bogle. Such a being we could have warded off with a rowan-wood cross tied with red thread. Instead, he turned out to be the devil himself. If not for that awful visitor, old MacDonald would probably still be alive."

"How so?" asked Holmes.

"Well, didn't he ask Archie and his pa to sail him over to Lamlash, even though that meant going through the Roost? And didn't he fall out of the boat in a drunken stupor? And when old MacDonald tried to save him, didn't he pull the man down with him into the black depths?"

"Perhaps you should start at the beginning, Mrs. McBane? Who was this man?"

She frowned as she tried to think back. "I don't recall his name precisely. Dingy, mayhaps? Or Digby. He was about forty years of age, unless I miss my guess. He had a dark, hard, dour sort of face, with black hair and a beard and sunburned features, with intense blue eyes. He was handsome, I suppose, in a rather Spanish sort of way. I remember his velveteen jacket, which was so rich that I wanted to rub my face across it – it he had not been wearing it, of course! He appeared on the island one night claiming that his ship had been wrecked off shore. He stayed with Archie and his dad for about a fortnight before announcing one afternoon that he was ready to return to the mainland, and insisting that the MacDonalds sail him over in their little boat. Archie told him that it was too late in the day for that, but that he reckoned they might reach Lamlash before nightfall."

"Do you have any other recollections about this Spanish visitor?

"Well, Archie was rather fond of him. I think they had a bit of a dust-up at first, but soon came to terms. And I think Archie looked up to him. The man had a dash of recklessness about him and was forever telling stories of adventures in faraway places. Berlin. The California gold fields. The Great Plains of America. Mind you, I did not hear these stories directly. But Archie would retell them to me the next day, as we sat in our nook overlooking the sea. I think Archie wished that it could have been him who was off having adventures, instead of stuck on little old Uffa."

"And Dr MacDonald did leave Uffa eventually, did he not?"

She snorted in derision. "To Paisley! A town of factories. It's not exactly Paris, is it, Mr. Holmes?"

He smiled. "No, it is not. Thank you for your time, Mrs. McBane."

When we departed Corriemains, Holmes appeared deep in thought, so I refrained from disturbing him. Instead, I contemplated what we had learned from Minnie McBane. I did not understand how the mysterious visitor fit into the picture. He may have inadvertently caused the death of Fergus MacDonald, but that tragic event seemed to have little bearing on the murder of a woman some twenty years later.

As we walked, I noted that the afternoon was wearing on. Such wind as there was had fallen completely away and the air became close and stagnant. The sun blazed down with a degree of heat, which was remarkable so early in the season, and a shimmering haze lay upon the upland moors, concealing the Irish mountains on the other side of the Channel. I pulled my handkerchief from my sleeve and wiped my brow. I silently wished for the breeze to return.

"You shall get your wish, Watson," said Holmes suddenly.

"You think the wind will pick up?"

"I fear so."

"Fear? It sounds like a blessing right now."

He shook his head. "It may all seem calm and peaceful right now, Watson. However, to those who are accustomed to read Nature's warning, there is a dark menace in the air and sky and sea."

"Surely you jest?" said I, dubiously.

"We shall see."

Holmes was soon to be proven correct. When we returned to Carracuil, I studied the oak barometer upon the wall. The mercury had sunk to the phenomenal point of twenty-eight inches, which even I knew heralded the onslaught of a fierce gale. At nine o'clock, a sharp breeze was blowing. At ten, it had freshened into a gale. By midnight, the most furious storm was raging. Nature's grim orchestra was playing its world-old piece with a compass, which ranged from the deep rumble of the thundering surge to the thin shriek of the scattered shingle and the keen piping of frightened sea birds.

For dinner, the three of us shared some rough fare from the larder, washed down with a whisky which our host said was brewed on the island by the Gibbs brothers. Afterwards, I retired to the solitary spare bedroom, for Holmes declared himself contented with the couch. Though, when I left him, he was staring at the kitchen fire with his amber-stemmed pipe in his mouth with no signs he ever planned to sleep.

It was a dreary night. Once I turned out my lamp, any moonlight, which might have brightened the room, was snuffed out by the storm. There was a great commotion outside, and I could have sworn that a great bat fluttered against the window, as if trying to find its way into the room. Perhaps the sensational blood-curdling novel I had been reading on the train had overstimulated my imagination. But my suspicion was that this visitation was a sure sign of misfortune. The question was... for whom?

THE TREASURY OF SHERLOCK HOLMES

§

When I woke, shortly after the first pale light of dawn was just appearing in the east, the gale had blown past. I discovered that Holmes had already risen and departed the croft. I breakfasted and then walked down to the pebble-strewn beach. It was a sight to see the great rollers sweeping in, over-topping one another like a herd of elephants, and then bursting with a roar. Each wave sent the small pebbles flying before them like buckshot and filled the whole air with drifting sea foam. It was as if the fierce old ocean was gnashing its teeth at being deprived of any victims in the night.

I was standing there, watching the scene, when I saw Holmes hurrying towards me. "There you are, Watson," said he, with a smile. "I think there is something you might like to see."

He indicated that I should follow him. The croft of Carracuil was tucked into a corner of the isle, walled off by the Combera cliffs, which rose straight out of the water to the height of a couple hundred feet. But there were footpaths which led to the top of these cliffs, and it was to that spot where Holmes led. The area was covered with greensward and commanded a noble view on every side. I admired this for a moment, but the dark clouds covered the sun, and the keen north wind came in with frequent gusts, and I was soon feeling rather cold. "Very nice, Holmes. However, I don't see how the view advances the case?"

"We didn't come for the view, Watson."

He led me over to the edge, and for a moment, I thought he was going to fall off, but at the last second, he stepped onto a small path that was barely distinguishable from its surroundings. This plummeted down the steepest part of the cliff, and I clung to the face for fear of misplacing my step. Below, I could see a mass of great green slippery rocks and small pools, which had been exposed by the lowering of the tide. Fortunately, we did not have far to go before Holmes turned into a small cave, almost hidden from view by a tangle of thistle. I followed him inside and gasped. For in that small natural chamber lay another skeleton.

When I had recovered from my shock. "I don't understand, Holmes. How did you find this place?"

"I found it because I expected it to be here."

"What do you mean?"

"It was plain to me that Mrs. Grice Paterson had discovered something of interest after the great storm. Her husband mentioned that she was acting differently. Something had disturbed her prior equanimity. As she had never before been to Scotland, it seemed unlikely that she could have a direct connection to Fergus MacDonald. Therefore, she must have found something else. And here it is," he concluded, with a flourish of his hand.

"And the skeleton?" I asked, motioning to where it lay upon a burlap sack. "To whom does it belong?"

"Surely that must be obvious, Watson? It is Mrs. McBane's Spanish devil. The man who dragged MacDonald to his death."

I shook my head. "But he drowned. How could he be found way up here?"

"If I am not mistaken, Mrs. Grice Paterson hid him here."

"To what end?"

"Ah, yes, that is the question, is it not, Watson? If we knew that, I suspect we would understand the motive for her murder. But there is something I want you to see."

He crouched down next to the skeleton and handed me his glass. I noted from the hip bones that they indisputably once belonged to a man, and one with a powerful frame. Holmes motioned towards the neck. I inspected that area carefully and was surprised to find a deep groove in the spinous process of the fourth cervical vertebrae. "By Jove, Holmes!" I exclaimed. "The man was garrotted."

He smiled. "Such was my first thought, Watson. However, as you know, I have made a study of how far injuries may be produced after death. A ligature would leave an impression in the soft tissues of the neck, of course, but why would it do so in the bone? No, it is far too deep."

I frowned with incomprehension. "So he was garrotted after he was already dead?"

"No, no, Watson. Consider what else might make such a mark."

I shook my head. "I can think of nothing."

"What of a neck pouch? One made of leather, but lined with a metal mesh and whose lanyard contained a steel wire core."

"I have never heard of such a thing."

"I have. People who are carrying something of great value wear them. People who are paranoid that mere leather can snap or be sliced by a clever cutpurse."

"So what does this signify?"

"We now know Mrs. Grice Paterson's secret, Watson. After Jock Gibbs found the skeleton of Fergus MacDonald, and Uffa's inhabitants gathered round to inspect it, Mrs. Grice Paterson continued to walk along the beach, where she stumbled upon the second skeleton. It is possible that she thought it was more of the first, but she is the wife of a naturalist, and surely must have soon come to the conclusion that these bones belonged to another individual. She likely did not yet know the story of the Spanish devil, but she found something around the man's neck that induced her to hide the rest of the bones, so that no one would know what she had discovered. It must have been something valuable. Her motive is now plain. It merely remains to retrace her footsteps, and we shall be led to her killer."

I looked about the floor of the cave. "I don't see any footprints, Holmes. The gale winds must have wiped them clear."

Holmes laughed. "Metaphorically, Watson. Metaphorically. It is time we turned our gaze further afield than little Uffa."

§

We hiked back down the hill to Carracuil, where Holmes explained to his client that he was going to follow a lead off the isle, but that he would keep the man notified of any progress in the case. The man simply nodded miserably. I reckoned Grice Paterson would remain in that state until Holmes solved the mystery of his wife's death.

Holmes and I then made our way over to Arden, where the Gibbs brothers were happy to take us back over to the mainland in their fishing boat. They explained that the sea would be a bit choppy and asked that – if required – we attempt to refrain from bringing up our breakfast within the confines of the bulwarks. Fortunately, both Holmes and I had a rather iron stomach when it came to such matters – though given the current state of cleanliness of the boat, I silently wondered why they cared?

Holmes pointed the Gibbs brothers towards the town of Ardrossan. This was the largest on the North Ayrshire coast, which is to say that it is a small place, mainly used as a port for exporting coal and pig iron to other parts of Europe and even the Americas. A modest shipyard was busy constructing fishing boats and small cargo ships. There was also a passenger ferry engaged in loading passengers bound for the Isle of Arran and distant Belfast.

After we disembarked from the Gibbs' boat, we set off into town. I was uncertain of our destination, until Holmes stopped and asked someone for the address of Mr. Robert Fullarton. I deduced this gentleman must be Minnie's brother. Holmes was silent regarding the nature of this call, so I merely observed and waited for him to explain in due time. Fullarton lived in a large house tucked behind the castle promontory. This appeared to my eyes to be the nicest part of town, suggesting that Fullarton was clearly well off. Holmes presented his card to the footman who answered the door and we were promptly shown into the drawing room of the prosperous grain retailer. Robert Fullarton was a short and rather plump man nearing fifty years of age. I could see some of his sister's features in him, but while the sea air had lashed her brown hair, his was slicked with pomade. Her face had been pleasantly flushed, while his was limpid as a fish. I wondered about Plutarch's dilemma.[52] Did Fullarton's intrinsic nature propel him to leave the rough ways of Uffa, or did turning away from Uffa lead him to this soft state?

While I was silently philosophizing, Fullarton opened the conversation. "What can I do for you, Mr. Holmes?" the man asked.

Holmes explained that he was investigating the death of Clare Grice Paterson. Unless the man was a masterful actor, I felt certain that he was much surprised by this news. "I am wondering, Mr. Fullarton, if you were familiar with the lady?"

"Only in passing," said he, with a wave of his hand. "She had become friends with my sister, and I was recently introduced to her at the funeral of old Fergus MacDonald."

"Ah, so you attended that?"

The man shrugged. "Everyone who has ever lived on Uffa attended, Mr. Holmes. It was only right. I had to pay my respects to his son."

"So you went out of propriety, not grief?"

Fullarton's mouth turned downwards. "Truth be told, Mr. Holmes, I doubt many people missed Fergus MacDonald. Even my late father, who lived near him for over fifty years, had little nice to say about that bitter old man."

"Does Archie feel the same?"

The man pursed his lips. "I think you should ask him that, sir."

"I intend to do so," Holmes replied.

"And if I may ask, what does the reappearance of Fergus' bones have to do with the death of Mrs. Grice Paterson? I doubt she had even heard of Uffa when old Fergus was still alive."

"It is an excellent question, Mr. Fullarton, and if I find the answer, I promise to let you know. So, you met her at the funeral. Any other time?"

"Well, funny you should ask, Mr. Holmes, but she took the same boat as I back to Ardrossan."

"Ah, yes? And did you converse?"

"Briefly."

"Can you recall the content of your conversation?" asked Holmes.

The man waved his hand casually. "It was about how she liked living on the island. Why I had left. Those sorts of things."

"Nothing else?"

"No. Wait, yes. She said she was on her way by rail to Glasgow and asked me if I knew the directions from the station to a particular locale. Unfortunately, I did not." He shrugged. "I don't know if she ever made it there or not. In fact, I never saw her again after we parted on the Ardrossan dock."

"And the name of the place to which she wished to visit?"

Fullarton bowed his head and furrowed his brow. Finally, he shook his head. "I am sorry, Mr. Holmes. The name has escaped me. As I said, it was a place with which I was unfamiliar."

"Very good. Thank you for your time, Mr. Fullarton. Should you recall the name, would you please send me a wire? The address is on my card. Oh, and one final question. Were you in Ardrossan two nights ago?"

The man frowned. "Of course. We had our Cooperative Benefit that night. It was a smashing success."

"I am happy to hear that," said Holmes pleasantly. "Good day, sir."

However, his amiable air did not last long once we had walked some ways from Fullarton's house. "Blast it, Watson!" he exclaimed. "Why is it that I seem to be the only person in the universe capable of making a simple recollection?"

"Not everyone has spent their time training their memory and constructing a carefully-ordered brain-attic, Holmes," said I, defending the man. "It is hardly something taught in the public schools."

He shook his head. "If Fullarton had only paid attention to Mrs. Grice Paterson, we might have obtained an essential piece of information. As it is, we will be forced to question the cabbies around Glasgow Central to see if any remember her. It could take days, if not weeks, and will require a considerable amount of luck. It is hardly the way to conduct an expedient investigation."

Fortunately, Holmes' criticism of Mr. Fullarton was premature, for the sounds of rapidly approaching footsteps soon caught our ears. We turned to see Fullarton's footman chasing after us. When he had recovered his breath, he looked at Holmes. "Mr. Fullarton said to tell you, sir, that he recalled part of the name. He said it had something to do with an 'arcade.'"

By the gleam in his eyes, I could tell that Holmes had made something of this piece of information, though I could hardly see how it helped us. Holmes thanked the man with a half-sovereign and turned to me with a smile. "I am close, Watson. I think one more stop will do it. We must go to Glasgow."

"To this 'arcade'?"

"No, to the offices of the *Herald*."

§

The train to Glasgow was brief and uneventful. Once we arrived, Holmes directed me to take two rooms at the Central Hotel. He said I would be of no help at the newspaper building, so I availed myself of the time to turn some more pages of my gripping novel. My eyes must have closed for a minute, but when I opened them, I found Holmes standing over me, a triumphant look upon his face.

"You know who did it," said I, simply.

"I have a strong suspicion, yes. But most importantly, Watson, I have the means to force a confession, for it may be difficult to find conclusive proof."

I raised my eyebrows. "Mrs. Grice Paterson's killer is going to simply admit to the crime?"

"I believe so."

"Would you care to share with me what you found at the *Herald*?"

He shook his head. "All in due time, Watson. Surely you don't want to spoil the surprise?"

When Holmes was in such a mood, I knew there was little chance to pry information out of him. However, over dinner at a café along Buchanan Street, I attempted to reconstruct his train of reasoning. "So who are our suspects, Holmes?"

"You tell me, Watson."

"Well, surely we can rule out Mr. Grice Paterson."

"Why?"

"He is clearly mourning the loss of his wife."

Holmes wagged his finger. "Great actors can fake such emotions with ease, Watson. There is a more sure method of establishing his innocence."

"Which is?"

"He hired me."

I laughed at Holmes' monstrous ego. "Perhaps he thought himself capable of hoodwinking you?"

He shrugged. "That would take a very brave man. Or a very foolish one. I don't believe Mr. Grice Paterson fits either description."

"Very well, then there is Minnie McBane."

"Her motive?" he asked.

"I don't know."

"That is because there isn't one. And surely her absence from the isle would not have passed unnoticed."

"Her husband then. He has a boat, and could easily dock it in some small harbour before catching a train to London."

Holmes smiled with appreciation. "That is very devious, Watson. No discernible motive, of course, but yes, he would have had the means. Still, I don't believe he is our man."

"The same logic applies to Tommy Gibbs, as well as his brothers."

"Indeed it does. All three Gibbs boys could have plausibly snuck down to London. But again, there is a paucity of reason for any of them to wish her harm."

"I suppose Robert Fullarton can be excluded. His alibi is watertight."

Holmes shook his head. "Not yet proven, Watson, but I nonetheless agree. Fullarton would not have given us the critical clue if he was guilty."

"So who does that leave?"

"You are forgetting one man, Watson. But tomorrow morning we shall pay him a visit."

§

We rose early and Holmes hired a carriage to take us to Paisley. Holmes wanted to call upon Dr MacDonald before he left for his morning rounds. When we arrived, the town was bustling with textile mill workers, busy supplying the world with imitation Kashmir shawls. Everywhere I looked, the ladies were festooned with the distinctive colourful teardrop-like patterns once made popular by our Queen when she was a young lady, but now sadly out of fashion in cosmopolitan London.

Dr MacDonald's modest house was situated very near Paisley Abbey, which was slowly emerging from centuries of post-Reformation decay as evidenced by scaffolding covering the restoration work transpiring upon the nave and transepts. Holmes hefted the knocker and the owner himself soon answered his call. Clearly he was either too frugal or too badly off to employ someone for such a task.

MacDonald proved to be a square-shouldered, long-legged man of forty. He was clad in a professional fashion, with a neat frock coat and well-pressed trousers. Behind a pair of steel-rimmed glasses, there was a hard glint to his grey eyes, such that I could still see a trace of the proud Uffa man underneath his now modest exterior.

Once Holmes had introduced us, the doctor invited us into his dining room, where he bade us sit while he prepared a pot of tea. While this was happening, I glanced around the room. The doctor had set up a Sholes and Glidden machine at one end of the table. There were no obvious signs of recent use, unless the papers were contained in the manila envelope that lay next to the typewriter. Once the tea was boiled and poured out, he joined us at the table. MacDonald took a sip of his tea and then asked how he could assist us.

In turn, Holmes took a sip of his tea before answering. "You grew up on the isle Uffa, did you not, Dr MacDonald?"

"I did indeed. However, farming and fishing were not in my blood, Mr. Holmes. As soon as I was able, I began to study at the University of Glasgow."

"But you were at home at the time of your father's accident?"

He looked at Holmes sharply. "Yes, that is true. I was there that day. I remember it well. Whether from caprice, or from some lessening in his funds, my father recalled me to Uffa that spring after only two winter sessions."

"Your mother?"

He shook his head. "Influenza. In '57."

"No siblings?"

"None."

"You must have been bitter, Doctor, to be trapped upon that little isle, with just sufficient education to wish for more? I assume your father did not share your passion for science?"

He snorted in amusement. "No, the stern old man was not much of a conversationalist, that be certs."

"And yet, you must have been surprised when his bones were suddenly found after all these years."

"You could say that, Mr. Holmes. I thought he would lie forever – in a dreamless and unruffled sleep – in the silent green depths of the Roost of Uffa, till the great trumpet sounded."

"But the sea gave up its dead," said Holmes, mildly.

"Aye. Perhaps the end of days is upon us."

"What about his partner in sleep?"

The man's eyes narrowed. "What do you mean?"

"Your houseguest at Carracuil? The man who drowned with your father? He was a Spaniard, I believe?"

The right corner of the man's mouth curled upwards. "You have been talking with Minnie. In fact, the man never said where he was from. By his accent, I would have taken him for an American. He certainly spent a considerable amount of time there, according to his tales." He paused to fill his pipe with tobacco and proceeded to light it.

"Ah, yes, Minnie told us he was quite the storyteller. California gold fields and shootouts on the Great Plains."

"And the barricade in Berlin.[53] And mutinous lascars. And hunting bears in Colorado."

"I wonder if he ever mentioned any adventures in France?"

Dr MacDonald licked his lips. "I believe he spent time in Marseilles. Certainly his ship, the *Proserpine*, was headed there before it was wrecked in a storm."

"Do you recall his name?"

"Of course. It was Charles Digby."

Holmes shook his head. "Perhaps that is the name he gave you. But would it surprise you if it was an alias?"

The doctor shrugged. "No, I suppose not."

"In fact, I believe Mr. Digby was in fact one Achille Wolff."

"The name sounds familiar," replied MacDonald, evenly.

"Yes, he was in the papers for a time. I found something about him just last night when searching through the archives from around the time of your father's death." Holmes reached into his breast pocket and withdrew a newspaper clipping. He handed it to me. "Would you read it aloud, Watson?"

I frowned at the twenty-two year-old *Herald* article, which appeared to be a translation from a French correspondence. I cleared my throat and followed Holmes' command. It ran this way:

"Fuller details have now come before the public of the

diamond robbery by which the Duchesse de Rochevieille lost her celebrated gem. The diamond is a pure brilliant weighing eighty-three and one-half carats, and is supposed to be the third largest in France and the seventeenth in Europe. It came into the possession of the family through the great-granduncle of the duchess, who fought under Bussy in India, and brought it back to Europe with him. It represented a fortune then, but its value now is simply enormous. It was taken, as will be remembered, from the jewel case of the duchess two months ago during the night, and though the police have made every effort, no real clue has been obtained as to the thief. They are very reticent upon the subject, but it seems that they have reason to suspect one Achille Wolff, an Americanized native of Lorraine, who had called at the chateau a short time before. He is an eccentric man, of bohemian habits, and it is just possible that his sudden disappearance at the time of the robbery may have been a coincidence. In appearance he is described as romantic-looking, with an artistic face, dark eyes and hair, and a brusque manner. A large reward is offered for his capture."

When I finished reading this, I looked up. Dr MacDonald was staring at Holmes in silence. They remained like this for a minute or two. At last he spoke. "That is an interesting story, Mr. Holmes. However, I fail to see what it has to do with me."

Holmes shook his head. "I know all, sir. It is futile to pretend any longer. You may tell your story now, and unburden yourself of the terrible guilt that you must feel, or you may tell it in the dock of the Saltmarket.[54] The choice is yours."

"This is a bluff upon your part, Mr. Holmes."

"I tell you, Doctor, that I can see it all transpiring as if it was painted before me."

"You have no proof."

Holmes snorted with wry amusement. "Do you believe that

it will be difficult to find a witness who will confirm your trip to London on the same day that Mrs. Grice Paterson was killed?"

"Coincidence."

"Do you believe the fifteen men of the jury will swallow such a tale, Doctor? I find that highly unlikely."

"I will take my chances. If it even comes to that. At the moment, all I hear is conjecture and speculation."

"And do you suppose that you have hidden the Duchesse's diamond so well that it cannot be discovered? I have found out your secret, and I assure you that I will recover the stone. When I do so, you will have a most difficult time explaining how precisely it was acquired. No, sir, I think my account of your actions will be most convincing to the Lord Justice."

Dr MacDonald's face turned an ashen grey as he listened to Holmes' words. He sat for some time with a furrowed brow and a sunken chin. Then, he lifted his head, his visage clear.

"You are right, Mr. Holmes. I have been consumed with remorse over my terrible actions, which were like those of a stranger who temporarily inhabited my body. I will tell you what happened." He shook his head. "I will never forget the cruel spring day when the *Proserpine* dropped its ill-fated passenger upon the shores of Uffa. How was I to guess the dark things that were to come upon us, Mr. Holmes? As you say, I was most unhappy there, trapped under the power of my malignant father. However, things are never so bad but that they might be worse."

"*Vogue la galère*," said Holmes.

MacDonald smiled wanly. "Precisely so. Digby said that to me once. I did not believe him at the time. For when my father attacked him, and the two of them went down into that clear water, locked in their terrible embrace, I was suddenly free to do whatever I wanted in life. I left Uffa at once, completely and forever. But then my father came back from the grave, to haunt me like some horrible nightmare."

"However, you knew that if your father returned, so too the

Frenchman. And you knew that he carried the diamond."

"Of course. Many years ago, I spied on Digby as he secretly gazed at the stone, long and lovingly. After my father's burial, I walked upon the beach for a while, but found nothing. I then climbed up to my old perch above the Combera cliffs in order to think. That is when I saw the footsteps leading down to the cave where Mrs. Grice Paterson had taken Digby's bones. I quickly inferred that there was only one reason for her to do so. She had found his pouch, or what remained of it, and it still held the stone.

"Removed from temptation, I have been an upright, righteous man for many years, Mr. Holmes. However, it was impossible to be a saint when faced with such riches. For a moment, the devil was busy in me, and I made a resolution that the diamond was mine by rights. Some might have been squeamish in the matter, but my conscience was untroubled by such sentimentality. My father was a madman, and a dangerous one to boot, and it seems that his madness had infected me." He gazed absently out of the window. I knew that he was not looking at the streets of Paisley, but rather the long-ago shores of Uffa.

"My practice was closed for the funeral," he continued. "It was a simple matter to extend that for the sake of bereavement. I then waited for her to make her move. I watched as she came over to Ardrossan, and I followed her to Glasgow."

"To the Argyll Arcade, home of Glasgow's diamond merchants," said Holmes.

"I didn't realize what she intended at first, or I would have accosted her before she ever reached the Arcade. Unfortunately for all involved, the merchants at the Arcade were unwilling to buy the stone. Such a thing does not walk into one's store every day, I suppose. Perhaps they told her of their suspicions about its origin. She returned to Uffa, and I resumed my watch. When she left again, this time for London, I again dogged her steps. I was determined to stop her from selling the diamond. Once she arrived at Euston Station, she set off for Fleet Street. Since she made no effort to visit Hatton Gardens, I can only suppose she was going to try to claim the reward through the offices of her bank. There was once a time when I too considered the reward a sufficient recompense for my efforts. However, I was no longer interested in such meagre offerings. Only the stone itself would slack my thirst."

He shook his head. "To be honest, I don't even recall striking her. Of course, once I saw what I had done, I knew she was dead, and did my best to make it appear like an accident. It seems that stratagem was not sufficient." He shrugged. "In my defence, I had little practice in such matters. I will not pretend any longer, Mr. Holmes, that I am a perfect and spotless man. I once had notions of right and wrong, but somehow the rough friction of the world has rubbed those away, like the varnish on a boat's hull. Or at least I thought that I once had such principles. But perhaps – like my father before me – I am congenitally shallow-hearted and hot-headed? All of the events which lead up to my father's death can be found in these reminiscences, which I have jotted down during the brief intervals from my professional work." He slid the manila envelope across the table, and Holmes silently placed it in his pocket.[55]

"I am so sick of the grey clouds and continual damp," MacDonald continued. "I dream of blue skies and fine weather, Mr. Holmes. I once heard that Chios was the nearest thing to paradise on this earth. I suppose I shall never see it now?"

"No, I suppose not. I think it is Barlinnie for you, I am afraid."[56]

Dr MacDonald nodded slowly. "And the stone, do you wish to see it?"

Holmes shrugged. "If you do not bring it forth voluntarily, Scotland Yard will find it eventually."

MacDonald grinned sardonically, and for a moment, his eyes blazed like a fiend out of a pit. "Yes, I suppose they won't let me keep it. It is a shame. It would suffice for the ache of not ever seeing Chios, if I could look on it every day." He slipped his hand into his coat pocket and plunked something down upon the table before us. It was an extraordinary diamond of the first water. The facets of the great white stone twinkled brilliantly as they caught the rays of the late morning sun coming through the window. I had never seen a gem of its ilk, not even the enormous beryls of the coronet belonging to Mr. Holder's noble client.

"There it is, Mr. Holmes, the cursed stone," said MacDonald. "I trust that when the trial comes, they may show that, so the jury understands the sore temptation which the devil had placed in my way. Perhaps it will serve as some slight extenuation of my errors while in this mortal flesh."

§

Dr MacDonald went quietly with us to the local police station, from where he was eventually transferred to London for trial. As Holmes predicted, he was locked away for the rest of his life. He would never see the blue skies of Greece. I truly cannot say whether I am sorry for him or not. For his deed was a terrible one, but who among us has not been tempted, and who knows what fragile forces hold us back from acting upon such dark desires?

Before we departed Scotland, Holmes and I briefly sailed back over to Uffa in order to bring closure to Mr. Grice Paterson. At first, he was astonished at the tale, and then he sobbed at the thought that his wife was killed while trying to surprise him for his birthday. We left him alone at the Carracuil croft. I never heard whether he finished his book.

As a brief epilogue, a week later, upon our return to London, Holmes awoke late to find me sitting at my desk, pen in hand, but paper blank.

"You have further questions about the adventures of the Grice Patersons, I think, Watson?"

I pushed back my chair and looked at him. "Certainly, Holmes. It was all rather jumbled at the end there."

"So you intend to lay the matter bare for public consumption?"

I shrugged. "I have considered it. I think there would be an interest in your methods."

"Well, you must start at the beginning, with the Brixton Road mystery."[57]

"Of course. I have already submitted a small brochure of that case to a few periodicals. But if there is a call for more, surely it would do to be prepared."

He sighed and threw himself in the chair opposite me. "Very well, Watson. What do you wish to know?"

"What was Achille Wolff doing visiting remote Uffa?"

"The full answer to that can be found in here," said he, handing me the manila envelope with MacDonald's notes. "Essentially, Wolff believed that he would avoid police pursuit by hiding in one of the most desolate and lonely spots in Europe. Of course, little did he know that his choice would put him in contact with two men as merciless as Fergus and Archie MacDonald. You might make something of Dr MacDonald's recollections. They are rather lurid."

"And did MacDonald kill his father and Achille Wolff?"

He shook his head. "Not if his remembrances are to be believed, and I see no reason for him to lie. Fergus and Wolff killed each other, when Fergus tried to take the diamond from him."

"How did the bones survive that long? I thought that seawater would dissolve them?"

"Certainly in warmer waters, Watson. However, in the extreme cold depths of the Firth of Clyde bodies may be partially protected against decomposition. A chemical process called saponification creates an adipocere – or grave wax – which can seal the bones off from degradation. Documented cases have recovered bones over five years later, but I admit that twenty is quite a remarkable amount of time. And it was a singular set of circumstances which brought them back to the sunlit world. One that I am certain Mr. Grice Paterson sorely wishes had never transpired."

"And the diamond?"

"You will be pleased to learn, Watson, that Scotland Yard has recently concluded its investigation into Mrs. Grice Paterson's death. The diamond has – after all these years – finally been returned to the Duchess of Rochevieille."

"And the reward?"

"I made sure it went to Mr. Grice Paterson. It is small recompense for the loss of his wife, of course, but will give him the freedom to finish his book."

I thought that rather generous of Holmes and told him so.

He shrugged. "It is not good to grow overly attached to baubles or treasures, Watson. The work alone is sufficient reward for me. May we continue to be so blessed with further cases of great interest."

§

'The year '87 furnished us with a long series of cases of greater or less interest, of which I retain the records. Among my headings under this one twelve months, I find an account of... the singular adventures of the Grice Patersons in the island of Uffa.... All these I may sketch out at some future date....'
–The Five Orange Pips

THE ADVENTURE OF THE QUEEN'S PENDANT

F or most of the six years of our acquaintance, I have routinely observed that my friend Mr. Sherlock Holmes had a rather poor opinion of the fairer sex. Of course, ever since he was beaten by the wit of a well-known adventuress he no longer made merry over the cleverness of women. But he little trusted them, and was less than an admirer of womankind. This unfortunate attitude was, I believe, due at least partly to his inability to truly solve the puzzle of the female's heart and mind. Furthermore, his estimation of women was little elevated by the recently concluded case of Miss Sutherland, whose sad delusions Holmes was reluctant to shatter.

However, it was but a fortnight later when a remarkable adventure forced Holmes to readjust his opinions about the affirmative role of womankind in modern society.[58] I had called upon my friend at his chambers in Baker Street one evening to inquire about any new cases which had come across his door. He welcomed me with a manner more expansive than typical and waved me to my former armchair.

"I see you are well, Watson, and that your wager was a successful one."

"My wager? Holmes, I fail to see how you could possibly know about that?"

He shook his head. "When a man enters my chambers with the corner of a racing ticket protruding from his breast pocket, it is a perfectly trivial matter to determine that he has been recently visiting his turf accountant."

I glanced down in order to confirm this observation. "But why successful?"

"Because you stopped afterwards and purchased a new hat to replace the one with the worn brim and the discoloured patches that you were wearing upon our last case together."

"That was days ago, Holmes. I could have bought this hat at any time."

"A tag bearing the maker's name is still evident, something that your neat wife would never allow. Therefore, I conclude that you have not yet been home after the purchase."

Snatching the hat from my head, I laughed appreciatively at another of my friend's prestidigitations. "I suppose I should be used to your mind-reading tricks by now, Holmes."

"You are an open book, I am afraid, Watson. Have a quiet cigar with me. The Matronas is excellent."

"And you, Holmes, have you been busy?"

He shrugged. "Nothing of note. Merely the little matter of the Marylebone blackmail case.[59] Instead, I have taken upon myself to learn a new skill."

"You cannot refer to the new water-colours I see scattered about?"

"On the contrary, Watson."

"But, Holmes, these are extraordinary. You say this is a new skill, but these appear the work of a master. The scene at Westminster Bridge is a masterwork."

He smiled. "I think I once mentioned that my mother was descended from an artist, so I suppose some of the family talent has been passed on. However, these are mere scribbles. Something to pass the time while awaiting something of real interest. And by the sound of the bell, perhaps a fresh client has arrived."

We soon heard Mrs. Hudson opening the door, followed by a step upon the stairs and a tapping at the door. Holmes called out for the newcomer to enter.

The man who came in was a compact fellow, with hale and bronzed skin, and a straightforward, tidy manner. He had a pair of wonderfully sharp and penetrating blue eyes, and was dressed in an expensive but well-worn light brown suit.

"Are you Mr. Holmes?" he asked my friend.

"I am," replied Holmes waving him to the nearest chair. "And this is my partner and helper, Dr Watson. You may speak freely in front of him."

The man nodded in my direction. "My name, Mr. Holmes, is Hugh Cavendish. I am a lecturer at University College and the curator of the Gower Street Museum. It is on behalf of the museum that I come to seek your counsel."

"But only after you inquired at Scotland Yard," said Holmes.

Our guest's eyebrows rose in surprise. "How could you possibly know that, sir?"

"You have a splattering of a distinctively-coloured mud upon the cuffs of your trousers and yet the weather has been dry. The sewers along Whitehall are being repaired, which is the most likely locale at which a man might acquire such a stain. However, Whitehall is not on the way from the museum to Baker Street. Therefore, it is evident that you first called upon the official police force."

Professor Cavendish smiled. "I see that Inspector Lestrade was correct. You are just the man to solve this puzzle."

"And what matter did Lestrade feel was not worthy of the attention of the C.I.D.?"

"This is an anonymous letter which I received this morning," said he, drawing forth a slip of paper from his dress-jacket. "I want you to read it and to have your advice about its contents."

"You are very welcome to it for what it is worth," shrugged Holmes. He took the note and passed it over to me. "Read it aloud, Watson."

I glanced down at the scribbles. "This is how the note runs, Holmes:

> 'Sir, -
> I should strongly advise you to keep a very careful watch over the many valuable things which are committed to your charge. I do not think that the present system of a single watchman is sufficient. Be upon your guard, or an irreparable misfortune may occur.' "

"Is that all?" asked Holmes of our visitor.

"Yes, that is all," replied Cavendish. "Inspector Lestrade thought this warning too vague for any action."

Holmes snorted in wry amusement. "The good inspector often fails to take notice of the most interesting cases. If we are fortunate, this may prove similar."

"Well," said I, "it is at least obvious that the note was written by one of the limited number of people who are aware that you have only one watchman at night."

Holmes shook his head. "No, Watson. That fact would be simple enough to ascertain without any especial knowledge. A burglar of any proficiency always reconnoitres a locale before striking. A close watch of how many individuals enter the museum every evening shortly before closing time would provide this answer without difficulty."

"Then who?" I asked, somewhat peevishly.

"It is far too early to speculate, Watson." He turned his attention back to his client. "I will require more information in order to provide any useful advice, Professor."

"I am happy to answer any questions you may have."

"First, may I see the letter, Watson?"

I handed it over and Holmes looked at it closely. First, he

sniffed it, and he then took up his lens in order to inspect it for minute details.

"Do you see anything of note, Mr. Holmes?" asked Cavendish.

Holmes shook his head. "The writer was careful to disguise his identity. There are no stains or other distinctive marks. The ink is a standard iron-gall and it was written with a J pen. Beyond that, it is too soon to tell if the note will divulge any other secrets. May I retain this for the time-being, Professor?"

"Of course, if you think there is something else to be learned from it."

"One never knows," replied Holmes. "Now, you are rather young to be the curator of a major museum, are you not? I would put you at no more than a year or two over thirty."

Professor Cavendish nodded. "Spot on, Mr. Holmes. I am in truth, thirty-one. I have been most fortunate in my endeavours. I have had some small success at Thebes and that led to my recent election to the post."

"Are you the Hugh Cavendish who lived for two years in a tomb in the Valley of the Kings?" I exclaimed. "And who then created a considerable sensation with the exhumation of the alleged mummy of Cleopatra from an inner room of the Temple of Horus at Philae?"

Our guest smiled modestly. "Yes, I am he. Unfortunately, the identity of my find is not yet conclusively proven. My rivals believe the last Pharaoh of Egypt to instead reside at the Temple of Osiris at Taposiris Magna near Alexandria."[60]

"I have read several of your articles upon the subject, sir," I continued. "You are considered to be one of the best men of the day at everything connected with Oriental archaeology."

"You are too kind, Dr Watson. I assure you that most of it was luck."

"And yet, I have found that a man typically makes his own luck," interjected Holmes. "You noted that you recently assumed your post at the museum?"

"That is correct. It was vacated by the recently announced

retirement of Professor Hayward. The professor is a profound scholar and a man of European reputation. Students from every part of the world frequented his lectures, and his admirable management of the collection entrusted to his care was a model to all learned societies. It was, therefore, a considerable surprise when, at the still-young age of fifty-five, Professor Hayward suddenly resigned his position and retired from those duties which had been both his livelihood and his pleasure."

"Surely that is a difficult act to follow?"

Cavendish nodded. "It is always a challenge to live up to the legacy of such an extremely eminent man, Mr. Holmes. The museum at Gower Street is not large, and there is always the threat of its contents being subsumed by the much grander collection of the British Museum."[61]

"At any rate," said Holmes, "this warning is meant in a friendly spirit, and I should certainly act upon it. Are the present precautions enough to insure you against robbery?"

"I should have thought so. The public are only admitted from ten until five o'clock, and during that time, there is a guardian to every two rooms. He stands at the door between them, and so commands them both."

"But at night?"

"When the public have all departed, we at once put up the great iron shutters, which are absolutely burglar-proof. The watchman is a capable fellow. He sits in the lodge, but he walks round every three hours. We keep one electric light burning in each room all night."

"You say the watchman is capable. Did you engage him yourself?"

Cavendish shook his head. "No, he has been with the museum for many years. However, he is a former lance corporal of horse in the Queen's Bays.[62] He even lost part of his leg in '57 during the Siege of Lucknow. He is as honest as they come, I assure you."

"Then it is difficult to suggest anything more – short of

keeping your day watches all night."

"Sadly, the modest finances of the museum could not afford that."

"It is unfortunate that Lestrade did not take this seriously. He could have at least put a special constable outside in Gower Street for a few nights," said Holmes, shaking his head. "As to the letter, if the writer wishes to be anonymous, I think he has a right to remain so. We must trust to the future to show some reason for the curious course which he has adopted."

"Would you at least come round the museum and inspect things yourself, Mr. Holmes? Perhaps you would see some vulnerability that has escaped our notice."

Holmes nodded thoughtfully. "I am typically employed to solve a crime, Professor Cavendish, not to prevent one. Nevertheless, I once performed a similar service for the British Museum many years ago, and I see no reason to not do the same for you. Will you come, Watson?"

"Of course, Holmes. If the professor would have me?"

"Two sets of eyes are often better than one, Doctor. Why, when I was working at Thebes, I completely missed the entrance to a shaft in one of the side *wadis*, or bays, of the valley. Fortunately, my photographer spotted an area of the hillside that was strikingly free of tumbled rocks and sand. At first it seemed to be a most unpromising spot, but ultimately it proved to be the locale of a minor tomb."

"If I might make one suggestion, Professor Cavendish?" said Holmes. "Do you think it would be possible to have your predecessor to meet us there?"

"Certainly. In truth, Professor Hayward and his daughter have not yet departed the suite of rooms which form the official residence of the curator."

"These rooms are nearby?"

"Directly connected."

"And when will you take up quarters?"

"Tomorrow, in fact. The professor and Ellen are moving to a recently-vacated villa in Upper Norwood, and as an itinerant bachelor, it won't take long to transfer in my few possessions."

Holmes lips curled in a smile. "Norwood? Not the Pondicherry Lodge?"

"Yes, that is the one. Do you know it?"

"Watson and I once paid a visit to its previous owner. We unfortunately found him in less-than-ideal health," said he, dryly.

"Did you solve his case?"

"Oh, yes. Though Inspector Jones took the official credit, and only Watson here got his due rewards."

I smiled at the fond memory. "Perhaps it is just as well that Lestrade was uninterested in this case, Holmes. Once you solve Professor Cavendish's problem, you will receive the sole acclaim in my account of the matter."

Holmes merely shook his head. "I hardly think this matter will be worthy of one of your superficial sketches, Watson. Come now, let us hail a coach."

§

I was little bothered by Holmes' dismissive attitude. Despite his protestations to the contrary, I strongly suspected that he secretly enjoyed the recognition brought by my brochure embodying the events of the Hope case. The coach ride over to Gower Street was quick and uneventful. The museum itself proved to be an austere two-storied brown brick building, with heavy black shutters over the sole entrance door. The latter was doublewide in order to allow passage of the larger artefacts.

Cavendish unlocked the doors and bade us enter. He asked us wait in the central hall while he inquired after Professor Hayward, and Holmes utilized this time to quietly question the night watchman, a man of some fifty years named Bryson, with thinning hair and tired brown eyes. He moved with a limp from a wooden lower right leg.

Cavendish soon returned with three individuals, two men

mismatched in age and a young woman, which he introduced to us. The elderly man was of course, Professor Hayward. The young woman, no more than a few years above twenty, was his daughter Ellen. She was exceptionally beautiful, blonde, tall and graceful, with a skin of that delicate tint the colour of old ivory, her cheeks highlighted with a hue of the lighter petals of the sulphur rose. The younger man, approaching thirty years of age, had a dark, hard, incisive face. He was Major Bryan Nelson, previously of the 58th Regiment, and I understood that he was soon to become her husband.

When Professor Hayward learned of our mission, he insisted on showing us around the museum's admirable collection, of which he had played a significant role in compiling over the last twenty-odd years. His daughter and her fiancée also decided to accompany us in our inspection. There were fifteen rooms in the building, but the Egyptian, the Semitic, and the central hall, which contained the Syrian and Babylonian collection, were the finest of them all. Professor Hayward was a quiet, dry, elderly man, with a clean-shaven face and an impassive manner, but his dark eyes sparkled and his features quickened into enthusiastic life as he pointed out to us the rarity and the beauty of some of his former specimens. His hand lingered so fondly over them, that one could read his pride in them and the grief in his heart now that they were passing from his care into that of another.

He had shown us in turn the mummies, papyri, rare scarabs, and inscriptions. We saw a magnificent blown-glass vase from the Seleucid Empire, a statue of the god Bel from Palmyra, and a *lamassu* from Dur-Sharrukin.[63] Finally, he approached a case that stood in the very centre of the hall, and he looked down through the glass with reverence in his attitude and manner.

"This is no novelty to an expert like yourself, Professor Cavendish," said he. "But I daresay that your friends, Mr. Holmes and Dr Watson, will be interested to see it."

Leaning over the case, I saw an object, some twenty inches in length, which consisted of twelve precious stones in a framework of silver with a silver chain and hooks at the ends. The stones were varying in sort and colour, but they were of all the same size. Their shapes, arrangement, and gradation of tint made me think of a box of paints. Each stone had some hieroglyphic scratched upon its surface.

"It looks like a pendant of some sort," I said.

"You are correct, sir, though perhaps amulet would be more accurate given its inscriptions. There are, as you see, twelve magnificent stones, all inscribed with mystical characters. Counting from the left-hand top corner, the stones are carnelian, peridot, spinel, chalcedony, lapis lazuli, onyx, moonstone, agate, heliotrope, topaz, sardonyx, and jasper. Through careful analysis, we are able to identify the origin of the stones, many from the proto-historic mines of Afghanistan and Anatolia. It is astonishing to consider that mankind's covetousness for beauty is as ancient as civilization itself. Imagine, if you will, a period four-and-a-half millennia ago, when a stone mined at Sar-i Sang in the Hindu Kush mountains made its way over three thousand miles to end up in the tombs of Uruk or of Thebes."

I was amazed at the variety and beauty of the stones. "Has the pendant any particular history?" I asked.

"Oh, yes," said Professor Hayward. "After all, I excavated it myself ten years ago from beneath the ziggurat at Uruk.[64] I had originally gone out to Mesopotamia in hopes of replicating the feats of Layard and finding something like the Library of Ashurbanipal.[65] I got a firman from the Ottoman governor and went out to the site.[66] It is a remote place, miles from the nearest modern village. The mighty Euphrates had once flowed past it, but the channel had shifted over the course of centuries and the bed is now dry. To the untrained observer the mud walls might not look like much, but the great Tell would catch anyone's eye. It was under that great conical mound where we found layers of earth moved by water, physical evidence of the Great Flood of Utnapishtum."

"Utnapishtum?" I interjected.

"Yes, Doctor. You see, it was the Sumerians who first wrote of the flood. These writings were the inspiration for the later legend of Noah. In any case, after we removed this dirt, we finally came across the secret chamber. According to the cylinder seals we found within, the tomb belonged to the legendary Queen Ninsun. Without being able to make an absolute assertion, we believe this to be the same woman who was the mother of the great hero Gilgamesh. Of course, we are not entirely certain that she was a queen. She might have been a priestess. Alternatively, the two might have been one and the same. There is much about the Sumerian religion that we currently do not fully understand. Nonetheless, we know they had a very special feeling of reverence for Ninsun. Although once a mortal woman, upon her death she was elevated to the status of a goddess, something much like how the princess Psyche was transformed into the immortal wife of Eros in the tales of Apuleius. Or how Lady Beatrice Portinari became a divine guide to the heavens in Dante's *Commedia*. It is a symbol for the redemptive power of the feminine spirit."

"How valuable are the stones?" I inquired.

"From a historic sense, Dr Watson, the stones are priceless. Conversely, from an intrinsic sense, they are of only middling value. The Sumerians were not acquainted with what we now consider to be the four most precious gems: diamond, ruby, sapphire, and emerald. These twelve would have been the rarest stones of the ancient world, though today, they are counted as but semi-precious. They might fetch twenty or so pounds each at a broker's on Tottenham Court Road if they were unrecognized for their ancient uniqueness.[67] However, each one is in fact a pristine example of its type. There is certainly nothing so fine in any collection in Europe. My friend, Major Nelson here, is a practical authority upon precious stones, and he would be able to vouch for their purity."

Major Nelson was standing beside his fiancée at the other side of the case. "Yes," said he, curtly. "I have never seen finer stones of their type."

"And the metal-work is also worthy of attention," continued Professor Hayward. "It is in fact not silver, but a natural alloy of silver with gold. It is called electrum and was mined in ancient Lydia, now Anatolia. The ancients excelled in…" he was apparently about to indicate the setting of the stones, when Major Nelson interrupted him.

"You will see a finer example of their gold-work in this dagger," said he, turning to another table, and we all joined him in his admiration of the item's embossed patterned sheath and delicately ornamented hilt. This, Professor Hayward explained, was typical of the natural inspiration of their artwork.

"You have quite the collection of artefacts, Professor," said Holmes. "I am surprised that the local governments have not asked for these treasures to be returned."

Hayward chuckled quietly. "You must not have had much interaction with the Ottomans, Mr. Holmes.[68] They are stagnated in their Byzantine bureaucracy and cannot even protect what they still have. Who was it that blew the roof off the Parthenon? Who has allowed their ancient ruins to be looted and plundered? No, it is in the best interest of the citizens of the world that archaeologists like myself remove as much as possible and see it safely ensconced in the great museums of Europe, and even America."

Holmes nodded, as if he accepted this line of reasoning. Altogether, it was an interesting and a novel experience to have objects of such rarity explained by so great an expert. However, when finally Professor Hayward had finished our tour, I realized I had performed little inspection of the security of the exhibits. Holmes also made little comment regarding the letter's promised misfortune. Instead, he assured Professor Cavendish that he would come round again the next day. As Holmes and I drove away in a hansom cab, I could not help pitying the new autocrat of the Gower Street Museum. It must be a heavy duty to have been entrusted with such a precious collection and know that its security was being actively threatened.

We rode in silence, and Holmes had his head sunk upon his breast, with the air of a man who is lost in thought. I knew well enough not to interrupt him in such a mood, despite my great curiosity about what Professor Cavendish's letter could mean. As was his way, Holmes would apprise me when his conclusions were more fully formed. We circled round to Baker Street, where I intended to have the cab drop Holmes before proceeding on to Paddington. However, Holmes pulled my sleeve and signalled to me that he wished for me to remain. Acceding to his wishes, I re-joined him in my former quarters.

"What is it, Holmes?" I asked after we sat down in front of the cold summer hearth.

He handed me a note, with a curious smile. "Have you an eye for handwriting, Watson?" said he. "You may recall the utility of graphology in the Reigate affair."

I looked at this paper, which proven to be the letter entrusted to my friend by Professor Cavendish. "You know I don't have your skill at this, Holmes. I am hardly likely to be able to infer how old the writer is, or how poor his health, merely from the strokes of his pen."

"Surely, you can make some superficial deductions from it?"

"Very well," I sighed. I examined the letter with intense concentration and attempted to work out precisely what Holmes found so interesting.

"Anything of note, Watson?"

I shook my head. "Other than the fact that I would wager it was written by a man, I could not venture anything else."

Holmes nodded. "Capital, Watson! That is an excellent start. We will make a graphologist out of you yet. I concur with your assessment that this note was written by a man."

"And how does that advance us?"

"Surely it is of some utility to know that Ellen Hayward did not write it?"

"You suspected Professor Hayward's daughter?" I exclaimed.

"You know my methods, Watson. I suspect everyone. Now, look at this." He put another piece of paper in front of me. "Look at the c in 'classical' and the c in 'cuneiform.' Look at the capital I in 'Inanna.' Look at the trick of putting in a dash instead of a stop! Compare this to the letter, with its 'careful' and 'charge.'"

"They are undoubtedly from the same hand – with some attempt at disguise in the case of this first one."

"Excellent, Watson," said Holmes. "The second is a pamphlet which was written by Professor Hayward describing the Sumerian treasures. I took it from the front desk of the museum."

I stared at him in amazement. Then I turned over the letter in my hand, and there, sure enough, was 'Aston Hayward' signed upon the other side. There could be no doubt in the mind of anyone who had the slightest knowledge of the science of handwriting that the Professor had penned the anonymous letter warning his successor against thieves. It was inexplicable, but it was certain.

"Why should he do it?" I asked.

"Precisely the question. If he had any such misgivings, why could he not come and tell Cavendish directly?"

"I don't know. Will you speak to Hayward about it?"

"A tricky business, Watson. He might choose to deny that he wrote it. And to what end? No crime has been committed," he concluded.

So he dismissed the subject, but Holmes was soon to be proven wrong.

§

All that night after my return home, I was wondering my brain as to what possible motive Professor Hayward could have for writing an anonymous warning letter to his successor? For that the writing belonged to him was as certain to me as if I had seen him actually doing it. He anticipated some danger to the collection. Was it because he foresaw it that he abandoned his charge of it? But if so, why should he hesitate to warn Cavendish in his own name? I puzzled and puzzled until at last I fell into a troubled sleep, which carried me well beyond my usual hour of rising.

I was aroused in a singular and effective method, for about nine o'clock my wife rushed into our room with an expression of consternation upon her face.

"John, you have received an urgent telegram from Mr. Holmes."

"What does it say?" I cried, springing up in bed.

"It says: 'Museum robbed. Queen's jewels. Collect Lestrade. Come as soon as you can.'" She looked up. "Whatever does he mean?"

"The jewels!" I exclaimed. As I dressed, I hurriedly explained the case upon which I had accompanied Holmes the night before.

She shook her head. "I know you are always so interested in Mr. Holmes' adventures, John, but I implore you to be careful. The prospect of vast wealth often drives men to acts of reckless disregard for human life. Think of how close you came to succumbing to the thorns of Tonga."

I smiled and clasped her hands. "Do not worry, my dear. I assure you that there are no Andaman islanders wandering the halls of the Gower Street Museum."

I was not long in following Holmes' instructions; however, upon my arrival at that edifice, a grumbling Inspector Lestrade in tow, there was no sign of my friend. The museum was closed up tight, but a vigorous thumping of the door summoned a brown-skinned man between twenty and thirty years of age, whose dark hair was tousled and whose brown eyes were tense with anxiety. I introduced Inspector Lestrade and myself.

"Thank goodness!" the man exclaimed. "I am Myers, the sub-curator. Professor Cavendish will be most relieved to hear you have arrived. He has been distraught. I will fetch him."

He rushed distractedly out of the room, and I heard him clatter up the stairs. In a few minutes, Cavendish joined us. He appeared a far cry from the evening prior, for his collar was undone at one end, his tie was flying, and his hat at the back of his head. I read the whole story in his frantic eyes.

"Dr Watson!" he gasped, as if he was out of breath. "But where is Mr. Holmes?"

"I am here," rang out the familiar strident voice. I turned to find Holmes in the company of an elderly gentleman. Holmes introduced him as Mr. Ellison, one of the partners of Matson and Company, the well-known gem merchants of Regent Street. "Now, Cavendish, take us to the scene of the crime," he commanded.

Moments later we were grouped round the case in which the pendant of Queen Ninsun had been exposed. The pendant had been taken out and laid upon the glass top of the case, and Holmes bent over it for an inspection.

"It is obvious that it has been tampered with," said Cavendish. "It caught my eye the moment that I passed through the room this morning. As you know, we examined it just yesterday evening, so it is certain that this has happened during the night."

It was, as he had said, obvious that someone had been at work upon it. The settings of the first four stones – the carnelian, peridot, spinel, and chalcedony – were rough and jagged as if someone had scraped all round them. The stones were in their places, but the beautiful metalwork, which we had admired only the night before, had been very clumsily pulled about.

"It looks to me," said Lestrade, "as if someone had been trying to take out the stones."

"My fear is," said Cavendish, "that he not only tried, but succeeded. I believe these four stones to be skilful imitations which have been put in the place of the originals."

I now understood that the same suspicion had evidently

been in the mind of my friend, for that explained why he had brought along the lapidarist. "Such a crime would take very careful planning, Professor," said Holmes. "The thief would have had to study the inscriptions and replicate them upon the paste jewels."

"Paste?" I exclaimed.

"Not actual paste, Dr Watson," interjected Mr. Ellison. "Rather a heavy and transparent flint glass that simulates the fire and brilliance of gemstones. The technique is an ancient one, and difficult to tell from the real thing by the naked eye. However, under magnification, one can typically detect microscopic air bubbles. There are other signs as well, of course."

"And your impression of these gems?" asked Holmes.

Ellison nodded and proceeded to carefully examine the four stones with the aid of his loupe. He now submitted them to several tests, and finally turned cheerfully to Cavendish. "I congratulate you, sir," said he, heartily. "I will pledge my reputation that all four of these stones are genuine, and of a most unusual degree of purity."

The colour began to come back to our client's frightened face, and he drew a long breath of relief. "By Jove!" he cried. "Then what in the world did the thief want?"

"Probably he meant to take the stones, but was interrupted," suggested Lestrade.

Holmes shook his head. "In that case one would expect him to take them out one at a time, but the setting of each of these has been loosened, and yet the stones are all here." He smiled. "It is certainly most extraordinary. I cannot recall a case just like it. Let us see if the watchman has anything to add."

Mr. Ellison was thanked and dismissed by Holmes while the commissionaire was called. As I previously noted, Bryson was a soldierly, honest-faced man. He seemed as concerned as Hugh Cavendish did in regards to the incident that had occurred upon his watch.

"No, sir, I never heard a sound," he answered, in reply to the questions of the Inspector Lestrade. "I made my rounds four times, as usual, but I saw nothing suspicious. I've been in my position ten years, but nothing of the kind has ever occurred before."

"Is the room lit at night?" asked the inspector.

"Yes, sir, the museum installed the most modern incandescent lights last year."

"No thief could have come through the windows?"

"Impossible, sir."

"Or passed you at the door?"

"No, sir; I never left my post except when I walked my rounds."

"What other openings are there in the museum?"

"There is only the door into the curator's private rooms."

"That is locked at night," Cavendish explained. "And in order to reach it anyone from the street would have to open the outside door as well."

"You remained within your rooms all night, sir?" asked Lestrade of the curator.

"No, as Mr. Holmes and Dr Watson know, I was scheduled to move into the quarters today. Last night they would have still been occupied by Professor Hayward and his daughter."

"And where are they now?"

"They left for Upper Norwood this morning by the seven o'clock train from Victoria."

"Convenient that," concluded Lestrade. "Did they have servants?"

"Yes, however, their quarters are entirely separate from the museum. They come in during the daytime only."

"Well, well," said the inspector, "this is certainly very obscure. However, there has been no harm done, since your Mr. Ellison swore that those stones are genuine. Therefore, the case appears to be merely one of malicious damage. This little bother seems to be something more in the purview of Mr. Holmes here. I would advise you to tighten your security and inform me if the thief makes another attempt."

On that pompous note, Lestrade departed. Holmes

watched him go with an enigmatic smile.

"What is it, Holmes?"

He merely shook his head. "Nothing, Watson. Only that Inspector Lestrade continues to display a shocking lack of imagination, despite the number of occasions upon which it would have well served him. He has forgotten the lessons of the mythical Lady St. Simon. Now then, Cavendish, let us go carefully round the premises, and see if we can find any trace to show us who your visitor may have been."

Holmes' investigation, which lasted all the morning, was careful and intelligent, but in the end, it led to nothing. He pointed out to Cavendish that there were two possible entrances to the museum that he had not considered. The one was from the cellars by a trap-door opening in the passage. The other through a skylight from the lumber-room, overlooking the very chamber to which the intruder had penetrated.

"But neither the cellar nor the lumber-room could be entered unless the thief was already within the locked doors," protested Cavendish.

"Very true," said Holmes. "However, I am afraid that concealing oneself while a museum is still open and waiting for it to close is one of the oldest tricks in the thieves' handbook. It was most recently employed in the disappearance of the Dee crystal from the Victoria and Albert."[69]

This theory proved to be not of any practical importance, for the accumulation of dust in the cellar and attic assured us that no soul had recently used either one or the other. Finally, we ended the inspection as we began, I for one without the slightest clue as to how, why, or by whom the tempering of the setting of these four jewels had been performed.

There remained one obvious course for Holmes to take, and he took it. Leaving Cavendish at the museum, he asked me to accompany him that afternoon upon a visit to Professor Hayward.

"What are we going to ask him?" I inquired as we settled

into a coach for the ride out to Norwood.

"I have with me both the warning letter and the pamphlet. It is my intention to confront the Professor openly with the accusation of having written the anonymous warning. I will ask him to explain the fact that he should have anticipated so exactly that which has in point of fact occurred."

"Do you believe Hayward responsible?"

Holmes shook his head. "No, it would be an odd criminal indeed who warns his victim before robbing him. But he must know something."

"Could Professor Cavendish be involved?"

Holmes shook his head. "I think not, Watson. Cavendish has a reputation for impeccable honesty and a considerable career before him. Furthermore, based upon inquiries I made last night, I have learned that the post of curator of the Gower Street Museum carries with it an annual income. It has admittedly sunk a bit recently with the fall in land, still it remains at that ideal sum which is large enough to encourage a researcher, but not so large to enervate him. If he had debts, I could possibly see it, but with Cavendish's connections, surely he would sell the pendant in its entirety to an illicit collector. He could get far more for the intact piece than for the separated stones."

"And why did you bring in Mr. Ellison?"

"Cavendish's message this morning said that the pendant had been damaged but that the stones were still in place. I immediately considered the possibility of a switch. I worked with Mr. Ellison on the house of Holland case.[70] As an expert in stones, he has always been prepared to advise both the police and consultants such as myself."

When we arrived at Pondicherry Lodge, it appeared far different from that moonlit night when we first visited in the company of Thaddeus Sholto and my Mary. It was still girt-round with a very high stone wall, but the broken glass had been cleared away, and the single narrow iron-clamped door was propped open. Holmes and I wandered up the gravel path through the grounds, whose pits had been filled in and the beds planted with flowers. The house remained enormous, square and prosaic, but a fresh coat of paint had lent it a far warmer appearance.

Holmes knocked upon the door, which was opened by a young maid. The servant informed us that Professor Hayward was away from home. Seeing our disappointment, she asked us if we should like to see his daughter. Answering in the affirmative, the maid promptly showed us into the modest drawing-room. We waited for a span approaching ten minutes before Miss Hayward appeared, and I was shocked to see how much she had changed in the fifteen hours since we had last seen her. Her young face was haggard and her bright eyes heavy with trouble.

"I am afraid that Father has gone to Wales," she said. "He seems to be tired, and has had a good deal to worry him. He left but an hour ago, shortly after we settled into the house."

"You look a little tired yourself, Miss Hayward," said my friend.

"I have been so anxious about father."

"What ails your father?" I asked.

She shook her head. "The Gower Street Museum has been his life for twenty years. It kept him going after my mother passed. I think he is unsure of what he will do with himself now that he has retired."

"And may I ask why he retired at such a young age?" interjected Holmes.

"Troubles with his heart. The mitral valve, I believe," she replied.

"Can you provide me with his Welsh address?"

"Yes, he is planning to stay with his brother, David Hayward, at 9, Beaumaris Villas, Anglesey."

Holmes made a note of the address, and we left without saying anything as to the object of our visit.

"Now what, Holmes?" I asked on the way back to London. "We are in no better position than we had been in the morning. Our only clue is the Professor's letter. Should we start for Anglesey in the morning?"

Holmes frowned and shook his head. "No, Watson. I suspect that the solution lies much nearer than Wales. Go home, and we will start fresh in the morning."

§

Holmes proved to be correct. For there was soon to be a new development that altered all of my half-formed theories as to Professor Hayward's guilt. Very early on the following morning I was aroused from my sleep by a tap upon the front door. It was a messenger with a note from Holmes: 'Do come round Gower Street,' it said. 'The matter is becoming more and more extraordinary.'

When I obeyed his summons and rode over to the museum, I found Holmes pacing excitedly up and down the central room. The old soldier who guarded the premises stood with military stiffness in a corner, while Professor Cavendish sat in a chair with his face buried in his hands.

"My dear Watson," Holmes cried. "I am so delighted that you have come, for this is a most remarkable business."

"What has happened, then?"

He waved his hand towards the case that contained the breastplate.

"See for yourself," said he.

I did so, and could not restrain a cry of surprise. The settings of the next four precious stones had been profaned in the same manner as the first ones. Of the twelve jewels, eight had now been tampered with in this singular fashion. Only the settings of the last four were neat and smooth. The others were most jagged and irregular.

"Have the stones been altered?" I asked.

"No. I have already examined them with my glass," replied Holmes. "I am certain that these upper four are the same which our expert, Mr. Ellison, pronounced to be genuine, for

I observed yesterday a little discoloration on the edge of the spinel, which is still evident. Since the villain has not extracted the first stones, there is no reason to think the middle ones have been transposed. You say that you heard nothing, Bryson?"

"No, sir," the commissionaire answered. "But when I made my final round after daylight broke I had a special look at these stones, and I saw at once that someone had been meddling with them. Then I called Professor Cavendish. I was backwards and forwards all night, and I never saw a soul or heard a sound."

Holmes nodded and turned to Professor Cavendish. "And where was your-sub curator, Myers?"

Cavendish shrugged. "Home, I assume. He came round about twenty minutes later, while I was awaiting your arrival. Myers typically arrives early and sets up the museum prior to opening."

"Has he been with the museum long?"

"Some years now. He was Professor Hayward's assistant during his last field excavation."

"Did Hayward recruit him locally in the East?"

"Oh, no. His father is a Londoner. His mother is a Chaldean, I think.[71] They met when Myers senior was working for Viscount Stratford, the Ambassador to the Ottoman Empire."

Holmes nodded thoughtfully. "Cavendish, I have concluded that the answer to this mystery lies with your predecessor."

"My predecessor?" said the man in surprise. "Whatever could Professor Hayward have to do with this?"

"He was the one who excavated the pendant. He will have some theory as to who would wish to harm it."

"Did you not call upon him yesterday? What did he have to say?"

"I am afraid that he had already left Upper Norwood. He has gone on to Wales."

"Wales?" said Cavendish, mystified. "He said nothing to me of such a trip. Whatever is he doing there?"

"His daughter told us he was resting his heart. I propose to visit him there."

"If you think it best, Mr. Holmes," said Cavendish, his face clearly doubting the wisdom of this plan.

"I do. We will return in the morning. We will meet you here at the museum. By the way, in case you are out when we arrive, I wonder if you have a spare key?"

"Of course, you may have mine, and I will retrieve the spare." He removed a key from his pocket and handed it to Holmes.

"And who else has such a means of ingress?"

Cavendish considered this. "Bryson, of course. And Myers, the sub-curator. That's all."

"Very good. Well, I doubt your vandal would be so bold as to strike again tonight. But keep the lights on in the hall, just the same."

With that, Holmes and I departed from Gower Street. Instead of taking a hansom cab, however, he took hold of my arm and steered me in the direction of Russell Square. "Walk with me, Watson. Now, what do you think of this?" he asked.

"It is the most objectless, futile, idiotic business that ever I heard of. It can only be the work of a monomaniac."

Holmes nodded slowly as he considered this. "Can you put forward any theory?"

A curious idea came into my head. "This object is a relic of great antiquity and sanctity," said I. "The inscriptions may have a mystical significance."

Holmes shook his head. "No, Watson, I fear there are no ancient Sumerian cultists running about the alleys of Fitzrovia."

"It need not be an antediluvian cult, Holmes. It might be some modern secret society, like the Rosicrucians, who believe that the stones may impart a special knowledge."

Holmes smiled. "You have become quite the romantic, Watson. I am unfamiliar with any such society based upon the Sumerians. The Rosicrucians look to ancient Egypt for their inspiration. No, I think the answer will prove to be a tad less outré."

"Well then, could it be that someone is seeking to return the stones to their homeland? One could conceive that a fanatic might believe that the looting of the museum is a just retribution for the removal of the artefacts from their place of origin."

"No, Watson, that also will not do," said Holmes. "I assume you are thinking of Myers, the half-Eastern assistant? He certainly has the means, and possibly the motive. Such a man might have pursued his patriotism for the country of his mother to such lengths, but why is he so reticent about it? Why just nibble around the stones and end up removing none of them? Why not make off with the pendant in its entirety? We must have a better solution than that, and we must find it for ourselves, for I do not think that Lestrade is likely to be of much help in these matters."

"Well, Holmes, what do you think of Bryson, the porter?"

"Have you any reason to suspect him?"

"Only that he is the sole person on the premises. *Quis custodiet ipsos custodes*?"[72]

"Juvenal, eh, Watson? But why should he indulge in such wanton destruction? Nothing has been taken away. He has no motive."

"Mania?"

"No, I have spoken with the man and will swear to his sanity. He would need to be a consummate actor in order to fool me."

"Have you any other theory, Holmes?"

"I have composed several theories thus far, but discarded most of them."

"Then I give it up."

"But I don't – and I have a plan by which we will make it all clear."

"To visit Professor Hayward?"

"No, that was merely a blind to ensure that everyone believes that we are away from London. I will tell you what we shall do, Watson. You know that skylight which overlooks the central hall? If Cavendish leaves the lights on in the hall, and you and I keep watch in the lumber-room above, I believe that we shall soon solve this mystery. If our enigmatic visitor is doing four stones at a time, he has four more still to do, and there is every reason to think that he will return tonight and complete the job. That is when we will take him."

"Excellent!" I cried.

"We will keep our own secret, and say nothing to the police, to Cavendish, or to Bryson. Will you join me?"

"With the utmost pleasure," said I. And so it was agreed.

§

It was ten o'clock that night when I returned to the Gower Street Museum, this time wearing my pair of silent rubber-soled tennis shoes. Holmes was unforthcoming regarding how precisely he had spent the remainder of the day while I was engaged in the routine task of calling upon my patients. He pulled out his pocket watch and consulted the time. He was, as I could see, in a state of suppressed nervous excitement, however, with a satisfied nod he quietly unlocked the front door using Cavendish's key.

He leaned over and spoke in a soft voice. "I know from my interrogation of him that Bryson makes his rounds at this time, and he never varies his route. If we are careful, we should be able to stay away from him. Follow me, Watson. The game is afoot!"

Via a roundabout route, he quietly led the way to the lumber-room, which overlooked the central hall of the museum, and we slipped inside. I was eager to discuss all the possibilities of the singular business that we had met to solve, but Holmes motioned me to silence. Holmes had brought with him some sacking so that we could lie at our ease and look straight down into the museum. The skylight was of unfrosted glass; however it was so covered with dust that it would be impossible for anyone looking up from below to detect that they were overlooked. We each cleared a small piece at the corners, which gave us a complete view of the room beneath. In the cold white light of the incandescent lamps, everything stood out hard and clear, and I could see the smallest detail of the contents of the various cases.

It was nearly twelve o'clock when at last the roaring stream of hansom cabs and the rush of hurrying feet became lower and more intermittent as the pleasure-seekers passed upon their way to their stations or to their homes. Such a vigil is an excellent history lesson, since one has no choice but to study at those objects that we usually overlook with such half-hearted interest during a typical visit to a museum. Through my little peephole I employed the hours in scrutinizing every specimen, from the huge mummy-case that leaned against the wall to those very jewels that had brought us there, gleaming and sparkling in their glass case immediately beneath us. There was much precious gold-work and many valuable stones scattered through the numerous cases, but those wonderful twelve jewels, which made up the pendant of Queen Ninsun, glowed and burned with a radiance that far eclipsed the others. I studied in turn the obelisks of Nimrud, the bronze friezes of Balawat, the copper statues from Ur, and the alabaster bas-relief lion-hunting sculptures from Nineveh, but my eyes would always come back to that wonderful Sumerian relic, and my mind to the singular mystery that surrounded it. I was lost in the thought of it when my companion suddenly drew his breath sharply in, and seized my arm in a convulsive grip. At the same instant I saw what it was which had excited him.

I have said that against the wall – on the left-hand side of the doorway as one entered – there stood a large mummy-case from Thebes. To my unutterable amazement, it was slowly opening. Ever so gradually the lid was swinging back, and the black slit which marked the opening was becoming wider and wider. So gently and carefully was it done that the movement was almost imperceptible. Then, as we breathlessly watched it, a white thin hand appeared at the opening, pushing back the painted lid, then another hand, and finally a face – a face which was familiar to us both – that of Professor Aston Hayward.

Stealthily he slunk out of the mummy-case, like a fox stealing from its burrow, his head turning incessantly to left and to right, stepping, then pausing, then stepping again. He was the very image of craft and of caution. Once some sound in the street struck him motionless, and he stood listening, with his ear turned, ready to dart back to the shelter behind him. Then he crept onwards again upon tiptoe, very, very softly and slowly, until he had reached the case in the centre of the room. There he took a bunch of keys from his pocket, unlocked the case, took out the Queen's pendant. Laying it upon the glass in front of him, he began to work upon it with some sort of small, glistening tool. He was so directly underneath us that his bent head covered his work, but I could guess from the movement of his hand that he was engaged in finishing the strange disfigurement that he had begun.

I was amazed to see this vandalism from the quarter where I would have least expected it. Professor Hayward, the very man who a two nights before had reverently bent over this unique relic, and who had impressed upon us its antiquity and its sanctity, was now engaged in this outrageous profanation. It was impossible, unthinkable – and yet there, in the white glare of the electric light beneath us, was that dark figure with the bent grey head and the twitching elbow. What possible motive could underlie these sinister nocturnal labours? Even I, who had none of the acute feelings of an expert, could hardly bear to look on and see this deliberate mutilation of so ancient a relic.

Finally, Holmes tugged at my sleeve as a signal that I was to follow him as he softly crept out of the lumber-room. It was not until we were upon the stairs that he opened his lips, and then I saw by his animated face how deep was his exhilaration.

"The monstrous barbarian!" I cried quietly. "Holmes, could you have believed it?"

"Not only that, Watson. I predicted it."

"What? How? As far as I can tell, Professor Hayward is a villain or a lunatic – one or the other."

Holmes smiled. "Perhaps. Come with me, Watson, and we shall get to the bottom of this black business."

The staircase led to the ground floor of the museum. Down this Holmes crept, having first kicked off his shoes, an example which I followed. We skulked together through room after room, until the large hall lay before us, with that dark figure still stooping and working at the central case. With an advance as cautious as Professor Hayward's own minutes earlier, we closed in upon him. However, as softly as we went we could not take him entirely unawares. We were still a dozen yards from him when he looked round with a start, and uttering a husky cry of terror, he ran frantically away though the museum's rooms.

We raced after him. "Bryson! Bryson!" roared Holmes, and far away down the vista of electric-lighted doors, we saw the stiff figure of the old soldier suddenly appear. Professor Hayward saw him also, and stopped running, throwing up his arms in a gesture of despair. At the same instant Holmes and I each laid a hand upon his shoulder.

"Yes, yes, gentlemen," he panted, "I will resist no longer."

Within moments, Professor Cavendish, whose face vacillated between astonishment and indignation, joined us. For the span of an entire minute, I could see that he dared not trust himself to speak. He spun and stomped off towards the great hall. Holmes and I walked on each side of the old Professor, the astonished commissionaire bringing up the rear.

When we reached the violated display case, Cavendish stopped and examined the Queen's pendant. The settings of three of the stones of the lower row had been turned back in the same manner as the others. The new curator held up the pendant and glanced furiously at our prisoner.

"How could you!" he cried. "How could you? What inhuman hypocrisy, what hateful depth of malice towards me!"

Professor Hayward mutely shook his head. "I don't wonder at your feelings," said he. "Call in the police. Take me to prison. I deserve it for this horrible deed."

"Very well," said Cavendish. He motioned for Bryson to go and alert a passing constable.

"Hold a minute, Professor Cavendish," interjected Holmes. "I may be able to shed some light on this matter if Professor Hayward is unwilling to do so."

"Whatever do you mean?"

"I can tell you the reason for this peculiar foray of your predecessor."

"So you anticipated it?"

"Oh, yes," said Holmes. "In fact, I knew that Professor Hayward was nearby when I announced my intention of leaving for Wales. I hoped that would draw him out for a final attempt, and so it did."

Cavendish looked dazed. "I am astounded, Mr. Holmes. Would you care to explain?"

"Of course, but first perhaps we might repair to your quarters?"

The curator nodded. "But this shall not be left exposed!" he cried. He picked the pendant up and carried it tenderly in his hand, while I walked beside Hayward, like a policeman with a malefactor. We passed into the curator's chambers, leaving the amazed old soldier Bryson to understand matters as best he could. Professor Hayward sat down in one of the armchairs, and turned so ghastly a colour that for the instant all my resentment was changed to concern. A stiff glass of brandy brought the life back to him once more.

"What do you have to say for yourself, Hayward," said Cavendish, severely.

"Nothing," said the man stubbornly.

Holmes smiled. "I understand the reason for your reticence, Professor; however, I assure you that it is unwarranted. I know all."

"How did he get in?" asked Cavendish.

"By taking a very great liberty with your private door," replied Holmes. "However, the object justified it. The object justified everything. I doubt that you will be angry when you know everything, Professor Cavendish; at least, you will not be angry with Hayward. He kept a spare key to your side door and also to the museum door, and did not give them up when he left. Therefore, it was not difficult for him to let himself into the museum whenever he liked. Today he used the key to come in late, after the crowd had cleared from the street. Then he hid himself in the mummy-case, and took refuge there whenever Bryson came round. I suspect that Professor Hayward was well aware that he could always hear the watch-man coming, for the tramp of Bryson's wooden leg is hardly inaudible. When a sufficient portion of his task was complete, Hayward then left in the same way as he came."

I shook my head and stared at the former curator. "He ran a terrible risk."

"He had to," said Holmes.

"But why?" interjected Cavendish. "What on earth was his object – why would Professor Hayward of all people do a thing like that?" he asked, pointing reproachfully at the mutilated pendant that lay before him on the table.

"I doubt that he could devise any other means. The alter-nates included a hideous public scandal, and a private sorrow, which would have clouded the life of his daughter. I believe that the Professor acted for the best, incredible as it may seem to you Cavendish, and I only ask your attention to enable me to prove it."

"I will hear what you have to say before I take any further steps," said Cavendish, grimly. "Though I cannot imagine what you might say that would prevent me from sending Bryson for Inspector Lestrade."

"When you know the facts of the matter, you may feel differently."

"I have the essential facts already."

Holmes shook his head. "And yet you understand nothing. Let me go back to what I learned today, and I will make it all clear to you. Believe me that what I say is the absolute and exact truth."

"Holmes, you have been holding back information," said I, with a measure of umbrage.

"My apologies, Watson. I will take you both completely into my confidence now. As I made clear at the beginning, any substitution of the stones would require a careful study of their inscriptions. Five individuals – Professor Hayward, his daughter, her fiancée, the sub-curator Myers, or possibly Mr. Bryson, could have only carried this out. And thus, I turned my attention to an inspection of their characters. I soon dismissed Myers and Bryson, however Major Nelson proved to be a much more interesting individual."

"But Holmes!" I protested. "The stones were not substituted. Mr. Ellison confirmed that."

"In point of fact, Watson, he did not. He confirmed only that the first four stones, whose settings were tampered with, were genuine. He had no reason to suspect any problem with the other eight stones, and thus did not inspect them. But I did."

"Do you mean to say that the other stones are false?"

"They were, Watson. Of course, the second set was replaced last night, and Professor Hayward has the final four genuine stones in his pocket as we speak."

Professor Cavendish shook his head. "You amaze me, Mr. Holmes. I cannot follow your reasoning."

Holmes smiled. "I appear to have picked up a bad habit from my friend Watson of telling a story the back-end round. Let me start at the beginning. You have met the person who calls himself Major Nelson. I say 'calls himself' because I have reason now to believe that it is not his genuine name. At first light this morning, I performed some research in the archives of the 58th Regiment and found that the original Major Nelson perished eight years ago at Laing's Nek.[73] This man assumed

Nelson's identity and obtained an introduction to Professor Hayward. I visited Miss Ellen today, and she shared with me the letters from colleagues in Paris and Berlin that had compelled the Professor to show Nelson some attention. Presently Nelson employed various means to ingratiate himself into Hayward's friendship and win the affection of his daughter. By his own attainments, which are considerable, Nelson succeeded in making himself a very welcome visitor at these rooms, which once housed Professor Hayward and his daughter. Miss Ellen was frank that he has a charm of manner and of conversation which would have made him conspicuous in any society, and her heart was soon lost."

"I don't understand what Major Nelson, or whoever he may be, has to do with the theft of the stones, Holmes?" I interjected. "We didn't catch Nelson in the act!"

Holmes smiled. "All in good time, Watson. It seems that Major Nelson was much interested in Oriental antiquities, and his knowledge of the subject justified his interest. Often when he spent the evening with the Haywards he would ask permission to go down into the museum and have an opportunity of privately inspecting the various specimens. You can imagine that Hayward, as an enthusiast, was in sympathy with such a request, and that he felt no surprise at the constancy of Nelson's visits. After his actual engagement to Ellen, there was hardly an evening which Nelson did not pass with the Haywards, and an hour or two were generally devoted to the museum. He had the free run of the place. This state of things was only terminated by the fact of Hayward's resignation of his official duties and his retirement to Norwood. Hayward's daughter mentioned that he had hoped to have the leisure to write a considerable work upon the archaeology of Mesopotamia, which he had been planning. But his plans were interrupted when he discovered the true nature and character of the man whom he had so imprudently introduced into his home."

Professor Cavendish shook his head. "I fail to see how this

relates to the stones, or Hayward's actions."

Holmes turned to the former curator. "Shall I go on, sir? As you can see, I have deduced the general outline of what transpired over the last few days. However, only you can provide the precise details."

Hayward's shoulders sagged and he shook his head mutely.

"Very well, Professor," said Holmes. "I will tell you what I believe took place. It was just a few days ago that you were made aware of your error. The discovery came to you through letters from your friends abroad, which showed you that Nelson's introductions to you had been forgeries. Aghast at the revelation, you asked yourself what motive this man could originally have had in practicing this elaborate deception upon you. You are not a rich man, nor does your daughter stand to inherit any vast sum. Too poor then for any fortune hunter to have marked you down. Why, then, had he come? And then you recalled that some of the most precious artefacts in Europe have been under your charge. You remembered also the ingenious excuses by which this man had made himself familiar with the cases in which they were kept. You decided that he was a rascal who was planning some gigantic robbery.

"But how could you, without devastating your own daughter, who was infatuated with Nelson, prevent him from carrying out any plan which he might have formed? Your device was a clumsy one, and yet you knew that if you wrote a letter to your successor under your own name, he would naturally have turned to you for details that you did not wish to give. You therefore resorted to an anonymous letter, begging Professor Cavendish to be upon his guard.

"However, shortly after you wrote it, you recognized that it would not be sufficient. You were due to depart from Gower Street soon, and you knew that Nelson would not stay his hand any longer. If he was to attempt a robbery, it would come immediately. You saw no other choice but to confront him. When I questioned your daughter earlier today, she told me that you gave orders that Major Nelson should be shown into your study instead of to the drawing room when he next called upon your rooms. I suspect that you told him that you knew all about him, and that you had taken steps to defeat his designs. You likely ordered him to break off all ties with Ellen and never again to set foot in your house.

"But you didn't prepare for a man of such iron nerve as Major Nelson. He admitted to being a villain, not just to you, but also to your daughter. Moreover, to your dismay she refused to abandon him. I could tell from the grim determination in her eyes that Ellen Hayward is not a woman who changes her mind easily. She had thrown in her lot with Nelson, for better or for worse. You were about to lose your daughter forever to this man. And then something remarkable occurred. Nelson did something entirely contrary to his very nature and every life action to date. He admitted that he had already absconded with the stones, substituting twelve others made especially to his order, which carefully imitated the originals. He returned them to your care. Since then you have been carrying them about in your pocket, desperately trying to figure out a way to quietly replace them."

Professor Hayward finally looked up and nodded wearily. "You are entirely correct, Mr. Holmes. There is little point in holding back, now that you know so much. You cannot conceive of my horror at the sight of the stones when he handed them to me. My hair rose and my flesh grew cold as I looked upon them. There could be no doubt that those twelve magnificent square stones engraved with their mystical characters were the jewels of Queen Ninsun. If the substitution was discovered, we would all be ruined.

"My position was a dreadful one. Here I was with these precious relics in my possession, and how could I return them without a scandal and an exposure? I knew the depth of my daughter's nature too well to suppose that I would ever be able to detach her from this man now that she had entirely given him her heart. I was not even sure how far it was right to detach her if she had such an ameliorating influence over him. How could I expose him without injuring her – and how far was I justified in exposing him when he had voluntarily put himself into my power? I thought and thought until at last, I formed a resolution, which may seem to you to be a foolish one, and yet, if I had to do it again, I believe it would be the best course open to me.

"My idea was to return the stones without anyone being the wiser. With my keys, I could get into the museum at any time, and I was confident that I could avoid Bryson, whose hours and methods were familiar to me. I determined to take no one into my confidence – not even my daughter – whom I instead told that I was about to visit my brother in Wales." Finally, his voice gave out, and Hayward bowed his head in shame.

Holmes took up the conclusion to the story. "That night Hayward made his way into the museum, where he replaced four of the stones. It was hard work, and took him all night, for whenever Bryson came round he was forced to conceal himself in the mummy-case. Hayward must have some knowledge of gold-work, but he was far less skilful than the original thief had been. Major Nelson had replaced the setting so exactly that I doubt anyone could have seen the difference. In contrast, the Professor's work was rude and clumsy. However, he must have counted upon the pendant not being carefully examined, or the roughness of the setting observed, until his mission was done. The next night he replaced four more stones. And tonight he would have finished his task, had it not been for the unfortunate situation that Cavendish employed me to investigate the threat of the anonymous letter."

We all turned to gaze at the bowed head of Professor Hayward. He finally looked up and stared into the eyes of his successor. "These last few days have been too much for me. I am convinced that I could not stand it any longer. It is a nightmare – a horrible nightmare – that I should be arrested as a burglar in what has been for so long my own museum. And yet, I cannot blame you, Professor Cavendish. You could not have done otherwise. My hope always was that I should get it all over before I was detected. This would have been my last night's work. Mr. Holmes has revealed so much of which I hoped to have kept concealed. I will leave it to your own generosity how far you will use the facts with which he supplied you. I appeal to you, gentlemen, to your sense of honour and of compassion, whether what you have learned should go any farther or not. My own happiness, my daughter's future, the hopes of this man's regeneration, all depend upon your decision."

"Which is," said Cavendish after a long pause, "that all is well that ends well and that the whole matter ends here and at once. Tomorrow, Mr. Ellison will be called back to tighten the loose settings, and so passes the greatest danger to which Queen Ninsun's pendant has been exposed since the sack of Uruk by the Parthians. Here is my hand, Professor Hayward, and I can only hope that under such difficult circumstances I should have carried myself as unselfishly and as well."

Holmes, however, was less generous with his clemency. He turned to Professor Hayward with a grave face. "I would hope for your sake, sir, that you are making the correct decision about your future son-in-law. A tiger does not easily change his stripes."

§

As we shared a hansom cab back towards Paddington, I had a few minutes to ask Holmes the remaining questions I had regarding the case. "I still cannot believe that Professor Hayward was simply trying to return the stones."

"You should have learned the lesson imparted by the case of Arthur Holder, Watson. He too was trying to rectify a great wrong when he was wrongly accused of the crime. He too would not speak in hopes of protecting one that he loved."

"You did once say that it has all been done before, Holmes."

"But surely we can consider this little case unique, Watson.

How often does one go looking for stolen treasure and instead find it being replaced where it belongs? It is a shame you cannot put this narrative to pen for fear of committing a grave indiscretion. For no amount of obfuscation of names could hide from your readers the true identity of Major Nelson."

"Did you suspect him from the beginning?"

"I certainly thought his manner odd when Professor Hayward was showing us the stones. I soon learned that Major Nelson was quite the villain. Perhaps not as dangerous as Sir George Burnwell, nor so devoid of heart or conscience. Nevertheless, much like poor Mary Holder before her, Ellen Hayward would have had little experience with such a scoundrel. As he breathed his words of love to her, she could have fallen under his power and been turned into his willing tool."

"But she didn't, Holmes. Quite the opposite, in fact. Instead, she touched his heart and transformed him into a better man."

He nodded slowly. "Let us hope that to be true, Watson. I shall certainly be following Major Nelson's future career with a great deal of interest, and should be most put out if he were to backslide. But here is your stop."

I climbed out of the cab in front of my chambers and motioned for the driver to hold for a moment. "You would be surprised by the many benefits of a strong marriage, Holmes. With a woman like that behind him, I foresee a future for Major Nelson filled with wide and deserved honours."

Holmes snorted in wry amusement. "If you insist, Watson. But I doubt that I shall ever have first-hand knowledge of such things." He waved to the driver, who immediately flicked the horse and set off in the direction towards Baker Street.

As I watched my solitary friend recede into the distance, I was glad to know that behind the door my loving wife waited patiently for my return. Before I entered, I thought for one final moment about Ellen Hayward and Major Nelson. I had told Holmes that I predicted great honours for the man. But if the truth were known, that honour would be due not to him, but rather to the gentle girl who, with the force of her love, plucked him back when he had gone so far down that dark road along which few return.

§

THE ADVENTURE OF
THE PIRATE'S CODE

I n my journals for the year 1889 resides one of the most peculiar cases ever handled by my friend, Mr. Sherlock Holmes. Taking into consideration the fact that it occurred but a few weeks following the events surrounding the near-recovery of the great Agra treasure, Holmes felt it unwise to set this case before my readers. He deemed that the similarity between the two cases, which occurred in close proximity to each other strained the boundaries of credulity. It was an opinion with which I ruefully agreed.

However, as Holmes often quoted to me, life is infinitely stranger than anything the mind of man could invent, and to this day, it remains one of my favourite of all our adventures together. For it harkens me back to a simpler time, when one man could set forth upon an adventure unto unknown shores and come back richer, if not materially, then at least spiritually. I also like to believe that I was more helpful than typical with the eventual solution of the case; an active partner rather than merely a sounding board for Holmes' theories.

"Are you expecting someone, Holmes?" said I, as I stood one morning in our bow-street window.

My friend looked up lazily from his armchair, where he was

engaged in the task of devouring the morning's agony pages. "No one who bother to announce themselves in advance," he replied, waving his hand to the pile of correspondence and telegrams from the night prior. "Why do you believe the person you see to be a client?"

On the day in question, I was still residing at our shared quarters in the waning days before my impending marriage. I had risen earlier than usual and had already finished my morning tea and black pudding. Feeling a bit cooped up inside, I had slouched over to the window in order to ascertain the state of the late March weather. The snow of February had recently passed from a white blanket to a meagre brown residue along the edge of the pavement suggesting that a vigorous constitutional around Regent's Park was a possibility. It was then that I noted the single gentleman running up Baker Street from the direction of the Metropolitan Station. He was a man of about five and forty, tall and rather portly, and thus an odd candidate for someone to be moving so rapidly. He was dressed in a provincial style, the cut of his suit many years out of fashion and yet still in fair shape, though a bit tight around the middle. It struck me as the garb of a man who rarely required the donning of formal attire in his day-to-day life.

"Because he appears to be much agitated, Holmes," I answered. "He puts me in the mind of some of your more distressed and anxious clients."

Holmes stood up and shoved his hands into the pockets of his mouse-coloured dressing gown. Finding his amber-stemmed brier pipe therein, he clamped it between his lips unlit and joined me at the window. "I concur with your opinion, Watson. He should be pulling on our bell any moment now."

Holmes prediction proved to be correct. Within a minute, our visitor was shown in by Billy.[74] The man who entered possessed a face that was heavily seamed by lines which might have once been caused by mirth, but now appeared to have been turned downwards by recent troubles. His brown eyes were hung with dark pouches, and his hair and beard were unkempt. His suit bore the stains of a recent journey.

Holmes waved the man to the settee, where he seemed overcome with emotion and unable to speak. Despite the earliness of the hour, I decided that a brandy would prove restorative and poured him one from the tantalus. The man accepted this gratefully and once finished, stared at my friend with hopeful eyes. "I apologize, Mr. Holmes, for collapsing upon your sofa in such a state, but there is not a moment to lose."

"Pray explain what matter will require us to accompany you to Bristol."

"Bristol!" the man exclaimed. "How could you possibly know that your services are needed in Bristol?"

"I have made a special study of accents, sir – one I hope to codify into a monograph someday – and you have the distinctive terminal 'a' sound of a Bristol man. One can consider this definitive once you also take into account the return ticket from Bristol's Temple Meads Station that I see protruding from your breast pocket. Given that you have clearly come straight from Paddington Station, it is plain that you departed upon the first morning train from Bristol. Only a matter of grave importance would have induced a tavern keeper – whose work runs much later than the average man – to travel to London at such an early hour."

The man shook his head in wonderment. "But how do you know about the tavern, sir? You must be able to read minds!"

Holmes smiled wanly. "Nothing quite so outrageous, I assure you, sir. My friend here, Dr Watson, could also make such a determination." He turned to me with a questioning look.

I nodded my acceptance of this challenge. Knowing Holmes' methods, and having recently read his treatise upon the '*Influences of Trade upon the Form of the Hand*,' I studied the man's fingers closely. "I note that the skin of his right thumb is worn smoother than that of the opposite hand. I conclude that this particular appearance is only produced by the habit-

THE TREASURY OF SHERLOCK HOLMES

ual polishing of drinking glasses."

Holmes smiled. "Capital, Watson! You are coming along nicely. This sign is not entirely pathognomonic of a barkeeper, as there are a few other occupations which can produce a similar finding. However, I felt that it was the most likely possibility."

The man was following this exchange with an open mouth which made him resemble nothing more than a fish. "You are just the man to help me find Jim, Mr. Holmes. You must come with me at once!" he implored.

Holmes nodded and reached over to his shelf, where he plucked down the Bradshaw's. Rapidly flipping through its well-worn pages, he finally stopped at the one he desired and pulled out his pocket watch. "The next train to Bristol does not depart for an hour, and the station is but a ten-minute hansom ride, so we have a few moments to hear about what happened to your son. I would advise that you start at the beginning."

"Holmes, he never said Jim was his son," I interjected.

"Who else, Watson, would elicit such concerns?"

"You are correct again, Mr. Holmes," said our visitor, a modicum of calm having descended upon him with the realization that there was an immutable delay to returning home caused by the railway's timetable. "My name is James Eggleson, sir. I keep the 'Captain Maynard' tavern in Bristol.[75] My wife and I were only blessed with one boy, Jim, who is now fourteen years of age. Jim used to always toe the line and stay out of any troubles. Our life was a good one, at least until the damned pirate showed up five weeks ago."

"A pirate?" I said wonderingly. "I thought their kind was extinct? Did they not vanish as the Age of Sail gave way to the steamship?"[76]

"Well, he never claimed as such, Doctor, at least not when sober. He always professed to be a simple merchant captain, George North by name. He was a silent man by custom, but he liked his rum and when he got up in his cups, he would tell the most outrageous stories of exploits in the West Indies, Goa, Madagascar, and Leghorn.[77] Tales of sailing under the black flag, hangings, walking the plank, and 'no peace beyond the Line.'[78] He seemed to be a relic of a rougher age.

"Although Captain North appeared to be on the wrong side of eighty years, you could tell that he had once been a tall, strong, heavy man. His skin was nut-brown with the sun, and his tarry pigtail fell over the shoulder of his soiled blue coat. His hands were ragged and scarred, with black, broken nails, and what looked to be a sabre cut across one cheek, the old scar livid white compared to the rest of his dirty skin. He simply appeared at the inn door one day, his sea-chest pulled behind him in a hand-barrow. He paid up-front with four guineas for a week's board, but one week soon turned into three, and no more money was forthcoming. Although Captain North never came out and said it directly, from various off-hand comments, I reckoned that he had most recently resided near Edinburgh.

"Most nights Captain North could be found in the darkest corner of the inn, away from the fire, and slowly drinking from the bottles of rum that I have brought over special from Bermuda. Though he referred to it as grog, he lingered over the taste of it, like he was a connoisseur and it the finest Imperial Tokay. He would always refuse to drink from one of my glasses, but rather insisted upon his own peculiar wooden cup. When I asked him about it, he claimed that it was his protection from poison. He said it so matter-of-factly that it was hard to even take offense at the implication that such a thing could befall him in my tavern.

"When he had consumed a sufficient quantity of rum, Captain North would sing snatches of old sea songs in a high, old tottering voice. The folks used to come from far round to hear his tales, which I think provided a small thrill in their otherwise quiet and tedious lives. When he got to talking, you could almost feel the howl of the gales and the long swash of the sea waves. But I could tell that he was scared of something. He paid my son tuppence a week to be on the lookout for a blind man. Captain North told Jim to keep a 'weather-eye' open and to let him know the moment any such man appeared. Jim was quite enraptured by these tales and took his watch most seriously. I think it took his mind off the death of his mother, who passed from the ague a few days after North appeared at our door. With her passing, I suddenly had twice the troubles, and did not pay Jim half of the attention that the lad probably required. That must have been what caused him to vanish."

"Do you have any idea what precipitated Jim's disappearance?"

"North's mad tales of buried treasure, that's what!" Eggleson exclaimed. "No lad could resist such fancies."

"And where is Captain North now?"

"He is dead!"

"What!" I exclaimed.

"Oh, yes, Dr Watson. Three nights past, a messenger boy arrived with a sort of note for him. Captain North took one look at this note, put his hand to his forehead, and fell over in an apoplectic fit. Within minutes, he was dead."

"What did the note say?"

Eggleson shook his head. "That is just the thing, Doctor. There was nothing on it. It was simply a piece of paper torn from the Bible."

"Do you still have it?" asked Holmes.

"Yes, I thought to bring it, in case it might provide you some clue." He reached into his pocket and handed a crumpled paper over to Holmes.

Holmes took up the paper and nodded in a gratified way. "Not a tome with which I am much familiar, but ripped from the end unless I miss my guess: 'I warn everyone who hears the words,' etcetera, etcetera." He then flipped it over. "And upon the rear we find an interesting splotch of black ink. What then, Mr. Eggleson?"

"Well, Captain North still owed me a considerable sum of

money for his arrears board, so before we notified the local constabulary, Jim and I searched his pockets. Those held only a few small coins, a pouch of Ship's tobacco, an oily clay pipe, a tinder box, and a pocket compass. Then my Jim noted that there was no key to the man's sea chest, so he pulled open the man's shirt at the neck, and sure enough, there was a key hanging from a bit of tarry string. We opened that chest right quick, and inside we found a canvas bag that jingled like gold. It was filled with all manners and sizes of coins, including half-crowns, doubloons, reals, ecus, livres, guineas, pieces of eight, all mixed together at random. I took what I was owed, though I had the devil of a time figuring out the proper sum with such an assorted lot.

"We then called the authorities, who promptly hauled away the body. However, they left everything else while attempting to ascertain whether Captain North had any relations who might inherit his possessions. When I awoke the following morning, Jim was gone. The lad has been known to wander off from time to time, so I thought nothing of it at first. But when he didn't return that night, I grew worried. Yesterday, I went to the local constabulary, but they were of no help. When he still didn't come home last night, I knew that I had to seek out the one man who people say can solve any mystery, even when the police are baffled."

Holmes smiled wryly. "My powers, Mr. Eggleson, may perhaps have been exaggerated by my biographer. Nevertheless, the next course of action is clear. Watson, we must go to Bristol."

Bidding our guest to pause for a moment, Holmes vanished into his room in order to change into his travelling-cloak and cap, while I did the same. When I returned to the sitting room, Holmes was handing a note to Billy. When questioned, he refused to say anything about it, other than to remark that he was preparing for certain eventualities.

§

The Great Western Main Line ran quickly through the Wessex countryside, and in less than two hours, we were riding the short distance from the Temple Meads Station to the harbour wharfs along the broad River Avon. The 'Captain Maynard' inn proved to be near the docks, and as the trap rolled along them, I looked out with interest at the great multitude of ships that lay along the quays. All sizes and nations were evident, sailors bustled along engaged in tasks unknown, and the smell of tar and salt was everywhere.

The tavern was set back a short ways from the street. It was a two-story grey painted structure, with a high pointed brown roof. The paint of the sign was rather faded, but neat white curtains framed the windows. A small garden, shaded by a yew tree, lay in front, while an oyster-shell path led to the front door. Eggleson pushed this open and led us inside. At this still early hour, the public house was empty, so I could observe the large, low main room clear of the tobacco smoke which I assumed obscured it upon most evenings. The sanded floor was swept clean, and the bar was clear of glasses.

"Your bar is most unique, Mr. Eggleson," remarked Holmes.

"Aye, that there is a genuine piece of a schooner," said Eggleson, a hint of pride in his voice. "It was salvaged from the *Trinidad* when she limped back into Bristol harbour in 1809. She was deemed to be no longer sea-worthy, so her timbers were broken up for use in other ships, but my grand-father managed to lay claim to that particular piece as partial repayment for an old debt owed to him by the ship's captain."

"So, your tavern has been operating for many years then?"

"Indeed. It has changed names and hands over the years, but it has always been a popular watering hole of the sailors. On the other side of the building is a small gap, through which a look-out may spy for the approach of any tide-waiters or press gangs coming towards the inn, and thereby warn the men within to make themselves scarce."[79]

Anything further Eggleson had to say upon the matter was

lost in the arrival of a vivacious lady approaching thirty years of age. She had lustrous black hair, large dark eyes, and an exquisite mouth. "Blast you, James Eggleson, for a fool," exclaimed the new arrival. "How am I to operate this grog shop without any of the keys?"

"I planned to return before opening time, Polly."

"And how was I to know such a thing?" said she saucily. "A note might be a nice consideration."

"Sorry about that, lass. My head has been awhirl since Jim vanished." He turned to the two of us. "This here is Polly Brewis. She is our barmaid. She has been indispensable since my wife passed."

"It is a pleasure to meet you, Miss Brewis," said Holmes, nodding his head gallantly. "Have you had any word from Jim this morn?"

She shook her head sadly. "No, it has been as quiet as a churchyard round here. Are you gentlemen here to help locate him?"

"That is my intent," replied Holmes gravely.

"Well, just let me know whether I may be of any assistance," said she, tossing her hair as she glided out of the room.

Holmes watched her go for a moment, a considering look in his eyes, and then turned back to Eggleson. "I suggest that we begin with a search of Jim's room," said Holmes. "We may find some hint as to the nature of his plans."

Eggleson nodded at this suggestion and led us up a creaking set of wooden stairs to a small chamber, which was filled with the typical detritus collected by a young lad, especially one with a nautical hankering. This included a pulley, several glass bottles, and a nice brass spy-glass. Finally, there was a stack of papers weighted down by a large clear glass deck prism.

Holmes asked us to wait at the door while he inspected the room's contents. I watched him work his way round the space in his usual methodical fashion. After a span of some five minutes, he straightened up and glanced at his client.

"Your son has some remarkable charcoal pencil drawings

here," said he, pointing to the small desk. "He drew them himself?"

"Aye, the lad is a talented artist. Always sketching things around town."

"What does that tell us, Holmes?" I asked.

He shook his head. "Too soon to tell, Watson. There is nothing more to be learned here. I suggest we now inspect Captain North's possessions."

"Very good, Mr. Holmes," said Eggleson. "It's just along this corridor." He showed us through a twisting passage to a room in the back of the inn which would have looked over the docks. Drawing a key from his pocket, Eggleson swung open the door to reveal a small cramped room. The bed had been shoved to the side and had clearly been utilized by the prior occupant as a storage area for all manner of discarded clothes rather than as a place of repose. A shabby hammock had been slung between two of the wooden beams. Only the floor was relatively free of flotsam and jetsam.

Eggleson shook his head. "Sorry about the mess, Mr. Holmes. Since Jim vanished two days ago, I haven't seen fit to clean up the Captain's room. And he never let anyone inside while he was alive. Said he couldn't abide a place that was too clean, as it wasn't how life on-board ship was meant to be. That's also why North chose the smallest room we have. Over here is his chest."

The sea-chest was like any other you might expect a former mariner to possess, banded in iron and the corners rounded by heavy and rough usage. The initial 'N' had been burned onto the top of the chest with a hot iron. Slowly and carefully, Holmes inserted the key handed to him by Eggleson and threw back the lid. A strong odour of tobacco wafted forth, reminiscent of Baker Street after one of Holmes' all-night ratiocination sessions. On the very top, there was a set of fine clothes, albeit many decades out of style. Under that I could see a great miscellany of items collected from the far reaches of the globe. In addition to several pouches of tobacco, there was a set of pewter utensils and a plate, as well as bone dice and gaming tokens. As expected in a sea-chest, there was also a quadrant, a brass compass, an ill-treated fifty-guinea watch, and an old sea-cloak, permanently whitened with salt. Finally, there were two brace of archaic pistols, a silver ingot, a gold ring inscribed with 'E.T.' and five curious sea shells crafted out of gold.

Holmes lifted up one of the latter and inspected it. "Akan jewellery, from the Gold Coast region of Africa. Quite unusual to find in England in its un-melted state. Captain North certainly made his way around the globe."

"Does it have any bearing upon Jim's disappearance?" I asked.

He shook his head. "Doubtful, Watson, though it establishes a measure of authenticity to North's tales, which may perhaps be relevant." He then lifted a wooden cup from the chest and studied it closely. He even brought it up to his nose and sniffed it. "This cup, Watson, is most interesting. I have rarely seen its equal," said he, handing it to me.

I turned it about in my hands, but could see nothing of note. I shook my head. "It looks like a simple wooden cup, Holmes."

"I recommend you fill it with water."

I glanced over at Mr. Eggleson, who shrugged uncomprehendingly. "I will fetch some." He returned momentarily and poured a bit into the wooden cup. As we watched, the clear liquid slowly turned a pale opalescent blue colour.

"By Jove, Holmes!" I exclaimed. "What is happening?"

He smiled. "I believe this to be a genuine specimen of the fabled *lignum nephriticum*. It once grew in certain well-guarded locales of New Spain, and is therefore further proof of Captain North's bona fides. Because of its unique property of turning water blue, this wood was legendary in the royal courts for its reputed medicinal properties. However, I believe Captain North was confused about its ability to protect him from poison, which is a function that I am certain to be more fiction than fact for any object known to man." Holmes turned his attention back to the chest and withdrew the oil-skin packet. He studied it for a moment before glancing up at Eggleson. "Did you untie this, sir?"

Our host shook his head. "No, as I told you, I took only the coins due me."

"Still, someone has been at this since Captain North died."

"Why do you say that, Holmes?" I asked.

He pointed the twine used to tie up a bundle wrapped in oil-cloth and looking like papers. "This is a simple reef knot, Watson. No sailor worth his salt, like our Captain George North, would be caught dead tying such a thing. North would have used a bowline knot."

"So who did?"

"The most likely culprit, of course, is young Jim. Now, let us see what he found inside."

He pulled apart the knot and rolled out the oilskin. Within was a wondrously strange item. It was a piece of unusual-appearing parchment, roughly one foot wide and nine inches high, and splattered with candle grease. The centre was covered with six lines of incomprehensible scrawl, while the four corners each held a small drawing. Starting from the upper left and moving clockwise was an ingot, a compass, an old coin, and an antique firearm. I reproduce a copy below:

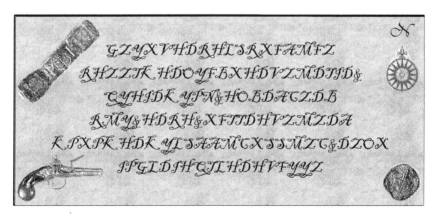

"What a remarkable piece of parchment!" I exclaimed.

"This is no parchment, Watson," said Holmes. He pulled his glass from his pocket and looked at the artefact closely. "It is a type of vellum, though the exact provenance of the hide used in its fabrication is not immediately apparent. It is clearly not made from the typical calfskin. If I had my microscope I might be able to determine with certainty. However, if I was forced to hazard a guess, I would wager that it derived from the skin of a man. If I am not mistaken, the lower left corner still bears a faint trace of a tattoo, which seems conclusive."

"No!" I exclaimed. "That is horrific, Holmes!"

"We appear to be dealing with a desperate lot, Watson."

"And do you believe that young Jim read this note?"

"Not only read it, but likely copied it. Do you see these pencil shavings?" he asked, pointing. Holmes turned to Eggleson. "Was Captain North often engaged in writing?"

Eggleson shook his head. "Honestly, Mr. Holmes, I am not even sure if the man could read. I never saw him pick up a pen."

Holmes nodded. "Then we must hypothesize that your son is responsible for the presence of these shavings. If we were to do a rubbing of the top page of his writing pad, we might prove it. Unfortunately, I noted no such pad in his room. He must have taken it with him. Give us a minute, Mr. Eggleson, to consider the implications of this item."

"But what is it, Holmes?" I asked, after the man departed.

"Clearly, Watson, it is a treasure map. And like any such item, at the end lies buried treasure."

§

It took a few minutes for this to sink in. But when it had, a thought occurred to me. "Holmes!" I exclaimed. "When the novel *Treasure Island* was first published, it was ascribed to one Captain George North! Do you think it could possibly be the same man?"[80]

"I think it not only possible, Watson, but probable. Of course, our old sea-dog here, barely literate, could not have actually written the tale himself. But what is to say that Mr. Stevenson did not hear it from the man's lips at Edinburgh? If we had more time, we might ask him. Let us take as our starting point the supposition that the events detailed in *Treasure Island* are more or less factual. When would the events chronicled in the book have taken place?"

I shook my head. "Stevenson left the exact date obscure, though it was plainly in the middle of the 1700's. Roughly 1750, or thereabouts."

"So there is no one alive who remembers that year," said Holmes.

"Certainly not, Holmes! Unless he also found Ponce de Leon's fountain."

"Then we might assume that this is not a direct memory, but rather an oral history passed down from father to son."

"Grandfather more likely," I argued. "Eggleson estimated that Captain North was over eighty, so we might assume he was born circa 1805. If so, his own father could not have sailed out to the Caribbean with a buccaneer crew unless he sired George when he was very advanced in his years. And I doubt many pirates lived to such an age."

Holmes nodded in agreement with this arithmetic. "Very good, Watson. In the passing down of the legend, however, Captain North plainly lost the means of deciphering the message and reclaiming the riches. Hence his retirement to this meagre room, his sea-chest drained of all but a few residual treasures. I have seen such things before down at Hurlstone. Captain North may not have been literate, but he could do the simple math. Presuming this meagre store represents his entire worldly possessions, he must have calculated that his resources would have been drained within the year. He therefore determined to sell the story of his ancestors to Mr. Stevenson. Such an action would have brought in a modest annual income from the royalties upon the book. But in so doing, North piqued the wrath of someone else with a claim to the treasure."

"How do you know that, Holmes?"

"The black spot, Watson. The pirates' warning sign. And this as of yet unknown party may be responsible for Jim's disappearance."

"But Holmes, do you really think that this leads to a buried treasure? I have heard that most of those legends were simply myths and fables."

He shook his head. "All myths have some basis in fact, Watson. Sir Francis Drake was forced to hide most of the treasure he seized from the mule trains of Nombre de Dios. William Kidd is widely considered to have buried some two-hundred bars of gold off the eastern seaboard of the Americas."

"But how might young Jim have gone searching for buried treasure, Holmes? A lad of fourteen could hardly have hired a ship to set sail for the West Indies!"

Holmes shrugged. "Perhaps the treasure lies closer to home. Some enterprising rascal may have shipped the bulk of his wealth back to mother England before embarking upon one last fatal cruise. If the pirate never returned to claim it, the treasure might still be there."

"Pirate treasure in England, Holmes? Surely not!"

"There are precedents, Watson. England may not be the wild coasts of the Americas, where every island is thought to hide some portion of Captain Kidd's buried treasure. However, in the beginning part of this century, old Spanish silver coins began to appear around the Gower peninsula of Wales, reportedly from a ship that crashed off the coast of Rhossili. Likewise, in 1588 the Spanish galleon *Florencia*, which held the paymaster's chest of the Armada, escaped the initial destruction of that fleet by sailing north, only to be lured by wreckers onto the coast of Scotland near Portencross. Most of the gold ingots that the *Florencia* carried to pay the Spanish troops have yet to be recovered and are rumoured to be buried somewhere near the town of Stevenston. However, there is only one method by which we might tell for certain. We must decipher the code upon the vellum. That will point us in the direction of Jim Eggleson junior."

I somewhat reluctantly picked up the horrible object and read the first dozen letters aloud: " 'G – Z – Y – X – T – I – F – P – I – K- Y – Z.' Holmes, this looks impossible!" I protested. "How could such a thing be cracked?"

"Not impossible, Watson. Merely difficult. As all good things are. Now, you would do me a considerable favour if you were to seek out a bookseller's and avail yourself a copy of Mr. Stevenson's masterpiece. I should like to hear how the clues to the treasure in the novel read. In the meantime, I will commence my attack upon this code."

Holmes and I repaired downstairs, where he claimed a secluded corner table at which to work. He laid out the mysterious message in front of him, and threw himself into an intricate and elaborate calculation using a pad of paper and a set of pencils that he acquired from Mr. Eggleson. Meanwhile, I set out upon his suggested errand. This task led me across a bridge and through the streets of the area of Bristol known as Redcliffe. Along the way, I passed numerous glassworks with blistering hot furnaces, as well as various interesting buildings. These included both a large gothic cathedral with a towering spire and another church with a precariously-leaning tower that looked as if it would collapse at any moment.

Eventually, I was successful in my mission and located a book-shop tucked away in a small alley next to a grogery called the 'Tin Pot.' A half-hour later I returned to the 'Captain Maynard' with a yellow-backed copy of *Treasure Island* in hand. I sat down at the table and silently waited for Holmes to acknowledge my existence, for I hesitated to break his concentration. I used the time to find the passage that he wished to hear.

He eventually set down his pen and looked over at me. "Well, what does it say, Watson?"

I flipped to the required page and read aloud:

" *'Tall tree, Spy-glass shoulder, bearing a point to the N. of*

N.N.E. Skeleton Island E.S.E. and by E. Ten feet.
The bar silver is in the north cache; you can find it by
the trend of the east hummock, ten fathoms south of the
black crag with the face on it.' "

I looked up and frowned. "How does that advance us, Holmes? Certainly Captain North could not have told Mr. Stevenson the actual locale?"

"No, but it is possible that he might have known some part of it. Therefore, knowing the language utilized in the novel may provide some hint as to the words expected to be found herein."

For another two hours I watched him as he covered sheet after sheet of paper with figures and letters, so completely absorbed in his task that he had evidently forgotten my presence entirely. Sometimes it seemed that he was making progress, and he whistled and sang at his work; sometimes he was puzzled and would sit for a long spell with a furrowed brow and a vacant eye. Finally he flung down his pen with a cry of irritation. "Curses, Watson!" he exclaimed. "It cannot be done."

"It is unbreakable?"

"Nothing is unbreakable, but it will take days, if not weeks, of constant work."

"We don't have days, Holmes. Every day that Jim Eggleson is gone makes it less likely that he will be found alive."

"I am aware of our timetable, Watson, he replied testily. "Now, here are the facts. We know that Jim found this code three nights ago and subsequently vanished. So where did he go?"

"He must have cracked the code," I exclaimed.

Holmes shook his head slowly. "I can say with certainty that this is no simple substitution cipher. If I had to speculate, I would opine that this is a polyalphabetic cipher, where each letter is encoded by a differentially-shifted alphabet. A fourteen year-old boy could never have cracked this in such a short time. Even Pascal or Gauss could not have done it."[81]

"How then?"

"The most likely explanation is that this message was encrypted with an Alberti cipher disk."[82]

"What is that?"

"The disk might be any size, but will always have two concentric circular plates mounted one on top of the other, the larger one stationary and the smaller one moveable. Each plate will have letters of the alphabet inscribed along the circumference. It is typically constructed of copper."

"But where would Jim have possibly found the one disk that could decode this particular message?"

"Hence the difficulty, Watson. I cannot fathom such a thing."

We sat there dejectedly for some time. I picked up the message and stared at it. The meaningless jumble of letters swirled together before me, and I instead fixed my eyes upon the drawings in the two corners of the vellum. And then a thought transfixed me. "Holmes!" I exclaimed. "Why is there a compass rose in the upper left?"

He frowned. "Need I remind you, Watson, that we believe this to be a message to a buried treasure? As in the novel, a portion of the directions will be marks upon the compass."

"But why include such a drawing? Once decrypted, we would still need an actual compass to follow."

He considered this for a moment. "What are you thinking, Watson?"

"It's not a compass!" I exclaimed. "It is the mark of the message's owner. Captain George *North*."

I had the pleasure of seeing a rare expression of surprise briefly cross Holmes' face. "By Jove, Watson! You are absolutely scintillating today! If the mark on the upper left indicates the owner of the message, then the mark in the lower left must guide us to the owner of the cipher disk." He cried out for our host. "Mr. Eggleson!"

When the man appeared forthwith, Holmes poised a question to him. "The matchlock here," said he pointing to the paper. "We believe it signifies a name. Do you know a man named 'Pistol' or something similar?"

Eggleson pondered this question. "No, Mr. Holmes," he said slowly. "No 'Pistol.' But there is old Frank Gunn."

Holmes glanced over at me with triumph in his eyes before turning back his attention to Eggleson. "And who then is Frank Gunn?"

§

Franklin Gunn proved to be a half-witted lodge keeper in the village of Abbots Leigh some three miles west of Bristol. Although pushing eighty years of age, Eggleson reported that Gunn came into town every Sunday to sing at St. Mary Red-cliffe and was the common target of pranks by local mischiev-ous boys. He confirmed that Jim would have been very much acquainted with the existence of Frank Gunn.

Holmes declared this to be our next destination and prom-ised to inform Eggleson at once should there be any develop-ments in the case. As Holmes and I rode out to Gunn's abode in a hired carriage, I asked Holmes the question that had been worrying me for some time, but which I was afraid to give voice while in Eggleson's company.

"Do you think young Jim is still alive, Holmes?"

He shook his head solemnly. "The matter is a desperate one. At best we can hope that he is a prisoner somewhere. How long do you suppose he can last without food and water?"

"As you well know, Holmes, a body can go quite some time without food. But water is another matter. It depends some-what on how warm the site of his prison, for hotter locales cause more insensible losses through sweat. However, this time of year, you could reliably say that a boy like Jim might last three or four days without hydration. Still, we have little time to waste."

Holmes nodded silently at this disheartening piece of in-formation and closed his eyes meditatively for the remainder of the short ride. This led us over Brunel's remarkable bridge spanning the Avon Gorge and through a fine set of woodlands which appeared to have been untouched since the days of the Saxon invaders. Eventually, a clearing upon the green slope of a hill revealed a curving drive that ran through the woods up to a fine Georgian mansion. Holmes instructed the driver to head around the back of the main structure where we found a small outbuilding. It was a simple dwelling, wooden-walled and single-roofed. There was one window beside the door, and a well-worn chair where a man might sit in nice weather.

The driver pulled up some distance from this cabin and after we had clambered from the carriage, Holmes bade the man wait. We approached the front door on foot, and Holmes had lifted his hand to knock when a quavering voice suddenly called out.

"You are too late."

"Too late for what?" asked Holmes sternly.

The door swung open to reveal an old man, who had seen at least seventy years upon this earth. His skin was browned by a steady exposure to the sun, though his eyes were a startling blue colour, like a shallow sea. He wore workman clothes that were rough and heavily patched. His hands held a musket so ancient and rusted I doubted that it was actually capable of being fired. However, given that the firearm was alarmingly pointed at Holmes' face, this was one theory I did not wish to put to a practical test. "Oh, you are not…" the man's sentence trailed off.

"We are not whom?" asked Holmes, his cool tone suggesting that he was unconcerned at the sight of the weapon aimed in his direction.

"Nobody," Gunn stammered.

"I see," said Holmes. "Very well, Mr. Gunn, we are here to purchase something from you."

The man lowered the musket slightly and narrowed his eyes. "Don't reckon I've got much that a pair of fine gentlemen such as yourselves wish to purchase."

"What about a brass disk, inscribed with letters, and roughly this size?" asked Holmes holding his hands together so that the thumbs and middle fingers formed a circle. "It would have had a smaller disk attached which rotated."

"I don't know what you are talking about," said the man crossly.

"Truly?" said Holmes, his voice mild. "That is most unfortunate. I have fifty pounds here that would have been yours."

"Fifty pounds?" said the man, a glimmer of interest appearing upon his face. "That is a mighty handsome sum, mister. If you are willing to pay fifty, perhaps you are willing to pay even more, eh? How about a hundred?"

"So you do have it?"

"Never said that, did I? But I might have heard of such a thing. A hundred pounds for the information."

"You drive a hard bargain, Mr. Gunn," said Holmes, calmly. "I am afraid that I don't have a hundred sovereigns on me at the moment. Would you take fifty, plus whatever my friend has in his wallet, plus this pocket watch? It is a Breguet from Paris, and reliably is worth a thousand pounds."

"A thousand pounds for a watch? Do you take me for an idiot, mister?"

"Not at all. In fact, I would very much hope that you will allow me to purchase it back from you tomorrow for a hundred pounds."

"So I am a pawnbroker now?"

Holmes spread his hands before him. "It seems a fair deal, Mr. Gunn, for merely a bit of information. If I return as promised, you will net over a hundred and fifty sovereigns."

The old man deliberated about this for a moment. "Very well, hand it over."

After Holmes finished raiding my wallet of its sole twenty pounds, he deposited it in combination with his fifty and the aforementioned watch into the man's waiting palm. "Now, where is the brass disk?" he inquired.

The man snorted in wry amusement. "You best ask Jim

Eggleson."

"What?" I exclaimed.

"Oh, yes, mister. That little rascal came to see me two mornings ago. He distracted me with a wheel of lovely Double Gloucester. When I was done consuming it, I found that he had absconded with my disk."

Holmes considered this new data for a moment. "And do you know the purpose of the disk, Mr. Gunn?"

"Nah. Just some piece of old junk left to me by my father, and his father before him." He shrugged. "To be honest, I am not even sure how exactly it came to be in my family's possession."

Holmes shook his head. "Mr. Gunn, need I remind you that you have been well paid for your information? A lodge-keeper could live on such as sum for two years, perhaps three. I advise you to utter no more falsehoods. Surely you know that the disks might be used to decipher a treasure map?"

The man pursed his lips. "Now where did you hear any such thing, mister? Have you been talking to Bench?"

"I assure you that we are unfamiliar with Mr. Bench."

The man spit upon the ground. "Good thing. David Bench is a nasty sort. You don't want to make his acquaintance." He stared at us with a sour look upon his face. "So if not Bench, then who?"

"Might I assume that Mr. Bench also has a significant interest in acquiring the pirate's treasure?" said Holmes mildly.

"Privateer," replied the man sullenly.

"I beg your pardon?" I interjected.

"None of them set out to be pirates. They were sent out to the Main all fair and legal. They had letters signed by Queen Anne herself giving them the right to plunder those ships. But George and his ministers revoked all that under Governor Rogers.[83] What choice did they have?"

"Choice?" I spluttered. "They could have taken the pardon."

"You don't understand, mister. That is like asking a bear to come down from the hills and put a chain round its neck. Such a thing would have been against their very nature."

"Are you saying that your grandfather sailed with one of the great pirate captains?" I asked. "Was it Thomas Tew? William Maze? James Flint?"

The man scoffed. "No such man as Captain John Flint. That's a writer's invention. The real captain was Edward Teach."

"Blackbeard?" I said, the disbelief plainly evidence in my voice. "Do you take us for fools, Mr. Gunn?"

He shook his head. "I do if you don't believe me. Where else would Blackbeard hide his treasure? He was born here in Redcliffe, wasn't he?[84] And at least a few of his fourteen wives lived here."

"Pray tell," said Holmes dryly.

The man took this invitation literally. "Aye, Teach first sailed with the Royal Navy out to New Providence. But he soon joined the crew of Captain Benjamin Hornigold, who quickly gave Teach command over the *Queen Anne's Revenge*. Teach was an enormous man, with a fiendish appearance, and a long black beard from which his nickname derived. The latter was twisted with colourful ribbons and slow burning fuses that wreathed his head in demonic smoke. His eyes were wild and fierce, such that a fury from hell could not look more frightful. He always carried a massive cutlass and three brace of matchlocks."

"And he hid his treasure in Bristol?" I said sceptically.

"Aye. It weren't on board his ship when they captured him, was it? And he wasn't about to bury it on some deserted island for any fool to dig up. No, he sent it back to England aboard the *Rose Emelye* with the only man he trusted – his quartermaster Jordan Foot. Foot hid it away just as Blackbeard ordered, but died before he could pass along the secret of how to find it. The treasure is lying there now, great heaps of coins and bars of gold, just waiting for someone to claim it."

"And how did you grandfather come into possession of the disk?"

The man narrowed his eyes furtively and shrugged. "I can't

rightly say. I don't even know how that scamp Jim knew that I had it. Or you gentlemen. My father made sure that I kept it a secret."

I turned to Holmes and muttered under my breath. "If Jim took the wheel, and used it to decipher the map, how are we to possibly determine where he went?"

Holmes nodded and turned back to the old man. "You must have stared at that disk many times, Mr. Gunn, did you not? Wondering how it could lead you to Blackbeard's treasure?"

"Aye. What man would not?"

"Do you know the letters inscribed upon it by heart? Could you replicate it upon a piece of paper?"

The man considered this for a moment. "I reckon I could."

"Then let me make you another deal, Mr. Gunn. If you draw it out for me, and I use it to track down young Jim Eggleson, I will make certain that he returns to you the original. But I will also do you one better. Should there also be some truth to this legend, and we utilize the disk to locate something that might be construed as a pirate treasure, whatever portion the Crown allows us to keep, one quarter share will belong to you."

"A quarter?" said Gunn sullenly. "That hardly seems fair. It's my disk."

"And how long has it been in your possession with it availing you of naught? If the treasure is as vast as your dreams, one quarter share should be more than sufficient. Certainly it is greater than what you currently possess, which is nothing."

The man pondered this for a moment. "Very well, come inside."

He led us into the small cabin and rummaged around until he located a pen and paper. He then set to work, carefully drawing concentric circles and transcribing letters within them. When he was complete, Gunn handed Holmes a paper with the following:

Holmes took the paper from Gunn and studied it for a moment before nodding. "It is as I suspected, Watson. An Alberti cipher disk." He turned back to the lodge-keeper. "I thank you for this Mister Gunn. Now take good care of my watch. I intend to return tomorrow in order to purchase it back from you. Come, Watson."

Holmes instructed the driver to make all haste back to central Bristol. When we were settled back in the carriage, I turned to my friend. "Was that watch really worth a thousand pounds, Holmes?"

He sniffed in amusement. "I would say so, Watson. It was a gift from the royal family of Holland for my assistance in the small matter of the purloined dispatch."

I was shocked that he would part with such a prize for even a brief time, but reckoned that the cause was a good one. I pointed to the drawing of the cipher disk. "So how does this work, Holmes?"

"You can see the stationary wheel is inscribed: 'ABCDEF-GILMNOPQRSTVXZ1234,' while the inner, movable wheel reads 'gklnprtvz&xysomqihfdbace.'"

"But why 'g,' Holmes?" I asked. "You could start at any letter upon the movable disk, could you not?"

"Because of the bar of *gold* upon the upper right corner of the vellum, Watson. Admittedly, this is – at the moment – a bit of a guess, however, it seems most likely. Though 'o' is also a possibility, should they have chosen to encode this in Spanish."

I thought about this for a moment. "But this is a simple substitution cipher, is it not? I do not understand why you were unable to break it without the disk?"

"Ah, that is the fiendish part, Watson. Because the guide letter changes by one position clockwise at a prescribed interval."

"And what interval would that be?"

"There were four drawings upon the vellum, were there not? We have elucidated the meaning of three of them. There must be a reason for the final item."

"A coin? What does that tell us?"

"Not just any coin, Watson. That is a Spanish 'pieces of *eight.*'"

I smiled as understanding washed over me. "So any 'A' in the first eight letters is encrypted as a 'g,' while any 'A' in the next eight would instead be a 'k.'"

"Precisely, Watson. And now, we may re-commence our attack upon Captain North's message."

From his coat pocket, Holmes drew forth his pencil and foolscap and handed them over to me. "Now let us see. The first letter we already knew to be an 'a.' Put that down, Watson. The 'z' conforms to the letter 'l,' and the 'y' to an 'o.' This is followed by the letters 'n' and 'g.' If I am not mistaken our first word is 'Along.' Capital!"

His eyes gleamed with excitement, and his thin, nervous fingers twitched as he rotated the letters of the 'disk' in his mind. As he deciphered the message and called out the letters, I scrawled down the words that were forming upon a sheet of scrap paper. But the next two were gibberish. "Holmes, we have a problem."

"What is it, Watson?"

"The next set of letters does not spell anything in English. You called out 'txesandi.'

He frowned as he considered this. "Let us proceed a bit further and see what transpires."

The following five letters did not help. They were 'sxore.' I handed him the paper gravely.

His bushy eyebrows twitched as he stared at the paper in

irritated silence for a long minute. "I have it!" he suddenly exclaimed in a happy tone. "The message writer – presumably the aforementioned Mr. Foot – was constrained in the choice of letters that he was able to utilize. For the disk has only twenty letters, does it not? It is missing an 'h, j, k, u, w, and y.' Therefore, he was forced to make additional substitutions. If the letter 'x' also can signify an 'h,' and if we use an 'i' for a 'y,' then we have a meaningful phrase, do we not? It spells out: along the sandy shore."

"By Jove!" I exclaimed. "You are correct, Holmes. Let us keep going!"

It took a bit of effort, further substituting 'u' for 'v' and 'z' for 'w,' but when complete, we had deciphered the mysterious message of Captain George North. The one which had set young Jim upon a potentially fateful path. I read it aloud:

> *"Along the sandy shore*
> *Full fathom thirteen score*
> *South and by southwest*
> *From the tilted tree nest*
> *Beneath a man who will never die*
> *Teach's treasures lie."*

§

I considered this riddle for a moment but could make nothing of it. "Whatever does it mean, Holmes?"

"It is, as I suspected, a series of instructions which presumably lead to the spot of Blackbeard's hidden treasure… or at least where said treasure once resided. Jim Eggleson was a most clever lad to make it this far, so we must presume that he has continued to follow the clues."

"How can you be certain of that?"

"The riddle, Watson, speaks of travelling in a south by southwest direction, and I noted no compass in Jim's room. A lad of his adventurous inclinations surely owned one, so we may presume that he took it with him when he set out upon his quest. If we continue to follow in his footsteps, we shall eventually locate him."

I frowned. "It says to start upon a sandy shore, Holmes. That sounds like the treasure must be buried upon some Caribbean isle after all."

"No, Watson, Mr. Gunn was quite clear that the treasure was brought back by Blackbeard's quartermaster to Bristol. We shall not need to engage a ship and sail to some distant coast. Let us return to Jim's father, and see if his local knowledge can shine any light upon this particular clue."

Before long the carriage dropped us before the 'Captain Maynard.' When we entered the main room of the tavern, the keeper looked up from his post behind the wooden bar with a hopeful glance.

Holmes shook his head. "The matter progresses, Mr. Eggleson, but we have not located Jim yet. Pray tell, if I spoke to you about a 'sandy shore' in relations to a locale either within or near Bristol, what would this suggest to you?"

The man pondered this for a moment. "I cannot rightly say, Mr. Holmes. I've not heard that term used before. Of course, Redcliffe is well known for the quality of its sand, which is used in the blowing of some of England's finest glass."

"Holmes, I passed numerous glassworks earlier!" I exclaimed. "And they were located along the shore of the river."

"Are there any forests in Redcliffe?" asked Holmes of our host.

"Forests? Not likely, Mr. Holmes," snorted Eggleson. "Every tree in the vicinity of Bristol was long ago cut down to feed the shipyards."

Holmes' brow contracted into a frown. "What then is the tilted tree?" he muttered under his breath.

And then it came to me. "Mr. Eggleson," I said, a measure of excitement rising in my voice. "When I was out earlier, I spied a church with a leaning bell-tower. Do you know it?"

"Of course, that is Temple Church. It's mainly ruins now, but once belonged to the Knights Templar. They say that the ghost of one of the knights still roams its grounds."

"That's it, Watson!" exclaimed Holmes. "The game's afoot!"

Without another word, Holmes bolted for the door, myself close upon his heels. Once outside, he paused in order for me to lead the way. I raced like a greyhound across the low bridge and through a warren of old lanes. My old leg wound was near eight years in the past, and I was once again reckoned fleet of foot, so that we sailed through the Redcliffe district like a pair of clippers. A leisurely walk of some ten minutes shrank to less than three.

We soon came upon the former graveyard facing the ruined, but still impressive, church. The bell-tower leaned alarmingly, as if ready to collapse at any moment. I wondered how the inhabitants of the building under its shadow felt about living under that sword of Damocles. As we strode across the still frozen garden grounds, Holmes grimaced. "I suspect that in the summer, Watson, the earth beneath our feet takes on a consistency akin to a marsh. The architect's poor choice of locale likely explains the church's unique lean. Nevertheless, we need to make our way up that tower to see if we may spy our quarry."

"Do you think it safe? It looks rather precarious."

Holmes nodded in agreement. "Nonetheless, it must be attempted." He paused and studied the barred and locked doorway. "Now, then, Watson. If you were a young lad such as Jim, how would you gain entrance to this structure?"

I studied the four sides of the tower and pointed excitedly to my candidate. "That window there!"

Holmes strode over to the spot in question and examined the area below the small orifice, some six feet off the ground. "I concur, Watson. Someone has crawled through this window in the last few days. See the footprints in the ground, all made by the same shoe? And these scuff marks where he found a sufficient purchase to scale the wall. Only a boy, or perhaps a midget, could possibly fit through such a narrow opening, and we must suppose this intruder must have been young Jim."

"Do you think he could still be trapped inside?"

Holmes shook his head. "Not if he was conscious, for his cries could be easily heard. And these two prints here are much deeper, suggesting that he jumped back down again."

"And where was he headed? Can you trace his steps?"

"Through the park, possibly. But not the city lanes, not after such a long time. No, we must deduce where Jim was headed."

"How?"

"By following his path to the top of the tower. We shall never fit through his spot of ingress, so help me force this door."

I eyed the sturdy-appearing gate. "Surely we could locate the keeper and ask him to open it?"

"Even if we had the time to find the man, what would you tell him, Watson? That we need to make a forbidden climb to the top of this tower because of words we decoded from a one-hundred-and-fifty year-old pirate treasure map? Would you believe such a story?"

"Good point, Holmes," said I, nodding tightly. "On three?"

It took only two tries for our combined weight to batter down the door, though the effort left my good shoulder feeling rather tender. Once inside, we found four walls of rough-hewn stone which soared well over a hundred feet above the ground. Along the edge, a rickety wooden staircase spiralled upwards, no railing to prevent a careless slip into the void. The earth at our feet was covered with a thick layer of dust, which allowed even my untrained eyes to follow the clear prints I presumed had been made by young Jim Eggleson.

"What are we looking for, Holmes?"

"Something that has been there for many years, Watson, and something expected to last through the span of time. Something notable, and most, importantly, something thirteen score fathoms – or one thousand five hundred and sixty feet – from this location in a south by southwest direction. But we must first make the climb in order to achieve the proper vantage point."

I shook my head. "Those stairs seem ready to collapse at any moment."

"They held Jim's weight, Watson."

"One slender lad does not equal two grown men, Holmes."

"Take heart, my friend. Would you rather wait at the bottom while I alone follow the map's clue?"

"Now that you mention it, I suppose I would like to see with my own eyes where it leads." I motioned to the stairs. "After you, Holmes."

Although the wood creaked alarmingly, as Holmes predicted, they managed to hold our combined mass. We soon reached the top of the tower and looked out over the rooftops of Bristol. Holmes, with his unerring sense of direction, quickly oriented himself on the specific bearing and a smile rose to his lips. "What do you say, Watson? Does that appear to be about a third of a mile away?"

I followed his gaze. There was only one structure which could possibly be our destination. "It looks like a good place to find a dead man, Holmes."

"It does indeed," said he, grimly. For we were staring directly at the mighty spire of the tallest building in Bristol – the church of St. Mary Redcliffe.

§

We quickly retraced our steps down the tower stairs and out of the church grounds. Again we raced through the warrens of Redcliff until we came upon the site of that beautiful Perpendicular Gothic church. Although the hour was late, the doors remained open, so that Holmes and I fortunately had no need to repeat our vandalism at the Temple.

We entered the structure, and despite the urgency of our mission, I involuntarily drew up for a moment to soak in the nave's glorious fluted columns which coalesced into the fan vault. Most of the day's light had fallen, such that the enormous stained glass windows were dark. Providentially, for the sake of our mission, the church was mainly empty, excepting only a shabbily-dressed blind man sitting bowed in prayer near the rear of the pews. I assumed him to be a beggar pleading for hope of a better life ahead.

And then the enormity of our task sunk in. "Where are we to locate the grave in question, Holmes? There must be hundreds in here!" I protested.

"The clue will point the way, Watson. We are looking for one belonging to a man 'who will never die.' "

I shook my head. "But that makes no sense. Every man must die."

Holmes shrugged. "Perhaps his reputation is immortal? I cannot say with certainty, Watson. However, I expect that the answer will be clear once we see it."

Of course, Holmes was correct. Upon his suggestion, we split up in order to cover more ground. He took the south transept and I, the north. I studied the name and inscriptions carved upon every grave and monument as thoroughly as possible, ever aware of the pressing nature of our quest, and hoping that Holmes' astute perceptiveness might spot something that I had missed. I wracked my brain trying to determine if any of the names I read were famous for any reason that echoed beyond the environs of Bristol.

And then I saw it. But it was not a man who was famous. Quite the opposite. "Holmes!" I called out. "Over here!"

He was at my side in an instant. "What is it, Watson?"

I pointed at the grave before me. It was a marble effigial monument stretching from the ground of the church up to twice a man's height. It was carved with false pillars and a tromp l'oeil vault, framing the figure of a reclining man. The basso relief above him depicted ships and sea scenes, while his name was spelled out below him.

Holmes frowned and shook his head. "I fail to see which portion of this particular sepulchre has caught your attention, Watson, other than it plainly belongs to a man of the sea. But those are plentiful here in Bristol."

"The name, Holmes! Look at the name! Captain John Argent Proceri."

"Spit it out, Watson!" Holmes snapped, testily.

"If you move the last name to the beginning, and translate both 'proceri' and 'argent' from Latin to English, this would be the grave of none other than Captain Long John Silver."

"And what is the relevance of that?"

"Silver is the villain of Stevenson's *Treasure Island*, Holmes! He will never die, because he never lived. He is a fictional character."

Holmes stared at the faux tomb for a moment, and then burst out with a boom of laughter. "Capital, Watson! You are scintillating today! We must presume that the name of Long John Silver was handed down through the North family, never realizing its association to this monument. We can give thanks to both the story that he spun Mr. Stevenson, as well as to the British school system, that you were able to render the translation and thus make the connection." His face grew serious. "Now let us see to opening Captain Silver's grave."

"Hold a minute, Holmes! How do we know that it will be empty? Pirates often buried their treasures under a body, sacrificed after a drawing of the lots, so that the man's ghost might forever defend the spot from treasure-seekers."

He shook his head. "Do not forget, Watson, that we are following in young Jim's footsteps. He is a clever lad, of that there is no question, but brave enough to push past a skeleton? And to do so without leaving any trace of his action? Do you see any bone dust on the floor?"

"They could have swept..." I speculated.

"Pshaw!" he ejaculated. "This floor is cleaned no more than weekly by the dirt I see before me. The more vexing question is how Jim opened it, for I see no signs of forced entry."

"A hidden latch?" said I, eagerly.

"Precisely. Recall the clue, Watson." He bent down before the tomb. "It says 'beneath a man who will never die.' Look carefully at the letters of the name below Silver's effigy. Each one has a minute crack between it and the facing marble."

"What does that signify?"

"It means that each letter is able to be depressed. I wager that if we press the letters in the correct combination, some queer mechanism will be engaged that opens the sepulchre."

"But what combination?"

He considered this for a moment, and then smiled. "How about spelling out the word 'die?' "

I shook my head. "There is no 'd' in John Argent Proceri."

"Not in English, Watson. In Latin."

"*Morior*? No, there is no 'm.' I have it, Holmes! *Intereo!*"

His long thin fingers rapidly pressed the letters in the specified order. Each sank smoothly into the marble as Holmes predicted. For a moment, nothing happened, and I began to wonder whether it mattered which of the repeated letters was pressed first. And then we heard a soft rumbling noise, followed by a sharp click. As we watched, the entire effigy sank back into the wall of the church, revealing a dark hole below.

"It's barren!" I exclaimed.

"Of a body, yes, Watson, but not entirely." He bent over the hole and peered down. "Here we find a ladder heading into the bowels of the earth. And the ancient mould upon its rungs has been recently disturbed."

"Does it lead to the crypt?"

"No, Watson, it is far too rough-hewn to be an official part of the church. This looks to be the work of an illicit smuggler, who likely colluded with the tomb's stonemason to create this passage. I doubt that the church fathers know what they have on their hands."

"We must follow it!" I exclaimed.

"Of course, Watson. But first, be so good as to borrow that candelabra."

While I was engaged in plundering one of the church's treasures, I noted that Holmes was scribbling a brief note onto his pocket pad. He then tore out the sheet and folded it in half before setting it next to the tomb.

"What are you doing, Holmes?"

"Preparing for eventualities, Watson," he replied vaguely. He motioned for the candle and I passed it to him. Holmes went first down the ladder. As soon as his head had passed from view, I followed. The shaft dropped some fifteen feet before ending in a passage tall enough for even Holmes to stand without stooping.

Holmes glanced at me and nodded tightly. "Ready, Watson?"

I wiped my hands upon my pants and replied in the affirmative. We followed the underground passage for some five hundred feet as it gently sloped downward. Finally, it appeared as if it were about to open into a great cave, though the single candle I carried could hardly illuminate the area. However, my attention was quickly diverted to the sight of a young lad lying unconscious immediately before the cave's entrance.

I sprang to his side and removed my coat to make a cushion for his head. I felt young Jim's wrist and was relieved to note a pulse, though it was rather thready, showing that his stream of life trickled thin and small. There was no motion in his eyelids to suggest that he was about to come round. I cursed that I carried no brandy with which to revive him. "We must remove him at once from the close air in this cave, Holmes. It is rank and stale."

Holmes nodding in agreement, together we lifted the lad and quickly transported him back to the base of the ladder. However, when I looked up, I got the shock of my life. For there was no light to be seen! The way back into the church had been sealed!

"Holmes!" I exclaimed. "What are we to do? We have been trapped, just like poor Jim!"

Holmes grimaced. "I was afraid of this very possibility."

"What? You anticipated this?"

He smiled wanly. "You should know by now, Watson, that meticulous planning is the key to all but the simplest of endeavours." He pulled out his pocket watch. "Ten o'clock will come round in just three more minutes. I counsel patience."

"And what is going to happen at ten o'clock?"

"Patience, Watson."

I shook my head in exasperation, nevertheless, Holmes would say no more. However, as Holmes said, it was a matter of but a few minutes before I heard a rumbling noise, louder than when we heard it above. Then, with a click, a ray of light appeared at the top of the shaft. To my astonishment, I saw the youthful face of our page-boy Billy looking down upon me. I had no time to consider his miraculous appearance, however, as Holmes had taken young Jim from me and was insisting I scale the ladder. I followed his instructions and, upon reaching the top, turned to receive Jim's limp body from Holmes, who had climbed most of the way with the boy upon his shoulder.

§

The rest of the tale is a simple one. Holmes sent Billy for a passing constable, who in turn was sent to fetch both a nearby fellow medico and then wire to Scotland Yard. Young Jim was promptly carted off for careful medical attention, though the simple remedy of the fresh air in the church was already bringing him around. By the time Lestrade and Gregson arrived several hours later in response to Holmes' summons, the local police force had already traced the man called David Bench. With a start, I recognized that he was none other than the beggar who had been supposedly praying in St. Mary Redcliffe when we first entered the church. At this point I was as perplexed as everyone else, so Holmes did us the courtesy of explaining.

It seemed that, from the very beginning, Holmes had anticipated the possibility of a sneak attack. Therefore, before we even had departed Baker Street, Holmes had handed written instructions to Billy. The lad was to follow after us to Bristol, all the while taking the utmost care to stay out of sight. Billy carried out his orders so thoroughly that I ever became aware of his presence. Fortunately, Billy tracked us to the church and watched silently as Bench closed the ingenious mechanism at the faux tomb of 'Long John Silver.' This trapped us inside, and it was hardly difficult to imagine that Bench had done the same to poor Jim Eggleson two days prior. Although Bench refused to confess, Billy's subsequent testimony was sufficient to ensure that Bench would serve ten to fifteen at Princetown Prison upon three counts of attempted murder.

During his trial, Bench was discovered be another descendent of a member of Blackbeard's crew, along with George North and Franklin Gunn. As the account was pieced together, Teach's quartermaster, Jordan Foot, refused to entrust the secret of the treasure's location to any one man. North's great-grandfather became the owner of the vellum note, Gunn's the cipher disk, while Bench's knew only that the two pieces needed to be brought together. Sadly, none of the men trusted the others sufficiently to work together, and without such co-operation, the riddle could never be solved.

Despite being a nasty sort, Bench knew that even if he could bring them together, his blindness prevented him from using either the code or the cipher disk. However, when North died, Bench realized his chance and began to follow young Jim as he went about his quest. He got around quite well for a man missing his vision, his other senses rather acute. Bench monitored Jim's progress as he went out to Gunn's lodge, and as Jim returned to Bristol to scale the Temple Church tower. And finally, he waited for Jim to open the false 'Silver' tomb and climb inside. Despite the great temptation that he must have felt, Bench likely decided that he could wait a few more days before collecting the long-lost treasure, and determined to wait until Jim had perished from starvation. Nonetheless, Bench kept close watch over the cave's entrance and when Holmes and I appeared, he repeated his treacherous action, intending to delay his acquisition of the gold for just a bit longer.

His treacherous plan might have worked, if not for the bravery and cleverness of our page boy. Once we had been trapped, Billy realized that he needed to effect the removal of Bench from the church. So Billy complained to a passing constable that Bench had accosted him, and the constable threw the man in gaol overnight. Billy then located Holmes' folded note and followed the instructions therein to re-open the trapdoor.

By the time Holmes was done explaining all of this, I was as eager as Lestrade and Gregson to descend the ladder and determine what precisely lay in that cave beneath our feet. A squad of trusty local policemen were stationed up top to ensure that we would be able to emerge again, and the Scotland Yarders followed Holmes and I back down the shaft.

Once we had successfully located Master Jim Eggleson, I began to worry that Blackbeard's cache might have been found years prior and already plundered, all trace of the great treasure gone. But such fears were unfounded. In the light of our combined torches, all around me I beheld great heaps of coin and quadrilaterals built of ingots of gold. There was the plunder of Spanish churches – enormous golden candlesticks and crosses encrusted with large and brilliant diamonds. Gold-hilted swords inlaid with jewels gave testament that the cavaliers of Spain did not go down without a fight. Wooden chests, silver porringers, and huge iron kettles were filled with all manners of silver and golden coins from a bygone era: doubloons, moidores, ducats, pistareens, and pieces of eight. These were admixed with rubies – great and small – emeralds, carnelians, agates, amethysts, stones of Goa, and a prodigious number of flawless pearls.

In the end, the authorities retrieved items worth some seven-hundred-thousand pounds. This vast sum proved to be worth even more that the estimated value of the lost Agra treasure.[85] The recovery was done under cover of night, in order to avoid setting off a mass hysteria of treasure hunters digging up every cellar in Bristol. Sadly, British law was clear upon the matter. Edward Teach had hidden his treasure with an intention to recover it later. As such, the legal code dictated that rights to the recovered treasure belonged solely to the Crown.

However, I have it on good authority that the Queen displayed a gracious beneficence worthy of her eminent rank. For young Jim Eggleson was richly rewarded for his role in the treasure's discovery. I am told that the 'Captain Maynard' is now the finest and most popular tavern in Bristol. Should I ever have another reason to pass through that town, I shall be certain to authenticate this report.

It was determined that Franklin Gunn had already been well-recompensed for his minor role. He had his one hundred and seventy crowns, for Holmes returned promptly the following morn to repurchase his watch. Meanwhile, Billy had been sent back to Baker Street by the last train the night prior, carrying a tidy reward of his own in his coat pockets.

Holmes and I followed after Billy the next day, only after we had ensured that Jim Eggleson was going to make a full recovery. On the carriage to London, Holmes leaned back in his seat and lit his amber-stemmed pipe. He puffed upon it contentedly for a moment before he spoke. "Never underestimate the fortitude of youth, Watson."

"While I am most gratified to see that young Jim is mending rapidly, Holmes, I do not believe that is the lesson of this case."

"No?" he said, raising his left eyebrow questioningly. "Then what, pray tell, is?"

"Never to go adventuring alone."

He shook his head. "A wise commandment, Watson. However, one that shall be more difficult to follow now that you are about to desert me for a wife."

"I still wish to be included in your cases whenever possible, Holmes," I protested vigorously.

"I am happy to hear that, Watson. I would be most dismayed to learn that matrimony had dulled your sense of adventure."

"Oxen and wain-ropes would not keep me from a good adventure, Holmes."

He smiled at that sentiment. "Oh, I almost forgot, Watson. I have a little something for you – to set you up in practice after your departure from Baker Street."

I frowned in mystification. "What is it?"

"I am aware that your resources are rather limited now that your half-pay wound pension has run its course. And of course, your fiancée's inheritance lies at the bottom of the Thames. Just reach up and bring down that Gladstone bag."

I did as instructed and when I opened it, I discovered that Holmes had somehow surreptitiously removed one of the sacks of coins from Teach's cave, worth perhaps some three or four hundred sterling.

"Holmes!" I exclaimed. "You didn't!"

"Given the vast quantities involved, I sincerely doubt this small sum will be missed." He shrugged and a twinkle appeared in his grey eyes. "Perhaps, Watson, there is a little bit of pirate in each of us."

§

THE HARROWING
INTERMISSION

I suffer under no delusions that the public – which has kindly shown a small degree of attention to the brief glimpses of my late, remarkable friend, Mr. Sherlock Holmes, that I have endeavoured on a handful of occasions to set down upon foolscap – has any particular interest in the solo meanderings of an invalided former Army surgeon, turned civil practitioner of minor repute. Therefore, I write these words for the sole purpose of chronicling the peculiar case that I had some trifling role in bringing to a successful conclusion, in the unlikely event that future students of crime wish to learn the truth behind the sensational accounts reported in the daily papers at the eventual conclusion of the inquest.

On the day in question, it was still mid-afternoon when had I finished with my final patient, for my practice was small and, in the light of Holmes' recent death, even less absorbing than typical. My wife was not due back from visiting her friend in Tunbridge Wells for a few hours, so I found myself with several hours free before I needed to be at Victoria in order to meet her train. The summer weather was fine, and my wounded limbs bothered me not a whit, therefore I determined to set out upon a constitutional ramble through London, without a particular destination in mind. I started from my consulting-room into Kensington Gardens and made my way past the Speke Obelisk, where my thoughts turned to the suspicious death of that great explorer over twenty years prior.[86] I wondered whether the coroner's decision would have been different if Holmes had been in active practice at the time? Surely, my friend, with his great interest in sensational literature, may have devised a theory regarding the matter, and I greatly wished that it were still possible to hear his thoughts.

I am not afraid to confess in these private notes that Holmes' death into the swirling chasm at the fall of Reichenbach had left a gaping and painful void in my life. My loving spouse attempted to assuage my prolonged bereavement by suggesting trips to the glades of New Forest and the piers of Southsea, but neither locale held any joy for me. As I mulled over these unhappy thoughts, I looked up and was surprised to find that my feet had unconsciously led me directly past the well-remembered door of our old haunts at 221B Baker Street. I stopped and gazed fondly at the broad bow window, which had been carefully restored by Mycroft after the fire set by Professor Moriarty's men. The blind was down, of course, and no lamp was lit, however for a brief moment I imagined that Holmes had but stepped out upon a case and would return any minute. I could climb the seventeen steps to the first floor flat, circle round the acid-charred chemical bench, and sit back in my armchair, ready once more to hear where our next adventure would take us.

However, I did not knock upon the door, nor ring the bell. There was no point. Holmes had perished nobly, bringing a fitting justice to his great adversary, and freeing society of the man's evils. Furthermore, I knew Mrs. Hudson was having a most difficult time accepting that Holmes was truly dead, and I had no wish to throw that long-suffering woman into a new set of hysterics. I instead turned my steps to the station, and by the time I met my sweet and amiable bride, her normally pale cheeks beaming red as she hurried through the crowd, all thoughts of Holmes had been banished from my mind.

The following morn, Mary slept in far later than typical, though she had mentioned the night prior that her trip had been rather taxing. The sun shone brightly through the shutters while I contented myself with a leisurely reading of the morning editions after my breakfast. One story in particular captured my attention. There had been a terrible tragedy at Covent Garden during the prior evening's performance of *Faust*. I read the account closely, for I was certain that Holmes would have been most interested in the grotesque facts of the case. I turned the details over in my mind, endeavouring to hit upon some theory that could reconcile them all but, where Holmes would have seen a spark of light, for my dull brain there was only an impenetrable gloom. I startled when I felt a touch upon my shoulder and I turned to see the smiling visage of my dainty wife.

"I thought your senses were more alert than that, John," said she. "Whatever is it that has you so entranced?"

"It is this harrowing account in the newspaper."

She coughed briefly and pulled out a chair to join me at the breakfast table. She waived away my offer of a piece of toast, which I was mildly surprised at, for she seemed thinner of late. "Tell me about it."

"I know only what I have read in the papers," said I, motioning to the sheets scattered about me. "They differ in some minor details, but agree upon the main facts. It seems that Josephine Taylor, the famous soprano, was murdered last night at the Opera House."

Mary's hand flew to her lips. "Oh my!" she exclaimed. "Did we not see her last year in von Weber's *Der Frieschütz*?"

"Indeed," I shook my head sadly. "But we shall not hear her dulcet tones again."

"And if I recall correctly, she was widowed last year. I read that this was to be her first return to the stage."

"And a tragic return it proved to be. It seems that the first three acts took place without any suspicious incident, but when the intermission was complete and the curtain rose upon the fourth act, Mrs. Taylor was not sitting at the spinning wheel preparing to sing her aria. Instead, the audience was dismayed to find her corpse hanging from a rope tied around the pin-rail! Her head hung at an appalling angle to her body, and her face was the colour of slate, with lips of purple."

Mary's face was flushed with righteous indignation at such a horrific event. "Who could have done such a thing? And why?"

I shook my head. "At present, it appears that the Yard has no suspects. However, the motive is plain. Do you recall the magnificent necklace that Mrs. Taylor was wearing when we saw her?"

"The one with the enormous blue star sapphire?"

"Just so. It seems that this necklace is Mrs. Taylor's prize possession. She never lets it out of her sight, and one of her conditions of performing was to be allowed to wear it upon the stage. However, when they pulled down her body, the necklace was missing."

We both sat quietly for a moment, as we contemplated the tragic end of Mrs. Taylor. Then Mary spoke, a slight tremble in her voice. "John, have you not always been fascinated by the promise of adventure, a diversion from the dull routine of every-day life? For many years, you were in the confidence of Mr. Holmes. This friendship obviously piqued your interest in some of the more outré crimes that have befallen our city since his tragic passing. What if you were to employ his methods and assist in discovering the solution to this calamity?"

I shook my head. "Mary, my dearest, I am touched that you hold me in such high regard that I could possibly replicate his skills. But I am no Holmes, nor could ever be."

"You sell yourself short, I think."

My gaze lingered upon the terrible headline. "One thing is certain. It is a great loss to London, and Europe as a whole, that Holmes is dead. If only he were still available to supplement, or even anticipate, the efforts of the Yard. For there are some points about this peculiar business which I am certain would have appealed to his particular tastes."

"Then tell him about it," said Mary plainly.

I glanced up in alarm. "Whatever are you talking about? Holmes is dead."

"Of course he is, dear," said she with great seriousness, her large blue eyes shining brightly. "But I fear that a piece of you has died with him. You have not taken up your pen since you detailed the events at the Reichenbach Falls. What once brought you such joy has been abandoned, replaced by walks past your old haunts on Baker Street."

I frowned. "How could you possibly know that I walked by Baker Street last night?"

She laughed. "When I find in my husband's coat pocket a new bottle of Behring's Antitoxin with a receipt from Portman's Apothecary at 239 Baker Street, I do not need the skills of Mr. Holmes to tell me what he has been doing in his free time."

I chuckled ruefully at this observation. I had myself forgotten that I had made a brief detour into the pharmacy for a restock of my supplies. "So what are you proposing, Mary?"

"Go around to the Covent Garden Theatre. Anstruther will cover your patients for the day." She paused and looked about the reading room until her gaze alit upon a pad of foolscap and a J pen. "I recall you once telling me of the time when Mr. Holmes sent you out to Dartmoor upon your own. Did he not instruct you to report the facts back to him in the fullest possible manner? This is no different. Write him a letter," she commanded, thrusting the paper and pen into my astonished hand. "The change would do you good. You have been looking pale and distracted, Dr John Watson, and you are in need of a remedy. As a wise man once said, 'physician, heal thyself!'"

Her tone was so forceful; I could only stammer my agreement that I would do as she suggested. Thus, from this point onwards, I shall simply relate refer to the two letters that I wrote to my friend, Mr. Sherlock Holmes. At first, Mary's exercise made me feel rather foolish, and at least twice, I set down the pen with a shake of my head. Nevertheless, I finally realized the profound wisdom in her words and obeyed her directive.

§

13 Earl's Terrace,[87] *Aug. 1st, 1891*

My Dear Holmes:

I will attempt to refrain from providing unnecessary descriptions in this letter to you, for I am well aware that you are eternally indifferent to poetry and would have me confine myself to the purest of facts. You have, upon occasion, commented that I never quite learned the trick that you do with your series of inferences. Therefore, I will need to pursue my inquiries after my own plodding fashion.

I began, of course, by taking a hansom cab over to Bow Street. Before the Opera House's Corinthian-pillared grand façade, a group of curious loafers had gathered. Although I assumed that Mrs. Taylor's corpse had been removed to the local morgue many hours prior, a morbid crowd still strived to obtain entrance, perhaps in hopes that the fatal rope might still be hanging from the rafters. Before making my own attempt at what I suppose I must admit was a similar mission, I glanced over at the inimitable white lamps outside the Police Station where you and I had once visited the filthy beggar Hugh Boone, as well as the maligned Dr Lowe. As I did so, I caught a glimpse of a passing man, rather over six feet in height and excessively lean, and for a moment I thought you had returned to aid me in this formidable task. However, the man then twisted his face in my direction, and I realized that his soft, rounded features were in no way similar to your narrow, hawk-like mien.

I shook my head and turned my attention back to the Opera House, where I had the happy experience of seeing Inspector

Lestrade emerge from its doors. He was as sallow, lean, and ferret-like as the first time I met him, but his visage reminded me of better days. His dark eyes lit up when he saw me, and he immediately came over to pump my hand warmly.

"Dr Watson," he exclaimed. "It is a great pleasure to find you here! I am most sorry that the Molesey Mystery has occupied my every waking moment. I have not had a chance to call upon you since we parted after the DeGrandin affair and offer my sincere condolences. Mr. Holmes and I did not always see eye to eye regarding our methods, but at the end, Mr. Holmes did the Yard a good turn. The papers in his pigeonhole M allowed Patterson to convict the whole gang. In one fell swoop, Mr. Holmes scoured away half the crime in London. Only a few men slipped through our fingers, but we'll catch them soon enough."

I congratulated him on his successes and inquired about the shocking murder that had taken place the prior evening. Lestrade shook his head in consternation. "You don't know the half of it, Doctor. You see, there was another murder in the middle of the night that I am certain was linked to this one."

I frowned. "I don't recall reading about any such murder in the papers?"

"We've kept it quiet for the moment, for the public is excited enough about Mrs. Taylor's death, which has the entire city talking."

"Why do you believe that the two murders are connected?"

He looked around furtively, as if to ensure that no one was listening in upon our conversation. "Do you know Harold Beechum?"

"The rubber magnate?"

"Aye. Also owner and proprietor of the Beechum Trading Company, one of the country's largest importers of spices, tea, and textiles from India. He was a very wealthy man."

"He is dead?"

"Indeed. He was slain most brutally in his home last night and something stolen."

"So he was killed during a robbery?"

"In a manner of speaking, Doctor. However, the thief was rather selective. Although Beechum's town home was filled with exotic tapestries, art, weapons, and silver, only one thing was taken... his walking-stick."

"What an odd thing to steal," said I, in a mystified tone.

"Well, Doctor, there is one fact that I am withholding, as Mr. Holmes was wont to do upon occasion," chuckled Lestrade. "You see, Beecham's Penang lawyer was topped with an enormous blue star sapphire."

"Like Mrs. Taylor's necklace!"

"Precisely," said Lestrade, coolly. "Mr. Holmes was always railing against coincidences, and I am inclined to agree with him this time."

"I think that wise," I replied, unassumingly. "Was Mr. Beechum also strangled?"

Lestrade shook his head. "No, it's hard to tell which murder was more horrific, Doctor. Mr. Beechum was stabbed in the eye with a curved Indian dagger. We are still attempting to ascertain if the assassin brought the dagger with him or if he simply used one from Mr. Beechum's extensive collection."

"How shocking. I now understand why you are keeping this quiet for the moment. But surely the general public has nothing to fear? It seems that the murderer has a most specific intention, which suggests the average Londoner is not at risk. Few people routinely carry around giant star sapphires."

The inspector nodded thoughtfully. "You might be right, Doctor, but we also don't want to tip our hand to the perpetrator of these crimes. For we have a solid idea of his identity, and now only need to bring him to justice."

"Indeed? Would you care to give me a hint? I can assure you that I will betray no secrets."

"Your discretion, Doctor, is undeniable. Very well, I can tell you this. I have just completed a most thorough examination of the theatre's proscenium and back-stage area. I even imitated our dearly departed friend and got down upon my hands and knees. And do you know what I found at the scene?" I shook my head in the negative. "An Indian rupee!" said Lestrade, a note of triumph in his voice. "Mr. Holmes himself could not have done a better job of the matter, I wager!"

"I presume that you are drawing a connection between the rupee found near Mrs. Taylor's body, the fact that Mr. Beechum was a merchant of wares from India, and the Indian dagger with which he was slain?"

"I am indeed, Doctor. The evidence is plain and obvious. An Indian fellow must have killed Mrs. Taylor and Beechum for their jewels."

"But why only those jewels? Why not the other things of value in Mr. Beechum's house?"

Lestrade shrugged. "How can I understand the workings of a madman's mind? Perhaps they have some sort of mystical significance to him. I assure you that we will ask the man when we catch him."

"Very good, Inspector. Say, I wonder if this case is worthy of a small brochure?"

Lestrade's eyebrows rose and his eyes sparkled with interest. "Do you mean like you did for Mr. Holmes?"

"Precisely."

"And who would be the protagonist of this story with Mr. Holmes sadly having passed on?"

I shrugged. "Clearly it would be the man responsible for solving the case. I assume that will be you, Inspector."

He nodded appreciatively, but his voice carried a measure of gruffness. "Well, surely I cannot officially condone any such activity, Doctor. I am, of course, a civil servant. However, I have no power to prevent such a publication."

"Of course," said I, agreeably. "Still, if I were to write such a tale, it would help with my descriptions if I could take a brief look about the scene of the crime." I paused for a moment. "Since I am here."

Lestrade appeared to consider this and then nodded. "Very well, Doctor. For old time's sake. It's hard to believe that it

THE TREASURY OF SHERLOCK HOLMES

THE TREASURY OF SHERLOCK HOLMES

THE TREASURY OF SHERLOCK HOLMES

THE TREASURY OF SHERLOCK HOLMES

THE TREASURY OF SHERLOCK HOLMES

THE TREASURY OF SHERLOCK HOLMES

THE TREASURY OF SHERLOCK HOLMES

has already been ten years since you and Mr. Holmes played a small part in helping me track down Jefferson Hope." My eyebrows rose at his rather fine characterization of your role in the matter. "I must question the singers, the orchestra, and the members of the crew in order to determine if anyone saw an Indian lurking about back-stage last night. However, I will ask Constable McBride to show you around for a few minutes. Of course, if you were to find anything of note, you must report it to me at once."

"I sincerely doubt that you overlooked anything, Inspector."

Nevertheless, when Lestrade departed, leaving me in the company of young McBride, I soon realized the error of my statement. With the constable's escort, I quickly passed through the cordon of police that was preventing curiosity-seekers from sneaking into the Opera House. When we arrived at the stage, I found that I was correct that Josephine Taylor's body had been removed. However, the creamy yellow-coloured agent of her demise had been left in place.

"That's no rope," I said in puzzlement.

"No, sir," replied McBride, though my statement had been a rhetorical one. "I believe it is some sort of long scarf."

"How odd. Why not use a simple rope? There are plenty scattered about."

The constable merely shrugged, as if my observation was beyond his mental powers and, not for the last time, did I wish that you were by my side, Holmes. You would immediately grasp the significance of this incongruous finding.

Then I noted one other peculiarity. Behind a large piece of wooden stage décor, I discovered the stub of a cheroot. On the grimy streets of London, it would have been one in a million, unnoticed by all. Nevertheless, in a theatre, where fire remained one of the most feared events, such an item was anathema. I bent down to get a closer look and absently patted my coat-pocket, before I realized that, unlike you, Holmes, I do not routinely carry a magnifying lens. Still, even without such an aid, I could plainly tell that the cigar was, in actuality, an Indian lunkah.

If only you could be here, Holmes! You would have been so stimulated by the sight. With your special knowledge of tobacco ashes and its forms, from this humble cigar you would have likely made many deductions, which have sadly completely escaped my eyes. I made a mental note to consult your monograph upon my return to Kensington. In those coloured plates, I might locate some supremely important point to serve as a clue to the identity of the criminal. I called over Constable McBride and attempted to explain the significance of the cigar. He seemed sceptical at first, but eventually agreed to place it in an evidence bag and have it taken round to Inspector Lestrade. Once that task was complete, I spent a few more minutes peering around the area of Mrs. Taylor's murder, but failed to uncover anything else of note.

Leaving the Opera House, I lingered on the pavement and contemplated my next move. I was at a loss, as I would normally have your orders, Holmes, suggesting how I might be of the most use. For a moment, I despaired at this fool's errand. I have no illusions about my role in our former partnership. I have no intrinsic genius of my own. At best, I merely stimulated one or two of your more brilliant conclusions, Holmes. If I were to be honest with myself, I should abandon this mystery to the professionals, return home to my loving wife, and resume seeing my needy patients. If Lestrade was correct, and an Indian was responsible for these murders, how was I conceivably to identify him? There must be thousands of such men in London alone. If you were here, Holmes, I have no doubt that you would quickly throw on an impenetrable disguise and infiltrate the regions of the city where he might be found. However, you would have laughed at the notion of me, with my distinctive lack of talent at dissimulation, attempting any such plan.

Then fate intervened. For as I stood there in front of Covent Garden, Inspector Bradstreet popped out of the doors of the

Bow Street Station, and looked around until he spotted me. He hurried across the road and shook my hand.

"Doctor Watson, Inspector Lestrade has just wired the station. With his compliments, he invites you to come round to Scotland Yard, for he has caught the murderer and thought you might wish to see the man."

I started in surprise, for I was well aware of your opinion, Holmes, on Lestrade's capabilities. Certainly, he possessed a bulldog tenacity and was quick and energetic, but such rapid results seemed extraordinary for a man whom you once said lacked imagination and was frequently out of his depth. Did you perhaps underestimate the man, Holmes?

I quickly thanked Bradstreet and caught a cab for the short ride to Whitehall. I was bursting with interest to learn Lestrade's news. When I entered the Yard, I was promptly directed to Lestrade's office. The inspector was sitting at his desk, his feet propped on top and a large cigar filling his mouth.

"Ah, Doctor!" he exclaimed in triumph, waving me to a chair. "It is a crying shame that Mr. Holmes is not here to see my handiwork today! Even he could not have done it so well, I think you will admit. Again, I cannot forbid you to write up the results of this affair."

"Pray tell me about it, Inspector."

"Well, as you know, after I left you to do your own little inspection, I asked around whether an Indian had been spotted in the theatre, and sure enough, one was seen by no less than five individuals. One of our police artists drew up a composite picture. We took it round to Mr. Beechum's house to see if anyone had seen the man in the area. And guess what we discovered, Doctor?"

"That he had?"

"Oh, yes, you could say that," Lestrade chortled. "The man in the sketch is none other than Chatter Ali, Beechum's Indian manservant!"

"His own *khitmutgar*!" I exclaimed.

"Exactly! Do you wish to take a look? We have him in a holding room." Lestrade stood up and I followed him into the hall and along a whitewashed passage with a line of doors on each side. "He's in the first one here," said Lestrade as he slid back a panel in the upper part of the door.

I glanced through and saw a small fellow with the dark skin, eyes, and hair typical of the Indian subcontinent. "What has he said?"

"Precious little," said Lestrade shrugging. "He is very quiet, almost inscrutable. He strikes me as rather sly."

"But can he explain his presence at Covent Garden?"

Lestrade snorted in amusement. "Indeed. He asserts that Beechum sent him round to the theatre with a message for Mrs. Taylor."

"Beechum and Taylor knew each other?"

"Perhaps, but that's of little importance, Doctor," said Lestrade with a shrug. "The important thing is that he freely admits he was there."

"And his message?"

"He claims that Beechum instructed him to tell her five words: 'He is in London. Beware.'"

"That is certainly suggestive."

The inspector snorted. "There is nothing in writing, mind you, Doctor, so we have no proof that such a dispatch ever existed. Only Ali's testimony, for what it's worth, since the sender of the supposed message is himself dead by Ali's hand."

"Allegedly."

Lestrade shook his head. "It will be proven soon enough, I assure you."

"And the pair of star sapphires?"

"Mark my words, Doctor. Ali will tell us where he hid them presently. Or he will regret it."

"And does Mr. Ali smoke Indian lunkahs?"

Lestrade stared at me in consternation. "Whatever does that matter, Doctor?"

"It would be most indicative if he did partake in tobacco,

considering the evidence at the scene."

He shrugged. "I smelled nothing on him, but it's entirely irrelevant. The other signs are incontrovertible. Anyone could have dropped that cheroot. Don't let yourself be distracted by red herrings, Doctor."

I frowned in silent disagreement with this conclusion, for I knew you, Holmes, would be unhappy with such an unexplained loose end. Meekly congratulating the inspector, I turned my steps towards home. Nevertheless, as I walked, I turned the events over in my mind. Lestrade had *a priori* determined Mr. Ali's guilt and therefore disregarded the man's testimony out of hand. However, what if there was, in fact, some other party that sought to harm both Josephine Taylor and Harold Beechum? Lestrade had failed to abide by your maxim, Holmes. He had not yet eliminated the possibility that Mr. Ali was telling the truth.

As I drew closer to home, I grew more and more concerned that Lestrade had, as in the case of poor Miss Flora Millar, arrested the wrong individual upon circumstantial evidence and thin testimony. If I was correct, a grave miscarriage of justice was about to transpire.[88] However, how was I to prevent it? If only you were here, Holmes, you would know the sure path forward.

As you are not, and having brought you up-to-date regarding these matters, I shall bring this first letter to a close, and start fresh with my continued observations in the morn.

§

13 Earl's Terrace, *Aug. 8th, 1891*

My Dear Holmes:

In my mind, I can hear you berating me for my faulty investigation to date. My only defence, my friend, is that I am but a simple physician and biographer. I may have lived with you for seven years, and witnessed your methods upon many an occasion, but I have never attempted to train myself systematically, as you have, in the arts of observation and deduction.

When I returned home the previous night, I found my wife resting in the large armchair in our cheery sitting room. She was engaged in a bit of needlework, and looked up at my entrance.

"Good evening, dear," she said. She coughed gently into her lacy handkerchief. "Did you find anything of interest for your report?"

"I did indeed." I explained to her everything that I have included to you in my first letter.

"So you believe that the lunkah is of some significance?"

"It would be a monstrous coincidence otherwise. For an Indian cigar to turn up at the scene of the murder, when all other signs point to an Indian connection?"

"So what will you do now?"

I thought about this for a minute. I strongly considered going around to Baker Street to see if either Mrs. Taylor or Mr. Beechum would have an entry in your now-abandoned index. Surely, it should be put to some use in your perpetual absence, Holmes. I hoped Mrs. Hudson was dusting it from time to time. However, there was perhaps a simpler method. I plucked Lawson's blue-covered volume from a line of reference books that I kept on the shelf behind my writing desk. It was the prior year's edition, but I hoped it would still serve. Turning over the pages rapidly, I came upon the first entry and read it aloud to Mary:

"Beechum, Harold. Formerly, Captain, 12th Gurkha Rifles. Commission resigned 1850. Born Manchester, 1826. Educated Eton and Oxford. Unmarried. Served in the Second Anglo-Sikh War. Founded Beechum Trading Company, 1851. Clubs: The Carlton, The Savage, The Anglo-Indian."

"So he was an Army officer?" said Mary. "I wonder if he would have known my father?"

"Perhaps," I replied nodding. "I certainly would have liked to. It is a great tragedy that his apoplexy took him before I could meet him."

"He would have loved you, John," she said, with a catch in her voice. "You are both so alike in your kindness. And the entry for Mrs. Taylor? What does it say?"

I flipped ahead in the book. "Taylor, Josephine, nee Beaulieu. Born Lyon, France, 1841. Married Rodney Taylor, 1860. Trained Académie d'Opéra, Paris. Soprano. Prima donna, Royal Opera. Notable roles: Violetta Valéry, *La Traviata*; Marguerite de Valois, *Les Huguenots*; The Queen of the Night, *Die Zauberflöte*; Antonia, *Les Contes d'Hoffmann*."

Mary shook her head. "I fail to see the connection, John. However, I am afraid my head is rather foggy. I am certain you will find it soon enough."

I glanced up at her in alarm. "Are you well, my dear?"

She shook her head. "A bit of a fever. I think it is nothing more than a little summer cold."

"You should rest!" I exclaimed. "I will give you some extract of willow bark and put you to bed immediately! It was thoughtless of me to burden you with my troubles."

She smiled wanly. "Nonsense, John. Your happiness is of the utmost importance to me. Nevertheless, perhaps when this is over we can take a lengthier vacation than our prior jaunts? I have always longed to do a cruise upon the Nile. On the way, I would like to stop and pay my respects at Mr. Holmes' final resting place. He was most important to you, and hence also to me. Afterwards, we could sojourn for a day or two and take the airs at Davos Platz?"

"Whatever you desire, my dear!" I replied without a moment's hesitation, though the thought of facing once more the great abyss at Reichenbach filled my mind with unease.

After Mary was tucked into bed, I turned my thoughts back to the mystery at hand. If Chatter Ali was to be believed, Mr. Beechum and Mrs. Taylor not only knew each other, but also had some unfathomable connection that led to their demises. But what was the connection? As I mulled it over, my eyes drifted down the page and alighted upon the entry for her husband, which read:

Taylor, Rodney. Formerly, Major, 12th Gurkha Rifles. Commission resigned 1850. Born, Southampton, 1825. Educated Eton and Oxford. Married Josephine Beaulieu, 1860. Served in the Second Anglo-Sikh War. Silent partner, Beechum Trading Company. Clubs: The Baldwin, The Lansdowne, The Anglo-Indian.

So Josephine Beaulieu was fourteen years his junior, I thought to myself, before realizing the implications of what I had just read. Harold Beechum was not connected to Mrs. Taylor herself, but rather to her deceased husband, Rodney! Moreover, the connections were numerous and sundry: they had been schoolmates, officers together in the Indian Army, and had resigned their commissions at the same time. They had founded an important company together, and they belonged to the same club. My next step was clear. I needed to gain entrance to the Anglo-Indian Club.

After checking on my still-sleeping wife, whose fever had finally broken, even if she first had drenched the sheets, the next thing I did the following morn was go round to the local telegraph office. There I composed a request to be sent to my old friend Colonel Hayter of the 66th Foot down at his house near Reigate. I returned home and before I could even finish my breakfast, there was a ring of the bell. A messenger boy handed me the reply:

My pleasure, old boy. No favour is too large. You will be expected at the A-I Club at one o'clock. My deepest sympathy at the passing of the good Mr. Holmes. He was the finest of men.
– Hayter

I needed to wipe a smote of dust from my eye before I could proceed. I glanced at my pocket watch and cursed that I still had four hours to wait before I could continue my investigation. I used that time wisely to bring my letter to you, Holmes, up to date.

The Palace of Westminster bell had not yet completed its chimes when I presented myself at St. James's Square and knocked upon the door of the club. I offered my calling card, and the footman who opened the door was plainly expecting me. He showed me up the stairs to a sizeable and luxurious room with large windows overlooking the greenery of the park. As could be found in any such gentleman's club, a gathering of comfortable arm-chairs, as well as assorted tables for card-playing, were in evidence. However, the similarities ended there, for the main room was outlandishly decorated with trophies from what were plainly some of the Empire's finest shots. Upon the walls, I could see the mounted heads of cheetahs, baboons, and even an elephant. A magnificent specimen of Bengal tiger seemed to follow my movements with uncannily real glass eyes.

As I moved through the room, I glanced over towards the cards table, where four men were engaged in a tense game of whist. At that moment, one of the players looked up at me, and it seemed that his piercing regard shone with recognition. He was an elderly man, with a thin, projecting nose, a high, bald forehead, and a huge grizzled moustache. I did not know him, so I continued upon my mission, and when I glanced back, his eyes had returned to the game. I finally sidled up to the deep mahogany bar, and ordered a brandy from the man pouring drinks. When he finished adding water from the gasogene and slid the glass over to me, I returned the favour with two silver crowns.

He eyed my offer but did not take them. "Drinks are on-the-house, sir," said the man, respectfully.

"For other services, then."

His hand lingered above the coins, obscuring them from view of any other patrons, but did not take them. "Such as?"

"Information."

He cocked his head. "Ah, well, that depends on what exactly

you wish to know. The price for such a thing is on a variable scale."

"I wish to know about Major Rodney Taylor," I said, using the man's former title.

The man's eyes narrowed. "You a reporter?"

"Nothing of the kind, I assure you. Merely a concerned citizen. I am assisting Inspector Lestrade of the Criminal Investigation Department." I hoped that I managed to conceal a blush at this small embellishment of my role to date.

The mention of Scotland Yard brought the man to attention, though I noted that the coins had also vanished. "What can I tell you, sir?"

"You are aware, I presume, that Major Taylor's widow was killed two nights ago?" He nodded silently. "I understand that the major himself died late last year. Do you know what killed him?"

"That's no secret, sir," said the man, his shoulders relaxing. "It was an undulant fever."

"So, there was nothing suspicious about his death? No mutterings by members of the club?"

He shook his head forcefully. "No, sir. Nothing of the kind."

"Have you also heard any recent news about Captain Beechum?"

"I know he hasn't yet arrived at the club today, nor yesterday at all, which is a mite unusual," said the man with a shrug. "But nothing more."

"Did you know that Major Taylor and Captain Beechum both served in the 12th Gurkha Rifles?" He nodded, so I continued. "Are there any other members of the club who served with them?"

He considered this for a moment. "Not at present, sir."

"But in the past?"

He nodded slowly. "Colonel Bloomsbury is 5th Bengal Lancers himself.[89] But I've heard that his father served in the 12th Rifles."

"Who is Colonel Bloomsbury?"

He motioned with a nod of his head. "The gentleman sitting at the table underneath Willie." When he saw the look of confusion in my eyes, he clarified to whom he referred. "The elephant."

I thanked the barkeeper for his assistance and glanced over towards the poor beast, where I found the man in question. I estimated that he was at least fifty years of age, with skin browned by the sun. His spine was ramrod stiff and his deeply lined face bore an expression of authority. His white hair was impeccably groomed with Macassar oil. He glanced up as I approached, a questioning expression in his brilliant blue eyes.

"Colonel Bloomsbury, sir, I am Dr John Watson, formerly of the Berkshires. It is a pleasure to make your acquaintance."

The muggy summer air in the upstairs room must have been approaching ninety upon the thermometer. Although the overhead fans, which appeared to have been constructed from native shields, desultorily spun around, the club was rather stifling with the strong smoke of numerous Indian cigars. However, not a drop of sweat could be seen on the Colonel's forehead.

He peered at me closely, such that I wondered if he was near-sighted and too proud to wear glasses. "Do I know you, Dr Watson? Your face is not familiar, I am afraid. Are you a recent member of the club? I am in London on a twelve month leave from a prolonged term of service in India, and have yet to meet all of the new boys."

"No, but I had a few questions that I wished to ask you. I hope it is not an inconvenience?"

"Not at all. I was just about to have a spot of tiffin. Would you care to join me?" he waived to the seat across from him. "You were in India?" he asked.

I shook my head. "Afghanistan."

"Even worse. Have you seen action?"

I instinctively touched my shoulder. "Maiwand."

"Ah, a bad business that," said he, a tone of respect in his voice. "But what can I do for you, Dr Watson?"

"I wondered if you were acquainted with Major Taylor and Captain Beechum, formerly of the 12th Gurkha Rifles?"

A series of fine lines appeared around his eyes as they tightened. "Solely by reputation."

"I was informed that your father may have served with them?"

He nodded slowly and studied me curiously. "That is correct."

"Major Taylor died last year, but his wife was more recently slain."

"I read the papers, Doctor. I could hardly fail to follow the story. It was quite lurid."

"And are you also abreast in regards to Captain Beechum's fate?"

He sighed heavily. "I assume from the tone of your question that he is dead."

The colonel's statement took me by surprise. "Why would you think that?"

"Because I know who killed them."

I gaped at the man in astonishment. "What? Why have you not gone to the police, sir?"

Bloomsbury shook his head. "I should clarify. I know why they were killed. But not the precise identity of the assassin. And in any case, he is not likely to strike again. Nor ever be caught."

"I don't understand."

"In some way, Doctor, you could claim that I shoulder some measure of the blame. For I should have warned them. But Beechum was a fool and Josephine even worse! Parading the stones about in public! And how was I to know the precise date when they would finally strike?"

"They?"

He smiled wanly. "I am afraid that I am telling the story the end ways around. If you would lend me your patience, I will start at the beginning."

"You have my undivided attention."

"Please understand that I only heard this story from my father's lips. I have no direct knowledge of its accuracy. But I see no reason why he would not have told me the truth in its entirety. My father was Lieutenant Clinton Bloomsbury. As you know, he served under Taylor and Beechum. They were stationed at Mayapore, in the northwest frontier. The year was 1849. It was a terrible time in India, those years leading up to the Mutiny. Do you know, Doctor, the tale of the dacoits?"

"The Thuggee?" said I, solemnly. "Only rumours and legends."

He shook his head grimly. "They were no legend. The dacoits ran rampant over the countryside. No traveller was safe. They would pose as humble pilgrims, joining a caravan for dozens, even hundreds of miles, before finding the perfect spot to strike. When they were done, they would carefully dispose of the bodies, and the caravan would vanish, as if it never existed. Estimates of the death toll are imprecise at best, but I have heard it confidently stated that it was at least two hundred thousand. They were a terrible plague on the land.

"One day, Taylor, Beechum, and my father received orders from Lucknow, penned by the hand of General Sleeman himself. Years earlier, the general had captured one of the dacoits, and the villain was eventually persuaded to turn King's evidence. Armed with this knowledge, General Sleeman and the Thuggee Department vigorously suppressed these cultists, hanging the chiefs and imprisoning the others in Jubbulpore. But some small bands held out, and it took years to track them all down. It seemed that the general had just learned of a group hiding at a temple deep in the jungle of the Sivalik Hills. The general's orders were to seek out this temple and subdue any dacoits they encountered, by whatever means necessary.

"The three of them set out from Mayapore with a small squad of sepoys under their command. They passed through Bhurtee and began to make their way along the steep banks of the Ganges.[90] After five exceedingly difficult weeks they finally located the temple. It was plainly an ancient place, frequented for certain dark rituals, but abandoned for most of the year, its altars and ornately-carved pinnacles an abode for only rhesus monkeys, vipers, and venomous spiders.

"Despite its remote locale, where few eyes would ever gaze upon it, the ancient masons did not shirk their duty to the temple's foul goddess. Impressive stonework friezes ran all about the shrine's inner wall, depicting images of wanton destruction. Their sepoys cowering outside, the three soldiers climbed the steps to the central part of the temple, moving amongst a forest of thick stone pillars, into the unholy shrine itself. There, the light of their torches reflected off a pantheon of strange demons, with monstrously coloured faces and eyes staring blindly from their dark niches.

"To the soldiers' eternal surprise – and I will say, eventual dismay – they also found under that roof of carved bones and skulls a magnificent treasure: a golden life-sized statue of Kali, that terrible goddess of destruction venerated by the dacoits. From her shiny neck hung a necklace of real skulls, bits of rotting flesh still attached. Her multitude of arms held a series of weapons as well as the wooden head of a decapitated man, its features plainly carved to resemble an Englishman. Her eyes were made from two enormous star sapphires, while the third eye upon her forehead, the *anja*, was nothing less than a great and flawless ruby. Each stone would have easily fetched at least twenty thousand pounds.[91] As my father told the story, he, Taylor, and Beechum agreed to split the gems equally and melt down the gold. Taylor and Beechum each took one of the sapphires, while my father claimed the ruby. Once his term in India was up, he brought the stone back to London with him. As did Beechum and Taylor with their respective prizes, as surely you know by now."

The colonel paused for a moment in order to light a cigar. I carefully noted that it was a lunkah similar to the one found at Covent Garden. Having shook off my amazement at the mention of this colossal sum, I seized the opportunity to ask a question. "May I see the ruby?"

He waved the wax vesta until it went out and dropped it in a nearby tray. From the way that he winced, I wondered if he had held it too long and burned his fingertips. "I am afraid not," Bloomsbury replied with a shake of his head. "Even I have never seen it. You see, Doctor, my father became convinced that those stones were cursed. Horrific mishaps followed in his footsteps. Therefore, he eventually had the ruby shipped off to Amsterdam, where it was cut into smaller pieces and sold off. It has been dispersed throughout Europe, possibly even the world, and can no longer bring any ruin to my family. However, as must be plain now, the same cannot be said for Beechum and Taylor. They should have heeded my father's advice many years ago. Plainly, the curse has finally caught up with them."

"Surely you are not suggesting a supernatural agency?"

He snorted in wry amusement. "Nothing of the sort, Doctor. I need not invent some divine force to explain the evils of men. As my father, Beechum, and Taylor were stripping the statue of its jewels and gold, the dacoits returned. Along with their small squad of sepoys, they took shelter behind the low wall of the temple. It was a close thing, with heavy losses on both sides, but eventually the dacoits were beaten back. Only a handful of sepoys made their way back with them to Mayapore. I understand that one man eventually attached himself to Beechum as a manservant. Unfortunately, for my father's comrades, not all of the dacoits were killed in the skirmish. At least one survived. And that man has plainly followed the tracks of the sacred jewels for many long years. Only now has he finally made his way to the streets of London and reclaimed his cult's lost treasures."

"How can you be certain of this?"

He shrugged. "What do you know of the dacoit method of assassination, Doctor?"

I shook my head. "Nothing."

"There were two techniques that they primarily employed.

The first was the garrotte, fashioned from their *rumal*."

"Their yellow head-scarfs," said I, translating aloud.

"Precisely," said Bloomsbury, nodding. "They were so notorious for their quick and quiet strangulations that they became known as the *phansigars*, or noose-operators."

My mind immediately flashed to the terrible death of Mrs. Taylor. "And the other?"

"They would stab the victims in the eye, and then throw the bodies in a nearby river or well. Tens of thousands of poor souls met their fates in this fashion."

"You horrify me," I exclaimed. I could hardly believe Colonel Bloomsbury's fantastic tale. It was like something out of a Collins novel.

"Now do you see why I failed to go to the police after Josephine Taylor's death? All I have is an appalling tale. But how would this help catch the assassin? He is surely on his way back to India by now, the sapphires securely in his clutches."

"But if the assassin could discover the names of Taylor and Beechum, are you not concerned that he will next go after your father?"

The colonel shook his head sadly. "They are too late for that. A greater power than Kali claimed him many years ago."

"You then? Your own safety must be a concern."

He shrugged unconcernedly. "Perhaps. Though my father took especial care to let everyone know that he had broken up and sold the ruby. I can scarcely credit that a dacoit assassin, who would have had innumerable opportunities to seek his revenge upon me while I was stationed in his home country, would strike me down now that I have returned to merry old England."

I could think of nothing else to ask the colonel, and he took this pause as a sign that our conversation had come to a conclusion. Bloomsbury pushed back his chair and slowly rose to his feet. "I am afraid that I have some other places to be, Doctor Watson. However, if I can be of any further assistance, you may call upon me at the Langham."

I thanked him for his time and watched as he jerkily moved towards the stairs. He was a cool customer, for certs. Nevertheless, I was convinced that he had withheld some portion of the story, and something about the man struck me as wrong. He was hardly the only man in London to smoke an Indian lunkah, but his possible connection to the crime was clear. Could it be a coincidence that the supposed Thuggee assassin happened to return to London concurrently with the Colonel's leave from India? Or was Bloomsbury the man that Beechum was attempting to warn Josephine Taylor about?

If only you could have been here to listen to his tale, Holmes, you would know in an instant what to make of it. However, Lestrade would never believe me. If I were to accuse the Colonel and, in so doing, suggest that Lestrade had arrested the wrong man, I would need incontrovertible proof.

Before I departed the Anglo-Indian Club, I swore that not another moment should have elapsed before I have done all that a man can possibly do to touch the core of the mystery. I asked myself: 'What would Holmes do?' What was the line of least resistance, which you so often avowed was the opening move for every investigation? Then I had it. I knew exactly what my next steps must be. I would take a leaf from your own book, Holmes, and mimic the actions you once took on behalf of a King. In pursuit of a higher cause, I would break the law.

You will not be surprised, Holmes, to find that, upon my return home, my wife was less than enthusiastic about my plan. I began by explaining to her what I had learned from Colonel Bloomsbury.

When my recitation was complete, she sighed in dismay. "With all this talk of cursed jewels, it again makes me happy again that Mr. Small threw the Agra treasure in the Thames."

"His selfish action was my selfish gain."

She brought her fingers to her lips. "Of course, I do still have the six fine pearls from the gold coronet, John. Do you think I should be cautious and dispose of them?"

I smiled and took her hands. "Ah, but our lives are blessed, are they not, Mary? For we have each other. No such scourge will ever bother us."

"But are you really going to break into the colonel's rooms? Think of the possible consequences, John. If you are arrested, your career would be ruined."

"I can think of no other way," said I, with a heavy voice.

"And if you are correct, my dear, and the Colonel discovers you in his suite, I fear for your safety."

"Do not forget, Mary, that I have been in some tight spots before in Holmes' company. Whenever he anticipated danger, he made certain to remind me to bring along my service revolver. You may be assured that I intend to do so tonight."

"But how will you know when to attempt your entry?"

I had considered this on the hansom ride back to Kensington. "I shall wait in the lobby until he goes out."

She shook her head. "But if he sees you, your plan will be ruined."

"I could disguise myself. I have often witnessed Holmes employ such methods. I could don a beard, or perhaps a pair of coloured pince-nez?"

"Ha!" Mary snorted in wry amusement. "Mr. Holmes had both natural talents in that direction, as well as some time practicing upon the stage, if his stories are to be believed. You have neither."

"What do you suggest?"

She studied me for a moment. "How much are you willing to sacrifice to see this through, John?"

"There are limits, of course. I would not see you put in harm's way."

"But everything else is fair game?"

"I suppose so," I slowly agreed.

And that is how I found myself, twenty minutes later, completely barren of face and sitting in a cab on my way to the Langham Hotel. I am not proud to admit that, at the last minute, I could not do the deed myself and was forced to hand the blade over to Mary in order to complete the removal

THE TREASURY OF SHERLOCK HOLMES

of the modest moustache that I had worn since my days at Netley. Before I departed, I glanced in the mirror and realized the truth in my wife's observation that sometimes the best disguise is not to add a distinctive feature, but rather to eliminate a characteristic one. I scarcely recognized myself. I was certain that, with the further effect of a complete change of clothes, the poor-sighted Colonel would never manage to identify me as the man he had met in the club earlier today.

I had not long to wait in the lobby before I spotted Colonel Bloomsbury walking down the stairs, with his slow high-stepping gait. Unlike at the Club, where I presumed he was too proud to show a hint of weakness, he supported himself with a heavy walking stick, its tip weighted with lead. I suspected that it could double as a formidable weapon. I waited a moment to ensure that he was not about to turn around, and then sprang over to the front desk and asked to speak with the hotel's manager. Two minutes later, I was standing in the small office of Mr. Huntsinger, where I presented my card. His sharp eyes glanced over my monogramed black medical bag, the bulge in the side of my top hat where my stethoscope was stowed, and the dark mark of silver nitrate that I had applied to my forefinger. He even sniffed once, and I am certain he could smell the iodoform that I had dashed upon my sleeve. If he had any doubts as to the veracity of my profession, I am certain that these signs set his mind at ease. Huntsinger asked my business at the hotel, and I explained that I had been rung up to do a private consultation with Colonel Bloomsbury. He informed me that the Colonel had just gone out and I should return at another time.

"Perhaps I could trouble you to allow me to wait in his room?"

The manager shook his head. "I am afraid that would be against the hotel's policies, Dr Watson."

"I see," said I, dejectedly. "That is a shame, for the Colonel was most adamant as to the urgency of his problem and I am a rather busy man. My stock of mercuric chloride is also rather low. Still, I fully understand that regulations come before the wishes of the guests." I spun around as if to depart.

Huntsinger looked pained. "Perhaps if you could tell me the nature of the Colonel's issue."

I frowned. "In confidence?"

"Of course, sir."

"Very well. Colonel Bloomsbury requires treatment for the Infinite Malady." From the expression upon Huntsinger's face it was plain he did not recognize this term. I cleared by throat. "Cupid's Disease," I said in a low voice.[92]

The manager's eyes widened in scandalized understanding. Within five minutes, he had personally showed me into Bloomsbury's rooms using the master key, and then had departed quietly. Once alone, I looked about the opulently appointed suite. I could not be certain how much longer Colonel Bloomsbury would absent himself from the hotel. He may have gone across town for a leisurely dinner, or simply stepped around the corner for an additional supply of lunkahs. I would need to be fast. I had already asked myself where a man such as the colonel would hide two items of inestimable value. A prompt and ready military man such as Bloomsbury would shun the obvious spots, such as the room-safe or beneath the bed covers. Accustomed to camp life, the colonel would require a receptacle that he could snatch up in a moment's notice.

Therefore, I immediately strode over to the writing desk, where the located a battered tin dispatch box with his name painted upon the lid. Throwing it open, I was gratified to find that my supposition was correct. Carefully wrapped in a white handkerchief were two enormous round sapphires, each with six-rayed stars shining luminously. There was little doubt of the provenance of such a pair of unique jewels.

Only one thing remained to do. The Langham was a thoroughly modern hotel, and each room was equipped with a candlestick telephone. I had a call routed to Scotland Yard, and within minutes, I had the relief of hearing Inspector Lestrade's voice on the line. I hurriedly explained that I had recovered the sapphires, and requested that he meet me immediately at the Langham, Room 402. Lestrade spluttered for a moment in speechless indignation, but like the good man that he was, he soon agreed to come round with all haste. I reckoned it would take him fifteen minutes to race straight up Regent Street to the hotel.

With my stomach a nervous bundle, but a fixed purpose, I sat in the darkened room and waited with solemn patience for the return of Colonel Bloomsbury. I moved the desk-chair round to face the door, and fingered my service revolver. I had to assume that the colonel was similarly armed, but that I would have the measure of surprise. For unlike the episode at the stone hut beneath Black Tor, I had not carelessly thrown aside my tobacco stub, nor could I possibly credit the colonel with any preternatural powers of observation approaching yours, Holmes.

While it seemed far longer, from an occasional glimpse at my father's old pocket watch, I knew that only ten minutes had passed before I heard the turn of a key in the door. The door suddenly was thrown open and Colonel Bloomsbury stood before me, his Adams .450 service pistol pointed at my heart. Although his hand trembled slightly, I had little doubt that at such a short range, he could hardly fail to miss. My gun was also trained upon him, but if I pulled my trigger, he would do the same.

"Good evening, Dr Watson," said he, amiably. "Mr. Huntsinger was kind enough to inform me that you had been shown into my rooms."

I inwardly cursed myself for this mental oversight, and knew that my only hope lay in sufficiently delaying him until Lestrade could arrive. "The game is up, Colonel Bloomsbury."

He shook his head. "I think not, sir. You see, I have just now surprised an armed thief in my room. Tragically, I was forced to shoot him in self-defence. The inquest will surely clear me of any wrong-doing."

"May I then ask a question before I die?"

He shrugged. "I would fain send you to the undiscovered country with your terrible curiosity unsatisfied. Even if such unwarranted prying was directly responsible for your demise."

"When you related your tale earlier today, you neglected to disclose your father's rank when he, Major Taylor, and Captain Beechum set out for the Kali Temple?"

He smiled maniacally, exposing a row of brown-stained teeth. "He was a lieutenant."

"Ah, strange for a man of his age to be their junior, is it not? For you are only ten years younger than Taylor and Beechum. So your father must have been at least ten years their senior."

He stared at me for a moment and then laughed. "What I told you was the honest truth, Doctor. To a certain point. However, you have hit upon the key point. My father was a brave man. He was a sergeant in the 5th Bengal Lancers. During the Battle of Mudki, he saved the life of General Hardinge, and for this action was promoted to lieutenant and transferred to the 12th Rifles. However, because he had come up from the ranks, those fine gentlemen, Taylor and Beechum, never considered him their equal. Thus, they had no qualms in betraying him as they did.

"Upon their return to England, my father was also a silent partner in Beechum's firm. Nevertheless, the two of them soon conspired to cheat him out of everything, while they multiplied their ill-gotten wealth a hundred-fold. My father used the proceeds from the Kali ruby to fight them in the courts, albeit to no avail. He died penniless, but not before he spent his last shilling purchasing a commission for me. I went out to India and joined his old regiment, but I never forgot my hatred for Beechum and Taylor. Sadly, Taylor died before I could enact my revenge. However, his beloved wife served equally well. All that remained was to arrange it so that it would appear as if a rouge dacoit was responsible for the murders, and from what I have read in the papers, it seems as if Scotland

Yard has obliged by arresting poor Chatter Ali." He gazed at me peculiarly. "But I admit to being curious why did you not believe my tale, Doctor?"

"Because I could tell that you were ill, Colonel."

He frowned. "Whatever are you talking about?"

"The symptoms are subtle, but readily apparent when you look closely for them. Your constricted pupils, the lightning pains in your fingertips, your jerky, high-stepping gait. Do you also have paroxysms of intense pain in your eyes?" He shook his head in angry denial. "You have tabes dorsalis, Colonel.[93] It is causing a softening of your brain, making you do things your personality would have once never considered. You must seek treatment immediately before the changes become permanent."

He sneered at me. "My father instructed me to always heed a doctor's advice. And I will certainly do so, just as soon as I have tied up these unfortunate loose ends," he concluded, cocking back the hammer of his pistol.

Nevertheless, I had stalled him long enough. Before he could pull the trigger, he felt the cold muzzle of a Webley Metropolitan pressed against his temple. I sagged in relief at the sound of Lestrade's strident tones. "Drop the gun, Colonel. I think it is high time that you and I have a little chat down at Scotland Yard."

When Lestrade was done securing Bloomsbury with a pair of steel handcuffs, I handed him the recovered jewels. He thanked me gruffly, and pushed his prisoner towards the door. Before he departed, however, Lestrade turned to me with a sly grin. "By the way, Doctor, if you don't mind my saying so, you look rather preposterous without your moustache. Mr. Holmes would get a good laugh if only he could see you now."

§

I suppose that is very true. Once I returned home, I found that Mary had turned in early. Therefore, I had only you,

Holmes, to tell of my small triumph. I sat at my writing desk, took up my pen, and – over the course of the next few days – finished setting down these final lines, all the while considering the pains and the pride with which I had composed them. But now that they are complete, there is no recipient to whom to send them. I suppose I will simply file them away in my yearbook for 1891, which is otherwise barren, excepting only my sad notes upon the final fall of Moriarty.

Neither Mrs. Taylor nor Mr. Beechum had specified the disposition of the sapphires in their wills, and as they were obtained in a less-than-legal fashion, I have on good authority that the British Government appropriated them. I doubted that there were any plans to restore them to the temple of Kali, but I never heard of their ultimate fate. As to the case itself, Lestrade took the public credit, though I had my own private satisfaction that I could employ your methods, Holmes, with some small measure of success.

I hope the powerful engine of your restless mind has finally found peace, my friend. I know that I have. But now I must check upon my dear Mary and ensure that she is swiftly recovering from her little summer cold.[94]

Very sincerely yours,
JOHN H. WATSON.

§

THE ADVENTURE OF THE SUNKEN INDIAMAN

W hen I review my notes for the year 1897, I find that it was that summer when my friend dealt with one of the most fantastic cases of his career. Mr. Sherlock Holmes had a well-known aversion to being separated from London for any significant length of time. Certainly, he travelled into the English countryside from time to time, such as when he camped beneath the tors of Dartmoor, or during our recent hikes amongst the prehistoric earthworks of the Cornish peninsula.

He was also known, upon occasion, to cross the Channel in order to help the French government, such as when he foiled the schemes of Baron Maupertins, or when he arrested the assassin Huret.[95] Moreover, of course, it cannot be denied that he once travelled to the New World in his days before setting up practice in Montague Street.

However, any longer voyages were strictly out of the question, save only his hiatus from active consultation from 1891 to 1894. Therefore, despite the many places which have claimed to have merited a visit from my friend, I am afraid that any such accounts in which Mr. Sherlock Holmes appears in various exotic locales, such as a California mining camp, or the islands of the Caribbean, are strictly products of a tale-teller's overactive imagination.[96] The case in question is perhaps the most vivid example of both Holmes' distaste for leaving London, and the peculiar nature and limitations of his inherent curiosity.

On the day in question, I was sitting in my armchair in front of the cold grate at Baker Street, for the air outside was already warm and steamy. Holmes was engaged in vociferously pasting newspaper extracts into his commonplace books, and I was half-heartedly perusing the morning edition of the *Times*. A sudden irritable exhalation from Holmes triggered me to glance in his direction.

After a moment's study, I elected to have a bit of merriment with my friend. "You are correct, Holmes, that this heat seems to be sapping the vigour of the commonplace London criminal."

Holmes' head suddenly snapped up and his piercing grey eyes locked onto me. "By what means…" he exclaimed, before mastering his surprise and clenching his thin lips together. He glared at me for a moment, and then began to laugh heartedly.

"Touché, Watson. I must be on my guard against further displays of this pawky humour of yours. I assume you have perceived that I would prefer to be engaged upon a case, rather than this admittedly necessary, but unquestionably tedious, docketing and arranging of papers?"

"You are not the only one who can harness his powers of observation, Holmes. Though, to be fair, I will admit that the task is far more straightforward when your subject is one whose habits you are already most familiar."

"And when the broadsheet in your hand is so lacking in lurid tales that the social outings of our illustrious heir royal are the lead story, one's case is complete. Well, you are absolutely spot-on, Watson. It is possible, however, that I may have something better before very many minutes have passed, for the unfamiliar tread upon our steps indicates a new client, or I am very much mistaken."

Holmes was correct, of course, and after a sharp tap at the door, he opened it to reveal a man of some seventy-odd years. Our visitor was rather thin and pale, and when he removed his top hat, unruly wisps of white hair stuck up from his balding pate. His face was heavily lined, but his piercing blue eyes were still full of life.

"Mr. Holmes?" the man inquired. "My name is Fletcher Hatley and I..."

The man was unable to complete his sentence, however, for Holmes held up his hand and waved Hatley into the basket-chair. After introducing the two of us, Holmes indicated that the man should proceed. "I presume you come upon a case, Mr. Hatley, and if you will be so good as to explain what precisely you have lost?"

"That's just the thing, Mr. Holmes," began the man, before he paused in surprise, his eyes widening. "But how could you know that I have lost something?"

Holmes smiled. "When a man enters my rooms wearing a well-cut suit of the finest materials, with a golden chain connecting to his pocket watch, and yet displays a shocking amount of dust upon his shirt cuffs and trouser knees, I deduce that he has spent his morning engaged in looking through rarely-visited parts of his home prior rushing over to Baker Street before his valet was able to correct the damage."

The man looked down in order to inspect the areas indicated by my friend and then smiled ruefully. "They said you were a man of careful observations, Mr. Holmes, and I see they weren't wrong. You are just the man I need. No one else could solve this mystery."

"Pray proceed," said Holmes, pressing his fingers together and his eyelids drooping with interest.

"I don't know what your professional charges are, Mr. Holmes, but I am prepared to engage your services for whatever time is needed until you can tell me what is missing from my library."

Holmes' grey eyes opened and his brow furrowed as he fixed Hatley with a frown. "Do you mean to say that you do not know for what I am supposed to be searching?"

Our guest nodded his head. "That's the peculiar thing about this matter, Mr. Holmes. I know that I have been burgled. I even know the name of the thief. However, I don't know what he took. I spent the morning searching the room myself before I thought of your name. I have read that you excel in these sorts of things. And so I hurried over here in a brougham before another moment passed."

"But why have you not gone to the police?" I interjected.

He shook his head. "I have been burgled once before, Dr Watson some dozen years ago. I recall having to fill out a report, upon which I was required to list all of the missing items. I assumed that Scotland Yard would not be much interested this time until I could tell them what precisely had been taken."

Holmes smiled and stood up. "I have nothing else of particular interest on hand at the moment, Mr. Hatley. Perhaps you would be so good as to explain further as we travel back to the scene of the crime?"

As Holmes moved over towards the coat rack, I stood and moved close to him. "It does not sound very promising, Holmes," said I, in a low voice. "I wonder if I should come?"

He turned to me with a look of astonishment upon his face. "On the contrary, Watson, this is most singular. Can you recall the last time we knew the identity of the felon, but not the nature of the crime? I wager that you would be amiss to sit this one out."

I nodded in diffident agreement, took up my coat and hat, and followed the two men out the door. At the curb, we climbed into the brougham that Hatley had waiting, which he directed to return to Hamilton Terrace. As we made the short drive, Hatley proceeded to elaborate upon the events that had transpired at his abode.

"I am a bachelor, and have only a modest staff of servants

to keep my townhouse in working order. The building is a fine one, which I inherited from my grandfather, who made a fortune around the turn of the past century in trade with the Far East. As such, I am not obligated to follow a profession myself, but instead have occupied my time with the writing of several historical works of small note. You may have perhaps seen my biography of Clive, *Raj of India*?[97] No? Well, it is not germane to the matter at hand, I suppose, save that the only items of significant worth in my house can be found in the library, where I spend the bulk of my days and evenings. I have a particular organization system for my notes, and therefore, when I am working on a book, the maids are forbidden from entering the room until it is complete, for fear that they will accidentally put the papers into disarray. To ensure that this rule is followed, I am of the habit of locking the door behind me when I leave."

"Surely the butler also has a key?" I inquired.

He nodded. "Yes, however, Wooten has been with my family for many years, and his father before him. I have no doubts of his loyalty."

"But there is someone whose loyalties you doubt?"

"Indeed, Mr. Holmes, and I will come to that in a moment. Yesterday was a typical day, and I worked upon my upcoming biography of Marlborough, *Nothing Greater*, until eleven o'clock at night.[98] I locked the door behind me, and went to sleep. When I awoke this morning, I took my breakfast, and then went to the library in order to re-commence writing. Imagine my surprise when I opened the door and found my papers scattered about the floor!"

Holmes leaned forward, interest plain upon his face. "Were there any signs that the door had been forced?"

"No, Mr. Holmes, the thief did not enter via the door, but rather one of the casement windows, which are large enough to admit a man. These are never opened when I am working, for fear that a gust of wind will disturb my notes. But one was open all the same, and there was a muddy boot-print upon the sill."

"That should make identifying our man much easier," said I. "Holmes is most skilled in tracing footsteps."

"That is not the problem, Doctor," said Hatley. "I only wish to know what the man took. You see, after I closed the window, I spent the next hour or so gathering up the papers and putting them back in their proper order. When this task was complete, I realized that nothing was missing from my desk."

"Perhaps they simply wished to copy some element of your notes?" I speculated. "Were there any shreds from a pencil, or broken tips of lead?"

Hatley shook his head. "Nothing of the sort. And while I am proud of my writings, Dr Watson, there is nothing secret about them. Anyone could come to the same conclusions if they made some trips to the London Library and did a close reading of the proper documents."

"What else of value do you keep in the library, Mr. Hatley?" inquired Holmes.

He shrugged. "The books themselves, mainly. My grandfather accumulated a rather fine collection over the years. However, I spend most of my waking hours in the library, Mr. Holmes, and I know their spines well. After another hour of searching, I am prepared to swear that no tome appears to be missing."

Holmes smiled. "Fascinating. Your case interests me very much, Mr. Hatley."

"But who is the thief?" I asked.

"A moment, Watson," said Holmes, holding up his hand. "We are just now arriving upon the scene."

Mr. Hatley's home proved to be a detached three-story brick structure situated upon a pleasant road lined with mature yew trees. A small drive ran along the left side of the building to a recessed coach house, its doors ajar. Holmes was the first to exit the brougham and motioned for Hatley and me to remain upon the pavement. His hands clasped behind his back, Holmes carefully stepped around the house as he studied both the windows and the ground.

He finally looked up. "I take it, Mr. Hatley, that you suspect your coachman?"

Hatley smiled and nodded. "That is correct, Mr. Holmes. How did you know that Mr. Lewis was the only member of my staff who was absent this morning when I called them together?"

Holmes waved his hand. "The casement windows that you mention illuminating the library are upon the first floor; therefore, your burglar would have needed a method to reach them. There are no marks upon the ground to suggest the use of a ladder or stilts, but it is plain from the wheel-tracks that a coach was parked under this window for a period of time last night. Furthermore, you possess your own coach, and yet you hired a brougham to take you to Baker Street. The deduction is a simple one."

"Very good, Mr. Holmes. In fact, Mr. Lewis is the newest member of my staff. He joined us only six weeks ago, when the previous man took ill and could not continue in his position."

"That is most suggestive, sir. And did you have any other reason to suspect Mr. Lewis's intentions before this morning?"

Hatley shook his head. "At the time, it seemed rather innocent, but Mr. Lewis was always very interested in the exploits of my grandfather. He repetitively asked Wooten, and even myself as we drove places, to tell him stories about what my grandfather was like."

"I thought you said that he was a merchant of some kind?" I asked. "I mean no offense, Mr. Hatley, but that is rarely an occupation known for producing fascinating tales."

The man smiled. "Perhaps it will be clearer, Dr Watson, if you would be so kind as to step up to the library?"

He led through the front entrance and up the stairs, where he paused in front of a door in order to draw a key from his pocket and unlock it. He swung the door open and motioned for us to enter. I found myself in a large, handsomely-appointed room. It was panelled from floor to ceiling with dark mahogany shelves, which held a vast collection of leather-bound books, admixed with an impressive display of nautical tools and décor. Several paintings, each of a clipper ship abreast tall waves, interrupted the shelving. Several ledges held exquisite models of similar ships as did assorted side tables, which were also littered with mariner's astrolabes, compasses, and sextants. Finally, the room held four comfortable armchairs gathered about a marble fireplace, and a large writing desk covered in stacks of books and loose papers.

"Your grandfather was a sailor, I presume?" I ventured.

Hatley nodded. "He was a farm boy from Farnham until he ran away to Portsmouth and shipped out on the *Royal Captain*, an East Indiaman. After he caught a taste of the sea, there was no going back. With a degree of daring and a steady nerve, Nathanial Hatley worked his way up the chain of command until he had not only a captaincy, but was also owner of his private ship. He had a great deal of good fortune, and the *Feather* managed to avoid the reefs, pirates, enemies, fires, and mutinies that have sent so many other ships to vanish beneath the waves. Instead, time and time again, it managed to bring home holds full of porcelain, tea, silk, pepper, and indigo. When Nathanial got too old to sail, and it was clear that my father did not intend to follow in his footsteps, he sold the *Feather*, and retreated to this room."

"Watson, your powers of observation are scintillating this morning," said Holmes chuckling. He strode across the room's large Isfahan carpet over to the desk where he glanced for a moment at the papers. He then turned and knelt at the windowsill, whipping his glass from his pocket and inspecting what I presumed was the boot-print of Mr. Lewis. With his glass in hand, Holmes meandered noiselessly about the room. It was clear that he was attempting to follow the man's tracks in hopes that they would inform us as to the prior location of the object of Lewis' attention.

Holmes finally rose and stretched out his back with a rueful shake of his head. "It is well that you did not call in the police,

THE TREASURY OF SHERLOCK HOLMES

Mr. Hatley, for they are like a herd of buffaloes. Once they are done with a scene, there is rarely anything left to observe. You did enough damage on your own, sir."

"So you cannot tell what he was after?" cried our host.

"At the moment, no, I cannot. However, he spent most of his time inspecting your bookshelves. The tables were untouched."

"But I told you, Mr. Holmes, that I am certain that no book is missing from this room!"

"In which case, there are two possibilities. The first is that he brought with him a duplicate book and swapped the two of them so you would not notice the difference."

Hatley frowned. "What would be the reason for such a switch?"

Holmes waved his hand. "There are many reasons. Your grandfather had both great wealth and great taste. Many of these books are over a century old. Perhaps your edition was a particularly valuable one, while the one substituted is a worthless modern one wrapped in an older spine. You don't happen to have a first folio of Shakespeare's, do you?"

"No," said Hatley, shaking his head. "Nothing so precious as to risk arrest and gaol. Mainly books about sailing and history."

"Then there is the other possibility. Your grandfather may have decided that the best way to hide something was in plain sight. If he had an important piece of paper, where better to conceal it than tucked into a book?"

I gazed around the rows of shelves, estimating that there were at least two thousand volumes. "Holmes, you don't propose looking through each one, do you?" I cried. "It would be like looking for a needle in a haystack!"

"Fortunately, we do not have to resort to such extreme measures, Watson. We may use the twin powers of observation and logic in order to narrow down the possibilities significantly. You can clearly appreciate that Mr. Lewis's prints are particularly heavy in front of this case here. And when you peruse the hundred or so volumes it contains what do you notice, Watson?"

I shook my head. "They all look similar to me, Holmes."

"Not so, Watson. Do you see that first volume of Gibbon's *Decline*?[99] Is the spine not more worn than its companions? As if it were a much-loved book, often taken down and consulted?" Holmes climbed the ladder and pulled down the volume in question. He flipped through it and, finding nothing of note, glanced up at our host. "Was there something special about this book, Mr. Hatley?"

Hatley's eyes widened and he nodded slowly. "It was my grandfather's favourite. I do not consult it often, myself, but I read it some ten years ago. And I was surprised to find a slip of chart-like paper tucked inside, plainly written in my grandfather's hand."

"What did it say?"

"I don't know, Mr. Holmes. If I recall correctly, there were some letters and numbers, as well as a few peculiar lines and a circle. However, it was all meaningless. I assumed it was merely something Nathanial had distractedly drawn while considering some other matter and then used as a bookmark. I couldn't bear to discard it, in his memory, so I tucked it back into the book where I had found it."

"Unfortunately, it has now vanished. Plainly, it was the object of Mr. Lewis's trespass. It seems likely that he even sought employment within your staff in order to scout the location of this paper."

Hatley shook his head. "But it wasn't of any importance!" he protested. "How could Lewis have even known of its existence?"

"An excellent question, Mr. Hatley, but one that I am unable to answer until we ascertain the true identity of Mr. Lewis."

"What do you mean?"

"If his object was a nefarious one, I sincerely doubt that the man used his real name when he applied for the coachman job. We might go so far as to even inquire if he was responsible for his predecessor's illness."

"But how are we to catch him, Holmes, if we don't even know who he is?" I asked.

"That is a simple matter, Watson. London may be a city of six million people, however, in many ways it is still but a series of small villages. Strange folk attract notice. The irregulars will assist us running him down. The question I find more interesting is what was on that paper which could have made it so valuable? You don't happen to have another copy, do you, Mr. Hatley?"

"No, however..." his sentence trailed off as his brow furrowed in grave deliberation.

"What is it?" asked Holmes, sharply.

"Upon his deathbed, my grandfather whispered something to me. I have not thought about it for many years. He told me that if I were ever in trouble, I should look to the *Feather*. He had sold the ship, of course, so I assumed he was delirious. I made nothing of it at the time."

Hatley may have dismissed it; however, by the gleam in Holmes' eyes, I could see that he thought this story was of great interest. He turned around and surveyed the room. "Tell me, Mr. Hatley, is one of these models a replica of your grandfather's ship?"

Hatley nodded and pointed to a three-masted ship mounted upon the fireplace mantel. Holmes strode over to it, lifted the ship down from its perch, and carried it back to the desk. He proceeded to prod at all of its various wooden parts, while Hatley and I crowded around and watched in wonderment at Holmes' actions. Finally, Holmes pressed upon two of the tiny cannons in unison, and I heard a small clicking sound as the tiny roof of the captain's stern cabin popped open. Holmes made a satisfied murmur and fished out a creased piece of chart paper, which he unfolded for our inspection.

"That's the same diagram I once found in the Gibbon!" Hatley exclaimed after a moment.

I gazed in wonder upon the mysterious paper, which I reproduce here:

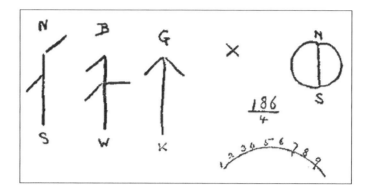

"Well, Watson, what do you make of it?" asked Holmes.

"I am at a loss, Holmes."

"Come now, Watson. It is plainly a treasure map."

Hatley staggered and had to steady himself by placing his hands upon the desk. "How can that be, Mr. Holmes?"

"You said that your grandfather had remarkable fortune. Perhaps even more than you know. At least that is how our Mr. Lewis saw it."

"But a treasure to what, Mr. Holmes?" Hatley exclaimed.

"For that, we shall have to ask Mr. Lewis. Would you mind, sir, if we were to hold onto this map for the moment? I assure you that we shall return it in forthwith. But it may perhaps help lead us to your burglar."

Hatley nodded his agreement and sank into his chair, plainly staggered by the implications of what had transpired in his library during the last half-day. Holmes took his leave and proceeded downstairs in order to question the butler, Wooten, about the particulars of Mr. Lewis. The butler described Lewis as being between forty and fifty years of age, medium height, and plain complexion, with a clean-shaven face and a lack of distinguishing features. His manner was taciturn, but not unpleasant, and he was efficient at his tasks of driving about town, keeping the horses groomed, and maintaining the carriage in working order. "He had excellent references," Wooten concluded.

"Did you check them yourself?" asked Holmes.

"No, sir."

Holmes shook his head. "A capital mistake. They were probably forged. I trust you will be more exacting with your next hire."

"Not much to go on, eh, Watson?" said Holmes, as a quick hansom ride took us back to our flat. Rather than turn inside, however, Holmes gave a sharp whistle, and within a few minutes, we were surrounded by a dozen ragged street arabs. Their small dirty faces managed a dignity as fine as that of many gentlemen of my acquaintance as Holmes gave a series of instructions to this irregular Baker Street division of the detective police force. He then handed them a shilling each before they buzzed away down the street like a murmuration of starlings.

§

We had scarcely climbed the steps back up to our lodgings when Mrs. Hudson entered with a telegram for Holmes. He ripped it open and after reading it, his eyebrows rose. He handed it over to me, and I read:

> "Come to the Diogenes Club when convenient.
> – MYCROFT."

Holmes sighed. "We best be off, Watson."

I frowned. "What is the rush, Holmes? It says 'when convenient.'"

"He means convenient for him, not for me."

Within minutes, we were back in a hansom cab and headed to Pall Mall, to that paradoxical abode of unsociable and unclubbable men. Holmes and I were welcomed inside by the doorman with the customary precaution against speaking, and he led us to the heavily-dampened walls of the Stranger's Room. Holmes' massive brother soon joined us, and the look upon his remarkably similar face was grave. Contrary to his typical courtesy, Mycroft failed to shake my hand, and instead launched into the business at hand.

"Do you recall the First Anglo-Mahratta War, Sherlock?"

"Would such knowledge make a pennyworth of difference to me or my work, Mycroft? However much I wish it were otherwise, my brain-attic is not infinite, and I simply cannot afford to take in useless lumber. Especially not when I can simply pay a visit to this fine establishment and put any such questions before my brother, whose appetite for geopolitics is far vaster than mine own."

Mycroft sighed heavily. "Very well then, let me tell you a story, Sherlock. It begins with Shah Jahan, the great Mughal Emperor, descendant of Genghis Khan himself. He was fabulously wealthy, even going so far as erecting the vast Taj Mahal at Agra in memory of his deceased wife. However, his reign proved to be the absolute pinnacle of that empire and, after his death in 1666, his successors became progressively less capable. By 1739, the Mughals were in complete decline. They could not resist an invasion led by Nader Shah of Persia, who sacked Delhi and occupied the Red Fort. In turn, after Nader Shah's assassination in 1747, his own Empire fell into anarchy. I will not bore you with the details – which are exceedingly complex – of what happened next, however, to make a long story short, in 1780 Captain Popham of the East India Company captured the Gwalior Fort from the Mahrattas. There he found one item of note from the time of Shah Jahan, which had made its roundabout way there via Persia and back again."

"What was it?" I asked, leaning forward in my excitement.

"The golden, gem-studded throne of Shah Jahan himself. The greatest treasure of the Indian subcontinent. The Peacock Throne."

My eyebrows rose in astonishment. "What happened to it?"

"Governor-General Hastings determined that it would be unwise to allow the throne to remain in India, where it might serve as a focal point of discontent. Therefore, he took the only course open to him. In 1782, the throne was loaded onto the swiftest East Indiaman clipper and sailed to England. Or such was his intention. Unfortunately, the ship carrying the throne, the *Cheshire*, was beset by stormy seas, and crashed into rocks off the Wild Coast. Many sailors died in the wreck itself, but a large party of some fifty men managed to make it to shore. However, despite aid from a friendly local tribe, the closest civilized town was an arduous trek through untraversed jungle. It took three months of walking and, when they arrived at Port Elizabeth, only five men remained of that party."

"Surely they were questioned as to the location of the wreck?" interjected Holmes.

"Of course," replied Mycroft acerbically. "Several of the men eventually returned to England, where they were interviewed by a predecessor of mine. It is relatively common knowledge that the shipwreck is located at the mouth of the Umzimvubu River. In fact, one attempt to salvage the ship was attempted in 1880, and another syndicate could be formed at any moment. Nonetheless, I am certain that they will not find the Peacock Throne."

"Why not?" asked my friend.

Mycroft smiled. "Because, according to our records, one of the *Cheshire's* boats managed to be launched before the ship foundered. It contained six sailors under the command of the first mate, one Lieutenant Nathanial Hatley."

"The grandfather of Fletcher Hatley!" I exclaimed.

He trained his steel-grey, deep-set eyes upon me. "Precisely, Dr Watson. And in addition to the six men, the boat also reportedly contained a large steel-banded box."

"The throne!" I deduced. "But where did they take it?"

"That is precisely the question, Doctor. When questioned, Lieutenant Hatley was very cagey. He denied any knowledge of the throne, as did the two men, Martin and Leamington, who made their way back to England with him. But Hatley subsequently became very wealthy, and we always wondered the origins of his sudden bounty."

"So you believe that Hatley plundered the throne?"

"Not exactly, Doctor. Hatley's wealth was not incredibly prodigious at first. Upon his return to England, he had only sufficient money to buy and outfit a trading vessel. Fortunately for him, his subsequent business interests proved to be quite successful. It is my theory that Hatley must have pried a gem or two off the throne before hiding it away. Ample enough to set him up in business, but certainly not an amount that would account for all the vast riches of the throne. Therefore the throne must remain safely stashed somewhere along the coast of Africa."

"Pray tell, Mycroft, what is your present interest in the matter?" inquired Holmes. "Surely you do not care about its intrinsic value?"

"What would it be worth?" I wondered aloud.

Mycroft waved his corpulent hand. "Inestimable, Doctor. Need I remind you that the magnificent Koh-i-Noor diamond, which now resides in the Queen's brooch, was once but an eye of one of the twelve peacock statues? Nevertheless, its symbolic value is even greater. The Peacock Throne may be lost, but I assure you that it is not forgotten for the followers of the Mughals. Its reappearance would stir up some strong emotions in the colony." He turned to his brother. "As you may know, Sherlock, if you could be bothered to read anything other than the agony pages, India is still recovering from a major famine. It would be a very poor moment to introduce such an element of chaos. I think it would not be hyperbole to say that we don't wish a tragic repeat of the Great Mutiny of recent memory."

Holmes' eyebrows rose. "You fear that the recovery of the throne could incite another rebellion?"

"I do indeed. Need I remind you of how many lives were lost in the first one? One hundred twenty woman and children at Cawnpore alone, Sherlock."[100]

"So you have been watching Mr. Hatley all of this time?"

Mycroft shook his head. "Not actively, of course, brother. Our resources are not so vast. However, his name is on a particular list of persons of interest. I heard from one of my sources this morning that he was inquiring after your services, Sherlock. Naturally, I wondered if he was suddenly short of money and setting out upon a treasure quest, aided by a particular consulting detective of some repute, thanks in no small part to his chronicler."

Holmes smiled sardonically. "The home of Mr. Hatley was burgled last night."

"Ah!" Mycroft's eyes widened with interest. "So there is another party in the game. I can only assume that something was removed that points to the hidden location of the Peacock Throne?"

"Perhaps," Holmes replied. "And you wish me to stop the thief before he can locate it?"

"This is not simply a request from your brother, Sherlock. You may consider it a task from the Government itself. If you succeed in retrieving the Throne, quietly I may add, I think it likely that a knighthood would be in order."

I was astonished at this munificent offer, and doubly so when Holmes dismissively waved his hand at the mention of such an honour. He nodded curtly at his brother and took his leave.

§

When we exited the Diogenes Club, Holmes threw back his head and laughed. "Here's a pretty problem, eh, Watson? It should teach you a valuable lesson that even the most trivial-appearing case may contain items of the most profound interest. In this instance, a simple robbery evolves into a matter of national importance."

"I stand corrected, Holmes. What is our next action?"

"If we are to arrest Mr. Lewis, it would be of considerable assistance if we were able to anticipate his next action. We must presume he is attempting to solve the map at this very moment. We must endeavour to do the same." He considered this for a moment and then pulled the strange diagram from his coat pocket. "Now then, Watson, what does this chart tell us?"

"Presumably, Hatley and his fellows buried the throne near the coast, and this is a map to the spot. Over the years, however, Hatley's descendants have forgotten how to interpret it."

"I concur with your analysis so far, Watson. Pray continue."

I studied the map for a minute. "The circle upon the right must give the compass bearings. The larger semicircle may be the curved edge of a reef or a rock. The figures above are the indications of how to reach the 'X' that marks the treasure. Possibly they may give the bearing as one-hundred-eighty-six feet from the '4' upon the semicircle?"

"And the three marks on the left-hand side? What do they tell us?"

I shook my head. "I cannot say. They are a mystery to me. Do you have a theory?"

"As a matter of fact, I do, Watson. Recall that Lieutenant Hatley drew this chart. He was a former officer in the Royal Navy. And how do naval ships communicate with one another when out of range of earshot?"

"By semaphore!"

"Very good, Watson. The semaphore was no crude system, but rather could communicate the most profound messages. 'England expects that every man shall do his duty,' and all that. This system was also a primitive version of a secret code, so that pirates and foreign ships could not interpret the signals. Now, I put to you that, if the Indiaman's semaphore code was changed every year for the sake of privacy, it may be conjectured that the marks upon this chart are signals from a long-forgotten three-armed semaphore."

"Holmes, the record of their meaning might be found in the old papers of the India Office!"

"Precisely, Watson. That is where we must begin our search."

The Foreign Office building was fortuitously situated very near to Mycroft's club along the Horse Guards Road. A quick walk brought us to the front of that Italianate-style palace, its rich decorations designed to impress foreign visitors to this 'drawing room' of the Empire. We strode across the marble pavement of the open courtyard, surrounded by three stories of red and grey columns and arch-supporting piers. Entering the Records Room via a gilded door stamped with the crest of a rampant lion within a medallion, we found ourselves confronted by what appeared to be many miles of shelving. We explained the nature of our quest to the old man, stooped and wizened, in charge of the records. It took him the better part an hour finally to locate the folio-sized tome that held the codes to the East Indiamen of the 1780's. The ultramarine-dyed leather cover was ornamented with gold leaf, a sign of the ostentatious wealth brought back by the Company from the Far East. From an inspection of the layer of dust coating the gilded top of its pages, it appeared that we were a step ahead of Mr. Lewis, for it was plain that no one had consulted this volume for at least a decade.

Holmes set the tone down upon the desk and carefully turned the pages, his keen grey eyes seeking symbols that matched the ones upon our chart. "Here, we have one, Watson!" he cried. "The middle symbol, between the 'B' and the 'W' is the number 'one.' Moreover, the first symbol, the one between the 'N' and 'S' is the number 'two.' Only the final symbol remains!" He turned another page and his thin, nervous fingers twitched with excitement. "Here we have it, Watson. The final symbol is the letter 'H.' Now what does that tell us?"

While Holmes was calling out the answers, I was scrawling them upon a sheet of loose foolscap, and I now stared at the still incomprehensible message: "Two, One, H," I said. "It is meaningless, Holmes!"

"On the contrary, Watson," said Holmes. "Do not forget that

we are not meant to read solely the semaphore's symbols, but rather as part of the larger message."

I wrote out the other letters onto my paper. "N, B, G, Two, One, H, S, W, K? It still tells me nothing," I protested.

From the twitching of his bushy eyebrows, I could tell that Holmes too was dissatisfied and a bit cross that the meaning of the chart remained an enigma. He clasped his hands behind his back and began to silently pace back and forth along the floor. "I am the dullest man alive, Watson!" he suddenly exclaimed, whipping his magnifying lens from his pocket. He closely inspected the map for a moment before looking up with a smile.

"You have broken the code?" I asked, eagerly.

"I believe so. I first recommend that you free your mind from the traditional method of reading left to right, Watson, and consider that the message may instead be vertical in nature, like flags upon a mast."

"N, Two, S?"

"Indeed. Now, where have we seen the 'N' and 'S' before, Watson?"

"Above and below the circle at the right of the chart."

"Very good. And what do we find upon the vast ocean that is – upon occasion – vaguely circular in shape?"

"An island?"

"Precisely. And what if that island was roughly two miles in diameter along the north – south dimension. Would that not help serve to identify it?"

"It would indeed!" I exclaimed. "However, there must be more than one island in the Indian Ocean that fits such a bill, Holmes. It could take a very long time to search them all."

"But that is not the sole clue, is it, Watson?"

"No, there is the mysterious 'B, One, W.' Do you know what that could mean?"

He smiled. "I admit that this took me a moment, Watson. I realized that we were making a simple mistake. For this paper is over a hundred years old and the iron gall ink has bled somewhat." He held forth his magnifying glass. "Perhaps you would care to look at it for yourself? I would counsel that you do so without any preconceived notions of what you might find."

I took the glass from him and bent over the chart, unsure of his meaning. I examined the 'B,' the 'W' and the semaphore symbol carefully. Then I saw it. "It's not a 'B!" I cried.

"Capital, Watson, you have outdone yourself! The supposed 'B' is, in fact, a sloppily written 'E' whose ink has bled to the point where it now more closely resembles an entirely different letter. But when the 'E' is restored, in conjunction with the first three symbols, the meaning becomes clear."

"The island is one mile in diameter in the east – west dimension!"

"And the number of possible locations grows exponentially smaller," concluded Holmes with a smile.

"But what of the last three letters, Holmes? What could 'G – H – K' possibly mean?"

He shook his head. "I do not know at the moment, Watson. Nevertheless, I suspect it eventually will help us narrow down the list to an even more precise locale. I suggest that, at this moment, we are missing a critical item to help us come to a definitive conclusion. We are in need of a good map."

§

A fifteen-minute hansom cab ride along the Strand and up Kingsway, pausing only long enough for Holmes to spring out and dash off a telegram, found us striding into the Reading Room at the British Library. We were met by Mr. Horace Oliver, a short, kindly gentleman who, by their familiar greetings, had apparently assisted Holmes upon at least one prior occasion.

"We are in need, Mr. Oliver, of a detailed map of the southern Indian Ocean."

"I have just the thing, Mr. Holmes," said Oliver, chuckling softly. "Right over here," he motioned, starting to lead us to the far corner of the room.

However, Holmes remained rooted to his spot. "Was there something amusing about my question?"

The man paused to consider this. "No, I suppose not, Mr. Holmes. But I thought it odd that you are the second man today to ask for such a map."

"What!" Holmes exclaimed. "Can you describe him?"

"Oh, yes," said the librarian. "He was around five and forty years, a bit taller than myself, with dull brown eyes and hair. He had no beard or moustache, nor any other marks of note. Of course, I can do you one better. I can give you his name. He signed the reader's registrar as a Mr. Randall Martin."

Holmes' eyes grew bright when he heard this description, which clearly matched that of the supposed Barney Lewis. He threw a pointed glance in my direction before asking his next question. "And you say that he asked for a map?"

Mr. Oliver nodded. "Yes, he asked for several maps, but the one that he stared at the longest was the Royal Scottish Geographical Society's 1885 sketch map of South Africa showing British possessions."

"May we see it?" asked Holmes, an eagerness to his voice, which I recognized from when he was hot with the thrill of the chase. Mr. Oliver scurried off to procure this request, and he promptly returned with the item in question. Holmes took the large map and with the help of some pins, he affixed it to the wall, as I had seen him do a hundred times at our flat with other case-related documents. He lit his black clay pipe and together we stared at it silently for several minutes.

"I don't see it, Holmes."

Suddenly he began to laugh, his braying evoking a sense of lunacy. "I say, Watson, you might have to examine me for a softening of the brain. For I almost failed to see the light of truth in this matter."

"Which is?"

"We are looking for something with the initials 'G – H – K' are we not? But what if those words are not in English?"

"What other language would they be in?"

"You are much better versed in history than I, Watson. Pray tell, in the year 1782, to whom did the tip of Africa belong?"

I considered this for a moment. "The Cape Colony would have been under the governance of the Dutch East India Company."

"Precisely. And thus, could the letters represent a Dutch name?"

"Such as?"

"Such as the *Goede Hoop Kaap*. Or, as we would call it, the Cape of Good Hope."

"Of course!" I exclaimed. "I will ask Mr. Oliver for a map of the Cape." I hurried over to the man's desk, and within minutes, he had secured what we needed. Here is a reproduction of that map:

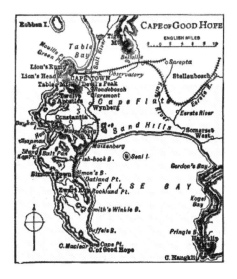

Holmes studied it for a moment, his eyes sparkling with pleasure. "This case grows upon me, Watson. There are decidedly some points of interest. Here we have several geographical features, which I want to commend to you in relation to Mr. Hatley's curious chart. First, there is the semicircle in the lower right corner. What does that suggest to you?"

"It has a similarity to the curved edge of the False Bay!" said

I, excitedly.

"Precisely, Watson. Therefore, we have now deciphered the meaning of the semaphores and their letters, as well as the semicircle. But several items remain."

"The 'X,'" I exclaimed. "It must mark the treasure!"

"Indeed. And where is that 'X' located upon the chart?" asked Holmes.

I considered this for a minute. "The figures about the semicircle! They must give the bearings! The treasure is to be found one-hundred-eighty-six feet from the '4' upon the semicircle!"

Holmes shook his head. "Not quite, Watson, for such a locale would surely be in the middle of the town itself. I highly doubt that Mr. Hatley's grandfather and his shipmates could have hidden such a large object where you hypothetically place it."

"Then where?" said I, crossly.

Holmes chuckled. "You are on the right track, my dear Watson. You are merely off on your units of measurement. What if the '186' refers to a furlong rather than a foot?"

I attempted to do the calculations in my head. "At 660 feet, per the imperial definition, that would make it some one hundred twenty thousand feet."

"One hundred twenty two thousand, seven hundred sixty, to be precise. Or a hair over twenty-three miles. Now what do we see upon the map that is twenty-three miles from where the number '4' would be found?"

I followed his finger as he traced the distance using the scale printed upon the map. "That little island!" I exclaimed.

"Robben Island," Holmes mused. "And unless I am greatly mistaken, I would estimate that it is about two miles in the north to south dimension and one mile from east to west, don't you think, Watson?"

"Indeed it is!"

"Now what do we know about Robben Island?"

I shook my head. "Nothing."

"Then let us see if Mr. Oliver can provide one final modicum of information."

The man proved to be happy to oblige. Reading from the very latest gazetteer that he had ready at his fingertips, Oliver informed us that the island's name was Dutch for 'seal.' He went on to relate that treacherous reefs, upon which the open Atlantic Ocean continuously thunders, surround the island. Many a ship has vanished under those restless waves. Due to this inhospitable locale, the Dutch settlers originally used the island as a prison for both natives and whites. After Great Britain annexed the Cape Colony in 1806, we first continued to use it for prisoners of the Cape Frontier Wars. However, since 1845, it has been utilized as a leper colony.

Holmes thanked the librarian for his assistance, and led me out the back entrance towards the leafy Russell Square. We had hardly made our way across Montague Street before I could contain my excitement no longer. "Holmes, now we know why Nathanial Hatley was forced to abandon the Peacock Throne upon Robben Island! His ship must have wrecked upon its reefs, and since Dutch forces occupied the isle there was no easy way by which to transport it. Instead, Hatley and his companions would have hidden it in a sea cave, or dug some hole. After England assumed control over the Cape, return still would not have been easy. Not with the British Army stationed on the island, nor a leper colony! So, Hatley drew his chart, and bided his time, but meanwhile, he gained sufficient wealth from his trading that a return to Robben Island was no longer fiscally necessary."

Holmes nodded. "Your hypothesis fits the known facts, Watson. Nevertheless, you are forgetting several features of note. Who precisely is Mr. Martin? How did he know of the existence of Mr. Hatley's chart? Moreover, how did he decipher it in advance of us? There were no signs that the East India Company semaphore records had been recently consulted."

"He must be the descendent of one of Nathanial Hatley's crewmates," I ventured.

"It is a solid theory, Watson. We must be certain to ask him ourselves when we catch him."

"And how do you propose to do that?"

"Tell me, Watson, if you had just discovered the locale of a remarkable treasure, what would be your next course of action?"

"I would take passage to Cape Town," I decided. "Holmes, we should check the shipping lines! I believe the African Steamship Company has offices at the end of Pall Mall...."

Holmes held up a hand to forestall me. "Before we canvas the commercial ships, Watson, I ask you to contemplate what you would do upon disembarking in Cape Town?"

"Well, I could not recover the throne myself. I would have to recruit a crew."

"Ah, but there is the rub, Watson. How can you, who have never set foot in Africa, be certain of their trustworthiness? Once the Delhi crown regalia are found, what prevents your hired crew from simply slitting your throat and keeping the riches of the Peacock Throne for themselves?"

I considered this for a moment. "He would need a crew made up of his own acquaintances. And that crew might already have its own ship!"

Holmes nodded. "That is how I read it, as well, Watson. Mr. Martin would have had a plan in place before seeking employment with Mr. Hatley. As we speak, he might be on his way to that ship."

"Then we must go at once if we are to thwart him!"

"But where, Watson?" said Holmes, calmly. "Surely you recall that the wharfs of London and Greenwich are a vast labyrinth of landing places. Where would you begin?"

"I don't know," said I, shaking my head. "Do you have a plan?"

"I have had one for some time. Why else do you think I enlisted the services of my unofficial force? The wharfingers shut up like oysters when talking to strangers, but street arabs are beneath their notice. One of their number is stationed at the Westminster wharf. Let us go see what he has to report."

§

The sun was low in the sky when we climbed aboard a hansom cab, Holmes promising the driver an extra sovereign if he could get us to the wharf in less than ten minutes. By the precipitous course the man took through St. Martin's Lane and Whitehall, I could see he took this as a personal challenge. When we successfully reached the north bank of the Thames, we found one of Holmes' irregulars bursting with news. It seemed that Holmes, suspecting that Captain Hatley's nautical career played a role in the mystery, had set them upon the task of learning the identities of all ships hired under furtive circumstances and sailing that night. Holmes listened patiently as the lad recited from memory the names of several such ships. Eventually, the little scarecrow mentioned that one of his brethren had located a steam launch called the *Hope,* stationed at the Pool, which had been employed to take a man out to a ship called the *Mayumba.* When Holmes heard that this ship was waiting in the Downs to sail out to the Cape Colony, his grey eyes gleamed brightly.

Holmes tossed the lad his reward and waved his hand to signal that I should follow him. We raced down the steps to where we found a launch of our own awaiting us. I drew up in surprise when I discovered that it was the black and red-streaked *Aurora* of puissant memory, Mr. Mordecai Smith at the rudder, and his eldest son, Jim, tending the engines. If possible, the man Smith looked even more sullen than when I had last laid eyes upon him, nine years prior, though his son had grown to become a fine strapping lad.

Holmes leapt aboard, with myself close behind, and ordered Smith to set off downstream with the engines fully stoked. As we got underway, Holmes leaned forward so I could hear his explanation. "I put in a good word for the two Smiths with Inspector Jones, and they got off with but a small fine for their role in the Pondicherry affair. Since then, Smith has owed me a turn, and his debt is being paid this evening. The telegram I sent instructed him to meet us here." He turned away from me. "Is the *Aurora* still the fastest clipper on the river, Mr. Smith?" called out Holmes over the noise of the engines and the waves.

"She will fly like the devil, sir, when you need her to," the man answered gruffly.

Holmes nodded and then smiled at me. "We should be able to catch them. It sounds as if Martin was only an hour or two ahead of us at the Library, and the *Mayumba* will require some last-minute provisioning before it can weigh anchor for such a long voyage."

We sped swiftly towards the Pool, with both Waterloo and Blackfriars Bridges quickly vanishing in the distance. As we approached the high spans of the Tower Bridge, Holmes pointed towards where a green launch was emerging from the St. Katherine Docks. It was similar in shape to the *Aurora* but with a yellow line and black funnels.

"There, Watson!" he exclaimed. "Do you spot the name *Hope* on its bow? That's our quarry!"

Two men were at work aboard the launch, one at the tiller and the other shovelling coals, both with black hair and beards. Neither matched the description of Martin, but they looked up at our rapid approach and the launch suddenly took flight. For a moment, I envisioned a repeat of our thrilling chase of Jonathan Small, but we had a superior head of steam, while the *Hope* was just getting underway. There was no chance of them outpacing us. Smith expertly maneuvered the *Aurora* until it swung around and cut off the *Hope*'s path. Their skipper was forced to put the helm hard down in order to avoid a collision, and the boat settled into the water. Holmes jumped onto the *Aurora*'s gunwale and called out, "The game is up, Martin! Surrender now and you will get a fair trial."

A man appeared at the stern of the boat from the small cabin, his hair dishevelled by the chase. "Like my great-grandfather did?" he screamed, his eyes gleaming maniacally. "And how will Hatley pay for the crimes of his grandfather?"

Holmes shook his head. "We know of no crimes other than your theft of the chart from Hatley's home."

"Of course not! For it was policemen like you that covered it up, for the right price."

"I assure you, Mr. Martin, that I am not a member of the official police force, but rather a private agent hired by Mr. Hatley to recover his stolen property."

"But it's not his, is it? It belonged equally to all three of them. At least it did until Nathanial Hatley had Thomas Leamington and Alan Martin killed so that he could keep it all for himself."

"That's a matter for the courts, Mr. Martin. I cannot arbitrate the supposed crimes of decades past."

"No!" Martin cried. "I will never bring the Government into this. They will take it all, and my great-grandfather will have died for nothing."

"There is no other way," said Holmes sternly. "Your skipper knows that proceeding any further signifies that he will be prosecuted for abetting a criminal. You will never reach the *Mayumba*."

Martin stared daggers at Holmes. "There is always another way! If I cannot have it, no one shall!" The man ducked into the cabin of the launch, and vanished from our sight.

"What the devil is he doing, Holmes?" I asked.

I could sense my friend becoming anxious as he considered what Martin had planned. Suddenly, Holmes suddenly began to wave to the men working the *Hope*. "Abandon ship!" he cried. "Get away from the boat, if you value your lives!"

The men stared at him for a moment, and then obeyed with alacrity by leaping into the Thames. Mordecai Smith required no additional alarm, for he was already reversing the propeller and backing the *Aurora* away from the *Hope*. And it was not a moment too soon, for less than a minute after Martin entered the cabin, an enormous eruption tore the boat in half. Even at our distance, the force was so great that if Holmes had not caught the lapel of my jacket, I would have been thrown overboard. Once I had regained my balance and cleared my head, I joined Holmes at the side of the boat, where he was gazing out over the rapidly sinking wreckage.

"What happened, Holmes?" I exclaimed.

Holmes shook his head. "One can hypothesize, Watson, that the launch must have been carrying a barrel of powder, intended to be utilized in blasting open any rocks on Robben Island that concealed the Throne. Martin plainly set it off, destroying both himself and what he believed to be the solitary copy of the treasure map, in the process."

"He must have been mad!"

"Fortunes have clouded the minds of greater men, Watson."

§

By the time that the *Aurora* had come about and pulled the two *Hope* crewmen from the water, their boat had completely vanished under the waves of the Thames. A few questions made it clear that the Larey brothers were completely ignorant of the crimes of their passenger. I have it on good authority that Holmes spoke to his brother and saw that the men were recompensed for the loss of their means of livelihood.

When Holmes and I had poured glasses of brandy and settled back into our armchairs at Baker Street, I told him that some features of the case remained unclear in my mind. Holmes raised his eyebrows and gestured with his free hand, inviting me to continue.

"So it seems that Mr. Martin was descended from one of the men who concealed the Peacock Throne. But how did he decipher the map?"

"Martin's great-grandfather must have kept his old semaphore signal-book. Once Martin saw the three-armed marks on the chart, he would have immediately recognized what they represented. Although he had a lead of several hours upon us, Martin naturally was not as quick as you and I at deciphering the remainder of the code."

"Do you think Martin was telling the truth about his ancestor being murdered by Hatley's grandfather?"

He shrugged. "That will likely take some time to determine, Watson, if we are able to do so at all. Careful records are few and far between from the days before Peel established the C.I.D. Perhaps a thorough search of Bow Street or Wapping High Street might eventually reveal something, but it would be purely of academic interest. At the moment, the only person outside of this room who knows of the existence of the map is Mr. Fletcher Hatley, and I can assure you that he will be easily persuaded to take this secret to his grave. He has no need of the fortune, and no reason to dredge up the possible misdeeds of his grandfather."

"What if Martin or Leamington had other descendants?"

"Are you suggesting that they should share in the illicit wealth gleaned from the throne? Need I remind you, Watson, that it legally belongs to the Crown? But if you wish, I shall make some inquiries, and if need be, request that Mr. Hatley settles a small pension upon them."

I nodded my head in agreement. "And the Throne? Are we not going to go out and locate it ourselves?" I asked.

"No, Watson, as you know, I have an aversion to leaving London for any significant length of time."

I was stunned at his apparent lack of interest in the treasure now that the crime had been solved and the criminal dealt with. "Aren't you planning at least to tell Mycroft? Surely he has men that he could send?"

Holmes considered this for a moment. "But who gains from such a thing, Watson? Does the Throne truly belong to the one who finds it? Certainly, it cannot be displayed in the British Museum for risk of inciting a storm of passions in India. Moreover, I assure you that Mycroft does not intend to return it there either. So, it would sit, forlorn, in some secret bunker." He shook his head. "No, Watson, perhaps some treasures are better left undiscovered. That way there are some mysteries left in the world."

"But if you can break the code, Holmes, then surely Mycroft can do the same! Did you not say that he was the equal to your intellect?"

"My superior, I should say," he replied with no hint of false modesty. "You are right, Watson. There is only one remedy for this. We shall simply have to tell poor Mycroft that the sole copy of the map was lost in the struggle to capture Mr. Martin. My brother will not be happy, but will have no recourse but to accept my explanation. Obviously, it goes without saying that this is one case which would be most unwise for you to write up for public consumption."

Holmes was correct, of course. The time had not yet come when the world was ready for the reappearance of the Peacock Throne. At his brother's urging, Mycroft had it quietly put it about that the Throne had been broken up during the chaos after the death of Nader Shah. Nonetheless, the map that leads to its final resting place was not lost. It remains safely tucked away in one of my tin dispatch boxes, which I have secured in one of London's finest banks.[101] And while Holmes might not be interested in seeing this treasure for his own eyes, I cannot profess to such aloofness. If I were a less busy man, I should be seriously inclined to go personally and look into the matter myself, without Holmes if need be. Who knows, perhaps someday I shall?[102]

§

THE ADVENTURE OF THE SILENT DRUM

It was a close day in early August 1903 when Mr. Sherlock Holmes appeared at my Queen Anne's Street practice. He was waiting for me in my consulting room when I entered from the breakfast nook in order to prepare for the first patient of the morning, and my delight at seeing him overcame my suspicions that he had picked the lock and let himself in. He rose and extended his iron-grasp in greeting. His thin shoulders were draped in a long grey cloak and the familiar close-fitting cloth cap covered his black hair. Noting that it was rather early for such a late riser as Holmes to be about upon a purely social call, I presumed that the game was once more afoot.

"Holmes!" I exclaimed. "What brings you here? A new case?"

His thin lips turned upwards in a smile as he fired a series of questions and observations at me. "It is good to see you too, Watson. A case indeed. Your wife showed me in, of course. If I am not mistaken, she is readying your travelling valise as we speak. You remain a prompt traveller, do you not, Watson? Even if you have seen half a century. How is your leg? Do I detect a trace of a limp?"

"I would thank you, Holmes, to not remind me of my advancing years. I am past the stage where the days bring any further wisdom. They now bring primarily greying whiskers. And where are we going?"

"So you have accumulated all of the knowledge that you require, my friend? I think not. Education never ends. There are still a few surprises in the world, I hope. And we shall find them in Devon, unless I miss my guess."

"Devon? Holmes, I cannot traipse off to Devon on the drop of a hat," I protested. "I have patients to see today."

He shook his head. "I have already spoken to Dr Moore Agar.[103] He shall look after your practice for a few days while we are gone."

Holmes, it seemed, had thought of everything. I suppose I should be flattered in a way. As I have noted before, I remained a fixture in Holmes' life, even if I had quit our chambers on Baker Street for a domestic arrangement into which Holmes had himself repeatedly vowed to never enter. Certainly, Holmes continued to take on cases without my assistance, but for those more difficult ones, he preferred to have me at his side. At the very least, my humble observations appeared to hone his interpretations and facilitated the impressive deductive leaps, which invariably brought both resolution and acclaim.

Once I had my valise in hand, donned my own travelling attire, and parted with my understanding wife, a fifteen-minute hansom ride deposited us at Paddington Station. Holmes had been rather loquacious during the drive, but only upon matters unrelated to the issue at hand. I seem to recall his comments upon illuminated manuscripts, the relative merits of various materials in the manufacture of pipes, and how the Emperor Ashoka's spread of Buddhism to Kalmykia influenced later Western philosophy.[104] For a man who once claimed to not permit any unnecessary cluttering of his brain-attic, I marvelled at the remarkable breadth of his especial knowledge.

Once Holmes had purchased tickets to Plymouth from the

Great Western Railway office, I waited on the platform while Holmes acquired a copy of every two-penny broadsheet he could find. This immense litter of papers in hand, we settled into our seats in the corner of a first-class carriage, where Holmes offered me his cigar case.

"The London criminal is a dull fellow, Watson. They are all too afraid to act anymore, for they know that I will soon find them out and send them on a one-way trip to Princetown or some other prison. But my sphere of influence has not extended to the countryside, it seems."

"What has occurred in Devon that is so urgent?" I asked. "Who is your client?"

"I received a telegram from my brother this morning. Unfortunately, Mycroft was most sparing of the details. He said he did not wish to influence my conclusions, as if such a thing were possible." A grimace appeared across his hawk-like features. "All I know is that we are expected at one of the manor houses of the Baronet of Yarcombe, a place called Buckland Abbey. Something has transpired there which Mycroft believes might be a matter of national security."

I frowned. "How could anything that occurred in such a remote locale have such global implications, Holmes?"

He shook his head. "I have insufficient data with which to speculate further, Watson. I suggest we peruse the morning editions for clues as to what might have so excited that humble representative of the British government."

However, this task ultimately proved to be futile. An inspection of the papers demonstrated that news of whatever had taken place at Buckland Abbey had yet to reach the offices of Fleet Street. Suddenly, Holmes rolled the papers into an enormous wad and tossed them onto the floor.

"It is futile, Watson," said he, a degree of irritation plain in his voice. He drummed his fingers upon his leg for a moment and then gave a rueful grin. "Still, the journey is not for aught." He pulled down a basket from the overhead rack. "You will be pleased to note that Mrs. Hudson has packed a basket full of treats for our luncheon. If I am not mistaken, I did hear you say recently that you missed her Merseyside pie, yes? Would you care for a glass of Beaune with that?"

§

Less than four hours later, the train carrying Mr. Sherlock Holmes and his contented biographer pulled into Plymouth Station. I will admit that after our fine repast, any attempt to focus upon Mr. Stoker's new Egyptian novel was futile, and I instead rested my eyes.[105] However, upon reaching that famous port town, I was immediately re-invigorated by the gentle breeze blowing off the Sound. This wind carried with it the briny smell of the Channel and the robust cries of adventures in far-off lands.

From there, we hired a comfortable landau to take us the dozen or so miles north to Buckland Abbey proper. On the way, we rattled through several clusters of small and ancient cottages. These I reckoned were sufficiently large to warrant the name of 'village' and suspected that may have been standing since the days of Elizabeth. Holmes gently chided me for sleeping as the train rounded the southern edge of Dartmoor, and he jokingly asked if I wished to stop in for a visit at Baskerville Hall when our mission was complete. The conversation continued in this vein until we finally passed through a thick copse of oak trees and arrived at our destination. The manor house was built from a warm stone, which shone gold in the slanting rays of the afternoon sun. A brick tower incorporating a curious Tudor arch still stood next to the front entrance, a reminder of an age when the occupants of these country houses might suddenly find themselves under siege. As if to remind us that this structure was well able to defend itself, an elevated arrow slit still guarded the door.

Holmes led the way as we descended from the coach and removed our bags from the back. He strode over to the front door and lifted the heavy brass knocker. Within seconds, a square-figured man of some thirty years, with a high forehead and reddish-brown hair, and dressed in formal livery opened the door.

"I am Mr. Sherlock Holmes, and this is my associate, Dr Watson," began my friend, holding forth his calling card. "We have been asked to investigate a matter of extreme urgency."

"Very good, sir. I am Verton, head butler of Buckland Abbey, at your service. If you would be so kind as to step inside for a moment, I will let the master know that you have arrived."

Holmes nodded and the man ushered us into a well-appointed entrance hall, lit by clerestory windows. There we admired a series of minor British landscapes and heraldic devices until the butler returned in the presence of a lithe person in his mid-sixties. He was an alert and vigorous man, neat and dapper, in a frock coat and gaiters, with a trim Vandyke beard and a pair of pince-nez.

Verton motioned to the man. "May I present Sir Francis George Augustus Fuller-Eliott-Drake."

The baronet smiled broadly and held out his hand. "Please, you must call me George. I am so glad that you are here, Mr. Holmes, and you as well, Dr Watson. We have been most anxious since the Drum went missing, and I will not sleep until it has been safely returned. I have been entrusted with a terrible legacy. If only it were possible to have it moved to London for safe-keeping."

"You must forgive us, Sir George," said Holmes. "We have been minimally briefed as to the reason for our visit. Perhaps you would start at the beginning?"

The man's brown eyes widened. "So you do not know about the Drum?"

Holmes shook his head. "No, I am afraid not. Do you refer to a drum in the literal sense?"

The man laughed, but it was not a chuckle of amusement. Rather, I thought I detected a hint of mania in his tone. "I do indeed. However, this is no mere orchestral instrument. It is the key to England's eternal well-being."

Holmes' grey eyes darted towards me, and in that gaze I could tell that he was silently wondering if the baronet had developed some *idée fixe.* He then looked back at our host. "I do not understand, Sir George. How is that possible?"

The man took a deep breath and then sighed it out slowly. "Perhaps it would be more apparent if you understood that I am a linear descendent of Sir Francis Drake? Buckland Abbey was his final home."

It was hard to credit that this small man was the heir of that great admiral. Holmes still appeared mystified, but I suddenly realized what had so upset the baronet. I began a low chant:

> "*Take my drum to England, hang et by the shore,*
> *Strike et when your powder's runnin' low,*
> *If the Dons sight Devon, I'll quit the port o' Heaven,*
> *An' drum them up the Channel*
> *As we drummed them long ago.*"[106]

The baronet threw a grateful glance in my direction. "Precisely, Dr Watson. Drake's Drum has been stolen from the Treasures Gallery."

"And what would be the value of such a historic artefact?" Holmes queried.

"No amount of money can replace such an item, Mr. Holmes," said the baronet despondently. "The Drum is the perpetual guardian of England's shores. The legend is most clear. If the Drum should be moved from its rightful home, England will fall."

§

As he led us deeper into the house to the site of the crime, Sir George elaborated upon the tale. As every English schoolboy – save perhaps the rather uncommon Mr. Sherlock Holmes – knew, Sir Francis Drake was one of the greatest privateers of the Elizabethan era. Even in his own day, Drake's exploits were legendary. Although of modest birth, he had gained control of

THE TREASURY OF SHERLOCK HOLMES

his own ship, the *Judith*, by the age of two and twenty. The following year, he sailed to the New World with plans to harass the Spanish Main. He and his men attacked along the Isthmus of Panama, debarkation point of the Spanish treasure galleons. There they captured such a vast quantity of silver and gold that they were unable to carry it all off. They were therefore forced to conceal most of it, in so doing igniting an infinite number of subsequent tales of buried treasures. With this success behind him, Drake set off in his new ship, the *Pelican*, to become the first Englishman to gaze upon the Pacific Ocean and circumnavigate the globe. When he returned to Plymouth in 1580, the treasure in his ship's hold was vaster than the entire annual income of the English throne. Queen Elizabeth was so happy that she had Drake knighted. After further state-sanctioned plundering of the Spanish colonies, Drake led a pre-emptive strike against the massing Spanish fleet at Cadiz, where he destroyed no less than thirty-seven ships. Drake was also second-in-command of the brave English fleet responsible for repulsing the dreadful Spanish Armada. His star was on the rise, but even the mighty Drake proved to be mortal. He finally perished from dysentery at the age of fifty-six while leading an attack upon Portobelo, Panama. Per his wishes, Drake's body was dressed in full armour, loaded into a lead coffin, and buried at sea. But he also ordered that the regimental snare drum which had accompanied him around the world be sent back to Buckland Abbey. With his dying words, he vowed to return should England ever be in danger and the drum be sounded.

Holmes snorted in amusement at this legend. Our host gazed at my friend. "You do not believe in the power of the Drum, Mr. Holmes?"

"I have been in active practice for some twenty-odd years, Sir George, and I have been confronted with many strange occurrences. There was a spectral hound in Dartmoor, a vampire in Sussex, even a miraculous cure in Westminster.[107] I assure you that they all proved to have more prosaic explanations than ghostly apparitions."

Sir George shook his head. "I am a rational man, myself, Mr. Holmes. I have been following the progress of Bateson and Marconi with considerable interest.[108] I freely admit that I myself have never heard the Drum sound. However, my ancestors were not fanciful men. Sir Thomas reported that he, and many others, heard the Drum roll when Napoleon was brought into Plymouth Sound as a prisoner aboard the HMS *Bellerophon*, before his final exile to Saint Helena."

"It seems that the Drum sounded a bit late if it waited until after the Emperor had been captured," said Holmes, dryly.

"Scoff all you want, Mr. Holmes," said our host, sadly. "The fact of the matter remains that the public believes that Sir Francis could return one day in our hour of need, but only if the Drum is ready to summon him. And the Drum has been stolen. The only possible reason for such a sacrilege is if the thief intends to shake the very spirit of the people of England. This is why I wired at once to my contacts in the government. And it appears that at least someone in a position of power takes these concerns seriously, Mr. Holmes, or you would not have been sent from London to our humble corner of the isle."

I nodded at the logic of this argument. "Holmes, Mycroft must believe that this is the work of some foreign agent."

Holmes frowned and shook his head. "Eduardo Lucas is dead. Hugo Oberstein is still in prison. Adolph Meyer has been banished from the country.[109] And I have never known Louis La Rothière, Luigi Lucarelli, or Gabriel Dukas to work so far from the corridors of power at Whitehall. No, Watson, this does not fit their typical *modus operandi*."

"Then who?"

"That is what we shall soon discover."

Our host stopped in front of a massive wooden door. "The Drum is kept in a special gallery at the end of the great hall, which you are about to enter," he explained.

Once the door was opened, my gazed was drawn upwards in wonder at the high ceiling. Like many halls, it had a large fireplace, ornate panelling, and decorative plasterwork, but the arches and windows were unlike anything else I had ever seen. "This is no manor house," I exclaimed.

"You are technically correct, Doctor," said the Baronet, smiling. "You are in the remains of an actual abbey."

"I do not understand."

"Like so many other such places, Buckland Abbey did not survive Henry VIII's Dissolution of the Monasteries in 1541. It was sold to one of the King's soldiers and courtiers, who converted it into the residence we know today. Unusually, rather than retain the outbuildings and demolish the church, the architects decided instead to incorporate the nave into the manor house. Hence, the beautiful room you see before you. In the eastern end, where the presbytery once lay, we have converted a side chapel into a room to hold our greatest treasure."

Sir George led us over to the indicated location, where we paused before another wooden door, barred with strips of heavy iron. Holmes knelt down in front of this door and closely examined it. "I see you have fitted it with a Chubb lock," said he.

The baronet nodded gravely. "It should have been impossible to pick."

Holmes shook his head. "Not impossible. Merely very difficult. I have done so before myself, but it takes both considerable skill and a prolonged period of uninterrupted time.[110] Furthermore, I see no evidence of the tell-tale scratches that such an endeavour would invariably leave. Who possesses keys to this door?"

"That is what is so troubling, Mr. Holmes," said the baronet frowning. "There is only one, and it is in my possession at all times."

"What about Verton? Surely it is his job to secure the plate?"

Sir George shook his head. "That is kept in a special bureau in the butler's pantry, not in the Gallery."

"How is the room cleaned?"

"I open it for one of the chambermaids, and remain inside

while she works. I assure you, Mr. Holmes, that I take my duty as the Drum's guardian most seriously."

Holmes nodded and I thought I detected a gleam of interest in his eyes. I knew that my friend's curiosity has been piqued by the mystery of this locked room. He then bent down and plucked one small item from the floor beside the chamber's entrance.

"What is it, Holmes?" I asked.

"It appears to be a sliver of red candle wax." He turned to the butler. "Do you recognize the wax, Verton?"

The man nodded. "Indeed, sir. We have a chandlery in one of the outbuildings beyond the great barn. That colour tallow is commonly employed to make the candles used throughout the house."

"So anyone could have dripped it here?"

"Yes, sir," answered Verton.

"Very good," said Holmes. "Let us see where the Drum was kept, Sir George."

Our host fished a key from around his neck and fitted it into the lock. He pushed the door open and invited Holmes and I to enter. Inside, we found a fifteen-foot square room bounded by walls and floor that incorporated the solid stone of the church that had once stood on this site. It was plain that there were no other exits, as the only small window was moulded into place and could admit only light. A few cases lined the walls, holding relics related to the life of Sir Francis Drake. Even from this distance, I could make out a small chest filled with silver pieces-of-eight, and a pennant displaying a golden deer's head. A chair carved from ancient wood completed the furnishings.

Holmes stopped the three of us at the door. "Who else has been in the room since you discovered the Drum missing, Sir George?"

"Only myself, Verton, and Constable Bowman."

Holmes nodded as he removed a tape measure and his large round magnifying glass from his pocket. According to the methods I have seen him enact many times before, he paced carefully about the room, stopping and kneeling in various places in order to examine marks invisible to my eyes. Finally, with a look of satisfaction upon his face, he returned the tape and glass to his pocket, and invited Sir George, Verton, and I into the room.

"Are you wearing the same shoes as last night, Sir George?" When our host nodded mutely, Holmes continued. "May I see your foot?"

Perplexed, the man held up his foot as Holmes requested. When Holmes was done with this inspection, he repeated the procedure with the butler Verton.

"Have you found something, Mr. Holmes?" asked Sir George anxiously.

"There is evidence of four different prints in the room. One is from a boot similar to what I have seen worn by local constables. Once we meet Bowman, we can confirm this hypothesis. The other cannot be explained at present."

"Perhaps it belongs to the chambermaid who is allowed to clean the room once a week?" suggested Verton.

"No," said Holmes shaking his head. "Not unless you have a maid with a gigantic foot. A print this size would typically belong to a man rather over six feet in stature. Now, where was the Drum kept?"

Sir George indicated a marble altar, the top and sides ornately carved with a variety of crosses, chi-rhos, and other mystical symbols emerging from the branches of an intricate tree. "Here, Mr. Holmes."

"How tall is it?"

"About like this," said Sir George, holding up his hands roughly two-feet apart.

"So one could not hide it under the fold of one's coat?"

"Absolutely not, Mr. Holmes."

"Can you describe it?" I asked.

"I can do one better, Doctor. I can show it to you. If you would turn around, you can see it in Sir Francis' portrait."

Holmes and I followed these instructions, and gazed upon

a painting of the great sea captain. I immediately saw that – despite the interval generations that had passed – there was a distinct similarity of face between our host and his famous ancestor. Sir Francis was dressed in the typical armour of the era, and his right arm rested upon a cylindrical shape. Drake's Drum appeared to have been constructed from a light-amber coloured wood, banded at the top and bottom by strips of a red wood. It was painted with an elaborate black shield that was interrupted by a silver wavy band, punctuated by two six-pointed stars, capped by a silver knight's helmet, and sprouting draconian wings. An intricate overlay of pearls bounded this shield. Finally, a Latin motto, *Sic Parvis Magna*, ran along the bottom.

As if reading our thoughts, Sir George translated for us, " 'Thus great things from small things come.' Our family motto. To commemorate that Sir Francis was not born noble, but achieved it on the strengths of his personal merits."

Holmes nodded and then moved over the former altar. "And this?" asked Holmes, indicating a small carved word. "How would you translate it?"

"NEMO," said Sir Fuller-Drake. "Obviously, it is Latin for 'no man.' As far as I am aware, it has been there since long before Sir Francis purchased the estate. If it once held some meaning, it has been lost to the mists of time."

"What about this symbol at the very centre of the carved tree's branches? I believe I also saw it carved into the walls in the Great Hall," said Holmes pointing to a symbol, which I have reproduced from memory below:

"That symbol can be seen throughout the estate, Mr.

Holmes. I believe it also dates from the days of the monastic order based here. It has no especial meaning to our family or to the Drum."

"Very good. I think we have seen what we can here, Sir George," said Holmes. "Perhaps we could repair to someplace comfortable and discuss the particulars of the theft itself?"

The man nodded and waited for Holmes and I to depart before carefully locking the door behind him. He saw me watching him and laughed depreciatingly.

"Old habits die hard, Dr Watson, even if there is nothing especially important left to guard." He turned to the butler. "Verton, see if Constable Bowman has arrived, and then request Lady Beatrice to please join us in the drawing room."

Sir George led us up a staircase next to what was once the south transept of the Abbey. We entered a comfortably adorned room on the first floor of the house and Sir George motioned for Holmes and I to be seated while he also sank into a chair.

Before Holmes could proceed with asking any further questions, a side-door opened and admitted a striking woman approaching four decades upon this earth. Her pale cheeks, green eyes, vivid flame-coloured hair, and delicate charm combined to produce a great beauty.

"Ah, Beatrice, my dear," said Sir George. "These men, Mr. Holmes and Dr Watson, have been sent up from London in order to recover the Drum."

A steely gaze studied us. "Do whatever you must, gentlemen. I am certain my father has told you about the importance of the Drum. Its loss would be devastating to Devon and England as a whole."

Her father nodded his agreement with this statement. "What questions do you have, Mr. Holmes?"

"Who lives in the house, Sir George?"

"Just the two of us. I have been a widower for the last five years."

Holmes turned to our host's daughter. "But you are married,

are you not, Lady Beatrice?"

Her eyebrows furrowed. "I am."

"And your husband? You do not live with him?"

"Lord Seaton is in the Transvaal, maintaining the peace against Boer raiders. Until he returns, I am residing here with Papa."

Holmes nodded and turned back to Sir George. "And the staff? It must be considerable to look after such an old rambling place as Buckland Abbey?"

"Well, Verton you already met, of course. There is Mrs. Thomas, the housekeeper, and Anne, the cook, not to mention two footmen and four chambermaids. However, they are all above reproach," he replied confidently. "The stables, gardens, and workshops have their own staffs, quartered on site, and who do not normally enter the main house."

"And yet the door to the Treasures Gallery abuts the entrance to the service wing, does it not? A servant would have easy access to the door."

Our host shook his head. "No, Mr. Holmes. I am afraid that you have not been properly informed regarding the timing of events. The Drum did not vanish overnight. It happened during the Armada Party."

"What is that, Sir George?" I asked.

"It is an event my family throws at Buckland Abbey every year. Last night was the three-hundred and fifteenth anniversary of our great victory over the Spanish dons. It was a magnificent festival. We even had fireworks for the first time, generously donated by my neighbour."

"And who attended such a soiree?"

"Everyone of note in all of Devon. The cream of society..."

"And does this list contain any of your enemies?" interrupted Holmes.

The baronet and his daughter exchanged a quick glance. "I hesitate to cast any aspersions, Mr. Holmes," replied he, slowly.

"Surely in matters of national security we must discard any

such qualms, Sir George."

The man nodded hesitatingly. "Very well. My neighbour, Sir Ralph Souza, was in attendance. He resides at Holywell House upon the River Tavy, less than three miles from here south of Milton Combe. We have frequently been rivals to represent the South Devon constituency in the House of Commons.[111] However, Sir Ralph is a gentleman. He would never stoop to such a thing."

Holmes shook his head. "You might be surprised, sir, to learn the things to which our aristocracy upon occasions stoops. I once caught the grandson of a Royal Duke tunnelling into the City and Suburban Bank. We can rule out no suspect, however unlikely, until we have gathered more facts."

"If you say so, Mr. Holmes," said our host, dubiously. "In any case, I checked on the Drum before the first guests arrived. Round five o'clock. It is a bit of a habit of mine, I suppose."

"Papa likes to meditate alone with the Drum," interjected Lady Beatrice. "I tease him that he is communing with the ghost of Sir Francis."

Sir George laughed wryly. "Metaphorically speaking, of course, Mr. Holmes. I assure you that no séances have taken place in this household. But Beatrice is correct that I like to gaze upon the Drum." He paused for a moment, and then sighed. "It is a difficult task, Mr. Holmes, being the descendent of such an illustrious man. How is one to live up to such a legacy? I have tried to do my bit for Queen and Country, and I like to think that our little corner of Devon is a better place for my efforts. However, I am well aware that I will be but an asterisk in the tome of history. While Sir Francis has entire pages written about his exploits. This is a matter that has occupied my mind of late."

Holmes pursed his lips. "I am afraid that I have no answers for you, Sir George. My own people were country squires of small repute, though I had a great uncle with some artistic talent. However, no one whose reputations I must attempt to match. I suppose that we must each discover our own path in this life, and while some guide you to great fame, there are equally valid routes that can lead to other forms of happiness. Furthermore, there are also many seemingly easy trails that can instead lead to ruin. It is of the greatest importance to avoid the latter."

I stared at Holmes with some surprise, for rarely had I found him in such a philosophical mood during an active case. "But if the Drum was in its place immediately before the party, when did it vanish?" I asked.

"It was sometime before midnight," replied Sir George. "That is when the last guest departed, and when I went to check on the Drum one final time before turning in for the night."

"That leaves a seven hour window. Plenty of time for the thief to make off with the Drum," Holmes mused.

Our host shook his head again. "You don't understand, Mr. Holmes. The Armada Party is held in the Great Hall. The door to the Treasures Gallery is in the passage to the serving area before the kitchens. Members of the staff were passing through there constantly. How could anyone have picked the lock during such a busy time?"

"I have some theories in that direction, Sir George."

"You do?" exclaimed the baronet. "What are they?"

Holmes shook his head. "I apologize, Sir George. Watson here will tell you that I do not like to reveal my hypotheses until they are fully formed. When I am ready to return the Drum to you, all will become clear, I expect."

"But even if someone could have opened the lock quickly, how could they have gotten the Drum out of the house, Mr. Holmes?" asked Lady Beatrice. "No one could have brought it out through the Great Hall. It would have been spotted in an instant."

"Though the kitchen!" I cried.

"No, Watson, the same objection applies," said Holmes, coolly. "The cook and her helpers would not have left their post. They would have recalled someone unusual passing through the kitchen, especially carrying something as large as the Drum. I assume, Sir George, you called for the local constable as soon as you discovered the Drum missing?"

He nodded vigorously. "Of course! Constable Bowman came round at once. He had the same thought as you, Doctor. He questioned the kitchen staff, and it is as Mr. Holmes suspected. No one saw any person that didn't belong in the kitchen."

"So he has no clues as to the identity of the thief?" asked Holmes.

"No, sir. That is why he suggested we wire to London immediately. Within an hour we had a return message that you would be coming out today in order to recover the Drum"

Holmes smiled. "I hope I can live up to your expectations, Sir George. Though I must warn you that such a thing might not be possible."

"What do you mean?" he cried.

"My friend has a theory that this was the work of a foreign agent. If that is the case, then the Drum may have already been destroyed. There would have been no reason for them to remove the Drum intact. They would have smashed it down to pieces small enough to smuggle out underneath their coat, even during the height of the party."

Sir George turned pale at this suggestion. "I thought you had discounted that theory, Mr. Holmes."

He shook his head. "It is improbable, but by no means impossible. I do favour an alternate hypothesis. However, if our villain were a more common thief, they would not have kept it in the Abbey. We will certainly not find it tucked under the bed of one of the chambermaids. This is Devonshire, sir. At its peak, only Cornwall was a greater hive of smugglers and scoundrels. A few miles scramble in any direction would bring our thief to some river or cove from whence the Drum could have been spirited away by a waiting accomplice in a boat."

If Holmes was attempting to relieve our host's distress, he was doing a poor job of it. "Do not fear, Sir George," said I. "I can count upon one hand how many men have ever beaten my friend. If the Drum can be found, Holmes is your man."

"You must do so, Mr. Holmes!" entreated Sir George. "I will not have it said that I lost the Drum which my ancestor left for the defence of our realm."

"I would ask free reign, Sir George, to conduct this investigation after my own fashion. You must give me command over the servants, and access to every part of this house."

"You may have it!"

"Then I would ask for the key to the Treasures Gallery."

Our host initially blanched at this request, but then reconsidered. "Very well, Mr. Holmes," said he, drawing it out from beneath his coat and handing it over. "Know that I would never do so, if only the Drum were still in its place. What will you do first?"

Holmes considered this for a moment and then pulled out his pocket watch. "It is now close to three o'clock. I think I shall go for a nice, cheery walk in the countryside."

§

Knowing my friend's whims, I attempted to calm down Sir George and his daughter, who were of the belief that Holmes was mocking their belief in the power of the Drum and was consequently little committed to recovering it. After Holmes had departed the room, I assured them that while Holmes' methods may seem a tad unusual, they almost always bore fruit. I counselled patience. By the time that I left them, I believe I had been successful in allaying their concerns.

When I descended the stairs in order to re-join Holmes, I found him deep in conversation with an anxious-looking person wearing a tight tweed suit. He had a clean-shaven, pale face, a slender body, and thin legs adorned with gaiters, looking much like an out-of-place member of Scotland Yard rather than a comfortable provincial criminal officer. Holmes was scribbling some notes onto a small pad, which he proceeded to rip out and hand over to the man, who looked them over before placing in his pocket.

"Ah, Watson," said Holmes. "This is Constable Rodney Bowman. He was just describing the methods he has employed upon this case, which I am pleased to note are quite advanced. Our friends at Scotland Yard could do with a bit of your energy, I think, sir."

"I don't know about that, Mr. Holmes," muttered the constable. "I am no further to solving this case than I was last night when Sir George called. If we don't find it straightaway, rumours will soon spread across the countryside and the locals' morale will sink like a Spanish galleon."

"Nonsense," said Holmes cheerily. "You have discovered the same clue that I have. The candle wax."

"The candle wax?" Bowman cried. "For certs, I saw it, Mr. Holmes, but how does that advance the case?"

"Ah, you must use some imagination, Constable. Perhaps this will set you on the path. Ask yourself, if the Drum was stolen between five o'clock and midnight from a room whose door was in a heavily-traversed and lighted passage, what need did the thief have for a candle?"

With that Parthian shot, Holmes strode off, leaving a puzzled-appearing constable standing by the door to the Abbey. I scurried after Holmes, who was following a path that led to an enormous building to the left of the manor house.

"Holmes," I cried. "What was that business about the wax?"

He looked at me with a disappointed gaze. "You too, Watson? I must say that I would have thought by now that the years of our association might have taught you a measure of my methods." He continued around the great barn and through an Elizabethan garden until we came to a semicircular series of outbuildings. "Here, Watson, we have all the necessary supports for a country estate. We passed the magnificent stables, which I estimate are from the fourteenth century. Amongst these workshops, we have the chandlery mentioned by Verton, and where there are horses, we must expect to find a smithy that keeps them shoed."

"Perhaps I am exceedingly dull today, Holmes, but I cannot see how a smithy possibly plays a role in the pilfering of Drake's Drum?"

My friend smiled. "You must use the same imagination that I advocated to Constable Bowman, Watson. Think back to the wax that I recovered from outside the door. What was its shape?"

"It was narrow, like a sliver."

"Precisely, my dear Watson. I put to you that when wax is dripped from a candle, it makes a far rounder shape, does it not?"

"Indeed."

"Therefore, the wax was not dripped from a candle. Now, Watson, if you wished to rapidly open a Chubb's lock – which, need I remind you, is the most difficult-to-pick lock currently made – what method would you employ?"

"I would use the key, of course."

"Capital! However, we have already seen that Sir George wears the key around his neck at all times. There can be only two explanations for such a quandary. Either Sir George himself has stolen the Drum, which I find altogether implausible, or a duplicate key has been made."

"By making an impression of the original in wax and then pouring metal into the cast!" I exclaimed.[112]

Holmes beamed that I had followed his train of logic. "It is rather elementary, Watson. But the motive still eludes me, hence my plans for a walk."

"To where?"

"Oh, just a ramble. I expect the views will be rather fine. However, you do not need to accompany me, Watson. I know that you have been feeling rheumatic of late and I doubt that your old war wound would be up for such a jaunt."

"What would you have me do in your absence? Shall I interview the staff?"

"No need, Watson. Constable Bowman has already performed that task, to no avail. There is a solution at hand,

I think, but certain elements must be found beyond these walls. However, if you could locate the library, I would ask that you seek out any accounts that it might possess regarding the history of Buckland Abbey. Do not forget the inestimable use we had for such a description during the Birlstone case."

He proceeded to pack his old and oily black pipe with shag tobacco from a pouch labelled 'Bradley's' and bid me farewell. I watched as he strode off into the distance and I could see him no more.

§

I therefore spent my time doing as Holmes instructed, though I could hardly see the point to it all. I had taken down and perused dozens of ancient manuscripts, but was unable to determine the significance of these musty records. Over two hours had passed and I was beginning to wonder if he had set me upon a fool's errand, when Holmes finally returned from his solitary excursion.

"Well, Holmes, what have you learned?" I inquired.

"One axiom of mine, Watson, which I have developed during the various cases which have taken me out of London, is that wherever one goes the locals are a wealth of information regarding the temperament of the community. Their memories hold vast swaths of data regarding minor grievances dating back generations. During my walk over to Yelverton, where I needed to dispatch several wires, I conversed with several illuminating individuals. I also marched for some ways upon Drake's Leat. Are you familiar with it?"

I admitted that I was not, so Holmes continued. "According to a local farmer from whom I purchased a draught of cider, the Leat is an aqueduct dug by Sir Francis Drake in 1591 in order to supply water to the city of Plymouth. Legend holds that Drake built the entire Leat himself in one night, and then rode into Plymouth upon a white stallion before the first flow of water arrived."

"I fail to see the significance, Holmes," said I with some asperity.

"The point, Watson, is that the legend of Sir Francis is very powerful in these parts. No local man would have dared risk disturbing the Drum, not for any amount of money. In a stroke, I have ruled out a great swath of possible culprits."

"So who remains upon the list?"

"The answer to that will hopefully arrive in response to my wires."

"And what is to be done until then?"

"Two things, Watson. First, I would request an account of the historical events that you have uncovered. And when we are done with this, I would propose a game of bowls."

It was therefore upon the expanse of lawn to the west of the manor house where Sir George and Constable Bowman located us an hour later. Despite the urgency of our mission in Devon, I will admit to becoming heatedly engaged in the game at hand, which I was leading twenty shots to eighteen. Our host was plainly exasperated by what he must have perceived to be an overly cavalier attitude displayed by my friend.

"Mr. Holmes!" said the baronet. "Need I remind you that this is a matter of national security? Every minute that passes reduces the chance of successfully recovering the Drum! Will you stand idly by while our nation's enemies steer for our shores?"

Holmes merely smiled. "I assure you, Sir George, that the Drum will be soon found."

"And why are my two footmen standing guard outside the Treasures Gallery?"

"Are they? Excellent. I am glad to see that my orders are being carried out."

"But they are guarding an empty room, and you have the sole key!"

Holmes shook his head. "If I possessed the sole key, Sir George, the Drum would not be missing. Hence the posting of the guards."

"We must solve this straightaway, Mr. Holmes," said the constable. "There will be a storm upon us soon."

Holmes frowned. "What makes you say that, Constable Bowman? The sky was clear when we arrived and those clouds are still far off."

Bowman nodded towards the horizon. "The dawn sky was a deep scarlet colour, Mr. Holmes. As the old adage goes: 'Red Sky at Night, Sailor's Delight. Red Sky at Morning, Sailor's Take Warning.' The clouds will be upon us soon. If you know who took the Drum and how to recover it, we should do it soon."

"Scarlet, eh?" said Holmes, glancing over at me. "An appropriate colour, though I hope to resolve the theft of the Drum without the spill of any blood. Very well, Constable, Sir George, to ease your worries, I will counsel you that my case is nearly complete. I am awaiting two things: the first is a messenger boy from Yelverton with a response to my wire, and the second is the arrival of your neighbour, Sir Ralph Souza."

"Sir Ralph?" exclaimed our host. "Surely you don't think him involved?"

"I have reason to believe that he may have witnessed something of great importance. Only he will be able to tell us for certain. Once those two pieces are on the board, please send Mr. Verton to me."

We had not long to wait. Less than forty additional minutes had passed – during which time Holmes had mounted a spirited attack and surpassed my score for the victory – before Verton appeared to inform us that Sir Ralph had arrived. He also handed Holmes a pair of sealed telegrams.

Holmes nodded his gratitude and instructed Verton to ask Sir George, Lady Beatrice, Constable Bowman, and Sir Ralph to meet us outside of the Treasures Gallery. When the man departed, Holmes tore open the notes. He read through them quickly and turned to me with a smile. "I think we have the answers now, Watson. It is time for the denouement."

As directed, the four men and Lady Beatrice were waiting for us when we made our way back into the house. Sir Ralph

CRAIG JANACEK

Souza proved to be a tall, pugnacious, barrel-shaped man with greying side-whiskers and a shock of greyish-brown hair compressed under a top hat. He wore a dark brown frock coat and vest, with an ornate gold pocket watch chain, and expensively tailored light brown pants.

"Why have I been summoned here, Mr. Holmes?" the man demanded as soon as my friend came into view.

"All in good time, sir," replied Holmes, dismissing the two footmen guarding the door with a wave. He then drew Sir George's key from his pocket and used it to open the door. Knowing Holmes' penchant for dramatic moments, I half-expected to see the Drum sitting atop the former altar.

As we entered the gallery, Holmes lingered by the door and shut it behind us. Just as he did so, I heard a far-off noise that sounded like the roll of a drum. I glanced up towards the clerestory window, and Holmes laid a comforting hand upon my shoulder.

"Simply thunder, Watson." He then turned to the gathered group and extended the key to its owner. "Sir George, would you be so good as to lock the door?" The man looked mystified, but complied with Holmes' order. Once complete, my friend turned to the constable. "And now, Constable Bowman, if you would please station yourself by the door and ensure that no one attempts to depart."

"Why would anyone attempt to leave, Mr. Holmes?" asked the mystified policeman.

Holmes smiled. "I have found that the natural instinct of the criminal once accused of maleficence is to attempt to flee the scene, no matter how futile such an attempt typically proves."

"Do you accuse someone in this room?" said Lady Beatrice, a heat rising in her voice.

"I intend to do so as soon as I have accomplished the task at hand."

"So you have solved it, Mr. Holmes?" cried Sir George.

"Let us say that I have high hopes of recovering the Drum

274

forthwith."

"How? Where is it?" exclaimed our host.

"Watson here is familiar with my maxim, which I find to be of inestimable assistance in such matters: Once you have eliminated the impossible, whatever remains, however improbable, must be the truth." He smiled broadly. "In this case, Constable Bowman has already established that it is impossible for an intact Drum to have left this room during the span of time between the two visits by Sir George. I concur with his assessment."

"But where then, Holmes?" I asked with a great deal of interest. "Surely you don't suggest that it is still in this room?"

"Where else, Watson? The legend holds that grave tidings will befall England if the Drum is destroyed or leaves the Abbey, and yet, the nation still stands. Therefore, it is logical to assume that the Drum remains within."

If Holmes had hoped for applause at this revelation, he was disappointed. The assembled group – myself included – merely looked around the room with mystified expressions. There was plainly nowhere to hide something the size of the Drum.

"Are you joking with us, Mr. Holmes?" cried Sir George!

"And I do not understand what this has to do with me, Mr. Holmes?" asked Sir Ralph, irritably. "Would you care to explain?"

"Your presence is essential, Sir Ralph. However, first a bit of history must be revealed." He turned to the group. "I asked Watson to do some reading about the origins of the Abbey. I was surprised to learn that it was originally built by the Cistercian order in 1278. Of course, Bernard of Clairvaux, who had a great fondness for secrets, founded the Cistercians. He also founded the Knights Templar, and his white monks were later famous for their skills as both metallurgists and engineers."

"Holmes, what possible role could this play in the disappearance of the Drum?" I exclaimed.

"Have you forgotten, Watson, the priest hole wherein we found Mr. John Douglas hiding, in the Jacobean manor house at Birlstone? Where do you think such ideas originated if not with the Cistercians?"

Sir George groaned. "There are indeed secret doorways built into Buckland Abbey, Mr. Holmes! Do you mean to tell me that there is another route, as of yet undiscovered, into this room?"

"Not exactly, Sir George, but you are close to the solution. The answer lies with 'no one.'"

"No one?" I exclaimed. "What do you mean?"

"I refer to the mysterious carving upon the former altar, Watson," said Holmes pointing. "To what end would the carvers have included the mysterious word 'NEMO' on this otherwise traditional piece of church architecture?"

"I am sure I do not know."

"Well, I had some time to contemplate this very question upon my walk and was certain it was the solution to our mystery. At first, I had the translation wrong. I thought it said, 'no man,' and was concerned that Lady Beatrice was involved in some fashion."

The lady in question threw her hand to her mouth in surprise. "Me, sir?" she cried. "How can you think I am guilty of such a crime?"

Holmes raised his hands in a supplicating manner. "I assure you, Lady Beatrice, that I soon discarded that theory. I am convinced you know no more regarding the Drum's disappearance than your father does. As I have already mentioned, the correct translation is 'no one.' However, what could that mean? I considered this question for some time before the answer became apparent." He paused and raised his eyebrows, as if to ask whether any of us were following his train of logic.

"I don't understand, Holmes!" I exclaimed.

"Very well, Watson. You and I shall demonstrate for our host. Imagine, if you will, that the year is 1278. An elderly Longshanks is on throne, following a period of civil strife known as the Second Baron's War. But the peace is short-lived, for the Despenser War that toppled his successor Edward II was not far in the future. The great abbeys should have been a place of refuge, but when armed bands are roving the lands, you never rely solely upon the mercy of man. Instead, you build a place to hide your most precious relics, should the sanctity of your walls be breached. However, what one man can close, so another can open. The mason responsible for the design of this chapel was a most brilliant individual. Now, I shall move into position behind the altar, playing the role of the medieval priest. Watson, you shall be my assistant. If you would be so kind as to kneel in prayer in front of the altar?"

I grumbled at this ridiculous request, but did as he commanded. "Alright, Holmes, what is this charade intended to accomplish?"

"What do you see before you, Watson?"

"A carved altar, just the same as anyone else."

"Look closely, Watson. Are there not two symbols at the very bottom that are repeated nowhere else?"

"The six-pointed stars!" I exclaimed. "Like the ones painted on the Drum!"

"Precisely, Watson. Moreover, very much like the marks upon the mysterious Greek cross carving. Before me upon the altar, I curiously find the sole example of the lambda and turned epsilon, which together complete the two upper symbols upon that cross. While I confess to not knowing their meaning, for my knowledge of Greek is rather limited, their presence alone is most suggestive. When I give the word, please reach out and press both of those stars. I will do the same with the two symbols I have before me. Now, Watson!" he cried.

I did as Holmes directed, more eagerly this time. To my great surprise, the top of the altar suddenly lifted upon one edge, like the lid to a chest. I heard an exclamation of surprise from behind me, but could not tear my eyes from the spectacle. As I watched, Holmes reached both arms into the hollow altar and – with a shout of triumph – he pulled forth the missing Drake's Drum.

§

The five of us sat in stunned silence for a moment, and then, everyone broke out in simultaneous questions. Holmes carefully set down the Drum and then moved around the altar, waving his arms to quiet the group. Once they had set-tled, Holmes continued. "You surely have some questions, Sir George. Pray ask them."

"I cannot thank you enough, Mr. Holmes, for finding the Drum!" he exclaimed. "But who put it there and why?"

"The 'why' is simple, Sir George. It was far too difficult to remove the Drum during the Armada Party in front of all of the witnesses. Hiding it was a far more expedient solution. The thieves could then later return, long after it any investiga-tion was abandoned, in order to claim it. The former question is what occupied my mind for some time. Of course, it must have been two individuals working together, for as Watson and I just demonstrated, no man alone could work the al-tar's secret mechanism. The assistant was most certainly your neighbour, Sir Ralph."

"What?" the man exclaimed. "How dare you, sir! If you re-peat that outside of this room I will have libel charges brought upon you that shall reduce you to penury."

Holmes shrugged. "You have motive, sir. According to local gossip, you loathe Sir George for defeating you in the most recent running for Parliament. And you despise his daughter, who refused your suit for her hand in marriage fifteen years ago."

"That is water under the bridge," bristled Sir Ralph. He waved his hand angrily. "You have no proof."

"You also had means," Holmes continued. "Was it not you who provided the fireworks which distracted the guests and staff long enough for you and your accomplice to slip into the

Treasures Gallery unnoticed?"

Sir Ralph shook his head. "So I provided the fireworks for the party. That proves nothing, other than my generosity."

"It was generous indeed," said Holmes severely. "For your family is relatively new to these parts, is it not? It has no ties to the glory days of Sir Francis Drake and the Armada of 1588, does it? Your ancestors are originally Portuguese, I believe. According to a wire I received, your great uncle was an exceptionally wealthy merchant who acquired Holywell House around the year 1800. He bought up many of the rotten boroughs in these parts and used them to gain a sufficient degree of governmental favour that he acquired a baronetcy. You are the rare man of these parts who would have no qualms about violating the sacred powers of the Drum."

The man crossed his arms and glared at my friend. "As I said, you have no proof. Only speculation and rumour."

My friend finally smiled. "No matter, Sir Ralph. If you will not confess to your role, I have no worries that your partner will do so for the both of you."

"Who is his partner?" cried Sir George.

Holmes turned to him. "Why, your butler Dick Verton, of course."

Sir George turned to the man with a look of horror upon his face. "Verton, tell me it isn't true! You have been with us for almost four years."

The man merely glowered at Holmes mutely and refused to answer the charge.

"It was Watson who found the solution," said my friend calmly.

"Whatever do you mean, Holmes?" I asked. "I did no such thing."

Holmes waved his hand. "Just tell them what you told me during our game of bowls about the origins of the Abbey, Watson. What happened after the monasteries were dissolved by Henry VIII?"

I could not tell what Holmes was driving at, but I had

learned that it was best to simply acquiesce to these sorts of whims, as there invariably was a point to them. "Well, Buckland was sold to Sir Richard Grenville the Elder, Marshall of Calais. Later, his grandson, Richard the Younger, who was a privateer and explorer – much like Sir Francis – inherited it. In fact, the two men were great rivals. First, Grenville attempted to establish a colony at Roanoke Island in the New World of Virginia. However, the experiment was a failure, and the colonists were evacuated back to England by Sir Francis. More importantly, it was Grenville who first proposed to the Privy Council the possibility of an attempt to sail into the Pacific Ocean. But it was Sir Francis who usurped this idea and, in so doing, made himself both rich and famous. Grenville never forgave him. Later, his debts mounting, Grenville sold Buckland Abbey to two intermediaries. Unbeknownst to him, these men were actually working for his despised enemy, Sir Francis Drake. And the home has been in the Drake family ever since."

"Very good, Watson. You see, I asked myself, how would Verton have known about the secret of the altar? It seems implausible that he could have stumbled across the mechanism himself, especially when it requires two people in order to function. I therefore took it upon myself to send a wire to London asking for an inquiry into his background. The response confirmed my suspicion. Until five years ago, there was no such person as Dick Verton. The man you see before you was a clerk for a firm off Cheapside Road in London. His first name is indeed Richard. However, his surname was altered, inverting the French and English components. The French 'Vert' from the English 'Green' and the English 'Town' from the French 'Ville.' Richard Greenville became Dick Verton."

Sir George's eyes bulged at this unexpected news. "Do you mean to say that Sir Richard Grenville was an ancestor of this man? I though the line was extinct."

"Not a direct descendent, of course, but yes, the blood is there," replied Holmes. "Most likely a by-blow during Sir Richard's wanderings far from home. Do not forget that this feat required both great cunning and courage in order to enact. In some ways, it was a worthy tribute to his ancestor. Sir Richard Grenville was an exceptionally brave sailor. Off the Azores, his lone galleon ran into a fifty-three ship Spanish fleet. Rather than flee, Grenville ordered his men to sail directly into the heart of the foe. They fought for hours, until it was clear that they could go on no longer. Grenville died of his wounds, and his captured ship was sunk soon after by a cyclone."

"I fail to see how stealing the Drum could be considered a homage?" said Sir George, irritably.

"Do you not recall the name of Richard Grenville's ship?" asked Holmes, mildly.

Our host shook his head, plainly confused by this nonsensical question. "His ship? Whatever does that have to do with anything?"

"Perhaps everything. For a man often names his most prized possession after something very dear to his heart. And certain traits may run deep within families. We have seen such spiritual throwbacks before, Watson and I, upon the moors of Devon."

"That seems rather fanciful, Holmes," said I.

"Does it? Well, I don't insist upon it. No doubt, I am wrong. And yet, I find it suggestive that Sir Richard Grenville called his ship the *Revenge*."

§

"So, in the end, the butler did it, eh, Holmes?" said I, contentedly settling into my first-class carriage seat headed to Paddington Station. The Drum was safely locked up back in the Treasures Gallery, and Dick Verton was under arrest by Constable Bowman. Holmes and I had taken the landau through the storm back to Plymouth in order to catch the final train to London. Holmes pulled out a newspaper to peruse during the trip, but I had a few final questions.

He shrugged. "Yes, perhaps an unlikely ending, for rarely do I find that a servant is the culprit. It is almost too obvious. But not without precedent, surely. As you may recall, Watson, one of my earliest cases hinged on the disappearance of the butler Brunton from Hurlstone Manor."

"But why did you suspect Verton?"

"Come now, Watson. Who else could have prepared the duplicate key that they utilized to effect rapid entrance to the Treasures Gallery? As we saw, Sir George carried it with him at all times. It could only have been copied during some brief interval while he was bathing. The sole possible candidates for such a caper would have been his daughter, Lady Beatrice, or the butler, Verton. Once I determined that Lady Beatrice had both little motive and a strong belief in the power of the Drum, my list of suspects became a short one indeed. Verton was also one of the few men who could have used the resources of the workshops in order to manufacture the key without raising questions. I am certain that Constable Bowman will confirm this with a careful questioning of the smithy staff. The level of patience required for this theft was most impressive. He insinuated himself into the Abbey's staff years ago, and carefully cultivated the assistance of Sir Ralph Souza for his schemes. Of course, Sir Ralph will get off with nothing more than a wrist slap, I suspect."

"I still don't understand why Verton did it. Revenge for something that transpired over three hundred years ago seems rather absurd."

"Memories run long in these parts, Watson. However, I suspect that his motives were more mercenary than simply revenge. The evidence suggests that Verton was planning anonymously to ransom the Drum. Sir George would have been forced to pay any sum that Verton demanded, in the name of national security. This would have ruined Sir George financially, and he would have been required to sell Buckland Abbey. Verton had already made inquiries via intermediaries regarding purchasing it. Therefore, in a sense, this was but a twisted scheme to regain something that Verton felt his ancestor had unfairly lost through the machinations of Sir Francis Drake. In fact, you might coin a new adage in response to this lesson: 'Never get involved in a business deal with a pirate.'"

"Privateer, Holmes. Their actions were sanctioned by the Queen."

"And yet, Watson, they were independent agents, roving the seas in the plunder trade only partly out of service to their Queen, and primarily for their own purposes."

"One might say the same about you, Holmes. Have you not said yourself that you are a private agent, free to choose to solve those crimes that interest you, and that you are not retained to repair the deficiencies of the Queen's official police force?"

Holmes stared at me for a moment, and then threw back his head in laughter. "I never get your limits, Watson." He smiled at me. "It goes without saying, Watson, that this is one tale which the government will never permit you to publish, for fears that your words may inspire some foreign potentate to replicate the feats of Verton and Souza and thereby weaken our national defences."

"But, Holmes, I thought you did not believe in the power of the Drum?"

He shook his head sadly. "I have grown to appreciate the power of mythology, Watson. It little matters whether Drake actually still patrols the waves, or whether Arthur and his knights will sally forth from Sewingshields Hill to guard our shores.[113] What matters is that the people of England believe it, and the power of this belief is what will maintain their morale far into the future, even in the face of insurmountable odds."[114]

"Just as the belief in the eternal powers of Mr. Sherlock Holmes guards the citizens of London against the more outrageous schemes of potential criminals?"

Holmes smiled. "We all have a role to play, Watson, each according to our means."

I leaned back in my seat, content in the successful conclusion of yet another adventure with my friend Mr. Sherlock Holmes. Just then, I heard the sound of a drum beating in the great distance.

Glancing over at Holmes, I saw him smile slightly and shake his head. "Simply thunder again, Watson." He turned his gaze back to the newspaper.

However, when I looked outside the train window, I could see that the clouds had retreated from the night sky. From where then would such a sound come, if not from Drake's Drum?

§

APPENDIX: ON DATES

A CHRONOLOGIC ORDER OF SHERLOCK HOLMES ADVENTURES (CANONICAL & NON-CANONICAL)

How best to read the various tales of Sherlock Holmes? The most obvious answer to that question is "the order in which they were written and published, beginning with A Study in Scarlet." However, Sir Arthur Conan Doyle, the first literary agent for Dr John H. Watson, did not publish the stories in a strict chronologic order, with many stories told primarily as flashbacks. Therefore, for the reader, either new to these wondrous tales or seeking to read them all again, I present the following option. By following this list, the reader is able to see for themselves the maturation of Holmes and Watson, from relatively young lads with all of London at their fingertips, to the mature gentlemen reflecting upon a lifetime of adventure.

I generally follow the dating laid out by the great Sherlockian editors William S. Baring-Gould in *The Annotated Sherlock Holmes* (1967) and Leslie S. Klinger in *The New Annotated Sherlock Holmes* (2005-6), which are themselves the product of consensus of other Sherlockians. These have often followed the vaguest of clues in the stories themselves in order to come to their conclusions. Dr Watson, for all his excellent qualities, was never his best with dates (he was known, from time to time, to even be off by a year or more). For point of reference, it is generally considered that Sherlock Holmes was born in 1854 (6 January, to be precise) and John Watson in 1852 (7 August, to be precise), making them at the time of their meeting in January 1881, approximately twenty-seven and twenty-nine years of age, respectively.

At the risk of being accused of vanity, into the list this literary agent interjects the timing for those stories (in bold) that I have been so fortunate as to unearth and publish.

Before 221B Baker Street (1874 – 1880)
- July 12 – September 22, 1874: The '*Gloria Scott*' (from *TMSH*). Recounted to Watson c. February 1888.
- April 4–22, 1875: **The Lost Legion** (from *TTI!*). Recounted to Watson c. December 1894.
- December 28 – January 7, 1875-76: **The Father of Evil** (from *TSS*). Recounted to Watson January 6, 1903.
- October 2, 1879: The Musgrave Ritual (from *TMSH*). Recounted to Watson c. February 1888.
- July 27 – December 4, 1880: **The Isle of Devils**

A Suite in Baker Street (1881 – 1889)
- March 4–7, 1881: A Study in Scarlet
- August 25, 1881: **The Adventure of the Tragic Act** (from *SAO*)
- December 3, 1881: **The Adventure of the Double-Edged Hoard** (from *FMFL*)
- April 6, 1883: The Adventure of the Speckled Band (from *TASH*)
- May 5-12, 1883: **The Adventure of the Monstrous Blood** (from *TFC*)
- August 23 – September 10, 1884: **The Gate of Gold**

- October 6–7, 1885: The Resident Patient (from *TMSH*)
- November 3–4, 1885: **The Adventure of the Mad Colonel** (from *TFC*)
- October 8, 1886: The Adventure of the Noble Bachelor (from *TASH*)

The Well-Remembered Door (The First Desertion) (1886 – 1888)[115]

- April 14–26, 1887: The Reigate Squires (from *TMSH*)
- May 20–22, 1887: A Scandal in Bohemia (from *TASH*)
- June 2–4, 1887: **The Adventure of the Dawn Discovery** (from *FMFL*)
- June 18–19, 1887: The Man with the Twisted Lip (from *TASH*)
- June 19-21, 1887: **The Adventure of the Missing Mana** (from *APRT*)
- September 29–30, 1887: The Five Orange Pips (from *TASH*)
- October 18–19, 1887: A Case of Identity (from *TASH*)
- October 21–22, 1887: **The Adventure of the Queen's Pendant** (from *TTI!*)
- October 29–30, 1887: The Red-Headed League (from *TASH*)
- November 19, 1887: The Adventure of the Dying Detective (from *HLB*)
- December 27, 1887: The Adventure of the Blue Carbuncle (from *TASH*)

The Return to Baker Street (1888 – 1889)

- January 7–8, 1888: The Valley of Fear
- April 7, 1888: The Yellow Face (from *TMSH*)
- April 14–15, 1888: **The Red Leech** (from *Assassination*)
- August 30-31, 1888: **The Adventure of the Loring Riddle**
- September 12, 1888: The Greek Interpreter (from *TMSH*)

- September 18–21, 1888: The Sign of Four
- September 25 – October 20, 1888: The Hound of the Baskervilles
- March 24, 1889: **The Adventure of the Pirate's Code** (from *TTI!*)
- April 5–20, 1889: The Adventure of the Copper Beeches (from *TASH*)

The Second Desertion (1889 – 1891)[116]

- June 15, 1889: The Stockbroker's Clerk (from *TMSH*)
- July 30 – August 1, 1889: The Naval Treaty (from *TMSH*)
- August 31 – September 2, 1889: The Cardboard Box (from *TMSH*)
- September 7–8, 1889: The Adventure of the Engineer's Thumb (from *TASH*)
- September 11–12, 1889: The Crooked Man (from *TMSH*)
- September 21–22, 1889: **The Adventure of the Fateful Malady** (from *TFC*)
- March 24–29, 1890: The Adventure of Wisteria Lodge (from *HLB*)
- June 8–9, 1890: The Boscombe Valley Mystery (from *TASH*)
- June 20 – July 4, 1890: **The Oak-Leaf Sprig** (from *ARW*)
- September 25–30, 1890: Silver Blaze (from *TMSH*)
- December 19–20, 1890: The Adventure of the Beryl Coronet (from *TASH*)
- December 25, 1890: **The Adventure of the Spanish Sovereign** (from *TSF*)
- April 24 – May 4, 1891: The Final Problem (from *TMSH*)

The Great Hiatus (1891 – 1894)

- August 1-8: 1891: **The Harrowing Intermission** (from *FMFL*)

The Great Return (1894 – 1902)

- April 5, 1894: The Adventure of the Empty House (from *TRSH*)
- October 7-9, 1894: **The Adventure of the Boulevard Assassin** (from *APRT*)
- October 20 – November 7, 1894: **The Adventure of the Double Detectives** (from *RTW*)
- November 14–15, 1894: The Adventure of the Golden Pince-Nez (from *TRSH*)
- September 18–22: 1894: The Adventure of the Second Stain (from *TRSH*)[117]
- September 22–25, 1894: **The Adventure of the Third Traitor** (from *AEW*)
- December 23, 1894: **The Adventure of the Manufactured Miracle** (from *TSF*)
- January 13-14, 1895: **The Adventure of the Dishonourable Discharge** (from *TSS*)
- February 13-15, 1895: **The Adventure of the Secret Tomb** (from *APRT*)
- April 5–6, 1895: The Adventure of the Three Students (from *TRSH*)
- April 13–20, 1895: The Adventure of the Solitary Cyclist (from *TRSH*)
- June 23-25, 1895: **The Problem of the Black Eye** (from *SAO*)
- July 3–5, 1895: The Adventure of Black Peter (from *TRSH*)
- August 20–21, 1895: The Adventure of the Norwood Builder (from *TRSH*)
- November 21–23, 1895: The Adventure of the Bruce-Partington Plans (from *HLB*)
- December 22, 1895: **The Adventure of the First Star** (from *TSF*)
- October 28, 1896: The Adventure of the Veiled Lodger (from *TCBSH*)
- November 19–21, 1896: The Adventure of the Sussex Vampire (from *TCBSH*)

- December 8–10, 1896: The Adventure of the Missing Three-Quarter (from *TRSH*)
- January 23, 1897: The Adventure of the Abbey Grange (from *TRSH*)
- March 16–20, 1897: The Adventure of the Devil's Foot (from *HLB*)
- May 2–3, 1897: **The Adventure of the Fatal Fire** (from *TSS*)
- July 7, 1897: **The Adventure of the Sunken Indiaman** (from *FMFL*)
- September 4-5, 1897: **The Mannering Towers Mystery** (from *SAO*)
- July 27 – August 13, 1898: The Adventure of the Dancing Men (from *TRSH*)
- July 28–30, 1898: The Adventure of the Retired Colourman (from *TCBSH*)
- January 5–14, 1899: The Adventure of Charles Augustus Milverton (from *TRSH*)
- February 2, 1899: **The Adventure of the African Horror** (from *RTW*)
- June 8–10, 1900: The Adventure of the Six Napoleons (from *TRSH*)
- October 4–5, 1900: The Problem of Thor Bridge (from *TCBSH*)
- November 4, 1900: **The Adventure of the Awakened Spirit** (from *TSS*)
- May 16–18, 1901: The Adventure of the Priory School (from *TRSH*)
- June 20-23, 1901: **The Adventure of the Fair Lad** (from *RTW*)
- May 6–7, 1902: The Adventure of Shoscombe Old Place (from *TCBSH*)
- June 26–27, 1902: The Adventure of the Three Garridebs (from *TCBSH*)
- July 1–18, 1902: The Disappearance of Lady Frances Carfax (from *HLB*)

- September 3–16, 1902: The Adventure of the Illustrious Client (from *TCBSH*)
- September 24–25, 1902: The Adventure of the Red Circle (from *HLB*)

The Final Desertion (1903)[118]
- January 7–12, 1903: The Adventure of the Blanched Soldier (from *TCBSH*)
- May 26–27, 1903: The Adventure of the Three Gables (from *TCBSH*)
- June 28, 1903: The Adventure of the Mazarin Stone (from *TCBSH*)
- August 2, 1903: **The Adventure of the Silent Drum** (from *TTI!*)
- September 6–22, 1903: The Adventure of the Creeping Man (from *TCBSH*)
- December 20-21, 1903: **The Adventure of the Barren Grave** (from *TFC*)

Retirement (1904 – 1918)
- January 6-18, 1904: **The Adventure of the Dead Man's Note** (from *APRT*)
- July 3–5, 1907: **The Cold Dish** (from *TSS*)
- September 2, 1907: **The Adventure of the Twelfth Hour** (from *SAO*)
- July 25 – August 1, 1907: The Lion's Mane (from *TCBSH*)
- June 21, 1909: **The Adventure of the Unfathomable Silence** (from *AEW*)
- October 31 – November 1, 1909: **The Adventure of the Pharaoh's Curse** (from *Assassination*)
- November 2–5, 1909: **The Problem of Threadneedle Street** (from *Assassination*)
- November 30 – December 1, 1909: **The Falling Curtain** (from *Assassination*)
- August 2, 1914: **The High Mountain** (from *AEW*)
- August 2, 1914: His Last Bow: The War Service of Sher-

lock Holmes (from *HLB*)
- March 19-22, 1915: **The Adventure of the Defenceless Prisoner** (from *AEW*)
- September 17, 1915: **Their Final Flourish** (from *AEW*)
- October 22, 1917: Preface (from *HLB*)
- December 22, 1918: **The Grand Gift of Sherlock** (from *TSF*)

THE COLLECTIONS

Literary Editor, Sir Arthur Conan Doyle (56 cases & 4 novels)
- *TASH: The Adventures of Sherlock Holmes* (12 cases, published 1891-92)
- *TMSH: The Memoirs of Sherlock Holmes* (12 cases, published 1892-93)
- *TRSH: The Return of Sherlock Holmes* (13 cases, published 1903-4)
- *HLB: His Last Bow: Some Reminiscences of Sherlock Holmes* (7 cases & 1 preface, published 1917)
- *TCBSH: The Case-Book of Sherlock Holmes* (12 cases, published 1921-27)

Literary Editor, Craig Janacek (45 cases & 2 novels)
- *The Assassination of Sherlock Holmes* (4 cases; published 2015)
- *Light in the Darkness*, comprising:
    - *TSF: The Season of Forgiveness* (3 cases & 1 letter; published 2014)
    - *TFC: The First of Criminals* (4 cases; published 2015-16)
- *The Treasury of Sherlock Holmes*, comprising:
    - *TTI!: Treasure Trove Indeed!* (4 cases; published 2016)
    - *FMFL: Fortunes Made and Fortunes Lost* (4 cases; published 2018)
- *The Gathering Gloom*, comprising:

- *TSS: The Schoolroom of Sorrow* (5 cases; published 2018)
  - *AEW: An East Wind* (5 cases; published 2019)
- *The Travels of Sherlock Holmes*, comprising:
  - *APRT: A Prompt and Ready Traveller* (4 cases; published 2019)
  - *RTW: Round the World* (4 cases; published 2020)
- *The Chronicles of Sherlock Holmes*, comprising:
  - *SAO: Seen and Observed* (4 cases; published 2020)
  - *TDC: Their Dark Crisis* (4 cases; published 2021)

§

ALSO BY CRAIG JANACEK

THE ADVENTURE OF THE DAWN DISCOVERY
THE HARROWING INTERMISSION[125]
THE ADVENTURE OF THE SUNKEN INDIAMAN[126]

THE SCHOOLROOM OF SORROW[127]
THE FATHER OF EVIL
THE ADVENTURE OF THE FATAL FIRE
THE ADVENTURE OF THE DISHONOURABLE DISCHARGE[128]
THE ADVENTURE OF THE AWAKENED SPIRIT[129]
THE COLD DISH

AN EAST WIND[130]
THE ADVENTURE OF THE THIRD TRAITOR[131]
THE ADVENTURE OF THE UNFATHOMABLE SILENCE[132]
THE HIGH MOUNTAIN
THE ADVENTURE OF THE DEFENCELESS PRISONER
THEIR FINAL FLOURISH

A PROMPT AND READY TRAVELLER[133]
THE ADVENTURE OF THE MISSING MANA
THE ADVENTURE OF THE BOULEVARD ASSASSIN
THE ADVENTURE OF THE SECRET TOMB
THE ADVENTURE OF THE DEAD MAN'S NOTE

ROUND THE WORLD[134]
THE OAK-LEAF SPRIG
THE ADVENTURE OF THE DOUBLE DETECTIVES
THE ADVENTURE OF THE AFRICAN HORROR
THE ADVENTURE OF THE FAIR LAD[135]

SEEN & OBSERVED
THE ADVENTURE OF THE TRAGIC ACT
THE PROBLEM OF THE BLACK EYE
THE MANNERING TOWERS MYSTERY
THE ADVENTURE OF THE TWELFTH HOUR

THE ASSASSINATION OF SHERLOCK HOLMES

THE ADVENTURE OF THE PHARAOH'S CURSE
THE PROBLEM OF THREADNEEDLE STREET
THE FALLING CURTAIN
(THE RED LEECH)

OTHER STORIES OF MR. SHERLOCK HOLMES
THE ADVENTURE OF THE LORING RIDDLE[136]

SET EUROPE SHAKING: Volume One of 'The Exploits and Adventures of Brigadier Gerard'
(Compiled and Edited by Craig Janacek, with Three New Tales)
HOW THE BRIGADIER WRESTLED THE BEAR OF BOULOGNE
HOW THE BRIGADIER FACED THE FIRING SQUAD
HOW THE BRIGADIER DUELLED FOR A DESPATCH

A MIGHTY SHADOW: Volume Two of 'The Exploits and Adventures of Brigadier Gerard'
(Compiled and Edited by Craig Janacek, with One New Tale)
HOW THE BRIGADIER COMMANDED THE EMPEROR

OTHER NOVELS
THE OXFORD DECEPTION
THE ANGER OF ACHILLES PETERSON

*Coming soon

§

FOOTNOTES

[1] The non-Canonical novel *The Gate of Gold* (Chapter I).

[2] The non-Canonical tale *The Adventure of the Manufactured Miracle*.

[3] The non-Canonical tale *The Red Leech*.

[4] The non-Canonical tale *The Adventure of the First Star*.

[5] "Of course, when people bury treasure nowadays they do it in the Post Office bank. But there are always some lunatics about. It would be a dull world without them." From *The Adventure of the Three Gables*.

[6] "The cursed greed which has been my besetting sin through life has withheld from her the treasure...." From Chapter IV of *The Sign of Four*.

[7] Many years after his death, the following narrative was found among the papers of Dr John H. Watson at his former home in Southsea. The paper was contained in an envelope, which was docketed, '*The Lost Legion. A Short Account of the Circumstances which occurred to Mr. Sherlock Holmes near Miss Vermilion's Farm in North-West Derbyshire in the Spring of 1875.*' The envelope was sealed, and on the other side was written in pencil – 'Excluded from '*Case-Book*;' excessively improbable for the acumen of the general public.'

[8] Sir Henry Rider Haggard (1856-1925) was one of the most popular Victorian authors of adventure novels. He published *The People of the Mist* in 1894, nine years after his novel *King's Solomon's Mines* pioneered the so-called 'Lost Word' literary genre. The latter was, of course, named after the eponymous 1912 novel by Sir Arthur Conan Doyle, Watson's first literary editor.

[9] Latin for 'Through Adversity to the Stars,' adopted in 1912 as the

motto of the Royal Air Force.

[10] In Tibetan Buddhist tradition, Shambhala is a mystical kingdom hidden within the hollow Earth. The Theosophical Society, founded in 1875, popularized the idea in the West.

[11] Scholars have determined that the case published as The 'Gloria Scott' took place in 1874, suggesting that Holmes's trip to Derbyshire likely transpired in early 1875.

[12] The careful scholar will note a great deal of similarities between certain aspects of this previously unpublished adventure of Holmes and a short story entitled 'The Terror of Blue John Gap.' The latter was written by Sir Arthur Conan Doyle, Watson's first literary editor, who published it in the August 1910 volume of the Strand Magazine. It can be surmised that Conan Doyle heard a verbal account of this case from Watson, and when he realized that Watson did not intend to publish it, Conan Doyle embellished it into a Gothic horror tale. For unknown reasons, Conan Doyle moved the action to the Blue John Cavern, which at the time was already a show cave open to the public. In fact, rumours hold that Constantine John Phipps, 2nd Baron Mulgrave (1744-1792) once threw a dinner party for his miners in the well-known cave!

[13] An archaic name for scarlet fever, an infection by the group A Streptococcal bacteria and associated with a sore throat, fever, headaches, swollen nodes, and a sandpapery rash.

[14] An archaic name for measles.

[15] There are two Bronze Age (c.1200 BCE) burial mounds on or near the summit of Mam Tor. I have been unable to locate any copies of Mr. Handsacre's planned book, so we must presume that he abandoned the idea.

[16] The second theory is now considered proven, and is known as Doggerland. The area was likely inhabited by humans during the Mesolithic period, and then flooded around c.6200 BCE.

[17] There is no known cavern called the 'Shivering' in the Castleton area. However, new caverns are still being discovered, the most recent being the 'Titan' which was found in 2006.

[18] There is some debate about the accuracy of this statement. Some scholars suggest that the Roman murrhine was actually a similar fluorite-based mineral imported from Persia, and that the source of the wine-flavour augmentation was not the stone itself, but rather a

myrrh-like resin applied to the stone during carving in order to prevent it from shattering.

[19] For the sake of Dr Watson's American readers, I should note that the term 'ironmonger' is used in Great Britain for a supplier of consumer goods, the equivalent of an American 'hardware store.'

[20] Cave-bears were giant bears whose range stretched across Europe, and whose fossils are often found in limestone caves. They became extinct about 24,000 years ago. Cave-bear bones have not been found around Castleton, however, bones from an auroch, a megafauna cattle-like beast from the same era, were excavated from Blue John Cavern.

[21] Latin for 'Entities must not be multiplied beyond necessity.' This is the 'razor' of William of Occam (.1287-1347).

[22] We have been unable to locate a place called 'Chargeford' in England, and we have no record that Holmes ever recounted the details of this ghost-hunt to Watson.

[23] It is postulated that the Romans derived *haruspicy* from the Etruscans. Such practices lasted at least until the destructive reign of Emperor Theodosius I (347-395), and did indeed make their way to England, based on an inscription found at Bath.

[24] Baron Thomas Babington Macaulay (1800-1859) wrote his *Lays of Ancient Rome* from 1834 to 1838.

[25] Taphophobia is the fear of being buried alive.

[26] Artus is a Breton name which means 'bear.' This also suggests a connection with King Arthur, who historically is considered to have been a Romano-British leader in the struggle against invading Anglo-Saxons during the late 5th and early 6th century.

[27] The Mithraic mysteries were a religion dedicated to the god Mithras that was extremely popular in the Roman Empire from the 1st to 4th centuries, especially amongst members of the Roman military.

[28] The oracle of Delphi, or Pythia, was famous for her prophecies. Modern science has suggested that subterranean vapours emitting from a chasm beneath the Temple of Apollo were responsible for her visions, though this theory has not been definitively proven.

[29] Holmes is vexingly vague here about whom precisely he confided in. Coming on the heels of his misogynistic statement, the reader is forced to wonder if this is some allusion to Miss Irene Adler?

[30] Watson unfortunately neglected to leave any additional notes on the disappearance of Mr. James Simmons.

[31] The origins of the 'Black Maria' nickname are obscure, but may derive from the fact that the police vans of the 1800's were painted either black or a very dark blue. The term was used in French detective novel *Monsieur Lecoq* (1868) by Emile Gaboriau, which Watson had read before his meeting with Holmes (Chapter II, *A Study in Scarlet*).

[32] The William murders were committed in 1811 in the neighbourhood of Ratcliffe Highway. Thomas De Quincey (1785-1859) popularized the crime in his sensational essay *'On Murder Considered as one of the Fine Arts,'* with which Holmes would surely have been intimately familiar. The Greenwich hammer attack may be a reference to the case of Edmund Walter Pook, who in 1871 was accused of murdering a maid in his parent's home. He was eventually found not guilty, though the murder was never solved, likely because Holmes had yet to finish university and establish himself in London as a consulting detective.

[33] A Regius Professorship is a unique feature of British institutions and refers to a special professorship position established by decree of the reigning monarch. The actual Regius Professor of History at Cambridge in 1881 was Sir John Seeley, who was never murdered. It can be concluded that Watson must have changed the name of the victim, and perhaps even the actual university, where this gruesome murder took place.

[34] The careful scholar will note many similarities between certain aspects of this previously unpublished adventure of Holmes and Watson and a short story entitled *'The Silver Hatchet.'* The latter was the product of a young writer known at the time simply as Dr Arthur Conan Doyle. Conan Doyle published this work in the 1883 Christmas edition of the *London Society* magazine. It may be surmised that he heard a verbal account of the case from his friend John Watson, for whom he would later serve as literary editor. As Watson had not yet decided to publish his adventures with Holmes, Conan Doyle must have been emboldened to embellish it into a Gothic horror tale, moving its setting to Budapest, so as to avoid any hint of referring to a still-recent event closer to home.

[35] Properly, the Elrington and Bosworth Professorship of Anglo-Saxon, Norse, and Celtic, which was established in 1878.

[36] Watson must have recorded this incorrectly, since *Bulmer's Direc-*

tory, which provides a history and geography of a particular area, was not published until 1883.

[37] The Holloway forgery case may be a reference to one of Holmes' first interactions with Inspector Lestrade, who had 'got[ten] himself in a fog over a forgery case' (Chapter 2, *A Study in Scarlet*).

[38] This is likely a mistake or purposeful misdirection on the part of Watson, as the excavations at the Sanctuary of Apollo at Delphi were not begun in earnest until 1893.

[39] This burial site has been lost to history, for while many Viking treasure hoards have been discovered in England over the years, no recorded site includes an actual burial. Two such sites have been found in Scotland, but not until 1924 and 1991.

[40] Whale Bay is the English name for Walvis Bay, a natural deep-water harbour in Western Africa. It was occupied by the British in 1878 and passed to the independent nation of Namibia in 1994.

[41] Holmes is clearly referring to the hallucinogenic mushroom *Amanita muscaria*. Most modern historians have discounted *Amanita's* role in the berserker trance, claiming that the effects of the mushroom do not precisely match the symptoms displayed by those warriors. However, the time of the berserker was almost one thousand years ago, and it may be hypothesized that the mushroom's hallucinogenic properties have altered over time. Or it may be that a related species of fungus was responsible, which has either since gone extinct, or is still unknown to science. The scholar will clearly recognize this possibility, especially as the precise nature of the *Radix pedis diaboli* has still yet to come to light (*The Adventure of the Devil's Foot*).

[42] Shockingly, surgical masks were not yet used in 1881. It was not until 1897 that the French Surgeon Paul Berger wore one, which he then published in an 1899 monograph entitled '*On the Use of a Mask in Operating.*'

[43] This surely explains why Watson did not include this early case as part of the original *Adventures* (published 1891 to 1892 in *The Strand*). Why he neglected to do so years later, after Professor Sidney surely must have died, remains a mystery.

[44] A paraphrase from *The Merchant of Venice* (Act II, Scene VII), which actually goes: 'All that glisters is not gold; Often have you heard that told: Many a man his life hath sold; But my outside to behold: Gilded tombs do worms enfold. Had you been as wise as bold, Young in

limbs, in judgment old; Your answer had not been inscroll'd; Fare you well, your suit is cold.'

[45] This appears to be a reference to the world's first electricity-generating wind turbine, constructed by James Blyth.

[46] The Roman Bath at No. 33 Surry Street, off the Strand near King's College. It is a natural spring and bricked cistern built in the era of James I. The Victorians, who were rather fond of such associations with classical artefacts, attributed it to the Romans.

[47] There is no such bank at Fleet Street, but may this be a pseudonym for Child & Co., founded in 1664.

[48] It is not clear where Watson heard the name of this train, as the *Caledonian* did not officially exist until the mid-twentieth century.

[49] Most likely, this would have been *Dracula* by Bram Stoker, published on 26 May 1897.

[50] The Vikings raided for slaves throughout the British Isles and Ireland from the 6th to 11th centuries.

[51] In fact, there are 206 bones in the human body, but we shall excuse Jock Gibbs' inexperience with such matters.

[52] Plutarch formulated the causality dilemma in his essay *The Symposiacs* (c. 100 CE), from an earlier question by Aristotle.

[53] A reference to the March Revolution of 1848, in which crowds of demonstrators erected barricades at Alexander Platz to protest King Frederick William IV's refusal to permit parliamentary elections, a constitution, and freedom of the press. A thirteen-hour battle ensued, leaving hundreds dead.

[54] The High Court of Justiciary meets in a building situated in Glasgow's Saltmarket.

[55] For reasons likely lost to history, Watson never published Holmes' involvement with the Rochevieille Diamond case. Instead, he turned the papers of Dr MacDonald over to his first literary editor, Sir Arthur Conan Doyle, who published them in 1891 in the *Temple Bar* magazine under the name '*Our Midnight Visitor.*'

[56] HM Prison Barlinnie opened in 1882 in Glasgow.

[57] *A Study in Scarlet* was not published until the end of 1887 in *Beeton's Christmas Annual*.

[58] The careful scholar will note a great deal of similarities between certain aspects of this previously unpublished adventure of Holmes

and a short story entitled 'The Jew's Breastplate.' The latter was the creation of Sir Arthur Conan Doyle, Watson's first literary editor, who published it in Tales of Terror and Mystery (1922). It may be surmised that Conan Doyle must have heard a verbal account of this case from Watson, and when he realized that Watson never intended to publish it, Conan Doyle embellished it into his own story. For unknown reasons, Conan Doyle moved the historical action from Mesopotamia to the Levant.

[59] Unfortunately, Watson never recorded any additional details regarding this case.

[60] The tomb of Cleopatra (51-30 BCE) has still not been conclusively identified.

[61] Since the Gower Street Museum no longer exists, we must assume that Professor Cavendish's fears were founded, and it was either subsumed by the British Museum, or perhaps by the nearby Petrie Museum of Egyptian Archaeology (founded in 1892).

[62] A nickname for the 2nd Dragoon Guards, a cavalry regiment of the British Army first raised in 1685.

[63] A lamassu is an Assyrian protective deity with a man's head, an ox's body, and the wings of a bird, much like the Greek androsphinx.

[64] There is no record of a significant treasure-filed tomb being excavated at Uruk. However, such a thing is certainly possible, as the tale is reminiscent of the discovery of Queen Puabi's Royal Tomb at Ur, which was excavated by British archaeologist Leonard Woolley between 1922 and 1934.

[65] Austin Henry Layard (1817-1894) was an English archaeologist who became famous as the excavator of Nimrud (from 1845-7) and Nineveh (from 1849-53). The latter contained the remarkable find of a collection of clay tablets containing a great variety of Cuneiform texts, including the Epic of Gilgamesh.

[66] A firman is a written permission to conduct an archaeological excavation granted by an official of various historical Islamic states.

[67] At twenty pounds each, the twelve stones would fetch only 240 pounds total. This is comparable to half of Mycroft's annual salary of 450 pounds, but hardly a vast sum.

[68] In 1903, Holmes would have a commission from the Sultan of Turkey, which presumably rectified this deficiency of knowledge.

[69] The British alchemist John Dee (1527-1608) owned a purple crys-

tal pendant that could reputedly cure diseases and foresee the future. However, this crystal is the property of the Science Museum, so Holmes must be talking about a different crystal owned by Dee.

[70] Presumably, the same case that Holmes references in *A Scandal in Bohemia* and *A Case of Identity*, since Holmes was rewarded with a large brilliant diamond ring.

[71] Chaldeans are an ethnic group of Syria, Iraq, and neighbouring countries who speak a neo-Aramaic language and typically followed the Syrian rites of Christianity.

[72] '*Quis custodiet ipsos custodies*' is a Latin phrase translated as 'Who watches the watchmen?' from the *Satires* of Juvenal (late first century CE).

[73] The Battle of Laing's Nek was fought during the First Boar War on 28 January 1881 and was a fiasco for the British forces.

[74] Billy is first mentioned in 1888 (*The Valley of Fear*), and then again 1901 (*The Problem of Thor Bridge*) and 1903 (*The Mazarin Stone*) suggesting that his tenure at Baker Street was a long one.

[75] Captain Robert Maynard (c.1684-1751) was in command of the two naval sloops, HMS *Ranger* and HMS *Jane*, which defeated the pirate Blackbeard in battle off the coast of North Carolina in 1718.

[76] Watson is correct. The Golden Age of Piracy vanished by the mid 1800's, when the United States Navy eliminated most pirates in the West Indies. However, privateers continued in some degree through the US Civil War.

[77] Goa is a state in southwest India. During the period of Portuguese rule, it became known as a pirate haven. For those fleeing increased scrutiny in the Caribbean, Madagascar became a pirate haven from c.1690 to 1723, and is still famed for its Pirate Cemetery. 'Leghorn' was an English name for the Italian city of Livorno, which was a free port during the reign of the Medici's.

[78] The origin of this phrase is a bit obscure, but it effectively meant that there was no peace on the high seas outside of European waters, where letters of marque conveyed unofficial power for privateers to capture ships of rival nations.

[79] Tide-waiters were customs inspectors working the docks.

[80] Interestingly, the manuscript for *Treasure Island* has been lost. It was published in book form on 14 November 1883, though it was first serialized in the children's magazine 'Young Folks' from 1881

to 1882 under the title *Treasure Island, or the Mutiny of the Hispaniola*, and was originally credited to one 'Captain George North.' Robert Louis Stevenson later claimed that he 'plagiarized' the idea of pirates and buried treasure from Washington Irving's story 'Wolfert Webber' (published 1824 in the collection *Tales of a Traveller*). The chronically-ill Stevenson left England in 1887 for San Francisco. By March 1888, when Holmes and Watson investigated this case, Stevenson was preparing to depart California for Samoa, where he would eventually die in 1894.

[81] Blaise Pascal (1623-1662) and Carl Friedrich Gauss (1777-1855) were two of the greatest mathematicians since antiquity.

[82] The Alberti cipher was invented c.1466 by the Italian Leon Battista Alberti (1404-1472), who is perhaps best known as the architect of the ground-breaking façade of the Basilica of Santa Maria Novella in Florence. His cipher was considered unbreakable without the encoding disk until the mid-nineteenth century.

[83] Woodes Rogers (c.1679-1732) was an English privateer, later commissioned to be first Royal Governor of the Bahamas and tasked with ridding the colony of pirates.

[84] There is not much verifiable about Blackbeard's identity. However he is thought to be one Edward Thatch, Jr. (c.1680-1718) originally of Bristol.

[85] The Agra treasure was estimated to be worth some £500,000 (Chapter Four, *The Sign of Four*).

[86] John Hanning Speke (1827-1864) was the first European to reach Lake Victoria. He died of a mysterious gunshot wound, officially ruled accidentally self-inflicted, the day before he was due to debate Sir Richard Francis Burton regarding the source of the Nile River.

[87] In *The Final Problem*, Watson claims that Holmes "came out with me into the garden, clambering over the wall which leads into Mortimer Street…." However, this is at odds with Watson's report that his practice during the Great Hiatus was in Kensington, as reported in *The Adventure of the Norwood Builder* and *The Red Headed-League*. We must assume that the latter was more accurate, and that the former specific locale was a misdirection. Arguably, the most famous 'Mortimer' in British history (excepting perhaps Dr James Mortimer of Devonshire) was Roger Mortimer, the 1st Earl of March (1287-1330), who led the Despenser Rebellion against King Edward II, and after the king's murder, was *de facto* ruler of England for three years. The

detail that Earl's Terrace in Kensington backs up on the gardens of Edwardes Square seems suggestive that this address is the undisguised locale of Watson's practice.

[88] In some ways, this case mirrors the later story of George Edalji, the half-Indian solicitor who was convicted of animal mutilation, until Sir Arthur Conan Doyle (Dr Watson's first literary agent) actively investigated the case and eventually achieved a pardon for Edalji.

[89] Much as there is no such unit as the 117th Foot (in which Colonel Barclay served in *The Adventure of the Crooked Man*), the 34th Bombay Infantry (in which Major John Sholto served in *The Sign of Four*), or a 1st Bangalore Pioneers (Colonel's Sebastian Moran's regiment in *The Adventure of the Empty House*), there is no such regiment as either the 5th Bengal Landers or the 12th Gurka Rifles. Why precisely Watson felt compelled to disguise the true names of these units, when he failed to do so with his own (the 5th Northumberland Fusiliers and the 66th Berkshire Regiment of Foot) is unknown.

[90] Neither Mayapore nor Bhurtee are actual towns in India, suggesting that Watson changed the names to avoid sending treasure hunters out in search of the Kali Temple.

[91] Due to the insidious nature of inflation, the seemingly small sum of £20,000 in 1891 would be worth some £2.3 million, or $3.3 million, in 2016.

[92] There was an extensive variety of terms used for the disease syphilis. 'Infinite Malady' comes from Shakespeare's *Timon of Athens* (Act III, Scene VI).

[93] Tabes dorsalis is a term for the slow nerve degeneration seen in the third and final stage of untreated syphilis. Watson's first literary agent, Sir Arthur Conan Doyle, completed a doctorate regarding tabes dorsalis in 1885.

[94] It may appear obvious to the astute reader, who is well aware that Mary does not live until Sherlock Holmes' triumphant return from the Great Hiatus in 1894, that she is ill with more than a mild summer cold. Watson appears to be ignoring – most likely due to emotional denial – the clues that his beloved wife is suffering from consumption, or tuberculosis. This scourge was also the cause of the death of Louisa Conan Doyle, Sir Arthur's first wife, in 1906.

[95] An account of the arrest of Huret can be found in the non-Canonical tale, *The Adventure of the Boulevard Assassin*.

[96] While it is unclear to what adventure Watson is referring with the mention of the Caribbean, the reference to a California mining camp appears to reference *A Double-Barrelled Detective Story* (1902), by the American author Mark Twain. Although Watson's discounts it, an account of the actual tale can be found in the non-Canonical tale *The Adventure of the Double Detectives*.

[97] Major-General Robert Clive (1725-1774), 1st Baron Clive, was a British solider and one of the most influential figures in the creation of British India.

[98] John Churchill (1650-1722), 1st Duke of Marlborough, was the British Commander-in-Chief during the War of the Spanish Succession, where he routinely defeated the armies of Louis XIV. The Duke of Wellington once said that he "could conceive of nothing greater than Marlborough at the head of an English army." He was also the ancestor of Winston Churchill.

[99] More properly, *The History of the Decline and Fall of the Roman Empire* (published in six volumes from 1776 to 1778) by Edward Gibbon (1737-1794), considered to be the first modern history due to its substantial use of primary sources and extensive footnotes.

[100] The Great Mutiny of 1857 is described vividly in both *The Sign of Four* and *The Adventure of the Crooked Man.*

[101] In *The Problem of Thor Bridge* Watson writes of his travel-worn and battered tin dispatch-box being secured "somewhere in the vaults of Cox and Co., at Charing Cross." However, here he implicitly states having more than one such reserve of stories.

[102] The same thought occurred to Watson's first literary editor, Sir Arthur Conan Doyle, who wrote of this treasure map in *Memories and Adventures: "Sidelights on Sherlock Holmes"* (1923). The fact that Conan Doyle was allowed to publish the map suggests that, in the interval years, Holmes reversed his decision and told Mycroft of his interpretation of the map, allowing the Peacock Throne to be safely recovered. If that is the case, it must remain hidden wherever the British government hoards such items. Conversely, it has also reported that the map in question was a clever fiction invented to entice treasure-hunters to invest in a salvage-company syndicate that purported to hunt for the ship. We may perhaps never know the full truth of the matter.

[103] Dr Moore Agar was introduced to Holmes and Watson in *The Adventure of the Devil's Foot*. Based on this aside by Holmes, Dr Agar ap-

pears to have taken over the role of covering Watson's practice, a part previously served by Drs Jackson and Anstruther.

[104] Ashoka (died 232 BCE) was an Indian emperor who sent Buddhist monks as far west as the Mediterranean. Kalmykia is a region of Russia in which Tibetan Buddhism remains the traditional religion.

[105] Watson appears to be referring to *The Jewel of Seven Stars*, published in 1903.

[106] These words come from an 1897 poem by Henry Newbolt, set to music as 'Songs of the Sea' by Charles Villiers Stanford in 1902.

[107] While the first two references are plain to any Sherlockian scholar, the last appears to be an allusion to the non-Canonical tale *The Adventure of the Manufactured Miracle*.

[108] William Bateson (1861-1926) was an English biologist and successor of Darwin. Guglielmo Marconi (1874-1937) was an Italian engineer, credited with inventing the radio.

[109] Lucas was slain in *The Adventure of the Second Stain*. Oberstein was jailed in *The Adventure of the Bruce-Partington Plans*. Meyer was banished after the events detailed in the non-Canonical *The Adventure of the Spanish Sovereign*.

[110] Invented in 1818, and not broken for thirty-three years, the Chubb lock was one of the most sophisticated locks of the era. While it was featured in both *A Scandal in Bohemia* and *The Adventure of the Golden Pince-Nez*, no Canonical story contains the details of where and when Holmes would have picked one on his own.

[111] Here we find evidence that Watson is obscuring some piece of the story, since the South Devon constituency was abolished in 1885.

[112] The lost-wax technique is a bit more complicated than Holmes and Watson make it out here. It was used throughout Europe and the ancient world until the 18th century, when the more difficult piece-mould process supplanted it. It is still used by artists such as Auguste Rodin (1840-1917) for his bronze sculptures.

[113] There are several possible candidates for the locale of the sleeping place of King Arthur and his Knights, who as 'The Once and Future King' is prophesied to return in the event of England's greatest need. The Isle of Avalon is one possibility, but so are caves under Alderley Edge in Cheshire, Sewingshields near Newcastle, and Freebrough Hill near Castleton.

[114] The legend holds that Drake's Drum was later heard both at the

onset of World War I in 1914 and upon the HMS *Royal Oak* in 1918 when the German Navy surrendered. It was also heard in 1940 during the miraculous Operation Dynamo evacuations of Dunkirk.

[115] The first desertion refers to the period of time when Watson married his first wife and returned to practice. During this time, some evidence suggests that he resided on Cavendish Avenue in St. John's Wood.

[116] The second desertion occurred when Watson wed Mary Morstan in the spring of 1889, approximately six months after the adventure they shared together. During this time, Watson's practice was reportedly located at Crawford Place in Marylebone (approximately May 1889 to May 1890), followed by Earl's Terrace (which backed up to 'Mortimer Street') in Kensington (approximately May 1890 to April 1894).

[117] The dating of *The Adventure of the Second Stain* is one of the most controversial of the entire Canon. Watson himself deliberately attempts to obscure the date: "It was, then, in a year, and even in a decade, that shall be nameless, that upon one Tuesday afternoon in autumn we found two visitors...." Baring-Gould places it on October 12–15, 1886 under the very reasonable hypothesis that it must have occurred during a year when two different men held the offices of Prime Minister and Foreign Secretary.

[118] While the identify of Watson's third wife is unclear, it is apparent that he wed her in late 1902, from which time, he practiced out of rooms at Queen Anne Street until his own eventual retirement to Southsea.

[119] Collected in paperback as *Light in the Darkness;* independently published by The New World Books (2017).

[120] Collected in paperback as *Light in the Darkness;* independently published by The New World Books (2017).

[121] First published in *The MX Book of New Sherlock Holmes Stories, Part I: 1881 to 1889;* David Marcum, Editor; MX Publishing (2015).

[122] Collected in paperback as *The Treasury of Sherlock Holmes;* independently published by The New World Books (2018).

[123] Collected in paperback as *The Treasury of Sherlock Holmes;* independently published by The New World Books (2018).

[124] First published in *The MX Book of New Sherlock Holmes Stories, Part IV: 2016 Annual;* David Marcum, Editor; MX Publishing (2016).

[125] First published in *Holmes Away from Home: Tales of the Great Hiatus;* David Marcum, Editor; Belanger Books (2016).

[126] First published in *The MX Book of New Sherlock Holmes Stories, Part VI: 2017 Annual;* David Marcum, Editor; MX Publishing (2017).

[127] Collected in paperback as *The Gathering Gloom;* independently published by The New World Books (2019).

[128] First published in *The MX Book of New Sherlock Holmes Stories, Part XI: Some Untold Cases;* David Marcum, Editor; MX Publishing (2018).

[129] First published in *The MX Book of New Sherlock Holmes Stories, Part VIII: Eliminate the Impossible;* David Marcum, Editor; MX Publishing (2017).

[130] Collected in paperback as *The Gathering Gloom;* independently published by The New World Books (2019).

[131] First published in *Sherlock Holmes: Adventures Beyond the Canon, Volume II;* David Marcum, Editor; Belanger Books (2018).

[132] First published in *Tales from the Stranger's Room 3;* David Ruffle, Editor; MX Publishing (2017).

[133] Collected in paperback as *The Travels of Sherlock Holmes;* independently published by The New World Books (2020).

[134] Collected in paperback as *The Travels of Sherlock Holmes;* independently published by The New World Books (2020).

[135] First published in *The MX Book of New Sherlock Holmes Stories, Part XVIII: Whatever Remains... Must Be the Truth;* David Marcum, Editor; MX Publishing (2019).

[136] First published in *The MX Book of New Sherlock Holmes Stories, Part XXIII: Some More Untold Cases 1888-1894;* David Marcum, Editor; MX Publishing (2020).

ACKNOWLEDGEMENT

First and foremost, I must give a grateful acknowledgment to Sir Arthur Conan Doyle (1859-1930) for the use of the Sherlock Holmes characters. Without his words, this could not have been written.

For reference, I consider Leslie S. Klinger's 'The New Annotated Sherlock Holmes' (2005 & 2006) to be the definitive edition, which builds upon William S. Baring-Gould's majestic 'The Annotated Sherlock Holmes' (1967). I also frequently consult Jack Tracy's 'The Encyclopedia Sherlockiana, or A Universal Dictionary of the State of Knowledge of Sherlock Holmes and His Biographer John H. Watson, M.D.' (1977), Matthew E. Bunson's 'Encyclopedia Sherlockiana, an A-to-Z Guide to the World of the Great Detective' (1994), and Bruce Wexler's 'The Mysterious World of Sherlock Holmes' (2008).

Of course, one work in particular was inspirational for these stories – 'Treasure Island' (1883) by Robert Louis Stevenson.

Finally, many of these stories owe a massive debt to David Marcum, author and editor of several wonderful compilations of Sherlockian tales, whose praise and encouragement prompted me to continue unearthing these lost cases of Mr. Sherlock Holmes, written long ago by his biographer Dr John H. Watson.

ABOUT THE AUTHOR

Craig Janacek

In the year 1998 CRAIG JANACEK took his degree of Doctor of Medicine of Vanderbilt University, and proceeded to Stanford to go through the training prescribed for paediatricians in practice. Having completed his studies there, he was duly attached to the University of California San Francisco as Professor.
The author of over a hundred and fifty  medical monographs upon a variety of obscure lesions, his travel-worn and battered tin dispatch-box is crammed with papers, nearly all of which are records of his fictional works. These include several collections of the Further Adventures of Sherlock Holmes ('Light in the Darkness', 'The Gathering Gloom', 'The Treasury of Sherlock Holmes', 'The Travels of Sherlock Holmes', & 'The Assassination of Sherlock Holmes'), two Dr Watson novels ('The Isle of Devils' & 'The Gate of Gold'), the complete and expanded Adventures and Exploits of Brigadier Gerard ('Set Europe Shaking' & 'A Mighty Shadow'), and two non-Holmes novels ('The Oxford Deception' & 'The Anger of Achilles Peterson').
His short stories have been published in several editions of 'The MX Book of New Sherlock Holmes Stories, Part I: 1881-1889' (2015), 'Part IV: 2016 Annual' (2016), 'Part VI: 2017 Annual' (2017), 'Part VIII: Eliminate the Impos-

sible' (2017), 'Part XI: Some Untold Cases' (2018), 'Part XVIII: Whatever Remains Must be the Truth' (2019), and 'Part XXIII: Some More Untold Cases' (2020). Other stories have appeared in 'Holmes Away From Holmes: Tales of the Great Hiatus' (2016), 'Tales from the Stranger's Room 3' (2017), and 'Sherlock Holmes: Adventures Beyond the Canon' (2018).

He lives near San Francisco, California with his wife and two children, where he is at work on his next story. Craig Janacek is a nom-de-plume.

ABOUT THE AUTHOR

Sir Arthur Conan Doyle

In the year 1885 ARTHUR CONAN DOYLE took his degree of Doctor of Medicine of the University of Edinburgh, and (after diversions in Greenland, West Africa, and Southsea) proceeded to Vienna and Paris to go through the training of an ophthal-mologist in practice. Having partially completed his studies there, he was duly attached to a consulting physician at 2  Devonshire Place, London. The patients were few in number and, to bide his time, he turned his attention to the writing of fiction.

The author of twenty-four novels, some two-hundred odd other fictions of all genres, and more than a thousand other works (including plays, poems, essays, pamphlets, articles, letters to the press, and architectural designs). Although he personally preferred some of his other works, he has been for-ever immortalized as the creator of one of the greatest and most famous characters to ever be set down in print – Mr. Sherlock Holmes.

In 1902, he was made a Knight Bachelor by King Edward VII. He is buried in Minstead, New Forest. The epitaph on his grave-stone reads simply: 'Steel true / Blade straight / Arthur Conan Doyle / Knight / Patriot, Physician and Man of Letters / 22 May 1859 – 7 July 1930.'

PRAISE FOR AUTHOR

" 'The Watson style is deceptively difficult to imitate. Good prac-titioners include....' I'm now adding the stories in Craig Janacek's series, 'The Midwinter Mysteries of Sherlock Holmes' as well."

- DAVID MARCUM, EDITOR OF 'THE MX BOOK OF NEW SHER-LOCK HOLMES STORIES', IN 'THE DISTRICT MESSENGER' (JAN-UARY 2014)

"Craig Janacek combines the puzzle mystery and the paranormal brilliantly in 'The Adventure of the Fair Lad.' "

- 'PUBLISHERS WEEKLY' (DECEMBER 2019)

THE FURTHER ADVENTURES OF SHERLOCK HOLMES

A large cache of manuscripts by the biographer of the world's first consulting detective, Mr. Sherlock Holmes, has been found! Restored, edited, and compiled into thematic collections, these tales augment and expand upon the Victorian world so vibrantly laid forth in the 60 original adventures. Setting forth from their base at 221B Baker Street, herein, Holmes and Watson come upon friends – old and new, and villains – both cunning and tragic. Fully annotated, these editions contain a cornucopia of scholarly insights which compare these newly unearthed tales by Dr John H. Watson to the classic adventures from the Canon of Sherlock Holmes.

Light In The Darkness

Sherlock Holmes returns! He must deal with a series of cases which encompass the broad range of the human experience, from the grim workings of physicians who have violated their oaths, to the magnanimous moods which every man – no matter how cool and emotionless – feels at the time of Christmas. Comprising the collections 'The First of Criminals' and 'The Season of Forgiveness,' all seven recently-unearthed adventures in this volume are narrated by Dr Watson in the in the finest tradition and spirit of such classics as 'The Adventure of the Speckled Band' and 'The Adventure of the Blue Carbuncle.'

THE FIRST OF CRIMINALS: Descend into the horrors that lurk in the minds of doctors who have gone terribly wrong in this quartet of stories featuring the world's first consulting detective, Sherlock Holmes, and his able assistant, Dr John H. Watson. This collection includes the tales 'The Adventure of the Monstrous Blood,' 'The Adventure of the Mad Colonel,' 'The Adventure of the Fateful Malady,' and 'The Adventure of the Barren Grave.'

THE SEASON OF FORGIVENESS: Celebrate the spirit of the season with the world's first consulting detective, Sherlock Holmes, and his able assistant, Dr John H. Watson. This collection includes the tales 'The Adventure of the Spanish Sovereign,' 'The Adventure of the Manufactured Miracle,' and 'The Adventure of the First Star.' It also includes 'The Grand Gift of Sherlock,' a final letter from Holmes to Watson at the very end of World War I, which is sure to delight bibliophiles with its depiction of Watson's bookcase and its moving testament to the enduring power of friendship. Also published as 'The Midwinter Mysteries of Sherlock Holmes.'

The Gathering Gloom

Embark on an exploration of the darker corners of the human experience with the world's first consulting detective, Sherlock Holmes, and his able assistant, Dr John H. Watson. Comprising the collections 'The Schoolroom of Sorrow' and 'An East Wind,' all ten recently-unearthed adventures are narrated by Dr Watson in the in the finest tradition and spirit of such classics as 'The Problem of Thor Bridge' and 'The Adventure of the Bruce-Partington Plans.'

THE SCHOOLROOM OF SORROW: Dive into the deepest abysses of the human soul with Mr. Sherlock Holmes and Dr John H. Watson. From the days before his career as a consulting detective to years of his restful retirement, Sherlock Holmes has all too often encountered terrible events that served to shape his philosophy. To Holmes, every adventure holds the possibility of teaching an earthly lesson regarding the nature of good and evil. This collection includes the tales 'The Father of Evil,' 'The Adventure of the Dishonourable Discharge,' 'The Adventure of the Fatal Fire,' 'The Adventure of the Awakened Spirit,' and 'The Cold Dish.'

AN EAST WIND: In the time of England's greatest need, Sherlock Holmes and Dr Watson stand ready. A great and awful war is brewing in the East, and foreign agents will do everything in their power to see England brought to its knees. Only the swift actions of Sherlock Holmes can prevent the empire's secrets from being sold to its enemies, thereby dooming thousands of brave young men to terrible deaths upon the fields of Flanders and in the frigid waters of the North Sea. This collection includes the tales 'The Adventure of the Third Traitor,' 'The Adventure of the Unfathomable Silence,' 'The High Mountain,' 'The Adventure of the Defenceless Prisoner,' and 'Their Final Flourish.'

The Treasury Of Sherlock Holmes

Embark upon quests for buried treasure with the world's first consulting detective, Sherlock Holmes, and his assistant, Dr John H. Watson. Comprising the collections 'Treasure Trove Indeed!' and 'Fortunes Made and Fortunes Lost,' all eight recently-unearthed adventures are narrated by Dr Watson in the in the finest tradition and spirit of such classics as 'The Musgrave Ritual' and 'The Adventure of the Six Napoleons.'

TREASURE TROVE INDEED!: Things get lost very easily in England. Across the realm, from the remote Peak District to the sea-faring shores of Bristol, from the ancient manors of Devonshire to the warrens of London, Sherlock Holmes is faced with a series of challenging cases. Ranging in time from his days at university until shortly before his retirement, these adventures span the gamut of Holmes and Watson's time together. This collection includes the tales 'The Lost Legion,' 'The Adventure of the Pirate's Code,' 'The Adventure of the Queen's Pendant,' and 'The Adventure of the Silent Drum.'

FORTUNES MADE & FORTUNES LOST: The pursuit of fortune may lead a man to riches or to ruin. From Cambridge to Scotland to London, Sherlock Holmes and Dr Watson must face the darker side of treasure hunting, as they contend with criminals driven mad by their quest of fortune and glory. The full brilliance of Sherlock Holmes is on display as he solves an ancient curse, the singular adventures of the Grice Patersons in the island of Uffa, and a mysterious cipher. Meanwhile, with Holmes thought lost over the Reichenbach Falls, Dr Watson must attempt to employ his methods in the solution of an exotic tragedy. This collection includes the tales 'The Adventure of the Double-Edged Hoard,' 'The Adventure of the Dawn Discovery,' 'The Harrowing Intermission,' and 'The Adventure of the Sunken Indiaman.'

The Travels Of Sherlock Holmes

Embark on a series of journeys with Mr. Sherlock Holmes and Dr John H. Watson. Although Holmes was at his best amongst the ghostly gas lamps and swirling yellow fog of London's streets, he was occasionally willing to venture forth to strange locales whenever a sufficiently-interesting adventure called. Comprising the collections 'A Prompt and Ready Traveller' and 'Round the World,' within are eight recently-unearthed cases which induced Holmes to set forth to the Continent, the Colonies, and even the Americas. All are narrated by Dr Watson in the finest tradition and spirit of such classics as 'The Disappearance of Lady Frances Carfax' and 'The Adventure of the Devil's Foot.'

A PROMPT & READY TRAVELLER: While Sherlock Holmes protested leaving London for too long, for fear of causing an unhealthy excitement among the criminal classes, Dr Watson was always a prompt and ready traveller, who could be counted upon to encourage his friend to take up a peculiar case, no matter where it might lead them. From a spiritual visit to the exotic Kingdom of Hawai'i to the dangerous boulevards of Paris, from to the dark catacombs of Rome to the posh resorts of Bermuda, Holmes and Watson must deal with private revenges and matters of grave international importance. This collection includes the tales 'The Adventure of the Missing Mana,' 'The Adventure of the Boulevard Assassin,' 'The Adventure of the Boulevard Assassin, 'The Adventure of the Secret Tomb,' and 'The Adventure of the Dead Man's Note.'

ROUND THE WORLD: Sherlock Holmes would recommend rejuvenating trips round the world for certain of his clients, but it took a strong force for him to do the same. And yet, occasionally, he would don his travelling cloak and ear-flapped cap and set forth to deal with challenging cases. These adventures include a faerie kidnapping in Ireland – featuring one of the most fantastic deductions of Holmes' career – and a trip to the American South to face the return of a terrible enemy – the K.K.K. Closer to home, the return of a tragic adversary – Dr Leon Sterndale – coincides with the emergence of a new horror. Finally, we learn the true story of whether or not Holmes ever visited the silver fields of California, as previously reported by an American author of some repute. This collection includes the tales 'The Oak-Leaf Sprig,' 'The Adventure of the Double Detectives,' 'The Adventure of the African Horror,' and 'The Adventure of the Fair Lad.'

The Assassination Of Sherlock Holmes

Embark on an epic adventure featuring the world's foremost

consulting detective, Sherlock Holmes, as told by Dr John H. Watson in the finest tradition of the Canonical stories. Comprising three parts, 'The Adventure of the Pharaoh's Curse,' 'The Problem of Threadneedle Street,' and 'The Falling Curtain,' these tales relate one of Holmes' final and most gripping adventures. This special Collected Edition also contains the previously unpublished tale 'The Red Leech.' For the first and only time, rather than a stranger, it is a desperate Dr Watson himself that is sitting in the client chair at 221B Baker Street. Can Holmes help save him from the clutches of the repulsive Red Leech?

THE ADVENTURE OF THE PHARAOH'S CURSE. October 1909. Sherlock Holmes has been retired to the South Downs for six years, resisting all entreaties to return to his career as the world's foremost consulting detective. But the brutal murder of one of his former colleagues from Scotland Yard has finally galvanized him back into action. Dr Watson at his side, Holmes journeys to London's British Museum, where a series of singular disappearances have taken place. With the museum staff convinced that the curse of a four thousand year-old pharaoh is emanating from the Egyptian Gallery, it is up to Holmes to prove that the worst horrors come from the minds of men. But will the echoes of the past prove to be his undoing?

THE PROBLEM OF THREADNEEDLE STREET. November 1909. Sherlock Holmes has been called out of retirement to successfully solve the mystery of the British Museum's Pharaonic curse. But while he longs to return to his villa on the South Downs, a new threat has arisen. A twisted riddle of the sphinx suggests that Holmes and Dr. Watson are wading through deep waters. And when the main vault at the Bank of England is inexplicably plundered, Holmes realizes that his enemies may be trying to bring down the nation itself. Only the piercing acumen of the world's foremost consulting detective could see that this theft was but the first blow, and that the villain is certain to mount another daring robbery. From a baffling series of seemingly unconnected events, Holmes must make the brilliant leaps of deduction required in order to determine where his adversary next plans to strike. Only then can Holmes set his own traps and turn the tables on his foe. But will Holmes be able to anticipate all of the forces that are aligning against him?

THE FALLING CURTAIN. November 1909. Sherlock Holmes has successfully prevented further robberies of England's greatest institutions and captured one of his most dangerous enemies, but something is still rotten in the streets of London. A series of attacks threaten not only his life, but the lives of those few individuals that he calls 'friend.' With Dr. Watson injured, his defenses crumbling, and Scotland Yard deaf to his appeals for succor, Holmes must call upon some irregular help and use every means at his disposal to determine what adversary is stalking him from the mists of the past. From the cells of Wandsworth to the heights of Tower Bridge, Holmes is once more on the hunt. But is he willing to make the sacrifice required to put a final end to this monstrous menace?

Made in the USA
Middletown, DE
25 March 2021

36190161R00198